THE
CENTURION

10/ 20/ 2018

To: B. M

5 P Q R

[signature]

THE CENTURION

A Tale of the Crucifixion

JOE MACK HIGH

This is a work of fiction. All of the characters, names, incidents, organizations, and dialogue in this novel are either the products of the author's imagination or are used fictitiously.

Archway Publishing books may be ordered through booksellers or by contacting:

Archway Publishing
1663 Liberty Drive
Bloomington, IN 47403
www.archwaypublishing.com
1 (888) 242-5904

ISBN: 978-1-4808-6547-1 (sc)
ISBN: 978-1-4808-6548-8 (hc)
ISBN: 978-1-4808-6546-4 (e)

Library of Congress Control Number: 2018909226

Print information available on the last page.

Archway Publishing rev. date: 8/21/2018

To my parents, whose hard work and sacrifice
allowed my sisters and me to inherit the promise, and
Arlie E. Cate, PhD, professor of philosophy.

ACKNOWLEDGMENTS

Little in this novel is original. It is the residual of myriad associations over time, the abstraction of eighty years of Sunday school, good and bad books and lectures, and innumerable conversations.

Many friends, including my son, reviewed sections and drafts and assured me it was worth reading.

I am especially grateful to Mary Bozeman Hodges and Cecilia Seale, who made a silk purse from a sow's ear. But I owe a special debt to Patsy Guy Hammontree, who taught a business major to write prose of sufficient quality for editing. As the centurion owed his success to those who assisted him along his way, I am indebted to family, friends, and strangers who helped me.

My great regret is that I did not have time to create a better product. Each time I read a paragraph, I see where it can be improved.

I did little research in the traditional meaning of the term but based the writing on recollections. I welcome criticisms and suggestions so that I may improve a second edition, time permitting.

PREFACE

I spent my early years in rural western North Carolina, an Eden on earth, amidst highly religious people. I learned later there was a depression, causing my father to move to East Tennessee to continue with the railroad. In North Carolina, I had attended small rural schools, but in East Tennessee, I enrolled in city schools, for which I was woefully unprepared. From that time forward, I was a poor student, an embarrassment to myself and a disappointment to my parents.

During my senior year in high school, the Japanese attacked Pearl Harbor. To please my parents, I agreed to delay enlisting until I graduated. My class reported to the recruiting station. All of them were accepted except me. I was eighteen and had to be nineteen to enlist. That was one of the saddest days of my life.

On my nineteenth birthday, two slots opened in the United States Marine Corps. I enlisted and spent almost three years with the Fleet Marine Force, making four assault landings as a telephone lineman, laying lines up and down the beaches and into command posts. I had a ringside view of the fighting. As my unit was preparing for the assault on Japan, the bombs were dropped on Hiroshima and Nagasaki. I was home by Thanksgiving.

To please my parents, I enrolled in a small liberal arts college. Much to my surprise, I survived the first semester, and by the time I began my sophomore year, I had fallen in love with the coursework. It opened new worlds for me. The teachers who influenced me most were the professor of philosophy and two professors of literature. I enrolled in at least one literature course and one philosophy course each semester until I graduated.

The high-water mark was a philosophy course using as textbooks Plato's *Republic*, the Old Testament book of Job, Shakespeare's *Hamlet*, and a heavy volume of readings in philosophy. The four Gospels of the New Testament were required, and for the first time, I studied the Bible as a textbook.

By the time I graduated, I had become a believer of sorts, basing my Christianity on the Hellenistic philosophers. I am convinced there is little difference between Greek philosophy and Christianity. More specifically, the teachings of Jesus seem to validate Stoic philosophy. That reconciliation is the main purpose of this book. It is, however, a work of fiction. In addition, I have tried to justify for Pilate and Judas better treatment than that afforded by history.

AUTHOR'S NOTE

In the New Testament of the Bible, in Acts 10:1, Luke refers to a centurion in Caesarea named Cornelius who commanded a cohort of the Roman Legion called "the Italian Cohort." For Luke to refer to "the Italian Cohort" implies it to be an elite unit, well known in Judea, with Cornelius its centurion. There is a reference in Matthew 27:54 to a centurion at the crucifixion. This novel assumes the centurion to be Cornelius.

PROLOGUE

My name is Cornelius, first centurion, First Cohort, the Italian Cohort, Tenth Legion, Fretensis. More than thirty years ago, I was in command at the crucifixion of Jesus, called by many the Christ.

My home is the Cydmus River Valley in Cilicia, a Roman province off the northeastern corner of the Great Sea. The rugged, snowcapped Taurus Mountains in a huge semicircle form the northern border of the great plain between the mountains and the sea. The river, fed by streams of the central mountains, empties onto the plain. Our farm lay in one of the valleys.

The farm was wedge shaped with two steep spurs forming boundaries and a good stream cascading down. Standing on any of the great outcroppings on the highest ridge and looking south, I could see a vast mosaic of small farms on the broad plain. Like a giant serpent, the river meandered through it, hidden among the trees. To the north, the far mountains were snowcapped during the summer, their ridges and spurs dark in heavy forests.

In the summer, my grandfather and I would climb the ridges. When he became too old, my father and I scaled them. The trees were more than a hundred feet tall, their heavy foliage blocking sunlight. The stillness was heavy, like that of an abandoned temple. The ground was soft, deep with decaying leaves. The rich musky smell of freshly turned earth recalls those summer days.

For my family, breakfast was important, for it enabled us to complete the day's work. The evening meal was of even greater importance. After a long day in the fields, it was good to sit at the table, feeling the tiredness diminish and the problems of the day fade away. It was there my grandparents and later my parents related their experiences, even to conversations at the time. I never tired of the stories, for they are who I am.

No matter where I journeyed, that valley was always my home and my country. For me, *home* and *country* have the same meaning. In Elysium, I shall be content if it is half so fair as the valley.

In the beginning, my family was not landowners but part of the land with the forests and fields. When my grandfather joined Pompey's navy, he set in motion events making him a landowner, severing him from the land, and just as surely as night follows day, leading to my being in command at the crucifixion. I begin with Animus, my grandfather, in Cilicia.

✝

The people of Rome, through their Senate, had made it into the great republic. Rome's legions and navy provided the Pax Romana, a canopy under which the commerce of the world joined all nations. The republic under Julius Caesar, Augustus Caesar, and the Great Pompey was becoming the Roman Empire. Senatus Populusque Romanus (SPQR), "For the Senate and the people of Rome," was becoming a casual greeting. Few in Rome were aware of the change, and certainly no one in Cilicia knew.

Cilician pirates threatened grain shipments from Egypt and other goods destined for Rome. Anxious about the wheat dole, people gathered in small groups, spreading rumors of food riots and starvation. The granaries were full, but the people shouted in unison, "Someone must do something."

The Senate gave Pompey unlimited power to defeat the pirates, but he needed a larger navy.

ANIMUS

It had been a hard winter. Weevils destroyed most of the acorns and the meal. There was never enough. Our family was starving.

A friend working in Tarsus had returned home to say goodbye to his family before joining the Roman navy. He told me Pompey was paying good money to sailors. I began thinking of joining. I had never been more than a few miles from home and did not know where Tarsus was or who Pompey was, but it was not a hard decision. On a spring morning, wearing my only tunic freshly laundered by my mother and sandals I had repaired the night before, I was ready to go. I said goodbye to my father and siblings and went to the kitchen to find my mother. She was wrapping the cheese and the acorn bread.

"You must not do that. It is all there is," I said.

"Oh, Animus, my son, my son," she said. "My heart is broken. The village has lost too many sons, and I lost my oldest. Now you are going. How can I bear the long nights startled awake thinking I hear the sound of your step on the threshold? And during the day, my heart will be anxious to catch the joy of your laughter outside the door."

She bowed her head. "Will I ever see you again? I am fearful that on some distant battlefield, in the darkness, you will be cold, wet, and hungry. Or worse, you will be mortally wounded, all alone with no one to lift your head or to hold your hand."

"I'll not go," I said.

She wiped her tears with her shawl. From a peg on the wall, she removed a worn pouch her father had carried and laid it on the table. "Animus, you have my blessing to go. This is my offering to the god who will look after you, thanking him for giving me all that I wanted in a son. You have been my life and my joy. May you do well. When darkness comes, remember I am praying for you, and when the sun rises, I am again praying for you."

Smiling through her tears, she slipped the cheese and the bread into the pouch along with the heavy kitchen knife her grandfather had made. She closed the pouch and lifted the strap over my head. I secured it at my side and embraced her, feeling the frailness in her thin shoulders.

"Thank you for all you have been to me," I said. "I will never forget. Each evening and each morning, I will remember you are praying for me. I am sure to return."

I kissed her on the forehead and turned toward the door. I did not want her to see my tears.

It was the last time I would see my mother.

✝

I was on my way to Tarsus and farther from home than I had ever been. On the road, I overtook a stranger who was about my age. He was barefooted and dressed only in a makeshift loincloth. His left hand was missing from well above the wrist. He wore a sleeve of heavy leather laced up that forearm. Together we walked toward Tarsus, carrying on a light conversation.

"My name is Animus," I said. "I've never been away from home. The land can no longer support my family, so I'm going to Tarsus to join Pompey's navy."

"I am Theron," he said. "I worked in Tarsus for three years but grew tired of the city and returned home. It seemed better to be poor at home than rich in Tarsus, but I've changed my mind."

By afternoon, we had walked a good distance. I had been curious about Theron's missing hand. Our comradeship had grown, so I felt I could inquire. "How did you lose your hand?"

"In a battle. My family had no money or influence, so I was conscripted into the militia of one of the Seleucid kings. We were to fight pirates raiding his villages. They gave us Greek shields and curved swords, then marched us straight into a pirate camp. We had no training, no armor. A big fellow charged toward me with his battle-ax raised. I took the blow on my shield, but the blade cut through and nearly took off my arm. A surgeon—I suppose he was a surgeon—cut off my hand and dressed the stump. I thought it would never stop bleeding."

Theron raised his left arm. "I should have sunk my blade into the big man's belly while both his hands were over his head. He knew what to do. I did not. As I could no longer hold a shield, I was useless to the king and released from the militia. I returned home, where my mother took care of the wound. Now that it has healed, I'm returning to Tarsus to find work."

We walked together, each deep in our own thoughts, speaking briefly from time to time.

Late in the afternoon, we arrived at a resting place with a good spring and a grassy area. We took a long drink and sat down.

Suddenly, from the bushes near the spring, three men rushed out while shouting, their knives drawn. I backed into a thornbush and slid my knife from the pouch. Theron raised his left arm and struck one of the bandits full in the face. The heavy leather crushed the bandit's nose and knocked his right eye from its place. Blood poured down his cheeks. He dropped his knife. In one swift motion, Theron seized the weapon and slit his attacker's throat. He turned and sank the knife deep into the right side of the second bandit's neck.

I charged at the third man, thrusting my knife into his lower belly until I felt his tunic against my hand. The bandit screamed. In a sawing motion, I pulled the blade upward. When it rested against a rib, I withdrew my weapon.

With a look of wild surprise, he grabbed at his abdomen with hands to keep his entrails from spilling to the ground. Collapsing to his knees, he whispered, "You were not supposed to—"

He fell face forward.

Theron removed a leather pouch from his victim and opened it. "The god of good fortune has smiled on us this day. It's a fine pouch, and there's money in it." He pointed to the men's tunics. "This one is worn and bloody but will dry. We can sell them if we need to. You take the better sandals."

He then laid the finer tunic on the ground and placed on it the sandals, knives, and belts. With relative ease, he wrapped the items with his right hand, and we walked to the eddy below the spring. I washed my hands and knife and splashed water onto my sandals to remove the blood. We cleaned the garments, footwear, and other items and then laid them on a large outcropping to dry.

"They had money and raiment," Theron said. "Why did they attack us?" He thought for a moment then answered his own question. "There are predators in the world just as there are on the farm, like the fox that kills chickens or lambs for the pleasure of killing. Most victims cannot fight back. This time, the predators became the victims. We need to drag the bodies into the bushes so the dogs and vultures can enjoy them in peace."

The sun was slipping below the horizon when we sat down to rest.

"My friend," I said, "had you not been here, I would be the one in the bushes. Most men would have run. Let me show my appreciation with something to eat."

I laid my pouch on the grass, removed the cheese and the bread, placed them on its cover, and cut two portions. I offered one to Theron as I said, "Please take it."

"No, there is not enough for you."

"Please," I said, "I cannot eat my share unless I see you eating yours. Help me celebrate being alive."

As we ate, Theron said, "Animus, my friend, you are a good man. You handled your bandit well." He smiled. "Most men would have run."

We ate slowly, making sure no crumb fell to the ground. I moistened the tip of my finger and picked up a bit of bread from the pouch. We drank from the spring. The sun had disappeared, and I remembered Mother's commitment to pray for me.

"Theron, my friend, it has been a good day," I said. "We are alive, the wind is not so cold, and the stars are bright. We've earned a night's sleep."

Each of us made our space as comfortable as possible and then curled up inside our tunics. We immediately fell asleep, despite the night breeze.

†

First light and the morning chill roused us. To loosen the stiffness from our legs and to gain some warmth, we walked back and forth while swinging our arms.

When it was good light, I removed the last of bread and cheese from my pouch, divided it, and handed a portion to Theron.

"May good fortune continue to favor us both," he said. "If all the world were as you, my friend, what a fine place it would be."

He walked to the outcropping, removed the tunic he had worn during the night, donned the other one and a pair of sandals, and placed the other items in his pouch. Picking up his tunic, he walked to the eddy, washed away the dried blood, wringing out water as best he could, folded it, and draped it over his pouch. He passed the strap over his head while announcing, "Let us be on our way. It has all the makings of a fine day. Tarsus by nightfall."

I picked up the bandit's sandals and placed them in my pouch. "Tarsus by nightfall will indeed make it a fine day."

We headed south.

†

By late afternoon, we had arrived at the outskirts of Tarsus.

Theron greeted a well-dressed citizen, an artisan by the cut of his tunic, a blacksmith by the smell of the forge about him. "My good sir, we are newly arrived in your city. Can you direct us to a public bath?"

"There is one about a hundred yards ahead," he replied. "Welcome to Tarsus. May your stay be a pleasant one."

"We thank you," said Theron. "It is good to be here."

At the bathhouse, Theron requested entrance for two and haggled over the price with the attendant until both agreed. He paid with proper coin from his pouch and motioned for me to follow.

We laundered our tunics and laid them on heated stones to dry. Then we enjoyed the warm waters. Theron said, "Let me invite you to a good meal to mark our arrival in Tarsus. We must find a proper place to celebrate."

He led me into an old section of the city. I did not recognize the dialect or traditional dress but savored the smell of food that filled the narrow, crowded street.

In front of an eating place filled with people talking and laughing, Theron stopped and said, "Follow me." He worked his way into the crowd and found the proprietor. They exchanged greetings, renewing an old acquaintance. Theron said, "Your best meal for me and my friend."

He led us to a courtyard and pointed to an empty table. In a mixture of Greek and local dialect, Theron ordered our meal. "We will dine on goat meat, vegetables, and bread and sour wine," he said. "The wine goes down well after a hard day in the sun. I learned to like it when I worked here."

I nodded assent rather than attempting to speak over the noise. I could not identify the spicy smell that filled the air, but it was pleasant and sharpened my hunger.

A woman in peasant raiment brought our food on a large tray, transferred it to the table, and set a wine jug and cups in front of Theron, who thanked her in dialect.

"Wash down the dust with this," he said, filling our cups with the dark liquid. I took a long drink. It had a slightly sour taste but had been sweetened and flavored with spice. It was good and did wash down the road dust.

"Take this," he said, breaking the pita in half. "I cannot eat my share until I see you eating yours." He smiled.

Using the bread as spoons, we devoured all that was in front of us.

Taking several coins from his pouch, Theron settled with the proprietor. To me he said, "Our bandit friends and good fortune continue to smile on us."

Theron found a hostel near the bathhouse and negotiated a night's lodging. It was sparse but offered more comfort than we had enjoyed the previous evening.

"It is dry, it is inside, and paid for. Who could ask for more?" said Theron, and we prepared for the night.

In the morning, Theron led me to the docks where a large ship was tied to a pier. "I am sure someone here can help you join the navy. Everyone speaks Greek, even the Romans."

He pointed beyond the wharf. "There is the Great Sea."

I was amazed. The great plain of the Cydmus River Valley could not compare to this endless expanse of water. Turning to Theron, I said, "My friend, if not for you, I would never have found my way to Tarsus or to this ship. I would be the one in the bushes at the spring. I wish there was some way I could repay you."

"You owe me nothing. The bread and cheese were payment enough. I gained two tunics and two pairs of sandals. I have enough money in this fine leather pouch to live six months. May the gods that brought you here return you to your home and family. May fortune follow you all the days of your life. The gods owe that to a good man." He paused. "Perhaps we shall meet again."

"May you be fortunate in your stay in Tarsus," I said. "You deserve as much. I shall never forget you. There may be a place where good friends meet again. If not, there should be."

Lifting the pouch above his head in a salute, Theron turned and disappeared into the crowd. I stood there, very much alone, adrift in a sea of strangers.

I walked away from the pier, found a secluded bench, and sat down. My good fortune overwhelmed me. Mother had placed the knife in my pouch. Meeting Theron could have been a chance occurrence, but how many would have acted as he did? Further, how many could have shown me Tarsus? A hand was guiding me and had led me here. Of that I had convinced myself.

It was past noon. I stood, straightened to my full height, squared my shoulders, and walked toward the ship.

On the pier, a sailor was handing out hardtack wafers to a group of waiting men. "Welcome to Pompey's navy. I have here his favorite fare. If you want more, there is more."

I held out my hand and received two wafers. "Is this the place to join the navy?"

"My friend, this is the place. We will board the ship soon."

I ate the wafers slowly, savoring the wheat taste. As I finished, another sailor ordered the group to board the ship.

On a Roman ship, I, along with other young men, joined Pompey's navy, placing my mark beside my name. I felt a burden lift.

I requested two more wafers, leaned against the ship's railing, and marveled at sights and sounds I had never known, savoring the taste of the hardtack. As darkness engulfed the ship, I made myself comfortable next to the rail. For the first time I could remember, I was not hungry. With a sense of contentment, I was soon asleep.

By late morning, the ship had completed resupply and slipped away from the pier, moving toward open sea. We joined Pompey's fleet and were transferred to a much larger ship.

I had expected everyone to be Cilician but saw men of every nationality, of every style of dress, obviously of the lowest class. All of them spoke Greek but with such different accents it might as well have been a foreign language.

An officer boarded our ship seeking men to operate a catapult. He examined our hands, selected a group, and proceeded to inspect each man's teeth, eyes, and muscle firmness.

"What did you do before you joined?" he asked. "Were you ever injured while working? Did you like your work?"

Men were rejected until only five remained to serve as his crew. I was among them.

The officer led us into his long boat, and we joined the captain's ship. He called for a meeting of all officers and crew. "My name is Aetus Marcus. I am a student of mathematics at the University of Alexandria. I spend my time studying the flight path of projectiles launched from a catapult," he said. "If we mount such a weapon at the front of this ship, we can launch firepots at pirate ships. I need your skill to maneuver this ship into position so we can hit a pirate ship."

As we sailed away from the fleet, Captain Marcus directed the crew in the installation of the catapult, aligning and bolting it to the deck at the prow of the ship. He turned to the five of us and said, "We are going to learn how to hit a pirate ship with a clay pot. Our success depends on you." Motioning us to follow, he said, "I'll show you to your quarters and get you something to eat. It is cramped, and the air is bad, but it is dry." From a basket nearby, he handed each of us several wafers, a piece of cheese, and a small cup. "The steward will provide you some wine. Welcome aboard this ship and to Pompey's navy."

I returned to the main deck, leaned against the rail, and enjoyed my meal. It had been less than a week since I left home. I watched the sun sink into the sea and wondered if Mother might be looking at the same sunset.

For the next few days, Captain Marcus trained the crew to align the ship with a target boat and the catapult crew to prepare and launch clay pots at it. I weighed each pot, then placed it in the cup on the arm of the catapult. For each launch, Captain Marcus made a record of the clicks on the windlass and the distance the pot traveled. Finally, after several days of practice, a series of launches splashed down within a few feet of the target, one hitting it. The next day, a series of launches all splashed down very near the boat, with several pots hitting it.

"Well done!" shouted the captain. "Let us join Pompey's fleet. We don't want the war to end before we get there. If we do well against the pirates, this war will be over before cold weather. We'll be home by spring planting."

Late the next day, the lookout shouted, "Roman sails ahead."

The catapult crew joined Captain Marcus at the prow to view the fleet, their sails a soft rose in the setting sun. The ship's first officer walked to the prow and stood beside us. "The fleet is beautiful in the sunset."

"Yes, it is," said Captain Marcus.

"We'll join it by morning," said the first officer. "None of you has been in battle."

"No. This is my first experience at sea."

"Captain, you have shown great skill in training the men."

Addressing all of us, he said, "The first encounter is always the most difficult. You think of all the things that can go wrong. You wonder what it feels like to be hit with an arrow. The greatest fear is that you will fail in your task or be paralyzed by fear. It will not happen. You will be so engrossed in what you are doing you will not be aware of the danger."

He turned to the captain. "Before we sailed, I made the obligatory sacrifice to Jupiter and requested the augurers read the signs. You will be pleased to know the augurers predicted, as they always do, a favorable outcome." He smiled and added, "It is possible Jupiter was attending to more important matters, but the sacrifice is there, should he be interested."

"I knew it was customary to make a sacrifice before an undertaking," said Captain Marcus, "but I was so engrossed in the resupply I overlooked everything else. Thank you for taking the initiative."

"Pompey ordered me to look after you. He told me of your application of the catapult. Your confidence impressed him. I have recruited the best officers and the best crew. Pompey assured me he was giving me the best ship in his fleet and that he expected me to see that you succeeded. We will take care of the ship. You take care of the catapult and the pirates."

"The catapult crew is ready," said the captain.

"I've served under Pompey since I was fifteen. He is good at what he does. When the Senate gave him authority to defeat the pirates, we knew the outcome. One day you will tell your grandchildren with great pride how you served under the great Pompey."

At break of day, Captain Marcus and the catapult crew were at the prow, amazed at the number of ships they saw, many of them pirate by their sail. The first officer pointed to a large pirate vessel, a trireme, maneuvering to board a Roman ship. "What are your orders, Captain?"

"Can you position us so that the pirate ship is between us and the Roman?"

"Yes, sir, in less than half an hour."

"Can you put us within fifty yards?" Captain Marcus asked.

"That is within arrow range, but we can do seventy-five yards without much danger."

"It is a trireme," said the third officer. "They have archers with crossbows aboard."

"Get me within seventy-five yards, and I will land a firepot on her main deck," said Captain Marcus.

"A ship this size has no chance against a trireme," said the third officer.

The first officer said, "Seventy-five yards with the pirate ship between us and the Roman. Yes, sir, within the half hour."

The third officer frowned and slapped the side of his leg with an arrow shaft fitted into a leather handle, then turned toward the rowers. No one strained at his oar. The ship moved sluggishly. He raised his stick and brought it down on the back of the nearest rower.

Captain Marcus stepped in front of the officer. "There will be none of that on this ship unless I order it." He turned toward the rowers and began walking back and forth along the gangway. "Put your backs into it!" he shouted, pointing again and again at the trireme. "Give me all you have. Get me close, and I will put a firepot on her main deck. This is the day we've been waiting for. From the foundation of the world, you were born for this day."

The men strained at the oars. The ship surged, and the trireme was soon between our vessel and the Roman.

Captain Marcus seated himself beside the catapult, removed some sheets from the chest, and studied the neat rows and columns representing distances traveled by pots in response to clicks on the windlass. With a series of hand signals to the helmsman, he maneuvered the ship into position. He shouted a number to the two men on the windlass. As they turned it to draw back the catapult arm, one man shouted the count as the claw dropped behind the next tooth, stopping when the count reached the number.

I prepared a good fire in the brazier and set on it a clay pot filled with pitch. With tongs from the water bucket, I placed it in the cup on the catapult arm and set ablaze the fabric around it. Captain Marcus held his hand high. When the ship's prow rose to the proper level, he dropped his hand. "Now!"

The catapult arm slammed against the crossbar, sending the pot toward the trireme, leaving a thin trail of black smoke. The crew cheered as the pot fell onto the main deck in a burst of flame and smoke. The captain leaped to his feet and joined the cheering.

As the pirate crew contained the fire, Captain Marcus ordered us to launch four additional pots. Some crashed onto the deck and burst into flames. The last one struck the sail, splashing burning pitch across it and setting it aflame. The pirates poured on buckets of sea water, but fire soon consumed the magnificent vessel.

Captain Marcus walked to the rail, listening to the cries of the pirate crew and galley slaves. He turned to his officers and crew. The rowers rested on their oars. "I am proud of you. We defeated a ship many times our size."

The day was far spent. I walked to the rail and watched the magnificent trireme burn until it slipped below the surface, along with all its men.

The following day, we prepared for the next encounter. I said to the captain, "Sir, the firepot that struck the sail yesterday and set it afire contained hot pitch. We should be sure the pitch is heated before launching the pots."

Captain Marcus looked up. "You are right. It needs to be burning to fire the sail."

"If I mount a Greek infantry shield over the brazier," I said, "it will hold three pots and keep the pitch heated."

"It is worth trying," said the captain. "Yesterday it took five launches. But if the first pot fires the sail, two should be sufficient, one to the sail and one to the deck. If there is a Greek shield aboard, I'll find it."

In a short time, the captain returned with a round metal Greek shield. The man at the water buckets extinguished the fire, and I nestled the shield on the top of the brazier, tested it for stability, then placed three pots in the center.

"Too much weight," I said. "We need to lower the brazier."

We spread the legs of the brazier, and I replaced the shield and firepots. My attempt to topple the firepots failed, and with tongs I lifted one from the brazier to the catapult. "It should work, but have the water bucket ready."

Each fleet spent the day improving its position. Captain Marcus stood at the prow of the ship with his evening ration. I joined him. The coolness of the breeze, the lapping of the waves at the prow, and the fading light added a sense of calm.

"Next time will be better, Animus," he said. "You were right; the pitch needs to be hot. I am pleased you are on the catapult."

"Thank you, sir. I am pleased to be there."

"I've been thinking about the men in the galley chained to their oars. The pirates deserved what happened to them. But imagine being chained and watching the fire come closer and closer. The Senate was right in giving Pompey authority to rid the sea of pirates."

Captain Marcus stared into the water below him. "There were probably three hundred rowers in the galley, all of them either drowned or burned to death. If I could collect in a vial their anguish and pain, how much would it weigh? A grain of wheat would weigh more. How can a single grain of wheat weigh more than the pain and anguish of all those men?"

I did not reply. After a long pause, he turned to me. "I'm not sure it is good to ponder such matters for any length of time. Let us end the day."

At first light the following day, everyone was at his station. The pirate fleet had repositioned with larger ships aligned, bow to stern, forming a shield for the smaller ones. With the captain's approval, the first officer turned our ship in that direction.

Standing at the prow, the first officer turned toward the captain and pointed to the line of vessels. Captain Marcus nodded. The first officer signaled the helmsman, who adjusted our course to align with the first ship. The rowers took their first stroke, and we surged forward.

"We will bear on the stern of the first ship in the line!" the first officer shouted. "When we get in range, you signal how to maneuver."

"Bear on the stern of the first ship," Captain Marcus said. "Slow at seventy-five yards. We will launch two pots into the sail that is broadside to us, then another to his main deck. Then I must adjust to come alongside."

The first officer repeated the order and walked to the stern of the ship.

I placed three pots on the Greek shield, with three additional ones close by. Adding wood to the fire, I watched the stern of the pirate ship draw closer. The captain removed one of the sheets from his chest and studied the neat rows and columns. Looking frequently at the pirate ship, he began signaling the first officer and the helmsman.

"Seventeen clicks!" he shouted.

"Seventeen clicks," repeated one of the men at the windlass. He began to rotate the drum, counting aloud each time the claw dropped.

I removed the tongs, grasped the nearest pot, and, careful not to spill pitch on the shield, lifted it onto the cup. With a burning stick, the point encased with pitch, I fired the pitch-smeared fabric. The heat from the brazier melted the pitch in the fabric, and it began to burn.

When the count reached seventeen, Captain Marcus held his hand aloft, waited for the ship to rise on the next swell, then dropped it, shouting, "Now!"

With a jarring crash, the catapult launched the pot. It struck the broad sail near the top, spreading burning pitch.

The crew readied the catapult for the next launch, and Captain Marcus shouted out, "Fifteen!" and signaled the first officer to slow the ship. I placed a heated pot in the catapult cup and fired the fabric.

When the count reached fifteen, Captain Marcus shouted, "Now!" The pot struck the burning sail and fell to the deck, spreading flames. The pirate crew fought the fire with buckets of sea water.

Captain Marcus signaled for a turn to the left and an increase in speed until we were a hundred yards from the stern of the second pirate ship. An occasional crossbow bolt pierced our sail or clattered to the deck.

The captain shouted, "Sixteen!" and the man at the windlass began his count. I placed a pot in the cup and fired it. Again, the captain shouted, "Now!"

That pot struck the sail of the second pirate ship, and the next hit the superstructure at the prow of the ship, fragmenting the pot and splashing burning pitch on several of the crew. Both ships were well ablaze.

The captain signaled the first officer to decrease the distance between our vessel and the third pirate ship, another magnificent trireme. He instructed the third officer to allow the rowers to rest on their oars, walked to the stern, and spoke with the first officer. He returned to the catapult, his face flushed. "We will to try to hit the trireme from here, out of the range of any ballista they might have."

He signaled for a maneuver to the right, stopping when the prow and catapult aligned with the center of the pirate ship, its sail now presenting a poor target.

I rekindled the fire in the brazier. Captain Marcus studied his paper and said, "Twenty-two."

The men on the windlass strained to reach twenty-two clicks as the cords of the windlass creaked loudly. Captain Marcus waited for the ship to rise with the swell and again shouted, "Now!"

The flaming pot crashed into the side of the ship about the center of the third bank of rowers. Much of the pitch must have entered the openings for the oars, for there was little fire on the outside. With twenty-three clicks, we landed two pots on the main deck.

The captain ordered the first officer to take control of the ship and withdraw. All three pirate vessels were engulfed in flames.

The next morning, there was not a pirate ship in sight. The following weeks were uneventful, as Pompey searched for the main pirate fleet. He was winning the war, scattering the main fleet into the eastern Great Sea.

Captain Marcus's ship had effectively used what he called "Pompey's fire." The encounters, even with large triremes, became routine but less frequent. The cries from the burning ships seemed louder with each success, and our men no longer cheered.

Between engagements, the captain sat by his chest, entering marks on the sheets and other documents. I had never witnessed anyone writing. The neat rows and columns fascinated me.

One day I asked, "What are you are doing?"

"I am writing." He removed from the chest a wax-coated wooden tablet and a stylus. He inscribed in the wax several letters of the Greek alphabet, showing me how to use the stylus. "A person must know the alphabet to write," he said. "You saw me make the letters. Form them just as I did. When you are ready, I will show you more."

He then handed me the tablet and stylus. I began to learn the Greek alphabet. One day I was practicing the alphabet when Livius, my friend on the windlass, asked, "What are you doing?"

"I'm learning to write so I can read," I said.

"Why do you want to write or read?" Livius said.

Captain Marcus, sitting nearby, said, "To make the catapult work, I must read and write."

"How could that make a catapult work?"

"My writing tells me the number of clicks needed to make a pot travel to a pirate ship. I tell you how many clicks to turn the windlass, and the pot hits the ship, because I write and read."

"I never have to hit anything with a clay pot," said Livius. "For a day's pay and something to eat, I don't need to read and to write."

I was the only one on the catapult who learned to read and write.

✝

On one occasion, all of us were at the catapult when Captain Marcus and the first officer joined us. "The ship has been under way for several months. Everyone has done well," said the captain. "I would like the ship to be distinctive. A red sail would do that. If we painted in yellow a large flaming firepot on the sail, it would announce to all the world who we are."

The first officer stared at the captain, then laughed and said, "By Jupiter, I should have thought of that. When the fleet regroups, I'll inquire of the captains whether they know of a red sail our size. I'll also take care of the yellow paint. By Jove, Captain, that is great. I wish I had thought of it."

Soon our ship displayed a distinctive red sail, the image of a large yellow flaming firepot in its center. The sail cost the first officer the promise of a cask of fine wine. He acquired the yellow paint with a requisition purportedly signed by his friend Pompey.

The reputation of the ship with the red sail soon spread throughout the pirate fleet.

✝

During one engagement, as the first officer was closing the distance with a large pirate vessel, the lookout shouted, "Pirate ship astern!"

The first officer said to the captain, "You must launch the firepot as soon as possible, and I will begin a turn to the left. I doubt we can complete the turn in time to launch a pot at the ship coming up behind us. I will order the second officer to prepare to repel boarders."

Captain Marcus consulted his chart and shouted, "Twenty-three!"

The men on the windlass were tightening the sinews, picking up the count with the next click. With the arm in position, I lifted a firepot to the cup and lit the fabric. It was burning briskly when the count reached twenty-three. Captain Marcus raised his hand, and as the prow of the ship rose, he shouted, "Now!"

The firepot catapulted toward the pirate ship's broad expanse of sail, striking the yard arm where it intersected the mast and breaking into a ball of fire and smoke. The sail was engulfed in flames.

Our ship had begun its turn, the rowers on the left pushing their oars to speed the maneuver. The men on the capstan started the count. The captain shouted, "Five!"

The catapult crew immediately had five clicks on the windlass, and I set a pot in the cup. The pirates, now less than fifty yards away, were showering us with arrows and crossbow bolts. As our ship's prow turned toward the oncoming pirate vessel and aligned with the edge of its sail, the captain shouted, "Now!"

The firepot struck the sail, splashed a small amount of pitch, fell to the deck, shattered, and spread fire around the mast.

Our officers rushed to the deck with shields and weapons. Every other rower on the right and left withdrew his oar and armed himself. As our ship continued its turn to the left, archers released arrows at the pirates. Others deflected or cut the grappling hooks as the ships came closer. The pirate ship came along our right side, its sail ablaze.

Captain Marcus shouted to the catapult crew, "Report to the second officer! We must defend the ship."

Some pirate arrows found their marks, wounding our men. Livius, standing in front of me, drew his sword. A bolt struck his lower body, penetrating nearly to the feathered guide. He sat down, yet with a wan smile and look of wonderment.

The second officer, arrow in hand, shouted and pointed to targets for the bowmen. I picked up a bow and quiver of arrows and ran to an opening between shields. I strung the bow, nocked an arrow, and found my target, a pirate swinging a grappling hook. I pulled the bow to the point of the arrow, felt its great strength, and let the arrow fly. It struck him in the left shoulder, knocking him off balance. Two more arrows penetrated well into his chest.

I drew another arrow and looked to the second officer. He pointed to a crewman directing some pirates preparing to board. My arrow penetrated deep into the man's chest. He dropped.

Flames engulfed the sail, and burning fragments fell on the pirate crew. The third officer shouted orders to the few rowers straining to propel the ship. Our vessel pulled away, the grappling hooks severed or trailing their lines.

I unstrung my bow and gave it, with the quiver and its few arrows, to the second officer, who was collecting weapons, and went to find Livius.

"Animus, I never thought I would be the one," he said. "I've seen similar wounds. I'll be dead by this time tomorrow, if I am fortunate, in two or three days if I am not."

He removed his tunic, folded it neatly, and placed it over his breechcloth to absorb the blood oozing from the wound. He looked down at the shaft. "It is not so long but has accomplished its purpose."

I sat on the deck beside him. The area around the shaft was red and slightly swollen.

"Livius, my friend, can I do anything for you? Let me fetch you some wine and take you to a more comfortable place."

"Yes, Animus," he said. "Place my pallet by the catapult so I can lean against it. Some wine would be good. The pain is not so great."

When I returned, Captain Marcus was standing beside him. "Livius, I am sorry. When I picked you to serve on the catapult, it was a good choice. Animus has some wine."

Turning to me, the captain said, "Look after him. Help him all you can. He was good on the catapult."

I handed a cup of wine to Livius. He drank, then lowered the cup and handed it to me. "That was good. I was thirsty."

I folded Livius's pallet, placed it next to one of the forward legs of the catapult, and helped him to it. I lowered him onto it, positioning him so he could look over the prow. Livius grimaced, then said, "This is much better. Some more wine would be nice."

I found a wineskin in the galley, filled his cup, then hung the wineskin on the catapult. The sun was sinking below the horizon. In the fading light, I could see his wound had become a deeper red and was badly swollen. He would have his wish. He would not live until sunset tomorrow.

I sat on a small box beside Livius and leaned against the other leg of the catapult. In the deepening twilight, he appeared to be sleeping. A tiredness seeped in, and I dozed. In the night, I was awakened by a groan. Leaning toward Livius, I whispered, "Are you all right?"

He made no reply. I smelled the sweet savor of the wound. I again leaned back and fell asleep only to be startled awake. "Livius, are you all right?"

"Animus, you are here! I thought I was alone. I am thirsty. Is there more wine?"

"Yes."

In the darkness, I retrieved the wineskin, located the cup, and filled it. With my left hand on his shoulder, I held the cup for him. He touched my arm, followed it to the cup, and grasped it. He swallowed the wine in great gulps. "The fever has started." After a prolonged silence, he added, "Animus, thank you for staying. Take my hand. I do not want to die alone."

I reached into the darkness, found his right hand, and closed my fingers around his. They were hot to my touch. After a few minutes, his grasp weakened. I squeezed his hand, and he pressed mine in return. I dozed, waking occasionally to squeeze his hand and feel his weak response.

Toward dawn, I woke with a start. Like a flash of light, a realization struck me. I had been the target of the bolt that took down Livius. Just before he was hit, I had stepped behind him. Had I stayed in the open, I would be the wounded one. My life had been spared at the cost of his.

I still held his hand in my own. It was hot, and I could smell the wound.

✝

In the morning light, the blood draining from the wound was dark brown, and its savor filled the air. By the end of the first day watch, Livius no longer responded. He lay against the leg of the catapult as though asleep, his chest gently rising and falling. I continued to hold his hand. His breathing became shallow and irregular. Near the end of the second watch, he took a long, deep breath, slowly exhaled, and breathed no more. I removed his hand from my own and folded both hands over his chest.

Late that afternoon, the catapult crew dressed him in his tunic and with a hemp line secured a firepot to his feet. We placed him on a board and carried him to the rail. After a moment, we tipped the board and let his body slip feet first into the sea. I watched as the white tunic disappeared into the clear blue water.

Subject to the captain's approval, the first officer selected one of the rowers to take Livius's place on the catapult.

✝

Once during a routine patrol, I asked the captain why all the pots had to have the same weight.

"Nature has laws," he said. "When we know the laws, we know how she responds. If the pot always weighs the same, it will always hit in the same place, if I use the same clicks—that's the law. At the university, I studied nature's laws. I hope to do that again when I return. My papers will help me." Then he asked, "Do you believe nature has laws?"

I thought a moment. "There must be laws, or things would not work."

"The more of nature's laws we know and follow, the better things work for us. I hope you find all the laws you will need."

The captain turned to the horizon. "Animus, the more we know, the more we can determine what will happen. The distance a stone travels is determined by both the weight of the stone and the push behind it. That is the reason for all those papers and for the practice. When we know what will happen, we can prepare for it. That is how we spend our time at the university. That is the purpose of it all, to learn the laws of nature so we can do better."

He looked at me. "It is worth thinking about. When I could predict the path of a stone or a firepot, I was sure I could hit a pirate ship. When I see the devastation of a firepot, I think I should have spent my time learning why a basket with the same weight as the stone would not travel as far, when each is propelled by the same push."

The captain stood his full height. "Let us end the day on that problem. May you rest well."

I knew a basket with the same weight as a stone would not travel as far but never thought why. I marveled that people spent their lives studying such matters.

✝

During the next few weeks, encounters with the pirates became less frequent. Captain Marcus learned Pompey was granting freedom to the crew of any pirate ship that surrendered its vessel and cargo. On our next encounter, we launched a firepot to cross the bow of the pirate ship. After it splashed into the sea, the captain said to the third officer, "Tell them to lower their sail."

The third officer refused. In a rage, he shouted, "Launch the firepot!"

Captain Marcus walked to the third officer and in a voice barely above a whisper, enunciating clearly each word, said, "Tell the ship to lower its sail or the next one will hit the ship."

The third officer hesitated a moment, then clamped under his left arm the stick he always carried. He formed both hands into a cup, raised them to his lips, and shouted the command at the top of his voice. The crew cheered as the pirates lowered their sail. The captain and third officer joined in the celebration.

†

During periods between engagements, I practiced the alphabet until I could form each letter and call it by name. The captain encouraged me, and soon I could write my name in both Greek and Latin.

When the ship entered a port to replenish food and water, Captain Marcus invited me to join him visiting the city. It hosted a small academy, and after several inquiries, we found it in an abandoned temple on a hill just outside the city. The teacher was an elderly man hosting many students, each studying a manuscript.

"My name is Aetus Marcus," the captain said. "I am a student of mathematics at the university in Alexandria. Your academy has a good name there. My friend here is a sailor on my ship. He has learned to write and to read Greek. He has never seen a Greek manuscript. Do you have one I can show him?"

"Welcome to our academy. We are honored by your presence. You have heard of our academy. That is encouraging. Please follow me. We have a number of manuscripts."

We followed him to the rear of the temple where a large room opened to the outside. In the shelves and on the tables were scrolls and manuscripts, some rolled and others lying flat. He walked to the nearest table and studied the open manuscript lying there.

"This is the beginning of *The Iliad*," he said. "It is easy to read." He stood aside.

Captain Marcus stepped to the table and studied the manuscript a moment, then motioned to me. I saw a parchment filled with Greek letters, all close together. The captain placed his index finger under the first letters in the upper left corner and moved it as he read aloud.

From the jumble of letters, Captain Marcus read words. It was a miracle, a feeling like that when Theron pointed out the Great Sea. I had seen a vast new sea and a new world.

After some polite conversation with the teacher, the captain thanked him for his hospitality, complimented him on his library and his academy, and wished him well. We returned to the ship. I was so overcome with what I had witnessed I said nothing.

Pompey's strategy succeeded. The pirate fleet was greatly diminished and sought refuge in the numerous inlets where the rugged Tarsus Mountains dropped into the sea. In the final battle, he trapped what remained of the fleet in a large bay, but before he could close the opening, several ships close to the shore slipped away. The lookout on our ship shouted a warning to the captain, who gave chase—the only time he had attempted to engage four ships in open water. After closing with the nearest ship, he launched a firepot over the pirate's bow. Then he shouted to the third officer, "Tell them to lower their sail or the next one will hit their ship."

The officer shouted the command. There was no response. The captain launched a second firepot, again close to the bow. On a signal from the captain, the third officer again ordered the ship to lower its sail. The pirate ship did so. We watched in amazement as the other ships also began lowering their sails.

It was an end to the war with the Cilician pirates in keeping with the best tradition of Pompey the Great.

Pompey won his war, and the fleet returned to its home port, but not before the first officer had extracted a cask of fine wine from one of the pirate ships to pay for the red sail.

A few days after arriving in port, Captain Marcus received word General Pompey was to visit our ship. The officers and the crew cleaned the ship and in their best dress received the general.

He was resplendent in a red tunic of the finest cloth, the leather of his armor rich in texture, its metal polished, his demeanor one of unquestioned command. In keeping with his style, he wore no toga to obscure his armor. He was the commander of the fleet that had cleared the Great Sea of the Cilician pirates.

General Pompey greeted the first officer as an old friend. "My heartfelt greetings, my friend, as first officer of this ship."

Motioning to Captain Marcus to join him, the general addressed all the ship's crew in his commanding voice. "On behalf of the Roman Senate, I make the following pronouncement and declaration. It is the will of the Senate that each of you be awarded Roman citizenship, that each of you be offered a tract of land in a Roman province of your choice, and that each of you be awarded a sum of money representing your share of the prize of the pirate ships and their cargos surrendering to this ship. I have here a list of those so surrendering, but you know their names better than I," he said, handing the list to an attending aide.

General Pompey addressed Captain Marcus. "Thank you for your service to Rome and to me as commander of this fleet. Your catapult did more to win this war than any of my ships. Not one of my other captains ever ordered successfully the surrender of an enemy ship with a voice command to lower its sail." He added, "As captain of this ship, you followed with great consistency my first commandment for victory: maneuver the adversary into a position where his ship is indefensible and maneuver your ship into a position where it is invulnerable. My other captains should follow this commandment as well. Your return to the university is their great gain and our great loss. May the gods who kept watch over you continue to do so."

An aide handed the general a tightly rolled document. "Captain Marcus, I have here a letter bearing my signet expressing my personal appreciation for your service. It is recognition of your contribution to the success of this fleet in its victory over the Cilician pirates. Accept it as a token of my esteem."

After brief conversation with the first officer, General Pompey again turned to the ship's crew. His voice supporting his demeanor, he expressed again his appreciation to Captain Marcus, the officers, and the crew for their role in winning the war. In a final gesture of genuine goodwill and with dignity in keeping with his rank, he raised his hand in formal salute and held it there for an extended period. As he lowered his hand, he said in his commanding voice, "For the Senate and the people of Rome." Then General Pompey, commander of the Roman Fleet, turned and with his officers and aides left the ship.

I was awed by what I had witnessed. It will always be one of the high points of my life. I had never seen anyone with an air of command like that evidenced by General Pompey. Every movement showed authority. I had never seen Roman officers in full military attire, resplendent in their armor, made more so in the brilliant sunshine. I also did not fully realize what had just transpired with the grant of citizenship, a grant of land, and a sum of money.

Some days later, amid the confusion of preparing to leave the navy, I made an occasion to speak alone with Captain Marcus. In my best Greek, I said, "I want to thank you for all you have done for me, especially teaching me to read and to write. I look forward to claiming my land and farming it. I plan to visit the university in Tarsus to learn more about the things you have shown me. I will never forget our visit to the academy and seeing you read from the manuscript. I look forward to the day when I can do the same."

I hesitated. "I would like for you to secure for Livius his share of the money. He told me of his family and where they live. I will make sure they receive it. He was a good man and my friend. I owe that to him. I give you my word it will be done."

"I am pleased you made the request," he said. "His name will be with the others. I know you will get the money to his family." Then he added, "I am saddened that now this must end. It has been a great venture. I have learned more than I ever imagined. Animus, I have great hope for you. You have a good spirit and learn well. Continue the effort. I wish we could meet again in a few years and talk."

I yet recall that benediction.

Some days later at the naval yard, leaving the ship for the last time, Captain Marcus led us to one of the many buildings. In a large room, with maps displayed on a row of tables, each member of the crew selected a site from numerous Roman lands and was issued a document granting ownership. The document was in Latin. I could read it. I had become a landowner in Cilicia. I rolled the document into a scroll and placed it inside my tunic.

We went to another building where my name was entered on a document granting me Roman citizenship. There was my name in beautiful Latin letters. Not only had I become a land owner, I was now a Roman citizen. I rolled that document and placed it inside my tunic.

Finally, in a well-guarded area, I walked to a table in a small doorway where each sailor received a leather pouch filled with gold coins. When the officer motioned for me to sign where the others had made their marks, I signed my name in neat, well-formed letters. I smiled as I returned the reed stylus to the officer and picked up my pouch. Its weight was significant. *There is a fortune here*, I thought.

Captain Marcus then led us to a small courtyard where, at one end, was a table with more pouches. He held up his hand for silence. "Thank you for your service. It has been my pleasure to serve with you. I am returning to the university. I am pleased to become a Roman citizen. I can now wear a toga with the best of my friends. As my home is the university, I have no need for a grant of land. Neither have I need for the money. The papers in my chest are worth far more. I have divided my share among all of you. I shall be forever in your debt."

I was deeply moved by the captain, a man of meager means, giving away more than he could earn in a lifetime. He then called each of us to the table, handed us a pouch, and thanked us for some personal contribution. The sincerity displayed in his conduct added to the solemnity of parting.

When my turn came, I said, "I shall be forever in your debt. Since I learned to read and to write, the world now is a different place. That means more to me than the settlement." Hesitating a moment, I added, "But not more than the land. I shall never forget."

When the third officer's turn came, he saluted the captain, laid on the table the stick he always carried, and said, "Should you need to discipline a student. I have no further need of it. It has been my pleasure to serve on your ship."

When the first officer stood before the table, Captain Marcus said, "Thank you for your tolerance and for obeying Pompey's command to watch over me. Someday we need to compare notes. May Jupiter and the augurers continue to smile on your ventures." He handed him his pouch.

Captain Marcus waited until the first officer returned to his place. He then raised his hand in salute, held it for a moment with all the dignity of Pompey's salute, and said in a loud and firm voice, "For the Senate and the people of Rome. *Ave atque vale.*"

Two men near the captain placed the small chest on the waiting cart. The crew watched as he and the cart disappeared into the crowd.

It was late fall, the war was over, and it was only a year and a half ago that I had left the farm. I would be home by spring.

A few days later, in an extended conversation with some Cilician pirates, I became interested in two of them. I said, "You are fortunate. Most of the pirate ships were sunk and the crews drowned."

The older one replied, "Our ship avoided Pompey, especially the one with the red sail. We were granted freedom when our captain surrendered."

"How did you come to be on the ship?"

The older laughed. "We grew up in a small village. Being on a ship was better—we ate regularly."

"What did you do in your village?" I asked.

"We worked for the owner of a small hillside farm, if it could be called a farm. Rocks mostly. It produced little. Our families moved away."

"When did you last eat?"

"Yesterday. A sailor gave us his wafers."

"I have not eaten today," I said. "Let us find a place to eat, and we can talk."

We walked into the old section of the city and found an eating place, the noise from within providing some assurance of its quality.

I worked my way through the crowd to a table in an open courtyard and ordered. It would be welcome fare after the hardtack and the poor wine.

After the meal, I explained I had been granted land in Cilicia. "I have not seen the land, and it is some distance from my home. I need help to make of it what I can. Whether the land is good or poor, I will pay you good wages for one year. I work hard and expect you to do the same. Do you understand?"

The men looked at each other, nodded in agreement, and the older said, "We promise to work as hard as you. This we swear before the gods that saved us from Pompey and from starvation."

"We will be in Cilicia before the winter rains. My name is Animus. I will present you to my family as friends but to everyone else as brothers. If we work hard, we can make a living."

The older pirate introduced himself. "My name is Cletus. I look forward to working for you."

The second pirate said, "I am Felix. I promise to work as hard as either of you."

I booked passage to Corinth and then from Corinth to Tarsus, where I purchased a large two-wheeled cart and two fine mules. I filled the cart with equipment, raiment, and supplies, among them a fine toga.

"Before we leave Tarsus," I said, "we need a good meal." I took them to the eating place where Theron and I had dined. The proprietor took us to the back of the establishment and seated us.

"Your best meal for the three of us." I said to my friends, "It may be our best meal for a while. Let us enjoy it."

After we ate, I found the hostel where Theron and I stayed, arranged for a night's lodging, and we passed the night, thankful we were no longer at sea.

The next morning, after preparing the cart, we were out of Tarsus by good light. The three of us sat on the bench seat. They talked of their ventures in Pompey's war, their families, and their work on the farm. At the spring where Theron and I had encountered the bandits, in spite of a new growth of brambles, we made a shelter from the cart's cover, prepared an evening meal, then slept the night through.

The second day, Cletus and Felix did the driving. Late in the afternoon, we arrived at my home.

Father and the siblings were surprised and delighted. "Animus, you are back!" shouted Father, his voice breaking. "We feared we would never see you again. The gods did answer our prayers. Oh, Animus, my son, my son, welcome home."

I embraced my brothers and sisters and wiped tears from my eyes. Despite my joy, I was distressed at seeing how gaunt they were and the shabby state of their raiment. From Pompey's generosity and good fortune, I could now improve their lot.

"Where is Mother?" I asked.

Everyone was silent. Father finally said, "Last winter was long and hard. It was colder than usual. Weevils again spoiled the acorns. We had little to go on. One morning your mother did not wake."

I turned aside and wiped tears, remembering how frail she was in that last embrace. I set it aside. I would mourn for her at another time when I could recall our good times.

I motioned for Cletus and Felix to dismount and introduced them as my friends as everyone helped unload the cart. I explained I had done well in Pompey's navy, owned a parcel of land on the Cydmus River, and could help them through the hard times.

"Here is good grain, wheat meal, and cheese," I said, "enough to last awhile, and clothing and sandals for everyone. The clothing for Mother, you can use. I can provide more when you need it. I am not that far away."

My sisters set about preparing the evening meal. They could not conceal their delight, laughing and talking at the same time.

"Oh, Animus, I've never seen so much, and it is all so good. Oh, if Mother could only be here, she would be the happiest of all," shouted one sister over the noise.

While my sisters prepared the meal, I talked with my oldest

brother. "Here is some money. Use it where it will do the most good. No one needs to know," I said, handing him a pouch.

He opened it and shook some coins into his open hand, then said, "Animus, I've never seen so much money. It will last forever."

After a pause, he added, "None of it will be squandered. I will care for everyone. I regret Mother is not here. Every morning and every evening, she expressed her concern for you. Welcome home, Animus. It is good to have you back."

By the time the meal was served, everyone had donned new raiment and leather sandals. All dined well and sufficiently for the first time since before my departure.

After the meal, we talked into the night. I related my experiences, telling stories about Captain Marcus, the catapult crew, and the great Pompey. My two friends joined in the conversation freely when the opportunity presented itself.

The next morning after a good breakfast, my friends and I said our goodbyes, made the parting embraces, and started toward the Cydmus River Valley. On arriving there, I located the land. It was a larger tract than I had imagined, covered in heavy forest, with a stream cascading down the mountain. The land itself sloped gently toward the river. This was some of the finest land in Cilicia.

Later that fall, before winter rains made travel difficult, I prepared for the journey to find Livius's family. I explained to Cletus and Felix the nature and purpose of my journey. Packing a quantity of wafers and cheese into a pouch and selecting the gentler of the two mules, I set out for eastern Cilicia, leaving my friends in charge of the land.

I followed Livius's directions and found the village where his family resided. I explained why I was there but did not mention the money.

After visiting with the family, I determined one of the older brothers was by far the most responsible. He operated a small livery in town. I met privately with him and explained the source of the money and that the amount was sufficient to provide a better life for all his family.

As our meeting came to an end, I said, "Livius was my friend. He was a good man. He served well the ship and accepted his death without complaint. Do not betray his dream. With his death, he purchased the opportunity to achieve it. No longer in the evening will there be the eternal hunger, nor at sunrise, the bone-weary tiredness. He made possible a better life for generations to come."

During the journey home, I was in a pensive mood. I had done for Livius what he would have done for me. Also, I sensed that somehow Livius had been with me during my visit, and even now was with me. I envisioned his giant form before me, saying, "Well done, Animus, my good friend. I am content. You may now let go my hand."

When I reached the Cydmus River, I turned north toward the farm. I was home at last.

✝

Over several years, my friends and I cleared the land and built for each a house with a large courtyard. True to my promise, I gave Cletus and Felix land close to the river. Each married and settled into a life prescribed by the season, the weather, and the crops.

As soon as my children could hold a tablet and stylus, I began teaching them to read and write. The boys could write their names before they were able to plow, the girls by the time they could cook.

Once a year, I journeyed to Tarsus. All the family joined in cleaning and oiling the harness, scrubbing the cart, and washing and currying the mules. As part of the ritual, I unpacked my toga and practiced its proper draping until the procedure appeared casual. In Tarsus, after purchasing supplies, I visited the university seeking counsel regarding a manuscript. I came to know the teachers and usually returned with a manuscript. It was my only indulgence.

In late summer and early fall, after the evening meal, sitting in the courtyard, I read to my children from one of the manuscripts, but only after I had mastered the material. In reviewing the day's work and planning for the days ahead, I observed that I had lived in the best of times. I had accomplished my purpose in life with a deep sense of belonging to the land, of being a part of the order of things, like the eternal forests of the Taurus Mountains. My children said I treated everyone as a member of my family. My neighbors said I was generous to a fault. My grandson, Cornelius, would later say I was a landmark on which to guide.

CYRUS AND MYRRINE

My name is Cyrus, youngest child of Animus. My two brothers and I worked the fields alongside our father while our mother and three sisters attended to the household, everyone with a daily routine.

By first light, everyone had finished the morning meal, and the men gathered in the courtyard. Father loved his ox like one of us. To conserve its strength, each of us carried the equipment. Father took the heaviest, usually the plow. Then, according to age, each son picked up the next heaviest. I, being the youngest, tended to the waterskin and led the ox. My father felt a kinship with that animal. As the hunter and his dog, the falconer and his bird, the cavalryman and his horse, so it was with Animus and his ox.

One morning when Father attempted to lift the plow to his shoulder, it fell heavily to the ground. A second attempt failed. He walked to the oxbow, lifted it to his shoulder, and walked from the courtyard. My oldest brother walked to the plow, lifted it to his shoulder, and followed. Father's joy of living was not diminished. It was for me, however, a sudden awakening to our ephemeral existence.

When his oldest son could do a man's work, Father's trip to Tarsus and the university included an arrangement for a teacher to spend time with us. In late summer, after the main crops were in and the fieldwork lighter, my mother and sisters prepared one of the rooms opening to the courtyard. For the next several weeks, the teacher was a member of our family.

After finishing morning chores, my parents and all the children gathered in the courtyard where the teacher took charge until the noon meal. He recited the history of Rome or of Athens or another city, the circumstance of a great battle, or the legends of a hero, real or mythical. After the noon meal, everyone returned to work, and then after the evening meal, all of us gathered in the courtyard again.

One evening Father asked, "Does everything follow a rule?"

The teacher thought for a moment, then said, "Everything does follow a rule. The sun rises, and the moon sets, the wheat seed grows, and each of us lives our life by rules. That is why the world works, and we are part of the world."

"How do we know?" Father asked.

"The rules exist and have existed from the beginning. Each mistake teaches us. We spend our lifetime learning. We learn that fire burns and a bee stings. If we learn well, the world is full of goodness; if we do not, the world becomes a difficult place."

Father thought a moment. "If you are still learning, how do you know they exist?"

"I do not know they exist as surely as I know a bee stings, but I will know for certain when I enter that other world."

After a few moments of silence, Father stood, indicating the session was over. Each wished the others a pleasant night and retired.

Father frequently spent afternoons with the teacher studying one of the manuscripts. Over the years, he became a student not only of the Greek language but also of the subject matter of the manuscripts. He grew careful in his speech, and his outbursts of temper became less frequent. The family became careful in their speech, especially in the use of swear words. My father never used a swear word in anger. Once as we sat around the evening fire in early fall after having read from a manuscript, as a benediction to the day's communion he said, "Language is too beautiful to tarnish with obscenities."

When winter rains threatened and before the roads became difficult, Father prepared the cart. With some sadness, we watched as the cart and our teacher disappeared in the distance.

One summer day, on returning to the house for the noon meal, Father faltered in his walking, steadied himself, and allowed me to assist him to the shade of a large tree. He sat on a stone, leaned against the trunk, looked over the valley, and entered that other world. He is content there, standing atop one of its giant outcroppings or walking along a field of ripe wheat, holding out his extended palm, passing it over the full heads, remarking what a fine crop it is.

At the proper time, my two older brothers left home, attended the university for a short period, joined a commercial venture, and seldom returned. I marveled that each was paid so much for doing so little. My sisters married and joined their husbands, giving up the rural life.

When my brothers were at home, my father had done the planning, but my mother had become the steward. She made sure we knew what to do, had the proper equipment with which to do it, and did it well and on time. She had a special ability to see a problem before it became a serious matter. Occasionally, she would remind me that had I done some task differently, it would have been easier or required less time.

She did have a special project. Shortly after their marriage and before the first child, she, with Father's help, constructed a small aqueduct, diverting part of the stream above the house to the courtyard near the kitchen.

It was a fine farm. On the hillside, the olive trees were mature and full of olives. In the vineyard, in neat rows, grapes grew in large clusters. The level ground, with its rich, black soil, did well. Frequently, when crops needed it, the water from the courtyard was diverted into the fields. The earth yielded up its goodness.

†

When I attended the university, the change was not difficult. Over the years, my teachers had prepared me, and I renewed their friendship. One of the teachers, Simmias of Tarsus, said, "A friend of mine in town is seeking a steward. I believe you would do well as one. Would you be interested in talking with him, Cyrus?"

"I never thought about anything but farming, but I would like to talk with him."

"Good. I will arrange a meeting. The man's name is Moshe Benjamin. He is the most successful merchant in Tarsus. You will find him an interesting man. He is Jewish, but that is of no concern."

A few days later, Simmias said he had arranged for me to meet Moshe. "Do not try to impress him. Do not even wear your toga. He is looking for a steward, not a husband for his daughter. Listen to what he says and answer his questions as best you can. You have the traits he is looking for. You will do well."

The meeting was to be in Moshe's office at his main warehouse in Tarsus. I arrived prior to the time. I had been in the warehouse previously, buying supplies, but had never been in the office. I introduced myself to one of the workers, who led me to an adjoining office and pointed to a chair.

In a few moments, he returned and led me into another office filled with papers, scrolls, and tablets. A tall, deeply bronzed man dressed in a plain tunic walked in. "Welcome to my humble office. My name is Moshe Benjamin. People call me Moshe. You are early. That is an admirable trait," he said. "Simmias speaks highly of you. I was raised in a small village in Palestine. When my family arrived here, Simmias taught us the ways of Tarsus. I shall be forever in his debt."

I was impressed by his air of command and that he spoke without accent. He was in his forties, his black hair cut in the Roman style, his bright eyes enhanced by his bronzed features.

"It is difficult to find good men. I understand you are from north of the city, that your family owns a fine farm there."

"Yes, sir. My father was granted the land for service with Pompey in the war against the Cilician pirates. He worked hard making it a fine farm. We are not landed people."

"Do not apologize," Moshe said. "Had your family been landed, you would not be here. I have lost good men by not employing them, but culling out bad ones takes so much time I cannot afford to look for good ones."

Moshe paused, then said, "Simmias says you are proficient in Greek and Latin. How did you come by those skills?"

"When each child was old enough to hold it, my father gave us a tablet and stylus. We could read and write Greek by the time we could do a day's work. When we were older, he brought a teacher from the university to spend time with us. Simmias spent several summers with us. He taught me Latin."

"Simmias is an old sophist and an authority on Stoic philosophy," Moshe said. "Not many of his kind are left. The world is poorer as a result. What do you think of his teaching?"

"At the university, after his sessions, the logic of his teaching was stronger than ever. Teachers holding other beliefs cannot overcome his arguments. The sessions with all the teachers present are the best to see Simmias discredit their argument with so little effort. I do not know whether it is their inexperience or that their beliefs are indefensible. I never miss one. He is like a magnificent mountain goat in a secluded clearing, defending his domain, surrounded by a pack of snarling, young sheep dogs. At the end of the day, he is still standing, the young dogs on the ground, whimpering, licking their wounds."

"Do you believe people are put here for a purpose, Cyrus?"

"Yes," I replied.

"Do you believe a person knows right from wrong and is supposed to do right?"

"The answer also is yes."

"Simmias does well at the university," Moshe said, indicating the meeting was over.

I stood and thanked him, adding, "I will think about your questions. I look forward to our next meeting."

Some days later, I said to Simmias, "I met with your friend, Moshe. He was complimentary of your work. He asked some questions. I've been thinking about the answers. I am curious why he asked the questions and how they relate to being a steward."

"I spoke with Moshe a few days after your meeting. He was impressed with your confidence and your spirit. Moshe is careful whom he hires. He believes a man's character is evidenced by what he does, and what he does is evidence of what he believes. He was impressed you are competent in Greek and Latin, which is unusual for anyone from the working class. You are fortunate your father taught you those skills."

Simmias hesitated, then said, "You should think about whether you want to work for Moshe. Working for him requires commitment. It is an unusual opportunity, and I am sure he will offer it to you. He rewards achievement. The harder you work, the more responsibility he will give you. The people who work for him love him and love their work. He has a fine reputation in Tarsus."

"Thank you for arranging the meeting," I said. "I will give it careful thought."

Simmias nodded. "Do not forget that you are here for a purpose. I am sure you will make the right decision."

Early the next day at the livery, I hitched a pair of mules to the cart and set out for the farm, arriving the following day. After the evening meal, my mother and I sat in the courtyard, each enjoying the companionship of the other.

I told her about Simmias's recommendation and about the meeting with Moshe. "I would like to work for Moshe, but what about the farm?"

"Do not worry about the farm," she said. "I knew when you left this day would come. Your father would want you to take the opportunity. That is why he taught you to read and to write and had the teachers visit us. Such opportunities do not drop from the sky. If you give it your best effort and do not succeed, Moshe will release you. A dissatisfied man working for him would result in two dissatisfied people. If it does not work, you will know it was not meant to be."

She paused a moment. "It is nice to have you home again, but with help from Cletus, Felix, and their children, we can manage the farm. If you work for Moshe, Tarsus is not that far away. You can come back to help if we need you."

"That is the reason I came home. I knew you would have worked out the answer before I arrived."

After returning to the university, I sought a meeting with Simmias. "How was your trip?" he asked.

"It is always good to be home, if only for the night. I thought about many things. I've decided to work for Moshe, if he offers me the opportunity. I need your assistance to know what to do."

"Be yourself," Simmias said. "Always be open and honest with everyone. You will do well. Go by his office as soon as you can. Early mornings are best. He will see you."

The next morning, I was at Moshe's office when it opened. He motioned for me to enter. "I am pleased to see you again, Cyrus. I hope you have good news."

"I hope it is good news," I said. "I have not yet worked out the answers to your questions, but Simmias helped me understand why you asked them. I believe I am here for a purpose, accountable for my actions, and if I do my best, I will succeed. I have worked long and hard enough to confirm that belief."

"Your answers are sufficient for now. I would like for you to work for me. Let me assure you your work will be interesting, and I will provide what you need to do it well. I need men who can take responsibility. You will be judged on how well you get things done."

"I must tell you something," I said, "that may have a bearing on my coming to work for you. Our farm is about two days north of the city. My mother manages the farm since my father's death. I am the youngest of the children. I must look after my mother and the farm. We discussed the situation. She says she can manage and for me to work for you. I assure you I will give my best effort."

"I am pleased to see you take responsibility for your mother and the farm," Moshe said. "If you need help, I will be pleased to do what I can. Thank you for letting me know."

"You are very kind. I will try that much harder."

"You may start work when you are ready," Moshe said. "I will introduce you to the people who will instruct you. I am pleased to welcome you to our business and look forward to a long and pleasant relationship."

"Thank you, sir. You will not be disappointed."

The next day, I met with Simmias and reported all that had happened. "Thank you for making the opportunity. Your counsel was what I needed. I am to start to work as soon as I can."

"I am pleased for you," Simmias said. "I visit Moshe frequently, and I am always here at the university, if I can be of assistance.

The next day, I reported for work, and Moshe introduced me to the steward over the wheat section of the warehouse. He was an older man, heavily built from years of working in commodities. Walking toward the section, he described his duties. "This is the time of year we begin receiving Egyptian wheat. It is a prize commodity. I verify the quality and seal the container. A ship is due in a few days, and I must be ready. I need to separate the wheat that is here, the good from the poor, and keep it organized."

In light provided by the high openings, I could see large clay pots in racks and others on their side and bags of wheat scattered about.

"I know what is here. It is marked in the seal of the clay pots or on the bag," said the steward. "This is the result of planning by our city leaders. While the shipyards were building the fleets, times were good. When they finished, there was no work and little money. People could afford only poor-quality wheat. Egyptian wheat was available at a fair price, but only the wealthy could afford it. To address the problem, the city leaders agreed to set the price for wheat low enough so that everyone could afford it."

He examined a bag of wheat. "The merchants knew what was about to happen and bought all the good wheat. By the time the law passed, there was no good wheat to be had at any price. The low price caused a scarcity in the supply, and the quality of the available wheat fell. The city leaders decided the low price had been a mistake and withdrew the law. I am still trying to recover."

Pointing to some racks, the steward said, "We have a few days to get everything in order. We need to repair the racks and build enough new ones to hold all the pots. Any pots containing poor-quality wheat need to be separated. The wheat in the bags is poor quality, but it will sell easily at the current price. I will mark on the floor an area for each grade of wheat in bags and mark the racks for the pots. As I grade the wheat, you make sure it gets to the proper place."

"I will see that it does."

"I'll contact the carpenters now so they will be here in the morning."

The next morning, the carpenters completed both the repairs and the construction of new racks. The steward then verified the grade of wheat in each container, and I directed the laborers in placing them in the racks. On several occasions, I helped the steward decipher letters and symbols on the wax seal of a container. By the end of the following day, the bags were in the designated place in neat stacks and the clay pots were in racks, also separated by quality. A section of new racks awaited the shipment of Egyptian wheat.

The shipment arrived a few days later, and the steward inspected the wax seal that filled the mouth of each jar. If he recognized the signet of the shipper, he accepted the jar. If he did not recognize the signet, or if he recognized the signet as one who occasionally shipped poor quality, he would verify the quality. By noon of the following day, all the pots containing Egyptian wheat were unloaded and neatly stored in the special racks.

"Cyrus, thank you for your help. Without it, I would not have been ready. You will begin working in another section tomorrow. It has been my pleasure. You will do well," said the steward.

Over the next year, I was assigned to stewards in other sections. Moshe was receiving reports about my work and was assigning me to areas to be trained. Frequently, on encountering Moshe in the warehouse, we would exchange greetings and a few comments, but he gave no indication that he was monitoring my progress. When I requested permission to spend a few days at home, my requests were granted. My interest in my work continued to grow.

✝

Moshe had constructed a large villa not far from his warehouse, complete with a manicured courtyard. Once a quarter, he invited his employees and their families to an evening at his villa, including a fine meal. He encouraged them to mingle, strengthening the bond among them. Some attributed his success to these events.

Papias was the master carpenter who had supervised construction of new racks in the wheat section. He began working at the shipyard as an apprentice during the construction of Cleopatra's fleet, becoming a master carpenter and overseer. He sent his sons to the university, where they did well and afterward joined businesses in the Tarsus area. When Cleopatra's fleet was almost complete, he talked with Moshe. He was working for Moshe when work on the fleet ended.

At one of the events, Papias introduced his daughter to me. "Cyrus, this is my daughter Myrrine. I've told her that you were one of the smartest men Moshe's ever hired."

I stood and said, "I am pleased to meet you. Your father is a fine carpenter. He has done some of the finest work I've ever seen. You should be very proud of him."

Myrrine replied, "My father is impressed with your work. He says you know both Greek and Latin and that you attended the university here. That is quite an accomplishment for someone who is not equestrian … Oh, my apology! That sounded like a criticism … I did not mean it so. I have tried to learn Greek. I can do the alphabet, but I am not sure it is correct. I wish I could read. There is so much to learn. I am talking too much. How did you learn Greek and Latin?"

"My father knew Greek. He taught me the alphabet and how to read. He also arranged for a teacher from the university to spend time at our farm. That teacher taught me Latin."

"I have a tablet and a stylus my father made," she said, "but he can neither read nor write, and neither can my mother. There is no one to help me."

"I can write the Greek alphabet on a sheet and give it to your father. We must be sure you know the alphabet."

"Oh, would you do that? No one ever offered to assist me. I

promise I will learn the alphabet by the next meeting, if you are coming," she said.

"I am pleased to do so."

Later, at the warehouse, after delivering documents to the office, I obtained from a worker a sheet of vellum, retrieved a reed pen and a vial of ink from one of the desks, and returned to my section of the warehouse. At a table there, I prepared three columns. The first was the capital letter of each letter in the Greek alphabet, the second, the small letter, and the third, the name of the letter. I then held the sheet up to better light. It was perfect.

I returned to the office, replaced the pen and the vial, rolled the vellum into a tight scroll, heated the wax, and sealed the document. In my finest style, I then penned "Myrrine" at the edge of the vellum.

The day of the event finally arrived. The night before, I had laundered the better of my two tunics and cleaned my sandals. During the day, to pass time, I assisted the laborers. That evening, I was among the first at Moshe's courtyard and joined several of the stewards and artisans, engaging in the gossip of the day. I positioned myself across the courtyard to watch the entrance. Papias entered with Myrrine following. She had a tablet in her hand.

I noticed how gracefully she walked, her head held high, eyes looking straight ahead, the way a laborer walks after a good day's effort, too proud of his work to let his shoulders droop or his eyes look down at the ground. She wore a long, sleeveless tunic, cream colored, which fit her body and displayed her tanned, well-formed arms. She saw me and nodded in recognition. She spoke to Papias, then walked toward me.

I was struck by her beauty, by the fine features of her face framed by dark hair. I noticed the high bridge of her nose, common among the people of the Taurus Mountains. Her fully developed shoulders and arms, the result of hard work, added to her grace.

"My father would be pleased if you would join us when the meal is ready," she said.

"I would be pleased to do so."

"Thank you for the alphabet," Myrrine said. "I have worked on the letters. I can make all the letters, but I am not sure how to pronounce the names. After the meal, would you help me?"

"I look forward to helping you. Once you know the alphabet, you can start making words. It is not that difficult."

She held up her tablet. "I'm ready to learn."

Papias motioned for us to join him. I was at ease, enjoying the meal and light conversation. After we ate, I said to him, "Thank you for letting me join you and Myrrine tonight. I usually eat with the young stewards, but this has been much better."

"It has been our pleasure," he replied. "Myrrine tells me you are helping her with the alphabet. I will leave both of you to that task." He rose and left the table.

"Let me write out the alphabet for you to see whether I am doing it right," said Myrrine.

She proceeded to engrave in the wax each letter of the alphabet, naming each letter as she completed it. When she mispronounced it, I corrected her. She repeated the letter names until I indicated she pronounced them correctly.

I then showed her how to make simple two-letter words and helped her pronounce them. We were both deeply engrossed in the effort when Papias approached, indicating it was time to go.

"I have learned more tonight than I ever thought I could learn at one time," said Myrrine. "You are a good teacher. Thank you for the paper with the alphabet."

"It has been my pleasure," I said, rising. "If you want to learn more, I can send you a list of the simplest words so you can practice writing."

"How kind of you," replied Myrrine. "That would be helpful. It has been a pleasant evening. It was good to see you again. Goodnight." She turned and joined her father.

A few days later, I made a list of the most frequently used two- and three-letter words. Again, I rolled the vellum into a tight scroll, carefully wrote her name on the outside edge, sealed it, and gave it to Papias.

During the next several weeks, I made a point to walk by the area where carpenters were working, hoping for an encounter with Papias but always careful not to distract him from his work. During that time, we had several conversations.

I learned Myrrine's father lived just outside Tarsus on a small plot inherited from his father, that the family had done well, and that Myrrine was the only child yet at home.

One day as I walked to the office, Papias said, "Cyrus, my wife and I would be pleased if you would join us Saturn's Day—*Saturday*—for the evening meal. Myrrine does our cooking, and she would also be pleased for you to join us."

"It will be my pleasure."

"You are our only guest. Do not wear your toga," said Papias. "Please arrive early, as Myrrine needs help with her writing. You know our house."

This was more than I expected. I had two days to prepare. That afternoon, I arranged to have the livery clean the cart and harness and curry the mules by Saturday. I prepared my best tunic.

Time passed slowly, but I finally arrived at Myrrine's house. It was, compared to my home on the farm, a small house on a small plot, built of wood and in good repair. Papias had used his skills to build it. I tied the mules to a secure stake as Myrrine walked to meet me.

"Thank you for coming. Welcome to our house. Your drive was pleasant, I am sure?"

"Yes, it was. Thank you for inviting me. I am early so I can help with your writing, if this is a good time."

"Father and Mother are working in the back. The meal is ready, but we plan to eat later. It is a good time," she said. "But first I would like for you to meet my mother."

On entering the room where her mother was working, Myrrine said, "Mother, this is Cyrus, who has been teaching me." Turning to me, she said, "Cyrus, this is my mother."

"I am very pleased to meet you. Myrrine is doing well at writing. She is a good student. You should be proud of her," I said.

After a few exchanges, Myrrine and I returned to the front of the house and sat on a covered bench. She unrolled the scroll with the columns of words and began pronouncing the two-letter words. The sound of the words was familiar to her, but occasionally I did correct her pronunciation.

As the light began to fade, Myrrine excused herself. "It is time to prepare the meal. My father made the table and benches. It is easier to eat and talk sitting at the table."

Myrrine prepared four places. When everything was ready, she called to her parents. The meal was a cordial affair. We sat a long time at the table and talked of many things, Myrrine's father telling of his experiences at the shipyard and with Moshe. I gave some of my own background but only enough to keep the conversation going. I was more interested in learning of Myrrine's family. It was late when Papias indicated it was time to go.

"It has been a most enjoyable evening," I said. "I have not enjoyed a meal as much in a long time. Thank you for the invitation. Goodnight."

I loosened the tether and climbed onto the cart. My heart sang all the way to the livery.

The Saturday-afternoon sessions and meal became routine. I was hopelessly in love. I liked everything about Myrrine—her interest in learning to read and write, her ability to prepare a fine meal from the simplest of fare, and, most of all, her pleasant demeanor. I knew her father was the force behind our growing relationship. I was thankful, for if Myrrine's father favored marriage, one would be arranged.

I began to think of reasons to justify the marriage. Of primary concern was the farm. Ownership of the land was too important to fall into the hands of a distant owner. The surest way to safeguard its ownership would be to have sons. Our marriage would also address other issues. There was my work with Moshe. I could not give my best effort to Moshe and at the same time look after the farm and my mother. Myrrine could help Mother manage the farm.

At the meal the following Saturday, I asked Papias if his daughter could go with me to meet my mother and see the farm. He did not conceal his pleasure in granting approval.

I arranged to be away from the warehouse for several days. I planned to arrive at the farm Friday evening, spend Saturday and Sunday there, and leave Monday morning for Tarsus, arriving late Tuesday. There were no hostels between Tarsus and home. I would have to arrange accommodations for overnight.

Myrrine took charge of the food, and I saw to the cart and mules. In the cart, I placed two large sections of tenting fabric, one to cover the cart in the event of rain, the other to provide a tent for the driver. I also included a light fabric to provide protection against the night wind. I made one last trip to the stable to make sure the cart was properly packed and ready.

At first light the next morning, I was at the livery where the attendant had hitched the mules. I mounted the cart and slapped the mules with slack in the reins.

The sun was well up by the time I arrived at Myrrine's house. She and her parents were in front. Papias had delayed going to work to see his daughter off. I dismounted and joined them. We exchanged greetings, and I picked up one of the baskets at Myrrine's feet. She picked up the other. I promised to take good care of her, then escorted her to the cart. I helped her to the seat, handed her the baskets, and walked around to mount from the driver side. We each raised a hand in a parting goodbye.

"Did you bring the tablet?" I asked.

"Yes, I keep it with me all the time, along with the scrolls. With you teaching me, it is easy to read and to write."

"The wheels are large, and the seat is padded, but it is still too rough to write. Let me tell you about the farm and my people so you will know what to expect," I said.

I told her about my father, Animus, serving in Pompey's navy, how he learned to read and to write, and how he become a Roman citizen with a land grant and money. I told her of Cletus and Felix, the Cilician pirates.

At noon, I pulled off the road under the shade of a large tree, dismounted, and walked around to help Myrrine. We both walked back and forth to relieve the tiredness of sitting. I picked up a basket, walked to some large stones nearby, cleared away some plant growth, and motioned to Myrrine to sit down. From the basket, she removed a pita loaf, some cheese, and two pears. She handed a portion to me, taking one for herself.

"This is good bread," I said. "Where did you get the wheat?"

"From the time of your visits, my father has been buying the best wheat. I grind the wheat and bake the loaves in the community oven. He said you would know the difference."

After we had finished eating, Myrrine removed two cups from the basket and poured the sour wine.

"That is the best wine I have ever tasted," I said. "Did you make it?"

"Father buys sour wine for special occasions, and I add honey and spices. I thought you might like it."

After finishing the wine, we were again on our way. Once the team had settled into a steady gait, Myrrine asked if she could learn to drive.

"Yes. I'll show you how. There is not much to learn."

I transferred the reins to her, showing her how to hold them to control the team. I held her hands, slapped the mules with the reins, and they picked up their pace. After a few minutes, I again took her hands and drew back on them, slowing the team to its normal pace. Myrrine placed a light kiss on my cheek.

My blood raced. I glanced at her. She was looking at me with a smile on her face.

I swallowed hard. "Let me tell you my plan. I've thought about it a long time."

Myrrine smiled and leaned toward me.

"I need someone to help me accomplish what I have in mind. I am sure I have a future with Moshe, but I need to keep the farm in the family. I cannot do both." I paused for a few moments, then turned to her. "Myrrine, I want someone to help me through this world. I would like for you to join me. Would you marry me?"

"Cyrus, after that first meeting when you offered to teach me to read and to write, I've been hoping you would ask. I was afraid something would happen, and you would leave, and I would be left behind."

I took the reins, brought the mules to a stop, and kissed her. Then I slapped the mules and picked up the pace to make the spring by late afternoon.

When we arrived, I placed the cart near the fire pit and asked Myrrine to get wood for a cooking fire while I took care of the team.

I unhitched the team, then watered, fed, and hobbled it. Myrrine placed wood by the fire pit. I started a fire, and in a few minutes, it was burning brightly. She removed a small pot from one of the baskets, filled it with water from the spring, and prepared a wheat porridge. Spice, honey, and milk made it a fine meal. We ate from the pot.

As the sun was slipping toward the horizon, Myrrine cleaned the utensils at the spring. With the tent fabrics and some rods, I soon built us a shelter.

I placed more wood on the fire, sat down, and leaned against one of the stones, motioning for Myrrine to join me. We sat for a while, watching the final rays of the sun as the fire gradually died, and talked of our plans.

In the flickering firelight, Myrrine raised her face to mine with her lips parted. I was swept away by the ecstasy of the kiss. Myrrine reached for my hand and slipped it inside her tunic. What we experienced was the hope and expectation of all the things meant to be.

Afterward, I saw the stars beyond the edge of the canopy, heard a familiar night song, and interpreted it to be a good omen. Myrrine was already asleep. I was at peace with the world.

It was yet dark when I awoke, sensing it was almost dawn. I lay still, refreshed after a good night's sleep. The warmth of Myrrine's body next to mine deepened my contentment.

When it became light enough, I eased myself out of the makeshift bed and started the day. We would be home by nightfall.

I brushed away the top layer of ashes in the pit, fanned the embers, and soon had a fire going. The bright flames drove away the coolness.

I took care of the team and hitched it to the cart. When I returned, Myrrine was placing a pot of water at the edge of the fire. She stood up, smiled, walked to me, and invited my embrace. I felt the strength of her body as I kissed her.

"I'll fix some porridge," she said, "and heat some wine."

After we had eaten, Myrrine cleaned the utensils in the eddy and packed the basket. I folded the tent and inspected the area. My spirits were high. I was ready for the world, regardless of obstacles.

During the day, we talked of many things, listening to the rhythm of the mules' hoofs, the creak of the harness and cart. Only with some effort did I keep control of my feelings. Time passed quickly, and late in the afternoon I recognized the outline of the ridges marking the farm. I had almost forgotten the beauty of the mountains. How good it would be to live out the rest of my days on the farm with Myrrine at my side. But that was yet to be.

I was in our courtyard before my mother realized we were there. When she saw me assisting a woman from the cart, she surely knew the purpose of this visit. She embraced me and waited for me to introduce the woman I had brought home.

"Mother, this is Myrrine. We hope to be married, if we can get everything arranged."

"Myrrine, I am pleased to meet you. I hope you had a good trip. Welcome to our home."

There was a coolness in her welcome, and I responded immediately, lest Myrrine detect it. "I have been teaching her to read and to write."

"He is a good teacher," Myrrine said. "You should be very proud of him. My father is impressed. I have some things for you. Cyrus, please hand down the other basket."

I handed it to her. She thanked me and said to Mother, "If you will lead the way to your kitchen, I would like to show you some things I brought from Tarsus."

Without a word, my mother led the way to the kitchen. I went to take care of the team.

When I entered the house, I was relieved to hear my mother and Myrrine talking and laughing.

"Myrrine brought me some very good flour and meal made from Egyptian wheat," Mother said. "She also brought salt, spices, special, cheese, pita bread, and some sour wine for you."

"If you like, I can help you with the evening meal," said Myrrine. "I've been sitting all day and need to move about. Tell me what I can do."

After a fine meal, we sat in the courtyard, and I built a fire in the pit. The air was cooler than in Tarsus.

I asked Myrrine, "Where did you get the wheat, the salt, and everything?"

"My father wanted to get your mother some things she might not have, being so far from Tarsus. He and Moshe made up most of the items. They wanted me to make a good impression."

"I am very pleased to have those things," Mother said. "We grow almost everything we need, but I do need items from Tarsus. Thank you and thank your father. He and his friend provided a fine selection. All of you are very kind."

"I'll sleep in my old room. Myrrine can sleep in sister's room," I said, hoping to avoid any awkwardness.

"That will be fine," said Myrrine.

"I'll show you to your room. We can get it ready in a few moments. I keep it ready for the family," said my mother, rising from her chair and motioning for Myrrine to follow.

When Myrrine returned, she looked at me and said, "Your mother keeps an orderly house. We will get along fine."

I took her hand and held it in both of mine. "Myrrine, I am so proud of you. I am sure Mother is worried about what will happen to me and to the farm. My brothers and sisters are married and gone. They visit occasionally, but they take no interest in the farm. I am the only one to help her. I wish I could live here with you for the rest of my days. What a joy that would be. But everything has happened in such a way that working for Moshe is what I feel I must do. I will work at it, but I need someone with me."

"Cyrus, I love you very much, and I promise to work as hard as you do. The farm is such a beautiful place, and this is a fine house. It is a far different world than I've known but a better one. Being with you is all I want."

"I'll show you the farm tomorrow," I said, "and we will meet some of the workers. Everyone is like a member of the family."

We embraced.

Myrrine was up at first light and went to the kitchen where my mother was already busy. She asked to help and Mother let her join in the work.

"I like the large kitchen and am amazed at the amounts of food," Myrrine said.

After breakfast, I showed her around the house, the outbuildings, and the large garden. Then I helped her into the cart and started a tour of the farm. It was late spring, and the laborers were already in the field. I pointed out the farms of the children of Cletus and Felix and waved to the laborers working in the fields.

We returned late in the morning in time for Myrrine to help with the noon meal for us and the laborers. She prepared six round loaves of bread and was amazed at the quantity of food.

"We'll eat before the men come in," said Mother.

When the laborers entered, Myrrine gave each half of a loaf and a spoon. I stood with the men around the table, each of us scooping with the bread or spoon the vegetables and some meat. We laughed, talked, and ate. After all were finished, each laborer thanked my mother and Myrrine, then filed out of the room. Everyone was glad it was springtime and there was work to do, glad to have enjoyed a good meal, and glad to see me again. After the meal, I joined them in the field.

Little food remained. "You see why we ate before the laborers arrived," said my mother.

I spent the afternoon with the laborers, especially the stewards. By the end of the day, I was reassured Mother was well in control and had the farm operation well in hand.

Myrrine and my mother spent the afternoon walking through the house and around the courtyard, Mother explaining the use of each room, if it was not apparent. Myrrine kept the light conversation going with stories from her father about me, and from her own encounters.

After the evening meal, we again sat around a small fire, Mother telling stories about me and my father.

The next day, I completed tasks my mother indicated needed to be done. Myrrine helped in the kitchen. The noon meal was a noisy, pleasant affair, the high point of the day.

Mother said she needed water to clean the table and floor in the dining area. When Myrrine volunteered to get the water, she gave directions to the creek and handed her two large buckets. She returned with the heavy buckets and completed the task. She also helped clean the kitchen, resolving if she became steward of the house, there would be a fountain in the courtyard.

Late in the afternoon, I packed the cart, making sure everything was ready for the return trip. After the evening meal, we again sat around the fire. Mother said, "You have my blessing to marry Myrrine. She is a good, strong girl and a pleasure to be with. I am sure she can manage the farm when the time comes. I do hope everything can be arranged."

"Thank you, Mother. I love her very much, and I'm counting on her to help me, but I needed your approval."

The next morning, when Myrrine entered the kitchen, Mother pointed to loaves of fresh baked bread. "I made those with the good wheat. It does make a difference. There is porridge on the stove."

I joined them, and we ate. Afterward, we sat at the table for some time, each with a cup of hot sour wine. Sitting there, the bond among us grew. I placed my hands on Mother's. "Thank you for all the things you did for me. You and Animus were good parents. I promise to do everything I can to help with the farm." I leaned over and kissed her on the forehead.

"I know you will, but your saying so makes me feel better. Animus believed our lives are planned from the beginning. All my days add up to a happy life, and all the days ahead will do the same. I look forward to sharing them with you and Myrrine. If it was meant to be, that will be the way it will be."

She looked at me. "Do not worry about me. I have good neighbors. If I need you, I'll send for you. I packed some things in the basket. It is not much, but it will get you through."

"It is time for us to get started," I said. "The cart is ready."

The three of us walked to the cart with Mother in the middle. Myrrine and I each embraced her.

"Thank you for filling the water buckets again," Mother said to Myrrine. "That was thoughtful of you. They are heavy."

She wiped the tears from her eyes as she waved goodbye, watching until our cart was out of sight.

By late afternoon, we arrived at the spring. While I took care of the team and cart, Myrrine unpacked the meal prepared by Mother. Together we enjoyed the meal, put up the tent, and prepared for the night. I built up the fire and sat against a large stone. Myrrine joined me, leaning against my chest, her head on my shoulder, and we watched the fire. When it was almost gone, Myrrine raised her lips to mine, grasped my hand in hers, and again slipped it under her tunic.

The next day, just before nightfall, we arrived at Myrrine's house. Papias heard the cart and called to his wife, and they waited while we dismounted.

"Welcome home. We are pleased to see you back," he said.

"Thank you for the welcome," I said. "It was a good trip. Myrrine was wonderful. My mother is pleased, and Myrrine is pleased. If you will allow me, I need to be at work in the morning to make up for the time I've lost. I'll visit you as soon as I can."

"Myrrine will tell us about the trip. I will see you in the morning," said Papias.

On my return to the city, I was ready to engage the world. With Myrrine at my side, nothing was impossible.

The next morning, I had difficulty adjusting to work. How could my own world have changed so much and the warehouse be the same as ever? I enjoyed my work more each day. The days seemed shorter, and I accomplished more. Papias reminded me that I was expected to join them Saturday afternoon.

I arrived at Myrrine's house at the usual time carrying a small scroll of verses. "Simmias found this among his scrolls. He said it would be easier to read than most manuscripts. He thought you might like it," I said. "Myrrine, you are beautiful."

"Cyrus, thank you for coming. Oh, thank you for the scroll! I can practice reading."

Myrrine's father and mother were waiting at the door and welcomed me with broad smiles. After a few minutes of light conversation, they excused themselves and returned to the back of the house.

I embraced Myrrine, ecstatic in her warmth and strength, and whispered, "I am so happy."

"I thought today would never come," she said. "It seems like it has been forever since we returned."

We sat on the padded bench, and she unrolled the scroll. "I am so excited. I've never seen a scroll like this. The writing is so beautiful."

"Simmias said it was written many years ago by a woman who loved the sound of the Greek language. When you read it aloud, you will hear how beautiful language can be."

Myrrine held the scroll firmly in both hands and began to read aloud. I helped her with new words. She read aloud the verses again, this time requiring almost no assistance.

She looked at me, her eyes sparkling. "Cyrus, it is so delightful. It sounds ... so pleasing, so elegant. I know what it says, but what does it mean?"

"It means different things to different people. Now you know what it is to read. And what it is to hear words read aloud. I've never heard Greek spoken so beautifully. Would you read it again?"

Myrrine again read the verses. I closed my eyes and listened to the rhythm of the language, visualizing the imagery created by the words. How could anyone, with only the careful selection and placement of words and phrases, create such magnificent sounds and striking images? From that day, I, like my father, became a student of the Greek language.

Myrrine interrupted my reverie. "It's time to prepare the meal."

As usual, she had prepared a fine meal. We all participated in the conversation, each enjoying the other's presence.

At a break in the conversation, Papias said, "My daughter tells me that you wish to be married."

"Yes, sir, I love her very much. My mother has given her blessing. I hope you approve."

"You have my permission. Her mother and I wish only for her happiness. June is the proper time for weddings. I will make the arrangements. It will be my pleasure to tell Moshe. He will be pleased. I look forward to your long, happy marriage," he said.

After an exchange of goodbyes, I walked to the cart. Turning toward the city, I loosened the reins to allow the mule to settle into a plodding gait. Elation flooded my being. With Myrrine at my side, all concerns were resolved. I was tempted to shout a raucous victory cry.

I had difficulty falling asleep that night.

✝

The wedding was to take place in the courtyard of Moshe's villa, and he invited his stewards and laborers. Papias arranged for the priest from the temple to Jupiter to conduct the ceremony, having built a small altar at one end of the courtyard.

Myrrine prepared several cakes as offerings to Jupiter. Her mother assisted in dressing her for the ceremony. Moshe provided a finely woven, long-sleeved tunic of the finest wool, reaching to the ground. He also provided a fine leather girdle with the simple Knot of Hercules to be untied by me, a symbol of our marriage and a protective amulet.

The priest arrived, surveyed the arrangements, and indicated his approval. Myrrine and her father stood before the altar, and with a word from the priest, her father stepped aside, giving Myrrine's hand to me. Facing each other with hands joined, we repeated in turn after the priest, "When and where you go, then and there will I go."

Myrrine stepped forward, sliced the cake, and placed the first piece on the altar, the priest saying a prayer. She then offered a portion to me. I, in turn, offered a portion to her. She then passed the cake among the guests.

The celebration began with a meal served in the courtyard. The east was beginning to lighten when the last guest departed. Like young colts during the first days after birth, Myrrine and I each found joy in being alive.

To provide a place for us, Moshe modified several rooms at the far end of the courtyard. I became chief steward. Moshe and I became closest of friends, but I never slacked in my dedication to my work. Moshe became the wealthiest man in Tarsus.

In early spring, Myrrine traveled to the farm, spending time there until the winter rains threatened. She spent winters in Tarsus. I visited the farm regularly and relied on Mother until she joined Animus. Then Myrrine became steward of the farm.

The farm prospered. The community had grown, and Myrrine was able to employ laborers to work the fields and women to help in the kitchen. When I was present, she delegated the kitchen to the women. We both tended the farm during the day but spent hours together at the evening meal or in the courtyard. Our time together was filled with all the wonder and joy we discovered that first night at the spring.

I presented each of our children with his own tablet and stylus. Myrrine helped them with the alphabet. When the oldest was capable of a day's work, late each summer, I brought with me from Tarsus a teacher from the university who became a member of our household. I continued this practice until our son, Cornelius, left for the university.

The years added to our contentment. We walked through the fields and the forest, leisurely traveling the whole distance, enjoying the sights and sounds, no bypasses taken to shorten the walk, no effort to accelerate the pace, lest the quality be diminished.

MOSHE, SAUL, AND SIMMIAS

MOSHE

My name is Cornelius, son of Cyrus, chief steward to the house of Moshe Benjamin. Moshe the Merchant, as he was called and as he called himself, was originally from Galilee in Palestine. There he served as guide and host to caravans passing through on the great trade route and became quite wealthy.

Merchants in those caravans talked of opportunities in Tarsus. Moshe sold his possessions and moved his family there, settling in the Jewish community. He employed a teacher from the university to instruct him and his family in the ways of the city. Soon he spoke with no accent and was a citizen of Tarsus.

Simmias, the teacher, assisted him in acquiring a large warehouse with a pier extending well into the bay. At that time, the Cydmus River flowed through the center of Tarsus, opening to the Great Sea, allowing ships to load and unload in the heart of the city. Caravans also passed through it, being just south of the Roman road through Cilicia. Tarsus rivaled Antioch and Alexandria.

Though Moshe was Jewish, it was not apparent. His wife and daughter seldom left the house, always spoke Aramaic, and dressed in traditional Palestinian style.

Moshe had provided my parents with rooms off the courtyard, and later provided one for me. After a day's work, discussions between my father and Moshe often turned to personal interests. Late one spring day, I was sitting with them in the courtyard.

Moshe said, "I do not consider myself religious by Jewish standards. Priests and scribes have made our religion a burden. Man cannot be free when religion takes his time, his money, and directs his life. I do not observe the dietary laws, the holy days, nor tithe my income, yet in my deepest being, I am as religious as the high priest in Jerusalem. Man is to make the world a better place. The great battles are fought in a man's heart as he strives to do that."

Looking beyond us, he said, "Among our sacred writings is the drama *Job*. Scholars have translated it, along with the other writings, into Greek. Do you know of the manuscript?"

"I never studied it," my father said, "but it may be at the university."

"In the drama," Moshe said, "Job is the richest and best man in the world. In heaven, in a discussion with Satan about the goodness of Job, God allows Satan to place Job on trial to test him, as Satan alleges Job is good only because God protects and rewards him. The issue was whether Job would continue to be good during a period of great adversity. Mankind was also on trial, for if Job failed, God's creation failed. The drama pits Satan against God, with God risking everything on the goodness of Job. Like the Greek dramas, it is very personal, as it addresses the purpose of our being here."

"I found the Greek dramas to be very personal," my father said.

Moshe continued, "During his testing, Job questions God's justice and wisdom. He learns he can never understand God's ways and is himself vindicated, his own ways being justified. Mankind, however, is yet on trial and the outlook is not encouraging."

"I attended Greek dramas," I said, "and was deeply moved. I would like to read it."

"You are welcome to my copy," said Moshe.

He then looked at my father. "In our business, we have made the world better. That is why we are successful. You are as religious as I am when it comes to believing that we are here to make the world better."

"You've put into words," my father said, "what I've spent half my life thinking but could never get the words right. What troubles me is whether there is a pattern to our lives and whether that pattern allows us to be free. I never found a sufficient answer, but the teachers at the university believed freedom is living out the pattern of our life because it is the right thing to do."

Moshe stared into the distance, the last rays of the sun giving his face a striking, hawk-like appearance. "Cyrus, we have done well, but sometimes I long for the hard life in Galilee. Life was difficult, but I was happy there. I am content here but feel, not so much remorse or sadness, but that I am missing in my life something very important without knowing what it is."

Moshe was silent. My father and I withdrew and allowed him to live again those happier days.

✝

One day as Moshe and my father were settling accounts, my father said, "A young steward in shipping is indebted to Crassus the Elder who put conditions in the loan document the borrower cannot possibly fulfill. His child is very ill, and he has expended considerable money for apothecaries. He is a good man, and we pay him well. Had I known, I would have helped him work out a solution. Is there a way we can we cause Crassus to forgive the debt?"

"Crassus is a disgrace to his toga and to the patrician's stripe in his tunic," said Moshe. "He has practiced greed until it is his personal signet. Perhaps we can use that trait to his disadvantage. Let us think on it."

A few days later, Moshe said, "Perhaps you can entice Crassus to borrow a large sum with the same terms he imposed on the young steward."

"I could tell him your ships are delayed at Corinth and request a sizable amount on your behalf, more than he can afford to lend. He will be forced to go to your Jewish friends. Would you provide them the money for him to borrow?"

"I will supply any amount," Moshe said, "but we must have Crassus's note come due prior to mine."

"I will circulate a rumor that your ships will be delayed at Corinth for weeks, possibly months," my father said. "Crassus must believe you will be forced to default before payment to his creditors is due. If his greed is sufficient and the security great enough, he may consent."

My father secured the loan from Crassus in the amount of 25,000 denarii due in ninety days, pledging as security Moshe's warehouse and its contents. Crassus, in turn, borrowed that sum from Moshe's lenders but was distressed to learn his was a sixty-day note. He demanded extra security, and my father offered Moshe's villa. On Moshe's default, Crassus would become the wealthiest man in Tarsus.

The Jewish lenders forwarded to Moshe the document signed by Crassus. On the sixtieth day, Moshe invited him to a meeting, my father and the young steward being present. Crassus arrived in a fine toga and tunic. He was of moderate height but carried evidence of an indolent lifestyle in his great girth. His face appeared small set between large jowls; his hands were thin and soft. Moshe gave him the loan document bearing his own signature. "Do you recognize this?"

Crassus stared at the document, clutching it so tightly in both hands his knuckles whitened.

Moshe again asked, "Do you recognize the document bearing your signature and signet?"

He replied, barely audible, "That is my signature and my signet on the document."

"The amount of the loan is 25,000 denarii, plus interest. In keeping with the terms, your lenders demand full and immediate payment," Moshe said.

"I cannot make payment," Crassus said.

"You default on the obligation?"

He replied weakly, "I default on the obligation."

"I offer you the following alternative to my giving this to the city consul. You will reimburse my steward the full amount of his indebtedness to you. You will return to me the document pledging my warehouse and my villa, and to the extent you are able, on current loans you will return the security to the owners. You will relocate yourself and your family to your lands in another province. You have one year to complete the arrangement. Will you accept these terms?"

"Yes," Crassus said. "They are more generous than those the consul would offer. I am no friend of his. My punishment would be especially harsh for defaulting on a debt, as I have always dealt harshly with any who defaulted on a debt to me. Thank you for offering me the alternative."

"Good," said Moshe. "Allow me a few days to prepare the document. It is written, 'An eye for an eye, a tooth for a tooth, a bruise for a bruise.' Justice has been done. You are free to go."

Over the next year, Crassus diligently carried out the terms of the agreement. The money and lands remaining he gave to the city of Tarsus to assist the destitute. He became known as a generous person and cordial in all relationships, and having lost his girth, he wore his tunic and toga with pride. On his departure, a large crowd was present to wish him well.

Before leaving, Crassus arranged a meeting at the warehouse with Moshe, my father being present. "Moshe, you showed me the error of my ways. I tried to make restitution to everyone I wronged. No effort could restore some, and for that I am truly sorry," he said. "I have learned compassion from seeing the plight of those I wronged, and used what means I had to ease their hardship. For those who had no hope, I did what I could for them, but many times it was woeful little. May the god of the unfortunate continue to use you as his high priest in Tarsus. Thank you, my friend."

Crassus turned and left the office. Moshe shook his head and said to my father, "There may yet be hope for mankind."

Job of the drama was the model for his living, and Moshe rivaled him in the way he lived his life. While in Jerusalem, many years later, I read the Greek translation of *Job*. As Moshe observed, it rivaled the Greek dramas in its intensity, and some parts exceeded them in imagery and the magnificent use of language.

SAUL

In addition to a daughter, Moshe had a son named Saul, about my age. He, too, was a student at the university, and we became great friends. We often joined Moshe and my father for breakfast and were aware of ships or caravans scheduled to arrive or to depart. We assisted when needed, but our studies were of primary concern.

Saul was much the better student. He well understood the subtleties and helped me greatly in learning. Instead of carousing and drinking with other students, Saul introduced me to the city. We dressed in the most casual style and mingled with the crowds. I never knew there were so many nationalities, so many languages, customs, and smells. In Tarsus, laborers were in great demand, and the streets were filled with artisans from every province. More than once I caught myself looking for the stranger with his left hand missing who had helped my grandfather.

Saul took great pleasure in visiting the Jewish and Arabic sections of Tarsus. He spoke Aramaic and introduced me to some of the best food in some of the most unlikely places.

One day Saul and I were invited to a local drinking establishment catering to young patricians. To my surprise, Saul suggested we attend. It was a raucous, cordial occasion with more than one wineskin circulating. For the first time, I mingled with students from the patrician class. To my astonishment, they had no idea of the excitement of the city or of the university. An evening with Simmias, or any teacher, would have been far more interesting.

Saul began to attend such events. At our breakfasts, he became argumentative and defensive. One day, with everyone present, Simmias, our teacher, asked Saul, "If I place a thin bar of marble on the table and place a weight on one end so that most of the bar extends beyond the table's edge, will the bar break?"

Saul replied, "If nothing strikes the bar, it should not break."

"If nothing strikes the bar, it will eventually break from its own weight. The significant question is, if nothing struck the bar, when did it begin to break?"

"It began to break the moment it was set in place," Saul said.

"You are correct," said Simmias. "Let me ask you another question. When did the derelict in the city street begin the long descent into dereliction?"

Saul looked down at his plate and did not answer, but from that time, he no longer attended the drinking events. Soon the old Saul returned.

One summer afternoon, he and I were helping load a ship due to sail the next day. Six of us were carrying a large crate when Saul lost his footing and released his handhold. The crate fell and tipped over, pinning him under its corner. We lifted the crate. A large splinter had pierced his upper right thigh. The wound did not bleed, but we were reluctant to remove the splinter.

A surgeon withdrew it but was unable to remove the many small splinters deep in the wound. It worsened and was slow to heal. With the help of an apothecary and the surgeon, Saul was finally able to walk without assistance.

The wound never healed completely, and Saul developed a distinctive gait in his walk. No longer able to do heavy work, he became a steward for his father.

Saul's stewardship included preparation and shipping of locally woven tenting fabric. The black, coarse Cilician wool, when spun with proper twist and woven with uniform tension, produced a fabric that allowed the passage of air when dry, swelling and keeping out water when wet—ideal for tent making.

Local weavers used upright looms with fixed width to weave the heavy fabric. Saul assigned those best at carding to card and those best at spinning to spin, producing a uniform yarn, and those best at weaving to weave. The group more than doubled its production of fabric uniform in weight, width, and of higher quality. Saul increased the pay to the artisans and at the same time lowered the cost of the fabric. Moshe's tenting became known from Antioch to Alexandria, and Tarsus became as well known for its tenting fabric as it had been for its shipbuilding.

At the villa, Saul and I frequently discussed with Simmias issues raised in sessions at the university. One day Simmias asked, "Saul, do you believe there is a natural law?"

"Yes, I do."

"Do you believe a person can avoid its influence?"

"No," Saul said. "We are all subject to it and violate it at our peril."

"From the day you were born, your father hoped you would study Judaism with teachers in Jerusalem," Simmias said. "He doesn't want you, necessarily, to become a scribe or a priest but to study Judaism as you studied philosophy. Teachers there rival those here. Have you considered doing so?"

"My father allowed me to do what I thought was best, and I have tried to do my best. The injury to my leg complicated matters. I am no longer confident what I can do. I always believed I would live out my days here in Tarsus. My father, deep in his heart, longs to return to Galilee and be among his own people. I am aware he would like for me to study in Jerusalem. Let me think about it."

"Please do," Simmias said. "In the great plan of things, your injury may have been to encourage you to take the next step. The time has come to take it."

It required some time, but Saul prepared for the trip to Jerusalem. He trained stewards in the production of tenting fabric, and he and Moshe spent more time together.

The day of Saul's departure arrived. As we sat at breakfast that morning, Moshe, my father, Saul, and I talked of many things. It was our last meal together. Moshe had prepared for Saul letters of introduction to the people at the temple in Jerusalem. A sense of new beginnings dispelled the sadness. Saul's ship, with two others, was to sail that afternoon. Breakfast was leisurely.

Moshe said, "We all knew this day would come. You were never destined to be a merchant, and for that I am well pleased. Your work in tenting gave us a new section in the warehouse. In that, you exceeded my greatest expectation. But you are different from the rest of us. You are a good student, and you excel in Simmias's domain. I believe you will find the studies with Gamaliel as interesting as those with Simmias. Our faith has many traditions and has survived many assaults. It is the true faith. I hope you will find it so. Study with Gamaliel as rigorously as you have done with Simmias. I look forward to the day we will discuss what you have learned."

"I, too, look forward to the day," Saul said.

"Your mother and I wish you well. The ship will afford you the best way to Antioch. Change to local dress and speak Aramaic. On the land routes, travel with a caravan. The people are good, but there are bandits in the hills." Moshe rose from the table. "It is time to go."

The four of us walked the short distance to the pier, Moshe and Saul leading the way.

At the pier, workers from the warehouse and villa wished Saul well. He worked his way through the group. When he reached the gangplank, he turned, waved, then boarded the ship.

The sail had been set and the ship strained at the lines. The gangplank was hauled on board and the lines cast off. The ship moved into the river channel and toward open sea. The crowd returned to work, but Moshe, my father, and I watched in silence until the sail disappeared behind the jut of land at the edge of the bay.

For Saul, it was the first of many journeys, and for me, his leaving meant my days at the university were drawing to an end.

SIMMIAS OF TARSUS

I had known Simmias for many years. My grandfather and father both had arranged for him to spend time with us on the farm. I renewed his friendship when I attended the university.

The University at Tarsus was among the finest in the world, a center of Stoic philosophy. Its teachers were well known among the city officials and spent many an evening at Moshe's villa. Among the best known was the old sophist who called himself Simmias of Tarsus.

He taught at universities in Athens and Alexandria and had traveled the world. He had been at Tarsus many years. He was a pleasant person with a head of white hair and skin like old parchment, his demeanor giving grace to his toga. At the time, he was what one expected an old sophist to be. Today, young sophists teach for the money and the easy life. *Sophist* no longer carries a favorable meaning.

Saul and I, and others, enjoyed many long sessions with him. His style was to ask a question, listen to our reply, and then ask another question, slightly different. By the end of such sessions, I had gained some knowledge of the subject matter. After Saul was injured, Simmias and Saul engaged in long discussions extending well into the night. After the day's work, I had difficulty staying awake and would excuse myself.

He taught us to read old Greek and Latin scrolls and codices. I spent many an afternoon with them, once finding a manuscript by Plato. I spent hours learning to read the first pages and took several days to read it through. At the conclusion, I wept as Plato describes the death of Socrates. I had looked on a new world. I have read it many times and each time learned more of that world.

Saul became a more serious student, seldom attending public forums or events at the university. Once Simmias said to Saul and me, "I am fearful it is the destiny of democracies and republics ultimately to fail. In those societies, authority resides with the people, but they delegate it to elected officials, and it is diffused."

"Do you believe Rome will cease to be a republic?" Saul asked.

"Rome is no longer a republic," Simmias said. "Consider the authority of the Senate. Authority is the ability to apportion resources, and the Senate is responsible for their proper apportionment. With authority goes responsibility. As authority is diffused, so is responsibility."

"But the Senate has the authority and the responsibility."

"That is an illusion," Simmias said. "In a republic, people elect those who reward them. Once elected, the representative's only interest is to gain personally from the allocation of public resources, with small cost to the republic but with great benefit to him. Instead of governing in the public interest, the elected provide for those who keep them in office. Is that not the way it is?"

"If power and authority reside with the people, as you say," said Saul, "when the elected officials fail, the people will replace them. If you have confidence in the people, the problem will solve itself."

I found myself first agreeing with Simmias as he spoke, and then with Saul as he spoke.

Simmias replied, "You are correct. Sooner or later, the people will remove the corrupt officials. But, Saul, it is at such a price, even when it succeeds, and success is never assured."

"If authority is with the people, why is success never assured?"

"The new leaders must be statesmen with courage. In my youth, Tarsus was like Athens, but now the officials of Tarsus no longer place the interest of the people first."

Saul did not respond, and I was unable either to ask a question or to give an opinion.

"Saul," Simmias said, "soon you will be going to Jerusalem. On people like you rests the hope of the world. There is a dearth of leaders. Humanity is in a giant maelstrom drifting faster and faster toward its vortex. While there is yet time, someone must guide us to shore. Surely there are young people with a vision of what should be and the courage to risk everything. Courage is the chief virtue, for without it, justice, wisdom, and temperance are of little benefit. Do you understand?"

Saul was silent for a time. "Simmias, knowing you is the high point of my life. I shall never meet another, and the world is much poorer from the dearth. Be assured I do understand. I am like the runner prior to a great contest. You have prepared me to run my finest race. I will exert every effort to win. Victory is never assured, but I will give it my greatest effort. I will keep the faith. There must be another world where old friends meet again and talk of great endeavors. We will discuss the matter further at that meeting."

"I look forward to the meeting," Simmias said. "We shall embrace as old friends. I have no doubt you will run your finest race and keep the faith. Watching you grow in learning and experience has been the high point in my life."

Over the years, I recalled that conversation many times. Rome is going the way of Athens. Legions are no longer loyal to Rome. During the time I served, the legion was the source of Rome's power. It was the best of times. As the loyalty of the legions has diminished, so has the power of Rome.

After Saul left, I continued discussions with Simmias. I learned men are destined to follow a calling. Working with Saul and the tentmakers, I had learned some men and women were better at one skill than another. Society includes those born to be workmen and masters of a trade, men like the weavers and workmen in Moshe's warehouse. Those who excelled in philosophy, people like Saul, were born to become leaders in government and in teaching. And some were born to be soldiers to provide security for the others. If everyone followed his calling, any city would be a good place to live. At one time, Taurus was such a city.

One evening, Simmias was sitting outside his room by a brazier. There was a chill in the air, and his toga was draped over his head. A wisp of white hair had fallen over his forehead and was visible in the firelight. I asked if I might join him. He looked my way and nodded.

We talked about Saul for a few moments, and then he asked, "What do you plan to do?"

I was caught off guard. "I will continue at the university."

"What do you plan to do when you leave the university? You will soon be twenty. Saul has gone, and you've spent enough time there."

"I haven't made up my mind. Like my father, I would like to work for Moshe." I paused. "Occasionally, I think of joining the legion."

"I suspected you were. You spend time at their camp, and I see you talking with the centurions. Being a legionnaire, especially a centurion, is a high calling. Only if you are born to be one can you be content with the life they lead. You see the respect afforded them in the city and here at the villa. That respect was earned; it is not granted like citizenship. Centurions, although Roman citizens, do not wear the toga. It would hide their red tunic and imply a preference for an easy life. Have you thought about it seriously?"

"Yes, I have," I replied. "I've talked with centurions at the camp. I've trained with the sword and the pilum. I am planning to enlist. I haven't picked the time."

"If you believe it is the right thing to do, let me encourage you," Simmias said. "You've seen enough of the world to know what it is, but the legion is different. There, the traits of a man are important, and you must have them all in abundance. You can read and write, and working for Moshe, you have acquired skills. You have some money, and you are a Roman citizen."

"I never thought that way about enlisting."

Simmias said, "Since Marius created the professional army, Marius's mules no longer must meet those requirements. But to become a centurion, it is necessary to have them, for the strength of the Roman legion derives from the ability of its centurions. The great legions represent Rome at its best."

"That is encouraging."

Simmias stared into the fire. "It is a disciplined life by any standard, the long marches, ignoring the heat and the cold, carrying the gear, engaging the enemy, following commands without question, always advancing, never retreating, and never surrendering."

A wave of fear swept through me. Could I endure the marches? Could I face an enemy intent on my destruction and not yield? Could I endure the pain of a severe wound and not cry out? Could I face death without a whimper? Could I never surrender? Why would anyone elect to face those choices? The palms of my hands became moist as I considered whether to enlist. Simmias could not know what I faced. I did not want him to know my fear. I would delay until next spring.

"I have sensed the pride," I said. "A centurion is different."

Simmias looked at me. "The disciplined life is the source of his pride, for it sets him apart from the great mass of humanity, which has no desire to lead such a life. Twenty years from now, you will wear the red tunic with pride and feel contentment a citizen will never know."

As suddenly as fear had engulfed me, elation swept it away. Joining the legion was the right thing to do. If there was a plan for my life, I must take the step. The next step would be easier, and all would fall into place. I would enlist.

As though reciting a passage, Simmias said, "Have one of your friends at the camp write a letter confirming your qualifications. That will make the enlistment easier. Your parents will give their blessing, as I will give mine."

Our eyes met, and I felt all apprehension fade away. "Simmias, sir, I know now what I must do. I will return in my red tunic. Your assurance was all I needed." I walked to my room, elated my future had been laid out.

With some sadness, I realized my days at the farm, in Tarsus, and at the university were at an end. I set in motion my plan to enlist in the Roman legion, to become one of Marius's mules, to be a centurion, to wear the red tunic, to be first centurion, First Cohort of a Roman legion.

The next morning, at breakfast, with some apprehension, I told my father and Moshe of my plan to join the legion. They reacted with encouragement and pride. A few days later, my father and I rode to the farm to spend two days with Mother and friends.

After the evening meal, we sat at the table, for although the winter was past, the wind from the mountains was cold. After a while, Mother said, "Cornelius, it is not just the danger that concerns me. I grew up in Tarsus, and I've seen men come back from the military ruined by dissipation and too much wine. It seemed that those who survived the battles or were wounded in battle returned better men than those who had easy service. I have often wondered what made the difference."

I placed my hand on hers, for I understood her concern. She was the one who insisted I master Greek and Latin and learn to read the manuscripts. "Mother, there is no need to worry. I have seen students throw away opportunities. I do not understand such things. There is too much to do, too much to learn to waste time."

Mother removed one of her hands and placed it on mine. I could see tears in her eyes. "Your father and I have tried to show you what is right. The teachers from the university helped. Your father believes stronger than I do we are here for a purpose. You believe your purpose is the legion. Without the legion to protect us, life would be uncertain. I've read about the Gauls sacking Rome when there were no legions to protect it." She retrieved from beside her a page taken from a manuscript and placed it on the table.

My heart ached from the deep feeling I had for her. Small wrinkles lined her face, and her hair was turning gray, but her eyes were as bright as ever, and she was as beautiful as ever.

"Cornelius, when you said you were to join the legion, I remembered your interest in stories of battles, especially Homer's description of Achilles preparing for battle. I removed from *The Iliad* that description. That is how I will envision you. Let me give this page to you to be a remembrance of all we have shared. When you return, together we will replace it in the book and lace the pages. I am a foolish old woman, but I wanted you to have something to remember the good times we shared."

I did not realize she knew how I loved to hear her read that passage. I looked at the manuscript and read the crowded Greek words describing the glory of armor draping a rejoicing world as a sheen of bronze filled the skies and empires trembled on hearing the marching feet of armies. I was almost to the point of tears, whether from the sentiment she had expressed or from my recollection of her reading the passage to me, or perhaps from my reading those lines once again.

She placed a small rod and long leather thong on the table. "Here is a scroll to roll it on and thong to tie it. I would have made a leather case had I time. I want it to be in good condition when you and I return it to the book."

I rolled the page and wrapped it with the thong. I would make or purchase a case for it. Gifts given with such care bear with them forever the spirit of the giver. It would always be with me, and on my return, together we would return it to its original place.

The conversation turned to happier themes, and we talked well into the night. With a sense of sadness that this was our last night together, we bade each other goodnight.

✝

I was awakened as Father set a lamp on the small table. He said, "It will be light soon."

I arose, embarrassed that I had overslept. I dressed and joined Mother and Father in the kitchen. In the soft light from two lamps, I could see the table laid out. Mother was standing at one end. I could see her eyes were swollen, but she had a smile on her face.

Father kept the conversation on his plans for the farm, casting a pleasant shroud over the sadness. We finished breakfast, and the three of us walked to the cart, Mother between us. It was light enough to see the road.

As I embraced my mother, I felt her stifled sobs and kissed her on her cheek, tasting the slight saltiness of her tears. "Goodbye, Mother. Thank you for all you have been to me. Do not worry."

I then mounted the cart, and Father started toward the gate.

We rode in silence until well into the morning. It was a beautiful spring day, and we had shed our cloaks when my father said, "Cornelius, your mother and I are very proud of you, not just for joining the legion, but for the way you conducted yourself during all the years growing up, especially your work for Moshe."

I did not reply. After a few moments, he reached under the seat and retrieved the knife that Grandfather Animus's mother had given him when he left to join Pompey's navy.

"Last night before we went to bed, I asked your mother if she would approve my giving this to you. Of course, she did. As I grew up, I looked at it many times. I do not know whether you ever examined it closely, but take a look at it."

I removed the blade from the sheath.

Father said, "It appears to be a Syrian sword someone made into a kitchen knife. They cut or broke the blade and ground it to shape it. The hilt and handle are pretty crude, but look at the blade."

I held the blade in the sunlight and saw a distinctive pattern in the metal itself. It consisted of tightly compressed lines resembling ripples on a pond or in an eddy of a stream. I had never noticed the pattern before, although when no one was around, I had looked at the knife many times. "I see the pattern."

"Your mother and I would like for you to have the knife. If you are agreeable and with Moshe's approval, I will ask one of the smiths to fashion it into a military knife. It is Damascus steel. The smith will know how to fashion it."

"With the page from *The Iliad* and with the knife, I will have something to recall the good days growing up," I said.

About noon, we enjoyed the food Mother had packed. Stopping only to water and rest the team, we arrived at the livery by midnight and walked the short distance to the villa.

The next morning, I went to the legion camp. Everyone there was enthusiastic about my decision and welcomed me. As Tarsus had no legion quartered there, it was not a place of enlistment. The centurions discussed the best place to enlist and finally agreed that, having attended the university, I should go to Rome. The training camps there were the best.

The centurion in command requested several days to prepare the letters to Sejanus, commander of the Praetorian Guard in Rome, listing my qualifications and adding his personal recommendation. My heart fairly sang as I returned to the warehouse.

†

During the next several days, I spent time with Moshe and my father and with Simmias. I worked at the warehouse when I could be of help. My departure hung like a cloud over the sun on an otherwise clear day.

One evening, I saw Simmias sitting in front of his room and asked if I might join him. He pointed to a chair. "Certainly. Your time here is growing short."

"Yes, the centurion at the camp is preparing letters for me. I wanted to spend some time with you."

"Thank you for doing so. I shall miss you as I miss Saul. Having such students is part of the reward in teaching," said Simmias.

"Sir, I want to thank you for your patience with me from the time you visited the farm. You made learning a pleasure. I wish I had been a better student."

"You are a good student," he said. "I have been thinking about all that has happened since my first visit to the farm. You have become a man. I hope you realize how far you have come."

"I realize my good fortune in having Myrrine and Cyrus for parents. I am appreciative of that."

"You are due credit," Simmias said. "You are destined to be a legionnaire. You have taken the first step. But there is more to our destiny than the calling. We are endowed with desires which help us. We are born with the desire to be a member of a family, to be among friends, to take pride in our calling, and to find enjoyment in being here. The family, however, is the foundation of our world, and we must respond. For those who have no family, they find a substitute. It shows us how to live and supports us as we learn. The stronger it is, the greater the likelihood of success. You were fortunate to be a member of a strong family. As you grow older, you will appreciate it more."

"We worked hard, yet there was time for talking and for being together," I said. "You knew Grandfather Animus and my parents. I never thought of my family being part of the plan. What of those who were not as fortunate?"

"It is not a matter of being fortunate or unfortunate," Simmias said. "It is the purpose of the family to prepare a child for its place. Had you been born into the family of a stonemason and destined to be a legionnaire, the family would have prepared you for that destiny. The legion needs engineers to build roads, bridges, and aqueducts. An individual with such a background would become centurion of one of the construction cohorts."

Simmias paused. "Communities need skills to become great, and every skill has its place in the community. When the family does not support a child, the community is poorer, and when too many families fail their children, the community is not a good place to live."

"So, everyone is destined to be someone special," I said, "to be needed by the community, to be someone great."

"Even when impaired by illness or some other reason, everyone is destined to be great. Do not underestimate the greatness of the blacksmith, the weaver, or the carpenter because he cannot read or write. Mastery of a skill leads to greatness. Everyone has the potential to be great. Remember that, Cornelius."

"In the Greek dramas, the tragedies, it is a tragedy," I said, "because the hero wastes his potential for greatness. A great man is brought low by his own weakness."

"You understand. I look forward to the day I see you a centurion. Do not waste your potential."

A day or so later during breakfast, my father announced he and Moshe would visit the smith that afternoon. It was early spring and a pleasant walk to the smith's shop.

Acrid smoke from the forge filled the air. The smith motioned to the apprentices to lower their hammers. I recognized him, for I had worked with him on several projects. He placed his smaller hammer on the anvil and motioned to one of the apprentices to return to the forge the tool he was working on, then walked toward his work bench. He picked up the knife and joined us, bringing with him a smile in a blackened face.

He was a giant of a man, as sturdy as his anvil, and much older than his apprentices. His tunic, dark with soot from the forge, was protected by a blackened leather apron adorned with a complex pattern of abrasions and discoloration. "Cornelius, I am pleased to see you. I understand you are joining the legion. We are all pleased. Your father gave me the knife that was your grandfather's."

"Yes, sir, my grandfather served in Pompey's navy. His mother gave it to him when he joined."

As he removed the knife from its sheath, he said, "It has been in your family more than a hundred years. It is Damascus steel and was probably smuggled out of Damascus unless taken from a battlefield when Alexander conquered Syria."

"My grandfather said only that it was a kitchen knife."

"I have only seen two items of Damascus steel," he said. "Both were swords. They were magnificent creations. My work was to clean and polish them. I have never had the pleasure of working Damascus steel. I know its reputation, and I know it when I see it. Many in Tarsus would give its weight in gold to possess it. This was once a sword. Someone broke the blade and ground it to make a knife. They destroyed a masterpiece to gain a kitchen knife. I am glad I was not present."

He positioned himself so all three of us could see the knife. "First, I will straighten the blade, then reshape it so that the back of the blade is more like the edge," he said, tracing with his index finger the changes he was suggesting, "and make a portion of the spine, from the point to here, a cutting edge."

"You have my approval. I look forward to seeing it." I had spoken out of turn and looked to Moshe and my father for their approval or a better suggestion.

They both laughed and nodded approval.

"Good, good," he said. "I will start first thing in the morning, although I am tempted to work through the night. Let me have three days, and I can make the hilt and handle."

For the next three days, I helped unload a ship recently arrived from Antioch. At breakfast on the third day, Moshe asked Cyrus and me to join him at his office in the afternoon to visit the smith. When we reached the shop, the apprentices were establishing order from the day's work. The smith welcomed us, held the knife up for us to see, then gave it to Moshe.

Moshe took it in both hands, walked to the opening to the shop, raised it in the good light, rotated it, then shifted it back and forth, studying the lines and pattern in the metal. He smiled, nodding his admiration and approval. He handed it to my father, who took the blade and examined it in like manner. He smiled, looked at the smith, and nodded approval, then passed the knife to me, handle first.

I took it, amazed at its brightness and its beauty. Holding the hilt in my right hand, I lifted the blade into the sunlight. I could see in the metal the compressed lines identifying it as Damascus steel. The guard and pommel were of bronze, giving the hilt a distinctive symmetry. The handle was of a fine-grained wood, apparently oak, plain but richly textured, in its plainness a work of art. I was amazed men could transform a kitchen knife into such a magnificent work.

The smith stepped toward me and took the knife. "Cornelius, I shall never forget this blade. Working the metal was a joy. The tang shows my name and signet. It may be the most significant monument I could have ever created for myself."

He took the knife by the blade, holding the hilt up for us to see. "My jeweler friend and I made a mold for the pommel and poured the bronze into it. It is part of the knife and will never slip off.

"I also double-tempered the blade in new olive oil," he added. "I was too embarrassed to use old tempering oil. You may use it to shave. It will provide an easier shave than that afforded by the barber. Let me show you something."

He went to the container holding water for tempering, filled the cup of his hand, and let some drops fall on the flat of the blade. Instead of spreading over the blade, the water beaded like drops of quicksilver.

"See?" he said. "Water rolls off the blade instead of flowing off, as on a steel surface. I always heard this is characteristic of Damascus steel."

He then walked to his work table, picked up a sheath, and slipped the knife into it. "One of the leather workers said you helped him with a difficult task and that he owed you a debt. He made this sheath as payment. It bears his signet here on the back." He pointed to a distinctive marking burnt into the leather. "There are no adornments or decorations on either the knife or the sheath. The design is simple and the surface plain."

He gave it to me. I took it in my left hand and offered him my right. Our eyes met. He knew I appreciated what he had done for me and that I was aware of his great skill.

I unfastened my belt, slipped the sheath onto it, again fastened it, and moved the sheath to my left side. I possessed one of the finest knives, if not the finest, in Tarsus, perhaps in all of Cilicia.

I resolved to dedicate my life and effort to becoming the best legionnaire I could be, as the smith had dedicated his life to becoming the best of smiths. If I succeeded in that effort, then the smith and I would have fulfilled our callings.

By the time we reached the villa, my step was firmer, my body more erect, and my face firmly set for the endeavor ahead. I suppressed the urge to shout for the entire world to hear, "Send unto me adversaries worthy of my encounter." I understood what Simmias meant by greatness. I resolved that I, too, would become great.

A few days later, I visited the legion camp. Both letters to Sejanus were ready. One was an official letter recommending me for enlistment, the other a personal letter from the centurion to Sejanus.

As we parted, I thanked them for the time and effort each had spent in training me in the use of weapons, especially the short sword and the pilum. In the last exchange, the centurion said, "If you ever meet a well-scarred, tough old mule of a legionnaire named Gaius, give him my regards. He and I marched many a mile and fought many an engagement chasing Arminius around Germany. He is a good man. Tell him I said, 'For the Senate and the people of Rome.' He will know what I mean."

I assured him I would, then turned and left the camp.

A few days later at breakfast, Moshe announced, "Cornelius, beginning today, we will be loading a ship destined for Corinth. It is scheduled to sail the day after tomorrow morning. May I book you as a member of the crew?"

"Please do. I am ready to go. Thank you for booking me."

To break the silence that suddenly descended, I added, "I will spend the morning getting ready, then spend the afternoon helping load the ship."

As we rose from the table, Moshe departed for the warehouse, but Father lingered. "Cornelius, I looked around Tarsus and found a leather pouch. It is old but in good condition and has a false bottom. I notice you are using Animus's old pouch. I also had a leather smith make a sheath for the scroll Mother gave you. It is thick leather and will protect the scroll."

I followed my father to his room. The pouch and the sheath were on a table. He handed me the pouch, then motioned for me to step outside. He followed, picking up the leather sheath.

"Mother and I are saddened to see you go," he said, "but we wish you well. Make sure the sheath fits the scroll. Bring it by the office if it does not. We can still alter it. Here is some money. See whether the false bottom works." He gave me a handful of gold coins, then turned and left for the warehouse.

I walked to my room, laid the pouch on my pallet, and picked up the scroll Mother had given me. I opened the sheath and slipped it inside. It fit perfectly. I laid the knife, the sheath with the scroll, and the letters to Sejanus on the pallet. I next laid a good tunic and a pair of sandals by the other items.

There was plenty of room in the pouch, but I decided not to take the extra pair of sandals. The pair I was wearing would last until I reached Rome. I sat awhile wondering about the trip to Rome. I had never been to sea, never served on a merchantman, and never been away from Tarsus. I was becoming apprehensive and reported to the warehouse to help load the ship.

The following day passed rapidly. When I returned to the villa, I walked by Simmias's room. He was sitting in front of it and motioned me over.

"Tomorrow is the day. Do not be anxious. From the day of your birth, this day would come. You will do well."

"It would be good just to let it all go and work for Moshe. I could be happy."

"No, Cornelius," Simmias replied, "you would not be content. In the back of your mind would be the fear you had betrayed yourself."

"You are kind to reassure me," I replied.

"Remember you are better prepared than most. You can yet learn from everyone you meet. Befriend them. It costs nothing." He stood and offered his hand, giving his blessing. "I am very proud of you and expect you to return in a red tunic."

"Thank you for all you have been to me," I said, taking his hand. "If we should not meet again, I will see you in the beyond."

I walked to Father's room where he and Moshe were finishing their evening meal. I joined them, for I was hungry. I enjoyed the meal and the casual conversation, then stood. "I am ready to go. I need only to place items in the new pouch. Will you have breakfast early?"

"We will have breakfast early," Moshe said. "We should be there at first light. Rest well. Until morning then, goodnight."

Someone had placed a lamp in my room. I opened the pouch and placed the coins in the false bottom, then packed the tunic to cushion the knife, the sheath containing the page from *The Iliad*, and the letters to Sejanus. I was ready to go. I extinguished the lamp and was immediately asleep.

I awoke to someone in the room. A servant indicated it was time to go. I dressed quickly, picked up the pouch, looked for the last time around the room, then joined Moshe and my father, who were waiting for me.

Breakfast was pleasant but subdued. We talked of pleasant things remembered. I expressed my appreciation for all each had done for me. Finally, Moshe stood. "It is time."

In the moonlight, we could see the way to the pier. A small crowd had gathered. On the ship, the sail was already set. I bade one last goodbye to everyone, shook hands with Moshe, embraced my father for the last time, then turned and walked up the gangplank.

The men pulled the gangplank on board and cast off the lines, and the ship moved slowly toward the channel, making a gentle surge as the river current caught the ship moving it toward the open sea. I took my place with the crew adjusting the sail to the wind. The sun was just rising above the city of Tarsus.

THE LEGION

When we reached the open sea, I became nauseated and found it necessary to spend the day at the prow to feel the slight breeze. By the following morning, the feeling had passed, and I resumed my duties, feeling at ease with my new tasks. We had a pleasant voyage and arrived in the bay at Corinth in less than three weeks. Most of our cargo was destined for Rome and had to be unloaded for portage across the isthmus and loaded on the other side. When this was completed, I reported to the captain and requested permission to leave the ship.

"Cornelius, it has been our pleasure to have you aboard. Most men with your training would not have engaged in the menial task of keeping the ship under way. Moshe ordered me to pay you a seaman's wage," he said, giving me a handful of coins. "May all the gods favor your journey."

As I walked toward the rail where the ship's longboat waited, the crew formed a passageway, and each held out his hand as I passed.

During most of the voyage, we were in sight of land. As we approached Corinth, islands became more numerous, rising sharply from the water with no delta or farmland between the mountains and the sea. *How different from Tarsus*, I thought. As we sailed into the harbor, I saw more ships than I could count. Corinth itself rose out of the bay with only a plateau on which the city itself was built. There was activity all along the shoreline and across the isthmus joining the two mountain ranges. I planned to walk across the narrow stretch of land and sign on a ship destined for Rome.

As I approached, I beheld a spectacle I could never have imagined. Toward the bay was a roadway paved with smooth stones much wider and better constructed than the Roman road through Cilicia. Hundreds of men and teams of oxen and mules responded to shouts of overseers and drivers. At the water's edge, workers loaded cargo onto a large platform with wheels the size of a chariot's. Men, oxen, and mules harnessed to the platform strained to move it forward. Once under way, the animals were unhitched, and the men continued to pull their load across the isthmus. On the other side, crews unloaded cargo. I could see ruts worn or carved into the road that provided a track on which the platforms could move back and forth. As platforms were unloaded, the cargo was immediately transferred to waiting longboats and carts and then hauled to ships or to piers in the harbor. I saw order in all the chaos.

Amidst the crowd, I purchased wine from a vendor who poured my drink into a cup with great skill from a large wineskin on his back. From another vendor, I purchased two dried fish, then walked to a small outcropping on higher ground and turned my attention to the activity on the isthmus.

I marveled at the steady flow of platforms, one occasionally carrying a large ship. How does man conceive of such an operation, much less put it into motion? I speculated whether the world would be a better place if every activity was as well planned and executed. Was this the order Simmias envisioned as the ideal society?

I watched until the sun dropped behind the mountain range, then walked to the other side of the isthmus. Activity along the passageway was slowing. I asked a harbormaster whether there were ships destined for Rome. He pointed out several, one a large merchant ship.

As the laborers collected into small groups, I walked up the hillside, picked up an armful of wood, and returned to the work area. I approached some men sitting around a small fire and inquired if I might join them, showing my load of wood. After receiving a favorable reply, I joined the outer circle. I understood most of the conversation but did not participate in it. After a while, I cleared some small stones from around me and, using my pouch for a pillow, fell asleep.

By daylight, there was already activity. I purchased bread of poor quality and some dried fish and ate breakfast, watching for a boat from the ship. When one arrived, I helped transfer cargo onto a platform at water's edge, then requested permission from the helmsman to board his craft. "I am seeking passage to Rome as a member of the crew. Is there need for one?"

The helmsman, a burly man with a bushy, short beard and similar hair, laughed. "Do we need one! By the time we are loaded and unloaded again, half the crew will be wasting their substance in Corinth."

I laughed. "That is fortunate for me. I have heard of nights spent in Corinth."

"You appear to be able to carry your weight," the helmsman said. "I will request of the captain you be assigned to my watch."

"I'll be pleased to join your watch. My name is Cornelius. I am from Tarsus. Thank you for your assistance."

"My name is Galen. I have visited Tarsus many times. It is a working town, not like Corinth. I am already short a man. Take your place there," he said, pointing to an empty seat.

I walked to the seat and retrieved the oar.

It was a week before the ship was loaded and set sail for Rome. Due to contrary winds, it required almost a week to navigate the long, narrow channel from the isthmus to the open sea. Once in open water, we enjoyed fine weather until nearing the narrow strait between Sicily and the mainland of Italy.

As we approached the strait, a sudden squall arose, requiring us to reduce sail. The captain kept enough sail to control the ship, but we were blown off course. Had we been within the strait, the squall would have blown us onto the rocky shore.

During the height of the storm, I lost my footing and decided to retrieve my sandals from my locker below. As I entered the sleeping area, a member of Galen's crew was removing my knife from my pouch. The noise from the storm concealed my approach. With my left arm, I grasped the man securely around his neck. He struggled violently for a few moments, then yielded to the pressure, dropped the knife, and hung in my arms, gasping for breath. I laid him on the deck, removed the laces from my sandals, bound his wrists in front of him, then carried him to a vertical brace. I looped another lace over a high pin in the brace and raised his hands to a point where his feet barely touched the deck, tugging at the lace to make sure it would hold him securely. I returned topside.

The squall had abated yet presented a danger to the ship. Everyone was at his station following orders to change the position of the sail, or to reef or loosen more sail. By late afternoon, the squall had passed, and the sun broke through. We raised the sail, and the captain ordered everyone to stand aside.

I thought of my shipmate tied in the sleeping area. As a member of Galen's crew, I had come to know him well. He was a good sailor, taking great enjoyment in the hard work of managing the sail. But I was angry that someone would steal my knife. The soul of the smith was in that blade. A gift created out of love and devotion carries with it an essential part of the creator, becoming part of the soul of the one who accepts it. Such a gift possesses more than its appearance, binding forever friends and loved ones over time and space.

The anger that my friend would steal from me offset any sympathy. Maneuvering the massive sail together, hour after hour, day after day, had created a bond exceeding that of casual friendship. I trusted him. If the theft were a transaction in the marketplace, the price he would pay would far exceed any possible gain.

Punishment in the military for stealing was severe, even death in some cases. It was especially so in closely knit groups such as a ship's crew. This man had betrayed himself by betraying a friend and so deserved the severest penalty.

When the ship's routine returned to normal, I reported to Galen what had happened. He and I went below and untied the offender.

"We've known for some time there was a thief among us," Galen said. "It was affecting the crew, for each was beginning to suspect the other. The captain will be pleased."

Galen approached the first officer, exchanged observations about the severity of the storm, then said, "During the storm, Cornelius found this man removing contents from his locker."

The first officer, after assessing the situation, led us to the captain and reported what had happened. The captain addressed the thief. "Are you guilty of the accusation by the first officer?"

He whimpered, "Yes, I am."

"I am surprised. You have given this ship good service," the captain said. "Punishment for thievery is removal of the left hand. I give you a choice. When we reach Rome, the first officer will cut off your left hand, or, as we pass through the strait, he will cast you from the stern of the ship. Which will you have?"

"Cast me from the ship. I would rather drown than be forever marked as a thief. Thank you, sir, for the choice."

"May the god of thieves grant you what you deserve," said the captain.

The captain returned to his duties. The ship was well off course, and no land was yet in sight. It was late the next day before we lay off the strait. The captain waited until the next morning before attempting passage.

As the ship passed through the narrowest point of the strait, the first officer directed the thief to the stern of the ship and, without ceremony, pushed him off. Several of us watched as the head of the man surfaced and gradually grew smaller. If the god of thieves smiled upon him, he would make it to shore.

A week later, we were at the mouth of the Tiber and unloaded the ship's cargo. We secured the ship for the night and received our pay. Galen brought his boat alongside and took ashore those of us not on duty. I was the last to leave and made my way to the stern. "Thank you for booking me on board, Galen. May the patron of good sailors watch over you."

"It was my pleasure, Cornelius," he said. "With your help, we found the thief. The spirit of the ship is much improved. May the gods favor you. Cast off."

I raised my hand in a casual salute and cast off the line.

I found an eating place, then a public bath. I enjoyed the warm waters, laundered my best tunic, and arranged to spend the night in the bathhouse.

Rome was two days distant, and I decided to allow two days for the journey rather than walk through the night. Late in the afternoon of the second day, as the road passed through a low gap in the hills, I saw that city. It was far, far larger and far, far grander that anything I had ever imagined. I understood why Rome ruled the world.

✝

I entered the city to find crowds anxiously going somewhere but no one working on a building or repairing a street, nor were there any street vendors.

I arranged to enter a public bath. A citizen noticed my slow Latin speech and asked where I was from. I told him Tarsus and inquired about work in Rome.

"No one in Rome works," he said. "Everyone is on the wheat dole. If you want to work, go back to Tarsus."

"I'm enlisting in the Roman legion. I am to report to the Praetorian Guard. Do you know how to get there?"

"My respects to you," he said. "The Guard is near the Senate north of here. May Mars smile on your venture."

By good light the next morning, I walked north and found the marketplace. A stranger pointed out the fortress. The guard let me pass, and an aide conducted me to a large room where Sejanus was holding counsel. I stood some distance away until he motioned me to him. After reading my letters, he inquired in Latin as to my background and education, then assigned me to an aide.

The fortress was massive, constructed of marble with polished floors. The legionnaires were impressive, dressed in fine tunics and polished armor, armed with the ceremonial hasta used before the Marius reforms—the long, heavy spear with the large steel point. This was a different legion from that described by Simmias.

In a formal ceremony, I joined the Roman army, took an oath to defend the republic, and received a legionnaire's plain white tunic.

That afternoon, in our new tunics, we marched to a training camp outside Rome. After being assigned sleeping quarters, we marched to a warehouse and were issued heavy sandals, a helmet, armor made of leather with metal plates attached, and a short sword. After an evening meal, we returned to the barracks. I examined my sword and helmet and noticed my sandals were extremely heavy and well laced, with small nails embedded in the sole.

We spent the next day learning the proper donning of armor and holding the shield and short sword, but we spent more time on the proper lacing of the sandals than on anything else.

On the second day, we marched about four miles to a drum beat, requiring about two hours. Each day, the tempo of the beat increased, as did the distance. By the end of the week, we completed twenty miles in five hours.

Simmias was right. It was a different world, but I had no difficulty with the hard work and the long hours. I heard oaths and swear words I had never heard and was amazed the magnificent Greek language could be so artfully crafted.

The following week, we marched to a training yard where each of us received a wooden sword similar to the standard sword but much heavier. I had practiced with such a sword at the legion camp in Tarsus and knew the basic offensive and defensive maneuvers. An older legionnaire was assigned to each recruit to train him. When my instructor demonstrated attack and defensive positions, I knew exactly what to do. I performed them with some precision and returned to the ready position. He then ordered moves he had not shown me. I executed them, if not well, at least adequately, though my right shoulder and arm were in great pain from the weight of the sword.

"Where did you learn these?" he asked.

"Sir, in Tarsus I spent time at the legion camp. The centurions there taught me."

"You were taught well," he said. "Follow me."

Arriving at a neighboring yard, he handed me a training pilum, similar to the standard pilum but much heavier. I assumed the ready position. He paced me through the basic moves.

"You have no need to go through the training exercises. It is good to see someone who knows what to do. Follow me."

We stopped before the centurion in command of the training yard.

"This recruit knows the basic moves."

"Where did you learn them?" asked the centurion.

I said in my best Latin, "Sir, I attended the university in Tarsus and while there spent time at the legion camp where the centurions taught me."

"At Tarsus? I have been there. I may know a centurion there."

He handed me a training sword and called out two maneuvers. I executed them with as much precision and speed as I could and returned to the ready position. He traded my sword for a pilum and called out a difficult pilum tactic. I performed it and returned to the ready position.

"You executed those better than some we sent to the fortress."

The centurion asked my name and requested I follow him to a tent at the end of the yard, his office by the papers and tablets present. He pointed to a bench, and I sat. He retrieved a tablet and asked questions about the studies at the university, my work on the farm and for Moshe, all the while making entries on his tablet. Finally, he asked, "With these qualifications, why did you join the legion?"

I hesitated.

"You answered the questions well. I, myself, would like to know why you joined the legion."

"All my family believe we are here for a purpose. I believe I was born to be a legionnaire."

"That is a remarkable answer. It may allow me to understand my life in the legion," he said. "I will direct your training so your time here will not be wasted. Report to this tent in the morning. It has been a pleasure meeting you. Welcome to the legion. My name is Domitus, centurion, Fourth Macedonia. I will be your advocate until your training is complete. You are free to go."

"Yes, sir." I stood, saluted, and left the tent. My arms and shoulders ached, and my lower legs pained me as I walked, but I was elated.

The next morning, before the appointed time, I was at the tent. Domitus arrived, resplendent in his centurion armor, and motioned me inside.

After seating himself, he said, "The trainers believe you should be in the advanced unit. It has been in training for almost a month. You have the right moves with the weapons, but can you adapt to the pace? If you believe you can, I will place you with it. You decide."

"I would like to join the advanced unit."

"Good," said Domitus. "I will introduce you to your centurion, Gaius. He joined us recently after serving with the Fifth Alaudae in Germany."

I followed Domitus to a far section of the training field, where he hailed the centurion. "Gaius, this is Cornelius. We discussed him last evening. He wants to join your group. He understands he must keep the pace."

Gaius was older than I expected, heavily built, his face deeply scarred. "Welcome to the legion and welcome to this unit," he said. "Get a sword and shield."

I selected one of the wooden swords and the best wicker shield among the lot and followed Gaius to an area where men were sparring. On the way, Gaius told me he had read the letter from the centurion in Tarsus, saying he was pleased to learn where his old friend was serving.

"Your friend said for me to tell you, 'For the Senate and the people of Rome.'"

Gaius stopped and stared at me, then broke into a hearty laugh.

"It is good to hear the greeting. It is not used here but is the greeting among the mules in the line—the real legion. For us it conveys all the best wishes at parting, or on meeting again, or even for a casual greeting between friends. If you should ever see my friend again, tell him Gaius said, 'For the Senate and the people of Rome.' Thank you for the greeting. It recalls the good days in Germany."

We arrived at the training yard, and Gaius interrupted two men sparring. "This is Cornelius. He joined our unit. Take him through the routine."

I faced the recruit. We were evenly matched in height and weight, but he was in much better condition. My best strategy was to save my strength by engaging defensively.

He was aggressive and used his sword well. I defended against his moves, and only twice did he land a serious body blow. The fatigue in my arms and shoulders was greater than the brief pain from his sword thrust.

Gaius ordered the engagement to stop, instructed the two recruits to resume their routine, and motioned for me to follow him. "You held your own well. For the rest of the week during our weapons drill, you work with the training posts to build your stamina. Join the unit in the marches and the drills. Next week, we will measure your skill. You are on your own."

I survived the marches with great pain and learned the unit drills. At every opportunity, I practiced long and hard with the sword at the training posts, even during rest periods. By the following week, I could hold my own.

The unit consisted primarily of men from patrician or wealthy backgrounds being trained for the Praetorian Guard. With few exceptions, I was cordially received. There were, however, some who felt I should not be there. I tried to gain their friendship, but the effort made matters worse. My farm background was apparent, and I was given the designation "the goat farmer." Several in that group were spoiling for a contest.

In the next training session, Gaius picked me as a constant and asked for volunteers to engage me. The adversarial group met briefly, and then one stepped forward, a fine-looking man, taller than I and somewhat heavier. We selected our practice swords and wicker shields. Gaius had previously indicated he was going to match me with one of that group, and I had prepared. As the weaker contestant, I planned for a defensive contest. One of the maneuvers the centurions at Tarsus taught was to catch the opponent's sword on the top edge of my shield, allowing a good thrust around the edge of his shield.

At Gaius's command, the contest began. I feigned an attack but allowed the opponent to press his. He was aggressive. I defended, each time slightly lowering my shield, inviting him to attack. He continued pressing hard, and I was having difficulty defending. But at the moment he began his thrust over my shield, I raised it, catching his sword blade with the top edge. At the same time, I pressed my shield against his, opening his right side. I caught him between his navel and rib cage, thrusting with all the strength I had. Had it been a real sword, it would have penetrated to its hilt.

The force knocked him to the ground, but he was not injured. I laid down my sword, removed my shield, stepped toward him, and offered him my hand. To my great surprise, he gripped it, rose to his feet, and said, "Goat farmers from Tarsus are dangerous."

From that day, I was accepted by the unit.

It was late summer when the unit finished its training. Gaius asked whether I preferred to join the Praetorian Guard as a parade legionnaire, protecting the wives of Roman officials was the way he described their duties, or to become a real legionnaire, a Marius mule. I jumped at the opportunity to be one of the mules. Gaius then had his scribe prepare a letter to the commander of the Fifth Alaudae Legion based in Germany, his old unit, recommending me.

One day before the group left for Germany, Gaius motioned me aside. "I acquired a special goatskin glove which served me well, and you will find a need for it. Stitched into its palm are rows of small metal splinters. Wear it when you draw your sword, for it will allow you to grip the hilt regardless of the blood on it. It saved my life more than once."

The glove was soft to the touch. I slipped it onto my right hand and felt its tight fit. I reached for a training sword lying on Gaius's table and felt the metal shards bite into the wooden grip. When I made two offensive moves, the glove held the sword firmly in my hand. I returned the sword to the table and removed the glove.

"Thank you for the gift. I shall carry it on my sword belt, and each time I slip it on, I will remember you." I saluted and said, "For the Senate and the people of Rome."

A few days later, a small detachment left the training camp for western Germany. I was pleased to be among them.

†

Several months later, after crossing the Alps through a high pass, we joined the Fifth Alaudae and reported to Germanicus, the legion commander. Our centurion handed him the mail pouch. Germanicus instructed an aide to provide us food and temporary lodging in a nearby tent.

The next morning, I was summoned to Germanicus's quarters where he was reviewing documents. "Among the papers was a letter from Gaius of this legion. He recommends you. I am assigning you to the Tenth Cohort. It is made up of old legionnaires waiting for their time to expire and recruits whose training is not up to our standard. They are all good legionnaires, but it better serves our purpose to place them in the same unit."

Germanicus paused. "I will not disclose your background. You are on your own to make of the assignment what you will." He summoned an aide and said, "Take this recruit to the Tenth."

As we walked past the rows of tents, the aide asked, "What did you do to be sent to the Tenth your first day?"

"I did not get a full term in the training camp. I need experience."

The aide laughed. "You will get lots of experience. Here we are." He directed me to enter a tent and addressed the centurion inside. "Germanicus sent you this recruit."

The centurion, sitting on a makeshift stool, looked up and spoke in Koine with a heavy accent. "What did you do to deserve assignment to this cohort?"

I replied in Latin, "I did not receive a full term of training."

"What is your name? Where are you from? In the legion, no one, not even Romans, speaks Latin. Speak Greek."

Using the Koine Greek, I said, "My name is Cornelius. I am from Cilicia."

The centurion stood, revealing a much larger man than I expected. "Welcome to the Tenth Cohort. My name is Remus. Do not be discouraged. It is a good unit, but we get some rotten assignments. I am pleased Germanicus sent me a good man for a change."

He motioned for me to follow him. "The Tenth Cohort is not at full strength, and neither are any of its centuries. The Sixth Century is most in need of men. It consists mostly of men waiting for their time to expire."

We entered a tent, and Remus addressed the group inside. "This is Cornelius. He is a new recruit in need of some training. He's fresh from Rome." He then left.

Speaking the street Koine, I asked where I was to sleep. An older man, his face deeply marred from the pox, stood and motioned to me to take the place next to him. He helped me remove my pack, unroll my bedding, and prepare for the night.

"My name is Titus. My time in the legion is nearly complete. Germanicus thinks us old ones are no longer fit for service. Welcome to the Sixth Century," he said. "You are in time for the evening meal. As long as we are at the base camp, we hire one of the camp followers to prepare meals. He does well, or at least it is better than our own cooking."

The meal was cordial, with each legionnaire introducing himself and making some small statement about his service. The food was better fare than that on the long march from Rome. I answered questions about happenings in Rome and rumors in the training camp, and was surprised when Titus asked about Sejanus.

"I met him only when I reported to the office of the guard. Other than that, I know nothing about him. He did look important with all the aides around him."

"There is a rumor," Titus said. "Sejanus is displeased with Germanicus in his conduct of the campaign against Arminius and the German tribes. I served in the Guard. Germanicus is Sejanus's lapdog and is not doing well. I wondered whether you had heard anything regarding the command of the Fifth Alaudae."

"I never heard anything about Sejanus and Germanicus," I said. "It was all I could do to survive the training."

✝

I quickly adapted to the routine. The Tenth Cohort collected large and small timbers to be used in preparing roads for winter. There were frequent forced marches attempting to engage Arminius, with the cohort guarding the legion's baggage train.

Arminius withdrew his forces. Snows began, and the legion moved into permanent structures. After a day in ice and snow, it was good to return to one. Meals were prepared in a central kitchen, and the crowded conditions provided warmth, but frequently the water-skin displayed ice formations.

This was my first winter in Germany. An additional tunic and heavy cloak helped, but Titus showed me how to survive the cold. The Tenth continued to gather timbers and occasionally assisted in repairing a permanent structure.

Finally, there were traces of spring, and mud became our adversary. It was a day worthy of celebration when we returned to our tents.

Arminius collected his forces and began attacking our patrols, capturing their baggage trains. By the time the legion arrived, he had vanished, taking the trains with him. Germanicus pursued Arminius over vast sections of Germany but never engaged his main force.

For the next few years, this was the pattern. Despite the cold in winters and the heat and insects in summers, I was content as one of

Marius's mules. The camaraderie of the hard work and the evening meals offset any displeasure. The eight men sharing the tent became as family to me.

Remus continued as centurion of the Tenth Cohort, with Titus still acting centurion of the Sixth Century. Germanicus sent inexperienced legionnaires to this cohort for training and old ones to serve out their time. There had been little change in the Sixth Century, except for the young ones, of whom I was now the oldest.

Germanicus had ordered the Tenth Cohort to provide escort for legion supply trains. One afternoon Remus announced Arminius had ambushed one of the trains, killing several drivers and capturing six grain carts.

As the century broke into groups, Titus said, "Arminius did it again. He is relying on Germanicus for supplies. You watch—the Sixth will be the escort."

As predicted, Remus visited our tent and ordered Titus to provide escort to Oberden and deliver a pouch to the commander. Titus called the Sixth Century to form an array, walked to the center front, and announced, "We are to leave in the morning for Oberden to escort the grain shipment. Be ready by first light. You are dismissed."

I returned to the tent and prepared for the trip. This was our cohort's first assignment as escort to a supply train. We had never been in a serious engagement. I laid out my armor. I had replaced my sandals only a few weeks before, so they were in good repair. I placed in my route pack the things I would need and slipped over my sword belt the glove Gaius had given me.

Titus instructed us to place our packs and helmets in the cart. "We are going to make the march to Oberden in one day, so travel as light as possible. There is not likely to be any trouble on the way."

By the time the evening meal was ready, all the packs and equipment had been placed in the cart.

Before dawn, someone shook my shoulder. I had slept fully dressed, anxious I could not lace my sandals in the dark. I rolled my bedding and laid it beside the things I did not need.

It was yet dark when I joined the group for breakfast. With the heat from the cooking fire, the hot porridge dispelled the chill.

Titus ordered us into an array of two ranks and marched us into the road to Oberden. The sky was overcast, and it was some time before we could see clearly the man in front. We spread out and no longer marched in step. Although the pace was rapid, walking was easy in the smooth ruts created by carts.

Late in the afternoon, we reached the camp at Oberden, marched to a shed, and prepared for the night. Before sunset, we ate with the garrison. An aide from the commander summoned Titus.

On his return, Titus led us back to our site. "The carts are being loaded. Recover your equipment and get a wicker shield from the cart. Be in full armor. We will leave at first light. Break the array."

I retrieved my pack and helmet and selected the best wicker shield from those remaining. I returned to the shed, found a place to lay the shield, and placed on it my helmet along with my marching pack. I tightened the laces on my sandals, wrapped myself in my heavy cloak, lay alongside my shield, pulled the pack from it to use as a pillow, and was immediately asleep.

It was dark when I awoke. I sensed it to be almost dawn, tightened the cloak about my shoulders, and thought about the return trip. If I planned a surprise attack on a supply train, where would I set the ambush? For most of the way, although it passed through deep forests, there was no undergrowth near the road, except where it rose for about a hundred yards through a gap in a low ridge. That would be the place. I would let the train enter the area, wait until both lead and rear elements were well within the overgrown section, capture the carts, and drive them through the lead. With the carts blocking the way, the rear section could not come to their aid.

I was reviewing my plan when Titus ordered us awake. We marched to the kitchen for a quick breakfast and returned to the shed. We then placed our packs in the cart, donned our armor, and picked up our helmets and shields. I folded the special glove over my belt.

Titus placed half the men in front of the carts and half behind to protect the rear, about twenty-five in each section. I was in the rear. The sky was again overcast, but there was enough light to see.

We stopped after about two hours, dropped the shields, and waited for the waterskin. The wicker shield was not heavy, but holding it at the proper height tired the muscles in my left arm. I removed the glove from my belt and slipped it onto my right hand. We resumed the march, and after about an hour, I recognized ahead the gap in the low ridge.

As soon as we entered the congested area, I heard shouts ahead. It was an ambush. No one was in command of the rear section. I ran to the front and ordered the carts to close the distance between them. I ordered five of the older legionnaires to move up the left side to protect the carts and to assist the lead section. I led five more to the right side of the train, urging the carts to move closer together.

We had the tribesmen in their flank. I caught the first man fully by surprise, thrust my sword deep into his exposed left side, and did the same to a second. A third tribesman, restricted by the under-growth, could not use his weapon. I thrust him straight on, through the throat. Five of my men moved ahead of me and disposed of the attackers. It was over in a matter of minutes. No tribesman escaped. The old legionnaires walked through the ambushers, finishing any who were not already dead. My men suffered no serious wounds.

Titus ordered several in the lead section to collect the weapons from the dead and place them on the baggage cart. He counted the dead, noting one of them wore a silver arm band.

I removed the glove and used my tunic to wipe blood from my sword blade as Titus approached. "There were thirty-seven of them," he said. "I did not see them in the undergrowth. They were on us before I knew it. It was as though you set an ambush for them. They would have caused us a problem had you not caught them in the flank. The crowded space was to our advantage."

He assessed the status of his men. "I will make a full repot to Remus. Germanicus will be pleased his carts made it through. Cornelius, you have had a day. Give me your hand," he said, extending to me his bloody right hand. To the group he shouted, "Resume your array."

We settled into the rhythm of the march. I had killed three men as routinely as a lunge at a training stake. I had imagined the engagement would be much different: a face-to-face encounter with a series of attacks and defenses until one had killed the other. We were fortunate the confrontation ended as it did. If there was to be a next time, I would suggest Titus designate someone to protect the carts. And the inexperienced legionnaires, myself included, would need practice at closing the carts and forming an array around them.

Titus's command to take the noon break interrupted my thoughts. The young ones ate in relative silence, shaken by the fierceness of the experience. The old ones in the lead section were laughing and talking. I had barely finished my ration when we were again on the march.

We rested again in the middle of the afternoon, and with little notice, returned to camp late in the day. As soon as the escort was dismissed, I washed the blood from my sword and glove at a large waterskin and returned to my tent. The evening meal was raucous and cordial, with everyone talking of the day's events.

✝

Late one afternoon, after spending the day carrying timbers, several of us sat in front of our tent. Titus said, "Cornelius, what you did on the trip from Oberden was remarkable. I've been in the legion twenty years, one of the first of the recruits when Marius made changes. On most campaigns, I've been a mule. I've seen good leaders and poor ones."

I started to speak, but Titus continued. "There are men in charge who know what to do but cannot get it done. They overestimate their ability or their resources. Germanicus has that trait. I've worn out too many sandals to believe he can bring Arminius to bay."

He stared into the distance. "Then there are those who know what must be done and know how to do it. Until the Fifth has that kind of leader, we will continue to chase Arminius."

Titus paused and looked at me. "You have the ability to get things done. It is a rare trait. People are born with it. I do not think it can be learned."

"Thank you for being good to me," I said. "Old ones know mistakes and successes. Young ones are lost in the forest. My family believes each of us is here for a purpose. I was born to be a legionnaire, to be here, and to do what I did at the ambush. Germanicus put me here in the Tenth. I will be the best mule I can, even to carrying timbers."

"I've never heard of such a plan," Titus said, "but hearing what you say, I believe it. I am at the end of my time. I am in charge of this century because I am one of the oldest in the cohort, but Remus should name you acting centurion. Germanicus abuses him and the cohort, but he handles it well. You can help him as you have helped me. Had I lost the grain shipment, I would be in trouble."

Titus stood. "It has been time well spent."

†

The days grew shorter, and the nights colder. We were gathering timbers one afternoon when an aide approached. "Germanicus wishes to see Cornelius."

Titus pointed in my direction.

As we walked the distance to the commander's quarters, the aide said, "I remember you. You are the recruit sent to the Tenth the very day he arrived. Are you in trouble?"

"I do not think so."

When we reached Germanicus's tent, the aide held open the flap. "Good luck."

Germanicus looked up. "Rest easy, Cornelius. Remus tells me you saved the grain shipment." He reached for a document on the table behind him. "I read again Gaius's letter. He assessed your abilities accurately. As Remus recommends, I appoint you acting centurion of the Sixth Century, Tenth Cohort. Continue the good work," he said.

I stood at attention, saluted, turned, and left.

My blood raced. I tried to reconcile Titus's assessment of Germanicus with what I had just experienced. He showed no interest in the details of the ambush—how many there were, how they set the ambush, what weapons they had. But he named me acting centurion of fifty men, many of them in the legion almost as long as I had been alive.

When I reached camp, some of the men were sitting in the late sunshine, resting from the day's effort. I waited for Titus to return, caught his attention, and nodded toward our tent.

"How did it go?" he asked.

"He appointed me acting centurion. I hope you do not take offense."

"No, I am pleased," Titus said. "Had you not responded the way you did in the ambush, I could be facing serious charges, perhaps Remus also."

"I am embarrassed to take the appointment. You've been in the legion longer than I have been alive."

"Cornelius, you are quite the hero, especially among us old ones. We are confident the legion will be in good hands after our time and look forward to ending our service in your command. I will make the announcement."

At the evening meal, Titus stood and called for attention. "I'm pleased to announce to the Sixth Century and to the Tenth Cohort the appointment by Germanicus of our own Cornelius as acting centurion of the Sixth. He has my blessing and the blessing of the escort detail."

I stood. "Thank you, Titus, my friend. With great pride, I assume command of the wood detail." The men cheered and laughed in response.

"I promise you the very best I have." I lifted my cup in salute. "For the Senate and the people of Rome."

✝

Our camp had grown into an elaborate post as the legion prepared for another winter. Engineers continued to add permanent structures to house us during the coldest weather.

Germanicus's sorties against Arminius stopped. However, whenever a shipment of supplies or grain left Oberden, the Sixth Century provided escort. It was a dangerous activity. Less experienced men protected the carts, while others engaged the enemy. I conducted regular inspections of clothing, equipment, and the physical condition of my century.

Germanicus continued to pursue Arminius over vast sections of Germany. The Fifth Alaudae continued its consumption of sandals and other valuable resources. There was never an engagement in which Germanicus selected either the battlefield or its timing.

The Tenth Cohort under Remus's leadership became more disciplined and more effective, continuing to provide escort to supply trains. Frequently in major engagements with Arminius's forces, we were assigned critical positions in the battle line. On those occasions, to the delight of the Tenth, the Ninth Cohort guarded the legion's baggage train.

Remus approved my suggestion that the Sixth Century remove its standard from the supply tent and place it in front of my tent. From that time, our escort detail carried its own battle standard. Soon there was competition to be named standard bearer.

As replacements arrived, Germanicus continued to assign the men near the end of their service to the Tenth Cohort, and Remus allocated many to the Sixth Century. There were usually about fifty men in my century divided into eight profiles, each with its own tent and baggage cart. Seven of the most experienced old legionnaires shared my tent.

The Sixth continued to escort supply trains. In later years, when a band of tribesmen appeared and we formed our array, their leader often lifted his weapon in salute and withdrew. Our standard bearer raised our standard in a return salute.

In winter, Remus attempted to secure for us heavy, hooded cloaks lined with animal skins. One day, a supply train arrived with sixty fur-lined cloaks. With those and winter leggings, our trips to Oberden were no longer so dangerous. I would always remember my century in deep snow wearing hooded, fur-lined cloaks as they escorted a supply train. The world will not see their like again.

✝

When the last of the snow melted and the pale green of new growth was everywhere, Germanicus prepared for another campaign against Arminius. The cohorts were all near full strength. One afternoon, Remus summoned me to his tent. "I am authorized to appoint you centurion of the Sixth Century. In the Fifth Legion, however, there is a custom that a new centurion must defend his appointment against all challengers. Are you agreeable?"

"Yes." Should I lose, I would yet be in the Sixth Century.

The next day, Remus arranged the centuries in a square and stepped into the center. "Cornelius, acting centurion of the Sixth Century, I appoint as centurion of the Sixth. He has agreed to defend his position. Does anyone challenge his appointment?"

Several legionnaires met at one corner of the square, then one came forward. He was taller and heavier than I, and his helmet and armor indicated he had been a long time in Germany. I had polished my helmet and the metal strips of my armor, the leather was clean and oiled, and my sandals were worn but freshly oiled. My tunic was clean. I looked the part of a fresh, arrogant patrician to be easily dispatched. I slipped on the glove Gaius had given me.

Remus handed each of us the standard infantry shield and the wooden training sword, then bid each of us well and stepped aside.

I slipped my left arm into the shield grips, grasped the sword, and felt the metal shards bite into the grip. My opponent held his shield away from his body. He had been fighting the local Chantii militia too long and had forgotten how to engage. I stepped forward and made a thrust. He was slow to defend. I lowered my sword and moved my shield outward, inviting an attack. He made a vicious thrust but was careless in protecting himself. Every legionnaire's move was designed to defeat the adversary.

I gripped my sword tightly and felt strength flow through my body like a flood. My opponent led with a hard thrust, opening his shield. I pressed my shield against his, opening it further and pinning his right arm against it. His right side was exposed. I aimed for his lowest rib. He went down with a grunt of pain and lay on the ground, jaws clenched.

I removed my shield and laid it on the ground with my sword on top. I helped my challenger remove his shield, then placed it and his sword next to mine. Then I assisted him to his feet and walked him to a camp stool nearby.

"I had the advantage, having done escort duty all winter. If you can handle the pain, I will take you to your tent," I said.

A few days later, with appropriate ceremony, Germanicus, commander of the Fifth Alaudae, awarded me the traditional red tunic of centurion. "Gaius would have been proud of you," he said.

✝

On a fine spring day, replacements arrived from Rome, including two cohorts of engineers who specialized in bridge building, having bridged the Rhine and other crossings. The news of their joining the Fifth Alaudae spread rapidly. At the evening meal, Titus announced there was a rumor that Sejanus was sending a prefect to bring the campaign against Arminius to a close. He predicted the prefect would be Pontius Pilate.

"When I served with the Praetorian Guard, Pilate gained a reputation serving as prefect with legions in Germany. I never saw him, but Sejanus sent him wherever he wanted to get something done. If the prefect is Pontius Pilate, we will have spent our last winter in Germany. Sejanus has grown weary of Germanicus's excuses."

Sometime later, Remus assembled the cohort. "Germanicus is going to bridge the Weser River. The Tenth Cohort is to deploy across it and provide security on that side. When the engineers finish the bridge, the Fifth will move across the Weser."

"I see the hand of Pontius Pilate in the bridging," said Titus at the evening meal. "Once we are across and moving into Arminius's home country, he will come out to meet us. Arminius never stands and fights. He pays a price, but it has cost Rome dearly. Mark my word, Pilate is already looking over Germanicus's shoulder. The god of war smiled on us this day."

"If that is so, I must be sure we are properly clothed," I said. "Titus, tomorrow you and I will inspect each man's clothing and equipment."

The profile prepared for inspection the next morning. When I arrived at the assembly site, the men were there in proper formation. With Titus at my side, I inspected each legionnaire's equipment and found it clean. I listed deficient sandals and equipment, then dismissed the men.

"I have the list of what we need," I said to Titus. "Get a cart and come to the front of the tent. Let's go to supply."

"Since you became centurion, the century has improved," Titus said. "The Tenth under Remus is a good unit, but engaging Arminius face-to-face will be a test. Arminius defeated three legions in the Teutoburg Forest."

"I am planning a ten-mile march with equipment, including the wooden shield. How will the men fare?"

"The old-timers will fare well. Anyone, even the new recruits, would die before dropping out. The escort marches kept us in good condition, but across the river there will be heavy engagements."

Titus stopped the cart in front of the supply tent. I dismounted and entered. It was filled with orderly stacks of all manner of military gear, the air filled with a good smell of cleaning oil and new metal. To my right, I saw a man of equestrian rank sitting at a table.

I approached him and asked in my best Greek, "Are you the supply officer?"

The gentleman looked up, and his face brightened. "I might be considered the supply officer, but, say, aren't you the young man who won his red tunic a few days ago?"

"Yes, sir, I am," I replied. "I had a good day."

"Germanicus told me of your success with the supply trains. The Fifth was the only legion in Germany last year that lost no carts. He also told me of your promotion to centurion and that you would defend against any challengers. I made a special effort to be there, for I had not witnessed a good engagement in a long time. Yours was a remarkable performance. You read your opponent well. Where did you train?" he asked.

"At the Praetorian Guard training camp outside Rome."

"My name is Pontius Pilate," he said, "prefect of the Fifth Alaudae. The supply officer stepped out for a few minutes. Can I be of help?"

"I need to pick up some replacement equipment. I can wait for the supply officer."

"He will return soon. Let me see your list," he said, reaching for my tablet. "It seems to be in order." He struck the tablet with his signet ring and returned it to me. "Do not be embarrassed being assigned to the Tenth Cohort. Germanicus is to cross the Weser to entice Arminius to attack. This is our last effort. We have lost too much time. The Fifth is to return to Rome. Before it is over, you will have earned your tunic. Here is the supply officer."

I handed the tablet to the supply officer, who hurried to the back of the tent and returned with several legionnaires. They brought the supplies to a table, matched them against my list, and loaded the cart.

I thanked the supply officer, expressed my appreciation to Pilate, and joined Titus, who could hardly contain his pleasure at the speed with which the order had been filled. From that day, when Remus had an order, he sent Titus and me to the supply tent.

After the men received their equipment, I announced the ten-mile march the following morning and told them to be ready by first light.

At the meal that evening, I told Titus the officer approving my order was Pontius Pilate. "By Jupiter," he said, "I was right. The Fifth will no longer wear out sandals chasing Arminius. Pilate will draw him out. We need to be ready."

The next day was a good one for the march, and it went well. Of the eighty now in my century, only three failed to keep the pace. I ordered them onto the cart with Titus, reassuring them they would soon rejoin their profile. On our return, I ordered the men to rejoin their group. The Sixth, its battle standard held high, marched proudly into camp.

On several occasions, I secured eighty of the heavy training swords from supply, paired each young legionnaire with an old one, and paced them through basic maneuvers.

On trips to the supply tent, I saw Pilate, and we had many conversations. Sejanus had appointed him prefect of the Fifth Alaudae. I found helpful Pilate's knowledge of the legion's organization and the function of its various officers.

Once when I asked about the legion's purpose, he replied, "To keep order. Without Roman law to administer justice and without the legions to enforce the law, there would be disorder. My duty as prefect is to administer Roman law. If I administer the law properly, there will be order in the world, and justice will prevail."

"Is there a force which supports Roman law, giving it authority to administer justice?" I asked.

"The Roman Senate supports the law. Roman law assures justice."

I wanted to hear more of his concepts of law and justice, for they were different from mine. "Over the years, laws change, and the Roman Senate changes. Does that mean justice changes?"

Pilate thought a moment. "I believe I am trapped by your question. If I say Roman law supports justice, then I imply that justice changes over the years with the law. If I say justice stays constant, then I can be unjust in administering Roman law as it changes."

"There must be a standard which permits a decision to be judged right or wrong, to be just or unjust, one that may have higher authority than the Roman Senate," I said.

Through our discussions, Pilate and I became good friends, but I was careful that my visits did not cloud my concept of being a centurion of the Tenth Cohort.

Once I was in the supply tent when Pilate hailed me and motioned me into his office. "You believe justice is not provided by the state but by an existing authority, that the military has no role in administering justice. In my view, the role of the prefect is to use the military to ensure laws are obeyed, and in so doing, I administer justice. You say justice is based on an authority defining right and wrong. I say justice is based on Roman law. There is a great difference in our concepts."

"I understand as prefect you enforce the law," I said. "I wish to correct an impression I may have left. I believe the military is more important than you do in providing order. Our difference is whether providing order also provides justice. We may be closer than it appears, for we are using words that carry different meanings for each of us."

"These discussions are enlightening," he said. Then he added, "Construction on the bridge is to start soon."

On the day before construction began, the Tenth Cohort in full campaign order marched to the Weser River, reaching it by nightfall. By noon the next day, the engineers had ferried us across, and we prepared a campsite close to the river.

That evening as we sat around the cooking fire, everyone's spirits were high. Titus stood facing the high ground. "Look where we are. The engineers have cleared all undergrowth. This will be the battlefield. Someone has planned to engage Arminius here. I see the mark of Pontius Pilate."

Engineers and legionnaires collected timbers, pilings, and poles, and once construction began, the bridge developed rapidly. In less than a week, it was complete, and the legion marched into Arminius's territory. The Tenth guarded the legion baggage train.

The third day after crossing the river, we had moved deep into Arminius's homeland. We saw small detachments of his cavalry watching our progress, and Germanicus's cavalry reported the gathering of Germanic tribes.

Germanicus then ordered a series of withdrawals to previous campsites, and on the third day, we withdrew to the clearing east of the Weser. Arminius would interpret the moves as a retreat and would attack with the legion's back to the river.

During the first withdrawal, we broke camp and marched to our previous campsite in a cold rain. There, the ditches and the rampart had been dug, but we constructed a palisade and set up the tents. It was a difficult day for everyone, especially the baggage train. The rain had ceased by the next morning, but the clouds remained. After a cold breakfast, we dismantled the camp. The second afternoon, we again set up the camp on a previous site. On the third afternoon, we set up camp north of the prepared field Titus had pointed out. That night, we had cooking fires to prepare our meal and to dry our raiment.

Titus had discerned Germanicus's plans. During the meal, he said, "I see Pilate's hand in the advance and withdrawal. Sejanus sent Pilate to defeat Arminius. He is drawing him into an engagement. Arminius may take the bait. We will know as early as tomorrow."

During the night, Arminius's forces moved to the high ground overlooking the river. His combined forces of infantry and cavalry numbered in excess of thirty thousand and covered the hillsides for almost a mile. He had taken the bait.

Germanicus's legion, including cavalry, numbered about sixty-five hundred and extended almost a mile, their backs to the river.

Late that evening, to present his plans, Germanicus summoned the centurions of the cohorts. His cavalry reported Arminius's tribesmen gathering near the river but with no effort to combine their forces. Based on that report, Germanicus planned to deploy his three best cohorts as the center—Cohorts One, Two, and Three—with three cohorts each constituting the right and the left wing. The Tenth Cohort would guard the baggage train. The three cohorts at the center would deploy in three ranks, the wings in two ranks, along the river to encourage Arminius to spread his forces. The legion would advance in formation until Arminius made his attack. Then the center would halt, and the wings would swing toward the center creating a giant U, funneling the tribesmen into the Roman center.

That evening, when Remus explained Germanicus's plan, my greatest fear was confirmed. The Tenth was to guard the base camp and baggage train. I felt as if I had betrayed my men. Our cohort was better than that, and the Sixth Century was as good as any in the line.

Well before dawn, everyone was preparing for battle. No cooking fires were allowed, so we washed down wafers with wine. One of Germanicus's aides entered Remus's tent. After a brief meeting, the aide departed, and Remus summoned the centurions. I finished the last of my wafer on the way to his tent.

As soon as all were present, Remus announced, "Mars and Jupiter have smiled on us. The Ninth Cohort is to guard the baggage train. We are the left flank. Be ready by sunup."

I inspected the equipment and supplies of my two archers and two slingers and sent a baggage cart to Remus's tent to load our pila and distribute them. We would be in the battle line, and my century was ready.

The eastern sky was beginning to lighten. In our tent, I laid out my armor. Titus motioned for me to follow him outside the tent. "Arminius was trained in Rome and is more experienced and more aggressive than Germanicus. He will try to outflank us. Once the battle begins, keep his forces always to our front. We cannot lose confidence. Place one of the old men beside each of the younger ones."

"Accompany me," I said, "to assure I instruct the leaders properly. We do not have much time."

I requested each leader to report to my tent. "Inform your units that we hold the extreme left flank of the legion. We cannot allow an attack on our own flank. Keep their forces always to our front. Place an old legionnaire beside the less experienced." I stepped back, saluted, and shouted, "For the Senate and the people of Rome!"

The leaders returned the salute. "For the Senate and the people of Rome!"

A light mist hung over the river, and the sun's first rays lit the tops of the trees beyond. I recalled Homer's description of Achilles as he prepared to do battle with Hector and the Trojans. I remembered Mother reading the passage from *The Iliad*, her voice becoming the sound of marching feet.

As I donned my armor, I pictured myself the gallant Achilles arming for battle. I reached for my greaves of heavy leather, and they became of the finest bronze. I fastened the iron buckle behind my heel, and it became a clasp of the finest silver. I passed over my head the strap holding my sword, the blade fashioned by a mighty Roman Vulcan with hammer blows that shook the seven hills of Rome, echoing down the thousand valleys of the Tiber. He twice plunged the blade into fires deep in the earth, twice removed it, cherry-red, twice plunged it into the anointing oil of kings. From the oil, twice withdrawn, he watched the temper line change the color of the blade, a blade now worthy of the death of heroes, then plunged it in the regal oil to cool.

As Achilles did, I lifted my helmet fashioned by Mars himself, with its transverse crest of feathers to gleam far and wide as bright as the sun. I set it well upon my brow, announcing to all the world the coming battle.

As he did, I spun on my heel to feel the fit of the armor and drew the fine blade to make sure my right arm was free to use it well. How light the armor, how light the blade, how light the shield! I was buoyed up with wings and would today deliver death to many heroes. Let the earth resound with marching feet and the din of battle. Let the skies be filled with the glory of armies anxious for encounter. I was unconquerable. I, Cornelius, like the mighty Achilles, was armed to do battle.

I took my place at the head of the Sixth Century with our battle standard to my left and marched to the battle line. I removed from my sword belt the glove Gaius gave me and slipped it on my right hand.

The Fifth Alaudae had deployed, its legionnaires shield to shield. Remus's Tenth Cohort was the Roman left, with my century the extreme left. Unit standards stood regularly along the battle line, and polished helmets and armor reflected the morning sun. Magnificent feathered crests made it a formidable array. I understood why Rome ruled the world. This was power and strength. Its beauty transfixed me. Being here was worth the hard going, the eternal fatigue, and the meager fare. This was the legion Simmias envisioned. This was my home. I could campaign forever. From the foundation of the world, I was to be here in this line as centurion of the Sixth Century.

Along the hillside facing the Roman line were Arminius's forces grouped by tribes, each with its own standards and distinct dress. Arminius and his staff, resplendent in colorful robes, were on a rise above the main force.

A century at the center of the Roman line moved aside. Pilate, followed by Germanicus and his vanguard, moved to the front of the line as if to lead an assault, then halted. Resplendent in his polished armor, flowing purple cloak, and feathered crest, he held his pilum in both hands and slowly raised it above his head in defiance of the overwhelming numbers. We began striking our shields in unison with the flat of our swords, the din filling the shallow valley. He then lowered his pilum. The din ceased, and in its place arose a raucous, angry, battle shout. The spirit of the Fifth Alaudae was at its zenith. It was unconquerable.

Pilate was Pontius, the *Pilum*.

Trumpets sounded from the hillside and one of Arminius's tribes, several thousand in number, moved down the slope. As they closed the distance, their front widened, and the pace increased. When his force came within arrow range, Roman archers and slingers positioned in front of our battle line began a rain of arrows and stones that took a toll and slowed their pace, withdrawing when the force was almost upon them. The legionnaires, each armed with two pila, then threw them. Many pierced shields, forcing the owners to discard them. When the first ranks of tribesmen reached the first ranks of legionnaires, many were without their shields, injured by the pila, the arrows, or the stones, and were carried forward by the momentum of the ranks behind them. The Roman line took the shock, wavered, and the enemy disappeared.

As the charging tribesmen spread out, a detachment several hundred in number moved in our direction. Our defense was for each legionnaire to take on his shield the shock of the opponent to his front, exposing the right side of that opponent to the sword of the legionnaire to his left.

The leader of the group, a young man wearing only a loin cloth, charged toward me, shouting and waving his sword. A glow like pale sunshine emanated from his face. I was entranced and delayed raising my shield. Titus, to my left, with his shield caught the blow and at the same time thrust the young man in his side. For a moment, Titus was defenseless against the opponent to his front who, with a full swing of his ax, struck Titus a glancing blow to the left side of his helmet and cut deep into the armor over his shoulder. Titus dropped his shield and fell to the ground. I was hard-pressed to hold my place in the line.

Germanicus's trumpets sounded, and the Roman line began to move forward. Groups of Arminius's tribesmen charged down the slope and were absorbed by the Roman line. The assaults increased, but each was singular and disappeared into the Roman line. The legion continued to advance.

Arminius ordered his remaining forces to charge. The Roman trumpets again sounded, and the center of the line stopped. The right and left wings began to turn, funneling the tribesmen into the center. Our wing closed on their right flank, restricting their use of weapons. My century pressed hard, exposing their right sides to our sword thrusts. As tribesmen fell, the legionnaires in the second line dispatched them. It was an efficient, bloody killing spree.

Seeing Roman cavalry approach, Arminius and his vanguard turned and rode away at full gallop. My century joined the flank of the Roman right wing encircling the tribesmen. A cry went up, and they dropped their weapons. It was not yet noon.

I walked along my century's line. A number of men were nursing cuts, but none serious enough to be cauterized. Two legionnaires removed Titus from under several tribesmen and laid him on his own shield. They removed his helmet and placed a cloak under his head. The wound was such it could not be cauterized. I knelt by his side and took his hand in mine. "Titus, my friend, my inaction cost you your life, and your action saved mine. My heart is broken."

Titus gripped my hand tightly. "Do not feel that way. I have no family. The legion was my family. I owe you the debt, for I died in battle. I will now enter Elysium. Remember me, Cornelius." He was silent for a moment. "For the Senate and the people of Rome."

I tightened my grip and, as my valediction, repeated, "For the Senate and the people of Rome." When he breathed his last, I crossed his hands on his chest. There was a smile on his face. Titus was already in Elysium.

Though we had become great friends, I knew nothing about his family or where he was from. If only I had thought to ask.

The injured who were able to walk and the seriously wounded on baggage carts crossed the Weser, returning to our permanent camp. The rest of us helped the wounded to the surgeon's tent and separated our fallen legionnaires from the tribesmen. We carried our dead to eight large funeral pyres built by engineers along the river. Six of the old ones lifted Titus's shield to their shoulders with him lying on it and walked parade-like to the nearest pyre, the rest of the century following in formation. Four of the younger ones climbed atop and set Titus to rest on his own shield. It was a fitting end for a soldier of the legion.

By late afternoon, the last fallen legionnaire had been placed and the pyres lighted. We watched as the fires increased in intensity. I would miss Titus's friendship, wisdom, and help. Without him, I could not see to all that needed my attention.

I turned to Otto, one of the old ones who shared my tent. He was reliable and had a following among the younger men. His time in the legion had expired, but he was waiting to return to Rome before being separated. "Otto," I said, "all of us will miss Titus, me most of all. You are as experienced as he was. Would you serve as acting centurion?"

"Nothing would please me more. However, may I place a condition on my service?"

"What is the condition?"

"That when we march with the standard, I carry it."

I took his hand. "Otto, you have earned it. For the Senate and the people of Rome."

By nightfall, the roar of the burning pyres was the only sound. The Sixth Cohort remained on the battlefield at the bridgehead to defend it from possible attack. In the light from the pyres, I could see the battlefield. Removing the dead legionnaires had been difficult, as the ground was soggy with blood. I calculated the number of men we lost. There were ten rows of twenty bodies on each of the eight pyres. Sixteen hundred lost, one death for every four legionnaires. It was a costly victory.

The price for Arminius, however, was far greater. We had taken six thousand prisoners. I estimated five thousand had escaped into the forest. From the thirty thousand on the hillside at the start, about twenty thousand of his men perished on the battlefield.

The greatest price, however, would be in the homes and communities throughout Germany and the republic. They would lament their dead for years to come.

Days later, the Tenth Cohort crossed back over the Weser River for the last time. Before leaving, I stood on the bridge and looked into the river. Small rivulets of bloody water drained from the bank into the clear water, staining it red. The reddened Weser carried the blood of our battle out to the sea. A thousand years from now, the water in the bay at Tarsus would be tinged with the blood of heroes. Someday all the seas would be red.

The Fifth Alaudae settled into base camp and prepared to depart for Rome. Baggage carts bearing the wounded and the injured who could walk had already started the march.

A few days after arriving at base camp, my century returned from an uneventful patrol along the west side of the Weser River. The camp follower for our tent prepared our evening meal, and after everyone had finished eating, I spoke. "Today, when we passed the battle site, the funeral pyres were still burning."

I thought of Titus's equipment still in my tent. I had not the will to return it. "Most of you know Titus gave his life to save mine. Today when I saw the smoke, I realized that among the sixteen hundred legionnaires placed on the pyres, there were many like him. I also saw blood from the battlefield, both Roman and German, seeping into the Weser. I am having difficulty justifying the price paid."

Otto sat across from me, his face illuminated by the light from the cooking fire. "Cornelius, many of us here are near the end of our service. Mine has already ended. Some of us have no family. For others, it has been years since we left them. If any of my family are yet alive, I do not know where they are. When we return to Rome and I must leave the Fifth, where will I go? What will I do? I have no skill but to be a legionnaire. All of us feel that way. What a joy it would be to die in battle on my last day in the legion." He raised his cup in salute, as did the others.

I raised my cup. "What of the younger ones, the men who had many years to serve? It is a waste to lose them in a battle just to punish an enemy who defeated three legions so long ago. Their families hope for their return."

One of the other old ones stood. "Everyone in the Fifth volunteered. At home, all of us faced a life of work on the farm or in a trade. That life had no meaning. Young legionnaires are as you, Cornelius. The legion gives meaning to their life. For those who gave their life at the Weser River, would they have exchanged places with any of their friends back home? I think not. The worst punishment a man can have is to believe his life has no meaning."

He paused. "Cornelius, it has given my life meaning to serve in the Sixth Century of the Tenth Cohort. When Germanicus points to a line on his map and says the Tenth Cohort is here, I am proud to be part of that. Each of us made it possible for him to draw that line at that place on that map. If you wish, say a requiem at the pyres, but do not disturb the ashes. All are in Elysium. I look forward to joining them." He then raised his cup in salute.

I stood, raised my cup, and said as a requiem for those at the Weser, those on other pyres, and the unmarked graves along the roads to Rome, "For the Senate and the people of Rome."

Training resumed with Otto as acting centurion directing the younger legionnaires. The Sixth resumed escort duty, but after two uneventful trips, Germanicus decided it was no longer necessary.

We began the journey to Rome. The discipline observed at the Weser River continued. We were Marius's mules, the real legion, marching twenty miles each morning, carrying forty pounds of personal baggage and forty pounds of camp equipment. Each afternoon, we constructed a new camp complete with rampart and palisade around it and prepared our own meal. The next day after breakfast, we dismantled the camp, loaded the baggage carts, picked up the camp equipment, and marched to the next site.

Simmias said discipline was the source of the legionnaire's pride. No one could do as much from dawn until nightfall, day after day. No other army could accomplish its purpose, regardless of enemy opposition, terrain, weather, or any other obstacle. I was part of the best in the world.

The evening meal was one of our pleasures. Each legionnaire was issued a quantity of wheat. A profile of eight men shared a tent and a cart on which to carry equipment, including a mill and a stove. After the day's effort, there was no greater contentment than sitting down to fare prepared from freshly ground wheat.

One evening some weeks later, Pilate rode into the Tenth Cohort's area dressed as an ordinary citizen. I welcomed him and offered him one of my wafers. He broke it in half and handed the rest to me.

"I am on my way to Rome," he said. "Sejanus is concerned about Palestine. He has offered me prefect for Judea and command of the Tenth Legion. I would like for you to join the Tenth with me. You've been under way a month and should be in Rome in two. After the parade, visit me at the praetorium. Meanwhile, consider joining me in Palestine."

We walked to his horse, and he said, "My appointment is an

opportunity for you. Continue your good work with Remus and the cohort. I will see you in Rome." He then mounted and rode toward the road.

I watched him disappear into the darkness. Titus was correct; Pilate was the one who should be in the legion's vanguard. I would join such a man for the pleasure of serving him.

Within two months, our legion was camped outside Rome. Everyone planned for a formal entry into the city. All armor was repaired or replaced, shields painted, and new feathered crests issued. I received a new red tunic.

In keeping with Germanicus's tradition of assigning unpleasant tasks to the Tenth Cohort, he ordered Remus to prepare and escort five thousand prisoners in the parade. Each of the cohort's six centuries would be responsible for more than eight hundred prisoners.

Remus called for a meeting of the centurions. On the way, Otto and I visited the prisoner enclosure. Their raiment hung in tatters on skeleton frames, and the stench was strong. How could such men have been part of the charge at the Weser River?

When we joined the others in Remus's tent, he said, "We are to put the prisoners through a public bath and into clean tunics, then escort them in the parade."

Since no one spoke, I said, "On our way here, we visited the enclosure. The prisoners are starving. If we offered them a meal, they would do what we asked."

"That's reasonable," Remus said. "Germanicus has agreed to supply the tunics. How can we feed so many?"

"Pilate helped when we needed equipment," I said. "With your approval, I will request he arrange for the feeding. To control the prisoners, we will need a few shortened hastae. The standard ones are too heavy and too long."

"That sounds reasonable," Remus said. "As everyone will be armed with his short sword, one hasta per profile should be adequate. I will prepare a request for food and shortened hastae. Germanicus will approve the order. Will you give it to Pilate?"

I agreed, and early the next morning, Remus handed me a requisition for meals for 5,200 prisoners, and one for fifty shortened hastae. I signed for a horse and went to the fortress. A guard directed me to Pilate.

He greeted me. "Well, Cornelius, this is a surprise. I did not expect to see you until after the parade. Can I be of assistance?"

"Yes, sir," I replied, saluting. "Germanicus has ordered the Tenth Cohort to prepare the prisoners for the parade and has issued these requisitions."

Pilate read the documents and leaned back in his chair. "I saw the state of the prisoners. I will obtain Sejanus's approval and have the cooks here at the barracks prepare the food. It will be ready two days hence. The quartermaster may have to prepare the hastae since they now are a ceremonial weapon."

I saluted. "Thank you, sir."

Back at camp, it occurred to me we had forgotten to requisition public bathhouses. I found Remus in his tent. "Good news, I hope," he said.

"The meals and the hastae will be ready the day after tomorrow morning, but we must also requisition bathhouses."

"By Jupiter, you are right! I'll take care of that."

That evening, Remus joined us as we ate. "I see you have dined well on wafers and wine. Tomorrow I'll send cheese and meat. Germanicus has gone to Sejanus for approval of the bathhouses."

Late the next evening, Remus joined us at the cooking fire. "Germanicus's aide gave me the requisition for the bathhouses. It is not approved. Pilate is our only hope to get the prisoners bathed."

The next morning, I was at Pilate's office well before he arrived. "It is good to see you so early in the day," he said. "What can I do for you?"

"We need six bathhouses to accommodate the prisoners," I said, handing Pilate the requisition. He reviewed the document.

"So, this is why Germanicus was here yesterday. The matter is easily handled." He reached for a stylus and prepared six requisitions, affixing to each Sejanus's seal. "Sometimes paperwork is a wonderful thing. The owners will recognize the signet."

"Yes, sir." I saluted and left his office. At the nearest bathhouse, I showed the proprietor the requisitions.

"Sejanus is paying," he said. "I will provide all six bathhouses. I can complete the arrangements by early afternoon."

I returned to Remus's tent. "With Pilate's help, everything is arranged. I am to get the locations of the bathhouses this afternoon."

Remus nodded and pointed to a stool in front of his desk. "It seemed Germanicus was going to spoil his own parade." He pointed to a large basket at the entrance to the tent. "There is a payment, enough for your century. Return the basket. They are expensive."

"Thank you, sir." I rode to my tent, left the basket with one of the older legionnaires, then returned to the bathhouse. The proprietor welcomed me and gave me the locations of the other houses. I signed each requisition.

I returned to my tent, placed the basket Remus gave me by the fire pit, and lifted the cloth. In it were six roasts of lamb, each wrapped loosely in its own cloth, neatly sliced, and six small cheese rounds, also sliced. It was a meal fit for Germanicus's table. I sent the evening's fare to each tent.

Early the next morning, Remus signed for six baggage carts. Otto and I rode in the lead cart to the praetorium. In the kitchen, we asked a young centurion about food for the prisoners.

"You are from the Fifth Alaudae," he said. "Welcome to Rome. We were pleased to prepare the food. Several of us worked all night to have everything ready. Pull to the back entrance, and we will assist in loading."

Our drivers maneuvered the carts to the platform for loading. The young centurion instructed his laborers to load three crates on each one.

"We prepared twenty-six hundred round pita loaves, thicker than normal," he said. "We cut them in half, opened each one, and filled the center with a hash of beef cubes and vegetables. I understand the prisoners are half-starved. This should get them ready for the parade."

"Thank you, Centurion," I said. "Judging by the size, it will take all afternoon to eat. Where is the weapons depot?"

"It is at the next loading platform," he said. "My respect to you for your service at the Weser River. I wish I could have been there. It has been my pleasure to help you."

I replied with a salute, which he returned.

The carts stopped alongside the next loading platform. I dismounted and opened the heavy door. An older legionnaire challenged my entry, blocking my way and demanding to know my purpose.

"I am from the Fifth Alaudae. We are here for the fifty hastae."

He stepped aside. "It is a pleasure to meet someone from the Fifth. Welcome to Rome. I was with the Nineteenth in the Teutoburg Forest."

"I never met anyone who survived that battle. How came you here?"

"It is the first thing and the last thing I think of each day. My cohort was fighting its way out of the main battle when we mired in a bog. I was waist deep when a cavalryman slashed my right shoulder. I sank in the mire and thought I was dying. I awoke freezing, but the battle was over. I worked my way out, salvaged some clothing, and managed my way to our camp. I could no longer use a sword effectively and was assigned to the Guard. It is an easy post, but I miss the hard going. My apology for burdening you with my woe. No one here knows."

"It is good to know details." I said. "No one talks about what happened there. It may have changed the history of the world."

"Your hastae are ready. It broke my heart to shorten the shaft of such a fine weapon, but I understand your purpose. I can help you load."

"Count out eight to a lot, and I will have the drivers load them. I am centurion of the Sixth Century of the Tenth Cohort. The Tenth Cohort held the left flank at the Weser; the Ninth guarded the baggage train. You understand why I make this clarification."

The legionnaire and I walked to the loading platform. "This is my acting centurion, Otto. He helped us hold the left flank." I said to Otto, "My friend here was with the Nineteenth. Compare experiences while I see to the loading."

When I returned, the two old ones were deep in conversation. As I approached, they turned to me. "Thank you for preparing the hastae," I said, "and for telling me of the Nineteenth."

"It has been a pleasure to be of service," he said.

As Otto and I started to mount our carts, I turned and then said in my best Latin, "For the Senate and the people of Rome."

His look of surprise told me he understood.

On returning to the campsite, I learned Remus needed an order to release the prisoners to escort them to the bathhouses. Given the lack of time, Remus suggested I accompany him to Germanicus's tent. It was late in the morning when we arrived, and Remus entered only to emerge a moment later. "Germanicus is strutting in his new armor," he said. "He is not pleased. He told me in no uncertain terms to take care of the task myself, no instruction, no order."

I remembered Pilate's observation concerning the advantages of paperwork. "Amid all the confusion getting ready for the parade," I said, "let me go back and request one of the aides issue the order. Wait here."

I walked to the back of a tent where legionnaires were coming and going, entered, and requested of an aide to see the first centurion. He pointed to an older man sitting at a desk. I approached him. After affixing a seal to an order, he looked up. "What can I do for you, Centurion?"

"I am with the Tenth Cohort. We are to take the prisoners to public baths, give them clean tunics, and escort them during the parade. We need an order to release the prisoners to us for the trip through the bath and one for the parade."

"Yes, I know. Tell Remus that for completing without complaint the unpleasant assignments and for improving the Tenth, I encouraged Germanicus to assign the left flank to the Tenth."

Reaching for some paper, he said, "Stand easy, Centurion. I'll

prepare the orders." He prepared the two orders and with little ceremony affixed Germanicus's seal. "The tunics are in the supply tent. I
was concerned we might not get them to the prisoners."

As Remus and I loaded the tunics, I said, "You know more
German phrases than I do. At the prisoner enclosure, you can explain what they need to do and that we have a meal for them when
they return."

It was noon when we arrived at the enclosure. After distributing
the hastae to his centurions, Remus walked to the guard in charge
of the prisoners and handed him the order. He led us to the entrance
where a large number of prisoners congregated.

In legionnaire Greek mixed with German phrases, Remus announced our plan and asked for volunteers to help in explaining it to
the others. Several prisoners stepped forward, and Remus chose eight
to assist us. He held up a pita from the nearest cart and explained this
was their meal when they returned.

When the prisoners arrived from the bathhouses in clean tunics,
they were given food. It was late in the afternoon when the last prisoner entered the enclosure with his pita. Remus gave the remaining
meals and tunics to centurions guarding the prisoners. He ordered the
drivers to return to the livery and marched the cohort to the camp
area. After Remus broke the array, I told him the first centurion had
suggested Germanicus assign the Tenth to hold the left flank.

That evening, one of the old ones said that Remus might promise
the prisoners another meal if the parade was well done. Early the next
morning, I visited Remus's tent and made this suggestion to him. He
inquired how it was to be arranged.

"I will ask Pilate to requisition the meals."

"Cornelius, I am reluctant to make such a promise."

"We must get the prisoners through the parade," I said. "We will
worry about the meals later." I returned to my tent and prepared for
the parade.

In full armor, I took my place in front of my century with Otto
to my left, proudly holding our battle standard. The century was in

perfect array with freshly painted shields, armor bright in the morning sun, and new feathered crests. Remus, magnificent in his centurion's raiment, took his place at the front. With the cohort's battle standard displayed proudly to his left, Remus marched us to the prisoner enclosure.

Remus handed the centurion the order to release the prisoners and called for the leaders he had selected to come to the gate. He instructed them how to organize for the parade and promised a meal if they conducted themselves as soldiers. They formed for the parade as eagerly as they had for their baths. Remus marched the cohort escorting five thousand prisoners to our place in the parade.

Germanicus, in bronze armor and helmet with a magnificently feathered crest, rode in a new chariot at the head of the legion. Trumpeters and drummers added to the spectacle. The route was lined with onlookers. Everyone in the city must have been present.

The Tenth Cohort was the last unit in the parade. In keeping with Remus's plan, there were six distinct groups of prisoners bracketed by a column of legionnaires on each side, with hastae pointing to the front. The men were instructed to deal as harshly with any citizen who might try to reach a prisoner as with any prisoner who attempted to flee.

My century was the last unit in the parade. I marched in the front center of the last group of prisoners, with Otto to my left carrying our standard. In the bright sunshine, the prisoners in their white tunics added to the spectacle. My pride that day was almost as great as that I felt at the Weser River. If the Fifth paraded daily or weekly, I would remain in it forever.

It was late afternoon when we returned the prisoners to their enclosure and Remus marched us to our campsite. That evening, everyone was in festive spirits.

The next morning, I signed for a horse and cart and drove to the fortress. I asked to see Pontius Pilate and was conducted to his office.

"Cornelius, how good to see you. Please come in," he said. "That was a great reception for Germanicus. He has a great following in the

Senate and in Rome. From where I watched, the prisoners appeared to be a fine lot. If I were Sejanus, I would try to enlist them as mercenaries. What brings you here so early?"

"The promise of a meal gave the prisoners incentive to cooperate in bathing and donning fresh tunics. On Sejanus's behalf, please request a meal for each prisoner to reward him for his performance in the parade."

Pilate pulled his chair closer to the desk and shut his eyes. I thought he would turn down my request, but then he looked at me and laughed. "I am pleased to do it," Pilate said. "Your audacity took me by surprise. That is a desirable but dangerous trait. You have used it well. Unfortunately, it is too scarce among our leaders."

"Thank you, sir."

He reached for a sheet of vellum and wrote the order, complete with Sejanus's signet. "I requested the delivery in two days."

I stood and saluted. "Thank you, sir."

"In the parade, you were impressive in your red tunic and the crest of a centurion," he said. "I saw Gaius the other day. He asked that I give you this greeting: For the Senate and the people of Rome. He said you would understand."

"Yes, sir. I do."

"Have you considered the post to Palestine? It is different than Germany but offers great opportunity."

"I am pleased to accept the posting. I trust your judgment in such matters."

"Good, good! I will arrange for you to be assigned to the barracks here. The paperwork may take a few days, but consider it done."

Pilate turned to papers on his desk. "There is much to do. I expect you to join me and my family for an evening meal in day or so. We will talk at that time. I look forward to our serving together when I am prefect of Judea."

After leaving Pilate's office, I gave the order to the centurion in charge of the kitchen. "Sir, I must have gained five thousand friends in the prison compound," he said. "I was fearful I had exceeded my authority when I prepared such fine meals, delivered in such a practical manner. For Pilate, I am pleased to execute the order."

"I am to join the Guard temporarily. I look forward to having a friend in the dining hall. Pilate is pleased with your work. He is a good friend to have."

My heart sang as I returned to the camp.

The next day, I followed the camp routine, but during the day, I went to my tent and carefully packed all my personal items.

The following morning, I signed for six carts and stopped by my tent to pick up my pouch. Otto joined me, and we went to the fortress. The centurion had again prepared a pita stuffed with a hash of meat and vegetables. I was not sure about the meat, but it was far better fare than we had at the campsite. While they were loading the carts, I went to the guard station and reported I had been assigned to the barracks and would check in tomorrow. I also requested permission to leave my pouch with them.

I returned to the kitchen and thanked the centurion. After loading the crates, we drove by a marketplace near the fortress, and I purchased a round of cheese, some pita loaves, and two wineskins of the best sour wine. We delivered the meals to the prison enclosure and assisted in distributing them. I wondered what would finally happen to the prisoners.

I reported to Remus that Otto and I had delivered the meals and assisted in distributing them, making sure all was in order. "After Pilate prepared the order for the meals, he offered me a posting to Palestine. I have decided to accept the assignment."

"Congratulations, Cornelius. I am pleased."

"My good friend," I said, "when I shared a tent with Titus, he taught me to be a legionnaire and a centurion. The years in Germany are the happiest I ever experienced. With your help, I have found my home. I shall never forget you or the Tenth Cohort, Fifth Alaudae. May the gods who look after legionnaires look after you."

"You earned your red tunic and will one day be first centurion of the First Cohort. I could see that from the first day," Remus said. "I had grown weary of bad assignments, but you made them an opportunity. The Tenth held the left flank. You can never know how much it means to me to say, 'At the Weser River, my cohort held the left flank.' That day is the high point of my life. I am not sure there is an Elysium, but if there is, I look forward to seeing you there."

I saluted him. "For the Senate and the people of Rome."

He returned the salute. "For the Senate and the people of Rome."

I then visited each cooking fire in my century, distributed the cheese and bread, and filled each cup. I returned to the cooking fire of my own profile and raised my cup. "Legionnaires, I salute you. With your assistance and that of Titus, I am a Marius mule and a centurion. I will someday be first centurion of the First Cohort of a legion, but I will never forget the debt I owe you. May the god of all legionnaires look after you and make for you a place in Elysium where we shall meet again."

Otto stood and raised his cup. "Cornelius, centurion, Sixth Century, we thank you for making ours the best in the Tenth Cohort, perhaps the best in the whole Fifth. I no longer plan to leave the legion. Someone with authority must order me out. Being standard bearer for the Sixth has been the high point of my life. I shall miss you at my right side."

"With Remus's permission, I am naming you acting centurion of the Sixth, Otto. You may select your standard bearer. I will rest well knowing the Sixth is in good hands." I raised my cup amid the shouts of approval. Remus then stepped into the firelight and appointed Otto acting centurion. I shared with him a portion of my cheese and pita, and we enjoyed the benediction of a farewell meal.

We talked long into the night. I felt contentment to be in Rome among such friends. Raising my cup one last time, I stood. "For the Senate and the people of Rome."

In turn, the group rose and lifted their cups. "For the Senate and the people of Rome." I turned and walked toward the fortress. In the east was the first hint of dawn.

✝

"Welcome to the praetorium," said the guard at the fortress. "The centurion told us you were to join us. We look forward to having someone from the Fifth Alaudae with us."

He pointed to my pouch and indicated I should follow him. "You were at the Weser River. That was indeed a great victory. The parade was proper recognition for Germanicus. It was my good fortune to be assigned to control the crowd at the Senate steps. I saw Germanicus receive the laurel wreath from Sejanus. I'll never forget it." He stopped before a small room and pointed to a wooden bunk. "This should be better than a bed roll."

By the time I stretched out on the pallet, I was asleep.

I awoke late in the morning and sat on the edge of the bunk, looking at a table, chair, and storage box. I set about transferring the contents of my pouch into the box. I selected a plain tunic and entered the bath, spending more than an hour in the warm waters. I donned the plain tunic, ventured into the city, and found a barber for a haircut and shave. After enjoying a fine meal, I looked unsuccessfully for a cobbler shop. I had hoped to purchase plain sandals, as my heavy ones readily disclosed my profession. I returned to the barracks clean-shaven and well fed.

As it was not yet dark, I climbed the stairs to the roof and walked to a parapet at its edge. The city was beautiful in the soft light. Suddenly I sensed the presence of someone and turned to see an attractive young woman dressed in a plain, sleeveless stola reaching to the floor. I smiled at her. "My apology. I hope I am not intruding. I was assigned to the barracks today and came up to look at the city."

"Oh, no, you are not intruding. You wear a plain tunic but a legionnaire's sandals," she said, stepping to the next parapet.

"I returned to Rome after serving with the Fifth Alaudae. I hope I did not frighten you."

"You were in the parade! What a magnificent spectacle."

"Yes, I was with the Tenth Cohort," I said, hoping she did not know the significance of the designation.

"That explains the heavy sandals. How did you gain entrance? Guardsmen do not wear the heavy marching sandals."

"I was a centurion with the Fifth Alaudae and have been assigned to the barracks until I am transferred."

"What is your name?"

"Cornelius."

"I've heard my father, Pontius Pilate, speak of you. He arrived in Rome several weeks ago, after service with the Fifth Alaudae. You were in the Battle at the Weser River."

"I know your father very well," I said. "He has helped me a number of times. Do you live nearby? It is getting late."

"We have living quarters on the floor below. The steps there lead to our place. I must be going, or Father will come looking for me."

"It was my pleasure to meet you."

"We shall meet again I am sure," she said, then turned and walked toward the steps.

I looked again at the dusky outline of the city, then turned to the parapet where the young woman stood, hoping she might be there.

The next morning, I had breakfast in the guards' dining hall. It was strange to have no duties to perform. When I returned to my room, there was an invitation to dine with Pontius Pilate that evening.

To pass time, I walked in the city, marveling at the buildings. I stopped in a cobbler shop, negotiated for a pair of worn sandals, and asked that they be cleaned and oiled. Late in the afternoon, I returned to the barber for a shave, then enjoyed a bath. When I returned to my quarters, it was time to dress for the evening meal. I donned my new red tunic and walked to Pilate's living quarters. Before entering, I straightened my tunic and made sure my new sandals were free of dust, should Pilate's daughter be present.

A well-dressed slave met me at the entrance and led me to a large room where the family was gathered. Pilate welcomed me. "Cornelius, this is my wife. Claudia, this is Cornelius of whom I have spoken many times. He served with the Fifth Alaudae."

Claudia bowed slightly. "Welcome to our home. You grace us with your presence."

Pilate then introduced me to his son, a fine-looking young man. I noticed he favored his right foot. "Avitus, this is Cornelius."

Avitus smiled. "Welcome to our home. My compliments on your red tunic. My father speaks highly of you."

Next, he introduced me to his daughter. "Portia, this is Cornelius, centurion with the Fifth Alaudae. He entered Rome with Germanicus."

Portia bowed slightly, then looked into my eyes. "Welcome to our home. I have looked forward to our meeting."

Claudia and the children withdrew to an adjoining room, and Pilate led me to a bench. "Things are developing more rapidly than I expected. Tiberius has consolidated his power, and Sejanus is to remain commander of the Praetorian Guard. He is second in power to Tiberius and anxious concerning the unrest in Palestine. He wants me to take command of the Tenth Legion Fretensis. He believes Quirinius, the legate in Syria, is too lenient with the Jews when there are three legions at his disposal," he said. "Do you see the opportunity? I have been schooled in Roman law and politics and served as prefect of the Fifth Alaudae. Your background is Greek. Palestine is more Greek than Roman."

Pilate paused. "I have assigned you to the Tenth Legion, which I am relocating to Caesarea Maritima. Depart as soon as possible. Go by way of Tarsus and visit your family and friends, then on to Caesarea. My family and I will follow."

He explained the administration of Judea had always been a problem. Rome's policy, and that of Tiberius, was to allow local administrators to govern so long as they were able to do so. In Palestine, however, the policy was complicated by local conflicts between Jewish rulers and the political administrators responsible to Rome. Sejanus wanted assurance unrest did not become a problem.

Finally, he stood. "The meal is ready."

It was an elegant, cordial affair. We were seated around a table, much to my pleasure, for I was fearful of falling asleep if we reclined on traditional cushions. We dined on foods I had never eaten, but they were very pleasant to the taste and easy to access.

Pilate, Avitus, and I returned to the large room and seated ourselves on cushions facing each other. They carried the conversation, discussing developments in the Senate and in the Guard, occasionally discussing development of Roman law. Pilate considered it the law of nations, man's first attempt to govern himself, and believed its proper administration assured justice for all.

At the appropriate time, I excused myself, expressing my enjoyment of the new experience. I was disappointed, however, that Portia had not returned. The hour was late when I entered the barracks.

I recalled when Titus had predicted Sejanus would appoint Pilate to assist Germanicus in defeating Arminius. Gossip around the barracks indicated that Germanicus was a member of the family of Augustus Caesar and of Tiberius. Sejanus, as commander of the Praetorian Guard, was considered a member of Rome's ruling family. There was more to Pilate's appointment to Palestine than merely an assignment to quell unrest.

I had nothing to lose casting my lot with Pilate. Having served my time as a Marius mule, I had become a centurion and enjoyed enough winters in Germany. I would commit to Pilate and prepare for the trip home.

The next morning, I inquired as to the status of my papers at Sejanus's office. My orders would be ready the next day.

After the noon meal and an afternoon nap, I ventured again to the rooftop to view the city. Portia stood by the parapet where I had first seen her. She wore a fine stola, and the breeze ruffled the edges of her head scarf. I walked to her and called her name.

"Oh, Cornelius, I hoped you would be here. I did not have the opportunity to talk to you last evening."

"I am pleased to see you again," I said.

"I wanted to caution you about the difference in your concepts and those of my father. My father and Avitus were taught by slaves familiar with Roman law and politics, and my father attended the best law academies in Rome. Father is not interested in Greek matters."

"I am aware of our differences," I said. "We had many discussions while he was in Germany."

"Among my father's slaves was a Greek he acquired as a gift. As my father and Avitus were not interested in such matters, my mother and I persuaded Father to let him become our teacher. He was a gentle old man who had studied and taught in Alexandria. Not only did we learn to read and write Greek and Latin, we also studied Greek philosophy and culture. My mother and I are aware of differences between Roman and Greek concepts."

"I understand."

Portia continued. "Mother's friends include wives and consorts to politicians and a few senators. There are rumors Sejanus will attempt to overthrow Tiberius, who has tired of the bickering between the Senate and his office. He wants to retire to Capri and enjoy the rest of his life on the island. He trusts Sejanus, but we are fearful he will discover the conspiracy. Although we believe Father is in no danger, we did not want you to go to Palestine without being aware of the rumors."

"Thank you for your concern," I said. "We are addressing Roman politics, but I am more interested in knowing about your Greek teacher. I would like to hear your experience."

Wisps of her dark hair escaped her scarf and reflected the evening sunlight. Her pale stola enhanced her olive skin, and her features were like images in a dream. She was beautiful.

"Mother is more interested in Greek philosophy than I. She says it gives meaning to her life, that Roman philosophy offers a life dedicated to Rome and the emperor. She is quite serious about it, but Father dismisses it as a woman's fantasy."

"I found Greek philosophy interesting," I said. "It prepared me for the legion, and I am content with the life."

Portia glanced my way and then looked again toward the city. "You are fortunate to find contentment in what you do. Mother is becoming that way. The Pontii family owns thousands of acres in southern Italy and thousands of slaves. Most of her family live an indolent life. Mother was among them until she studied the Greek manuscripts. She has become more tolerant of the failings of others and is sympathetic to the circumstances of house slaves. She enjoys discussions with her friends who also read the manuscripts. She believes she was born to be Father's wife. I wish I were more like her."

"Will you accompany your father to Palestine?"

"Yes, as will my mother," she said. "Avitus is to attend one of the academies here. I do not look forward to Palestine. I hear it is a harsh land."

"You will reside in the fortress at Caesarea on the coast. It may not be so harsh."

"I must go," Portia said. "I look forward to our meeting in Palestine to discuss more pleasing matters. May you have a safe trip and a pleasant time visiting your family. I have enjoyed this visit. I talked more than I planned to. You were kind to listen." She looked into my eyes. "Last evening, you were impressive in your red tunic. It is my pleasure to know a centurion."

When she left, a strange sadness engulfed me.

On my return to the barracks, the guardsmen were preparing to attend one of the many feasts and celebrations commemorating Germanicus's victory. They encouraged me to go, especially as I had been present at the battle. The hour was late, but I was already dressed for such an occasion and had no duties to perform. I consented and followed the group into a large, enclosed courtyard lit by torches and arrayed with palm trees, statuary, and walkways. In the open center was a large table filled with platters of food beautifully displayed. At one end of the table were rows of goblets filled with dark red wine. I was amazed at the number of people in large and small gatherings, talking and laughing.

At the table, each of us took a goblet. I had not tasted such rich wine since that served by Moshe the Merchant. The others drained a second goblet, but I drank mine in sips, listening to a spirited, good-natured argument regarding an issue before the Senate. I moved to a different group of young men who were ranking drivers in the upcoming chariot race, each adamant about the qualification of his favorite.

After finishing my second goblet, I became lightheaded and found a place to sit in the garden portion of the courtyard. More than once, I steadied myself by grasping the rim of a pot or the base of a statue. Overlooking my bench was the sculpture of a muscular Roman god with an angry countenance. Under the gaze of the alabaster god, I extended both hands to my sides to steady myself. I could not believe two goblets of wine resulted in my becoming so dizzy. There was a difference between the flat, sour wine of the legion and the fine, rich wine of Rome.

On nearby benches, in the flickering light, couples engaged in lovemaking. I looked away lest they see me staring. I closed my eyes tightly to clear my vision. When I opened them again, I could see other couples engaged in lovemaking. I looked to the ground at my feet.

A young woman dressed in a lightly woven man's tunic, open in the front, approached me. Her hair was honey colored, and her skin fair like the women of Germany. She appeared to be an apparition, but as she drew closer, her open tunic revealed most of her well-formed breasts. She bent over in front of me and allowed her breasts to brush along my right arm. The sensation of falling vanished, and my blood began to race.

I raised myself enough to lift my tunic to my waist and loosened my loin cloth. I returned to my sitting position and assisted her in straddling my legs. I embraced her around her waist and held her tightly against me.

It was over as quickly as it began. Breathing heavily, I again placed my hands to my side to steady myself. The young woman laughed softly as she lifted herself to a standing position and walked away.

I sat there some time, tightening my loin cloth and straightening my tunic. When I finally stood, a wave of nausea dropped me to my knees. I crawled behind the bench and retched. The sensation of falling overwhelmed me, and I lay down, avoiding the mass of vomit. I looked up only to see the angry countenance of the alabaster god, ghostlike in the uneven light, gazing down at my prostrate position. Under his watchful eye, I fell asleep.

It was yet dark when I woke. Most of the torches had burned out. The sour savor of my vomit reminded me of my great effort to crawl behind the bench. I tried to sit up, but my head ached as from hammer blows, and I felt another wave of nausea. I lay back down.

Jaws clenched, I rose to a sitting position. I held onto the stone god who had watched over me during the night, avoiding his scornful gaze. With slow steps, I made my way to the courtyard gate. The eastern sky was beginning to lighten, and I could see the street.

When I entered the barracks, the guard said, "I see you made it back. We wondered where you were. Can I assist you?"

I gave him a weak smile. "No, I can make it from here."

I walked to my bunk and sat down, propping my head with my hands. I had betrayed myself. What I had witnessed in the garden, including my own actions, reminded me of a pack of dogs with a bitch among them in heat. What if I became the butt of gossip around the barracks and the tale reached Pilate? And if Portia should hear, how would she react? I resolved to leave for Corinth without delay to reduce the chance anyone might recognize me and make the association.

The next morning, I awoke well past noon, changed to a clean tunic, rolled my soiled one, and dropped it into a half-filled bucket by an outside drain spout. I encountered only a few guards in the kitchen. The smell of hot grease caused the nausea to return. I poured a little sour wine, picked up a wheat wafer, and ate alone.

My head still ached, and the wafer and wine sat heavily in my stomach. I returned to my bunk and again fell asleep, only to be startled awake many times by an apparition of the young woman or the countenance of the angry god.

After breakfast the next morning, I bathed and then laundered my tunic. By the time I hung the tunic to dry, I felt better. It was early afternoon when I walked to the commander's office to learn the status of my documents. To my great pleasure, they were ready, and I sat a while in the office reviewing them.

When I returned to the barracks, the guard handed me a sealed message from Pilate requesting I join him for the evening meal. I hoped Pilate and Portia had not learned of the incident in the garden. Since that night, I had felt a sense of colossal failure. I recalled the death of Titus and the smile on his face as he thanked me for his plight. Was my failure to respond as I should the answer to his prayer to die in battle? Was failure to conduct myself with honor somehow a flaw not of my own making? Are we to weave into an acceptable design flaws in the pattern of our lives?

I envisioned one of Saul's weavers who, despite a flaw in the yarn, created an intricate pattern, adding to the beautiful design as the fabric moved toward the completed roll, the flaw known only to the weaver. The days of my life were as the weaver's shuttle passing so rapidly back and forth through the warp of time. If I remained true to that for which I had been born and which I had been taught, the flaws, whether in the yarn of my days or of my own making, would be lost in the intricacy. No failure on my part must break either the delicate warp yarns or the yarn in the shuttle.

I walked slowly up the stairs to Pilate's quarters. The guard spoke cordially as he let me pass to the large room where Pilate and his family waited.

"Welcome, Cornelius," said Pilate. "The invitation came on short notice. Sejanus mentioned you had picked up your papers. I was anxious you might get away before we had a chance to wish you well. Thank you for coming."

"I am pleased to be here. The best time for sailing is drawing to a close, and I would like to be home before bad weather comes."

Portia smiled and nodded in my direction. She and Claudia

excused themselves and withdrew. Pilate and I reclined on a series of cushions.

"I am pleased you accepted the assignment. Tiberius remains on Capri with most of his household. Sejanus assumes more of his functions. I grow weary of keeping him in good stead with Tiberius," he said. "We have discussed my purpose in going to Judea. It is a great opportunity. My days as an aide to Sejanus may be over."

"I pledge my support," I said, "but I will need your counsel."

"I hoped you would feel that way."

I recalled the concerns of Claudia and Portia regarding Sejanus and said, "Judea is far from Rome. You will have the freedom to administer the province. If the fortunes of Sejanus change, your reputation assures you of Tiberius's support."

"I would like to continue the discussion, but the meal is ready."

We joined Claudia and Portia, all of us reclining at the table, and enjoyed a fine Roman meal. Claudia suggested that Portia take me to the rooftop before sunset to see the city, and we excused ourselves.

Portia leaned on the parapet, looking eastward. She and the city were resplendent in the dying light. "Your departure arrived quicker than I expected. You are different from Father's other guests. They are officials with important posts in government or in the Guard and are awed by their own importance. Father is within Sejanus's circle, and they try to ingratiate themselves. They are hypocrites, and Rome is a sham. Greed and corruption are the order of the day. Yet you are genuine. I hope you never change."

"How good of you to say that. Having earned my tunic during a campaign, I am never sure how I am received," I said. "Your comments are reassuring."

"Sejanus has dined with us a number of times. Mother and I do not trust him. He dislikes the Jews because they have never acknowledged their defeat by Rome. Father does not see that in him. His confidence in Father grew when Father helped Germanicus defeat Arminius. We believe Sejanus is sending him to Palestine to punish the Jews, in spite of Tiberius's liberal policies."

I was hesitant to reply, as I knew Pilate was pleased with the assignment. "I understand why you and your mother are concerned. But being prefect with a province to govern will allow your father to enhance his own reputation. There will be portents to warn him should things change."

We stood in silence, watching shadows fill the streets below. Twilight wrapped Portia in a soft glow, making her presence ephemeral and spirit-like. I longed to take her in my arms and reassure her everything would work for her good.

"Bring some of the Greek manuscripts to Caesarea," I said. "Together we will read them. I never had anyone with whom I could discuss such matters."

"I will," she said, "but it is far off." She looked into my eyes. "I shall miss you more than you know. Have a safe journey. We had best return to the house."

As we walked toward the stairs, I marveled at her beauty. I felt somehow in my misconduct I had betrayed her.

PALESTINE AND GALILEE

Early the next morning, I ate my last meal at the barracks, returned to my quarters, donned my plain tunic and new sandals, and packed all my gear. I had only the glove Gaius gave me to remind me of the Fifth Legion, but my time with the Sixth Century, with Titus, and engaging in the battle at the Weser River were part of me. I lifted the strap of the pouch over my head and set out for the harbor, two days distant.

I set a good pace and arrived by late afternoon of the second day. I asked the harbor master about ships destined for Corinth. He pointed out two. I inquired as to when the larger would depart.

"It is to sail with the morning tide. That good ship has made the voyage many times. Neptune seems to favor her."

At the pier, I found the captain and arranged passage. He led me to a hold already loaded and covered, except for an entrance. "You can sleep here. Find yourself a place on the cargo. Beginning in the morning, assist the crew in controlling the sail. You can eat with the crew."

In the hold, I found a crate that afforded sleeping space, placed my pouch on it, and returned topside.

"I can help with the loading," I said to the captain.

He sent me to the steward who set me to work, and we finished loading by dark. Dock laborers returned to their warehouse, and the crew boarded the ship. The captain inspected the ship, preparing to sail before dawn. One of the crew gave each of us a portion of bread and cheese and a cup of wine. Afterward, I stretched out on the crate and welcomed sleep.

The weather was good, the wind steady, and in less than two weeks, we were in the long, enclosed bay leading to Corinth. The ship was too large to transport across the isthmus, so I joined the unloading.

After receiving my wages, I walked across the isthmus along the portage route. At the port, I inquired about Moshe's ships. There were two, one that had just arrived from Tarsus and another that was loading. I boarded that one and found the captain. "I request passage to Tarsus. I can assist in loading."

"Cornelius, what a surprise. You've grown up. I am short crew, so it is my pleasure to have you on board. Join the rest of the crew on the pier. You know what to do."

We worked until dark, and I bunked with the crew. We finished loading late the next day and prepared to sail the following morning. Once the ship was on its course, I asked the captain about Moshe.

"Better than ever. He has added several ships since you left. Your father and mother are doing well. I see them after each trip. I miss you and Saul when we are loading and unloading. I understand you joined the legion. Are you coming home?"

"No, sir. I am on my way to Palestine but plan to spend a few days at home," I said.

"Everyone will be pleased to see you."

We arrived in Tarsus without event. I prepared to assist unloading, but the captain said, "Cornelius, do not waste time. You can pick up your wages tomorrow. It was a pleasure to have you with us. May the gods continue to favor you."

I took the first long boat, disembarked at the pier, and walked to the warehouse. Moshe was in his office, and after a cordial exchange, I inquired about my father. He said Father's office was now at the villa and he was probably there, although it was late in the day.

Father was in his office, and both of us went to find Mother. We talked until Mother excused herself to prepare the evening meal.

After we had eaten, Moshe and Simmias joined us, and, sitting in a secluded part of the courtyard, we talked well into the night.

Early the next day, after receiving my wages, I selected a horse and, keeping a good pace, rode to the farm, arriving well past dusk. By the time I had dismounted and stretched my legs, an older woman stood in the doorway. Although she had aged, I recognized Aunt Julia.

"I'm Cornelius, Cyrus's youngest," I said to her. "May I come in?"

"Cornelius!" she said, laughing. "Of course, you may come in. What a surprise. Come in, come in. There is porridge left from supper and plenty of bread. It is still warm."

"If you made the porridge, it was worth coming all this way to enjoy it."

"Yes, I made it. It goes well with the cooler fall weather. The other day, I was preparing a chicken whose heart was upside down. I shouted when I saw it, for I knew something good was about to happen. And here you are. I even made extra for supper tonight." She filled a large bowl and handed it to me.

I pulled a stool to the table. "I spent too many winters in Germany. The winters there are so cold I am not yet warm. This porridge will finally take away the chill. On those long, cold nights, I remembered your porridge, and that memory kept me warm."

"You have not changed," she said. "I missed you. I did not realize how much until you were gone. While you finish the porridge, I'll find someone to put up the horse and then fix your bed in Myrrine's old room."

"Do not wake anyone. I'll put the horse in the shed and feed him. The porridge will keep," I said. When I returned to the kitchen to finish eating, I enjoyed each spoonful.

Aunt Julia removed a lamp from the shelf and lit it from the one on the table. "Everything is ready. You know where the room is. Is there anything else I can do for you?"

"In the morning, I will eat with the laborers. After breakfast, I will climb the highest outcropping on the back ridge, sit on its edge, and enjoy a meal you have prepared, if you would do so."

"That would please me," she said. "I have loved you as one of my own."

I picked up the lamp and gently kissed her on the forehead. "Goodnight. It is good to be home again."

The next morning, I laced my sandals, straightened my tunic, and walked to the kitchen. Julia and Uncle Lucius were carrying platters of food to the table.

"Come in," he said. "Julia said you would eat with us. It's good to have you here, like old times."

Three young children sat at a small table in the corner. Julia waved for six laborers to enter. Each introduced himself and gave his relationship to Cyrus. They had been children when I last saw them. We ate heartily, scooping up meat stew with pieces of bread or enjoying a large bowl of porridge. I had forgotten the camaraderie enjoyed around the table. After everyone had eaten, Lucius bade me good day, the laborers thanked Julia for their breakfast, and all filed out, including the children.

After they left, Julia sat across from me. I was amazed at the quantity of food she had prepared and its quality. She wiped her hands on her large apron and sighed. "That is done and done well. I must start the noon meal," she said. "But there is time to visit. It is good to have you here."

Years of hard work showed in her features, and I saw in her eyes a look of resigned hopelessness. A wave of sympathy engulfed me, for Julia represented all women who spend their daily lives in the drudgery of laboring without complaint. I reached across the table and placed my hand on hers. She had been a cook in this house for more years than I had been alive. I felt a great love for her. I could not bring myself to speak.

Julia smiled. "Thank you for coming. I catch myself thinking about times past. Those were good days. I am happy here helping Lucius, but those days have a special meaning. Your mother misses you more than I do. When she sees a traveler on the road to Tarsus, she will walk to the gate and watch until he passes."

She stood. "It is time to prepare for your trip. I'll get a seed pouch for your food. You may want to take a cloak. There is one by the door."

I went to my room, tightened the laces in my sandals, and slipped the knife onto my belt. When I returned to the kitchen, Julia had placed a seed pouch on the table along with a cloak. I passed its strap over my head and draped the cloak over my shoulders. "I'll be back for the evening meal."

I went into the courtyard, passed through the gate, and turned toward the high ridge. It was a fine fall day. I took a deep breath and smelled decaying leaves and wood smoke. I walked toward the ridge with the highest outcropping and began the climb.

I kept to the crest as there were fewer leaves to obscure the path. Morning sun filtered through the trees, warming me. I removed my cloak. I would need it later, if I made it to the crest. The air there would be much colder, and the wind severe.

I maintained a slow, steady pace and soon reached the first out-cropping. At the edge, I could see below the fields and buildings. Oak leaves displayed a deep russet red, and the softer hardwoods, yellow and pale red. I looked up to the mountain crest where the color was already gone. Dark trunks added a somber tone, enhanced by the dark green, almost black, of the evergreens filling the coves.

After resting a few minutes, I climbed to the second outcropping at a slow pace, resting several times. At the cove, I drank from the creek. When I stepped onto the uneven surface of the second out-cropping, I felt a chill, despite the warm rays of the sun. I stood at its edge, careful of my footing, for the drop here was much farther than the first one. The fields below were many shades of brown with an occasional deep green or bright yellow.

I sat on a smooth stone, for my legs were tired and my breathing labored. When I began to feel the chill, I started the last climb, rest-ing frequently. With each stop, the air was colder, the wind stronger. Although thirsty, I did not go to the cove. The spring at the foot of the highest outcropping never diminished, and its water was so cold if I drank too rapidly, my head would ache.

At the base of the highest outcropping, I put on the cloak and rested a few minutes. Then I lay on the ground at the spring and drank the sweetest water I ever tasted. I walked toward the ridge and started for the top. The climb was steep, and the air seared my throat. When I reached the summit, it was past noon, yet the sun was low in the sky. I pulled the cloak around me.

This was the view I had longed to see, the snowcapped Taurus Mountains to the north, the great plain of the Cydmus to the south. The mountains were clear, but the valley and plain were filled with a light haze that softened the colors. I studied the vista for some minutes until the wind gusts threatened my balance and made me shiver. I withdrew to a rock formation and found a recess that blocked the wind. I sat in the sun's rays, wrapped in my cloak, waiting for the chill to pass.

As I looked over this valley, I thought of changes in Tarsus and Rome, in people and government, and land. My own failures had contributed to the decay. *Yet here the land is clean and pure*, I thought. *This is my country, my home. This is where I belong.* As the spring at the base of this outcropping had not changed, I resolved that from this day forward I would never change.

The sun warmed me, and I opened my pouch to find two pieces of cheese, fresh baked bread, and a metal goblet of porridge thinned with milk, truly a meal fit for a king.

If I did not start back soon, I would not be out of the forest by dark. Wrapping the cloak around me, I walked to the edge of the outcropping and looked again into the valley. *If Elysium is half so fair, I shall be content.*

I stopped at the spring for one last drink and wondered if ever I would drink from it again.

†

That evening after the meal, all adjourned to the courtyard and sat around a brazier with a good fire blazing. We had assisted Julia in cleaning the kitchen so she could join us. The children sat wide-eyed, for they had never experienced a stranger eating and sleeping in their midst.

Lucius talked of what had been accomplished that day in the fields, but the children never took their eyes off me. They were fine looking, the oldest a girl of about fifteen, the boys younger, about ten and twelve. All were full muscled from hard work. They had not spoken since we sat down.

When the conversation lagged, I explained to the children that I once lived in this house, worked in the fields, and ate meals prepared by their mother. Not only had I traveled to Tarsus and the Great Sea, sailed to Corinth and Rome, but I had also been a soldier in Germany, a place much like the valley, except the winters were very cold and lasted nearly six months. The boys followed my every word, mouths open.

"Were you in battle?" the youngest asked.

I told them about Pontius Pilate and the battle at the Weser River, which started a steady stream of questions from the boys. The girl never spoke.

Finally, Lucius stood, said, "That is enough for one evening. Everyone to bed. There is much to do tomorrow. Tell Cornelius goodnight."

As the children walked toward the house, Julia and Lucius expressed again their pleasure in having me present. I wished them all goodnight and added more wood to the fire. It had been an enjoyable evening. Among all the family, I sensed contentment, even peace and happiness, despite their hard lives.

During my time with Pontius Pilate and his family, I never sensed peace and contentment. The slaves in that household had an easier life than Julia, but their demeanor was hardly one of contentment. I had felt a sense of contentment in the legion. How could Julia and I be content and the slaves of Pilate not be? Perhaps Julia and I felt we were destined to have these lives.

The fire had burned low, and cold was creeping in. I was tired from the day's climb, my legs stiff and a little sore. I stood by the brazier, enjoying the remaining heat.

The next day, I visited the stewards and laborers. The farm was as impressive as ever. I had not forgotten my love for these people and these mountains. That evening was a pleasant one around the fire, each one adding to the discussion, even the girl. When Lucius announced the day was over, I said I would leave for Tarsus the next morning. The children voiced their disappointment.

After breakfast with the laborers, the children and their parents walked me to the courtyard where a horse had been saddled and bridled. The two boys proudly announced they had gotten up when Julia did and prepared it.

I mounted and said goodbye. As the horse cantered through the gate, I turned and waved. These were my people, and this was my way. I arrived at the livery in Tarsus well after dark.

The next morning, I spent time in the courtyard thinking about differences between their world and my own. I had grown accustomed to a hard life. The life here seemed now like a dream. I needed to talk with Simmias.

In the open area near his room, I found him reading a manuscript. "Cornelius, thank you for coming by. The legion has changed you."

I sat in the chair across from him. "You once told me legionnaires are different, that they have a sense of contentment others never know. I am beginning to understand. I am no longer part of the life here. I love the valley, the farm, and the people, but here it is different. I am a stranger."

"Do not be concerned," Simmias said. "People who commit their lives, their every effort, to an endeavor are changed by it. It becomes their existence. They find contentment on a level others only dream about. Others do not understand dedication and commitment. For them, it is too great a price to pay. Be happy you have found your calling. But be aware you are different, and be tolerant of the rest of us. You have learned what one of our philosophers meant many years ago when he said that no man crosses the same river twice, for at the second crossing, both the man and the river have changed. Your visit with us has been as the second crossing. Appreciate us for who and what we are, as we appreciate you for who and what you are."

I pictured myself at the farm, standing on one of the narrow, fragile bridges over the Cydmus, looking into the fast-flowing water. How clearly Simmias had made his point. Since I last crossed the river, I had changed, and the river had changed. "My dear friend, what you said will help me to appreciate everyone here, you especially. I shall miss these conversations. To me they are as old manuscripts, and I will recall them many times."

After the noon meal, Moshe said, "There is a heavy merchant vessel leaving for Antioch late tomorrow. I can book you as a member of the crew." He paused. "I have a Palestinian tunic and mantle for you. There is also a turban, but it is not necessary that you wear it. The tunic is longer than a Roman one and has full sleeves. The mantle is a large square cloth, used for warmth, cover in sleeping, everything. Change to Palestinian dress at Antioch. It would serve you well to join a caravan from there to Caesarea or to Jerusalem. Do not travel alone. Use the journey south to become familiar with the customs. When you are settled in Caesarea, employ a rabbi or a scribe to teach you Aramaic. Everyone speaks Greek, but Aramaic is the language of the people."

"Please list me as one of the crew," I said. "Thank you for the garments. I will don them in Antioch."

"The wealthy are very wealthy. As a centurion, you will be among them. Most, however, are extremely poor, craftsmen trying to earn enough for the next day. Many of the trades are unacceptable to the religious, and those people are ostracized as unclean and fit neither for society nor to enter the temple," Moshe said. "You will become aware of this, if you travel with a caravan. The people are friendly and generous. I wish I could accompany you. Perhaps someday I will return."

Moshe, my parents, Simmias, and I spent a last evening together. As we parted, Mother placed her hand on my arm. "I wanted to talk with you alone. I am so very proud of you, yet I am filled with sadness. I endeavored to treat you children the same, but you were my favorite.

There was something in your spirit that reminded me of myself as I was growing up."

I put my arm around her waist, overcome with deep love.

"More and more I think about the days gone by," she said, "recalling pleasant memories of hard work on the farm, sessions with the visiting teachers, and most of all my reading to you from the manuscripts. I worry about your brothers and sisters. Somehow, they seem to have abandoned all the things we did as a family. They have all done well, but I am afraid the easy life and good living have taken something from them."

She wiped tears from her eyes. "You are different now, but that difference reassures me you still hold to the things we aspired to be. Palestine is so far away, and you still have many years to serve. I may never see you again."

"I hold fast to what you taught me," I said. "Do not worry. I know who I am, what I am destined to be. With you and Father as spectators to witness my race, how can I fail?"

"These last days are to me like those of an old mare put out to pasture who sometimes gallops as fast as she can for the pleasure of it. Thank you for staying. Do not worry about me or about your father. You are our great joy. Keep faith with all who have gone before."

She rose with some effort, and I extended my hand for her to grasp, then embraced her. "Thank you for what you said. Thank you and Father for giving me a good start. I will never forget."

Moshe, my father, and I had breakfast, as we did long ago. After a light noon meal, they accompanied me to the ship. As we bade each other goodbye, I wondered if I would see either of them again. Then, I was on my way to Palestine.

✝

At Antioch, I changed garments and walked south along the trade route, joining a large merchant caravan of camels, pack donkeys, horses, individuals, and families. There was little conversation, for traveling was hard and the road rough. The hot sun dried our mouths and throats. Moshe had said Palestine was a harsh land.

At sundown, the caravan stopped, dispersed into small groups, and prepared for the night. I was spreading my mantle when an individual said in Koine Greek, "My name is Joseph, and I bid you welcome. Our group is going to Galilee. Will you join us?"

"You are very kind. My name is Cornelius. I arrived in Antioch today on my way to Caesarea. I have never been in Palestine."

Joseph's group included day laborers dressed in worn tunics, many without mantles, some without sandals. Two moved to provide me a place in the circle close to a fire fed by dry animal dung.

"We are returning to Galilee," Joseph said. "We have been working in Antioch."

No one was preparing food. "I have not had a meal since this morning," I said.

"Please eat," Joseph said. "We ate in Antioch."

I opened my pouch and counted out four dried fish, laying them on the edge of my mantle. I broke one and offered half to Joseph.

"You are very generous, but you will need it for the journey."

"I cannot eat in your presence if you do not eat."

Joseph reached for the fish. I passed a portion to the others, removed one for myself, broke it in half, and returned half to my pouch. One of the laborers produced a waterskin, and I drank in turn. The water tasted of animal urine. I was thirsty, but two swallows were sufficient.

The spring at the base of the high outcropping I had climbed only days before would become a cascade sufficient to fill all the waterskins of all the caravans in Palestine. This harsh landscape denied these people the good things of life. How would Simmias reconcile their lot? Could an ideal society be achieved in places such as this?

My reverie was interrupted with everyone preparing for the night. Those who had mantles spread them; those without slept in their tunics. I wrapped mine around me and lay down, marveling at the brightness of the stars.

Before dawn, I awoke to activity, but none among the laborers. I removed from my pouch some cheese and bread and enjoyed them as the stars dimmed.

Dawn came quickly. The laborers passed the waterskin, and, as the water was almost gone, I did not drink. The sun cleared the horizon, and our caravan was under way.

When we passed through a village, one of the laborers purchased bread and dried fish, and I replenished my supply. Another laborer filled the waterskin at a well. A local youth with his own bucket filled containers for the animals.

We walked briskly to rejoin the caravan and to our position near the front. When shadows lengthened, we stopped. The laborers seated themselves in a circle in a small, open area, again inviting me to join them. The man who had purchased the bread and the fish cut them in equal portions and passed a share to each. I removed from my pouch a portion of pita and fish, careful to eat in the same manner as they did. We passed the waterskin, but the water was no better than before.

As we were preparing for the night, Joseph said, "You managed well the day's travel. By your sandals and the cut of your hair, you are Roman, though you wear the tunic and mantle of a Palestinian. By the manner of your walking, you must be a soldier. It is strange you would travel with a caravan as a Jew."

"I am a Roman soldier and will soon join a legion in Caesarea. Thank you for allowing me travel with you."

"It is our pleasure. We live in the hill country. Most soldiers are in the cities," Joseph said. "The land is too poor to farm, so many Palestinians like us go to the cities to find work, anything to earn money. In Antioch, we earned enough to last a few weeks. Unless we find work closer to home, we will return to the city."

"It is the same everywhere," I said. "If each of us could work and earn enough to live, the world would be a better place."

"Tomorrow the caravan will head east toward Galilee and the inland route south to Jerusalem. You will continue south along the coastal road to Caesarea," Joseph said. "I will tell my children about traveling with the Roman soldier who looked like us. May the God of Israel keep you safe."

The next day, the main caravan turned east toward Galilee, and I continued on the coastal road. The caravan passed a well, and I stopped and ate. After eating, I was walking rapidly to overtake it when I came upon a woman with two small children sitting beside the road. Her tunic was worn and her head scarf faded. Her eyes were wide, her lips compressed into a thin line, her cheekbones made prominent by the gauntness of her face. The children were listless, with tunics sorely in need of laundering.

"You are with the caravan ahead. May I be of assistance?" I asked.

She looked down and whispered, "It is no use. I cannot keep up."

"You cannot remain here. May I assist you?"

"It is no use. The children are tired. I am tired. Perhaps another will be along."

"If you allow me, I will carry the children. Can you walk?"

"I cannot overtake the caravan."

"It is a short distance ahead. We will join it when it stops for the night."

I knelt in front of the children, smiled, and opened my arms. Reluctantly the older child came, followed by the younger. I picked them up and said to the woman, "I will walk beside you."

We continued in silence. The children were thin, and their tunics smelled of urine and waste. Soon they were asleep on my shoulders.

When the caravan stopped for the night, we joined it. I knelt, letting the children stand slowly. I motioned the woman to sit. The only baggage she carried was in a small head scarf.

"I have food enough for the four of us."

"I cannot refuse for the children, but I have no money."

"That is of no concern," I said.

I prepared four portions. The children took theirs, but the woman was reluctant.

"I have never accepted food from a Gentile."

"The food is more Jewish than Gentile."

She took her portion.

I spread my mantle. "The children may sleep on this. I have no water, but we will stop at the first well tomorrow. I will be close by."

I withdrew to a level place nearby and lay down. I was tired, and my shoulders ached.

The next morning when I awoke, the woman was sitting and staring at the children as they slept. She turned to me and smiled. "I had best wake them. I hope you rested well. You were kind to us. We do not associate with Gentiles, but during the night, I resolved to be thankful. Forgive me for appearing ungrateful."

"You needed help," I said. "We must eat. It will soon be time to travel." I prepared four portions and handed one to each, taking one for myself.

When the caravan began to move, I lifted the youngest one, and the woman led her other child. Later we entered a village and drank from the well. At a small market, I replenished my food.

At times during the day, I carried both children. Their mother kept the pace. When the caravan stopped for the night, I again prepared food for each. After we had eaten and the young ones were asleep, the woman spoke. "My husband was a laborer in Antioch. A building timber fell on his leg. The wound would not heal. He developed a fever and died. I spent our money on apothecaries and surgeons. I have family in Cana, but I am fearful they are poorer than I," she said. "Without your help, I would yet be beside the road. My heart has softened toward Gentiles. I pray my God will bless you in the days ahead. Our religion commands us to be kind to strangers. You have shown more kindness to me than my fellow Jews in the caravan."

Two days later, the woman and the children left the caravan at the road to Cana. I gave her what remained of the wages I received working on the ship. When I looked back for the last time, she was still beside the road.

In Caesarea, I offered my documents to the centurion at the fortress who looked at me, suspicious that a Jew would present orders. After reviewing my papers, he said, "Welcome to Caesarea, Centurion. Your garments confused me. I see you were at the Weser River. I wish I could have been there. We are pleased to have you here. You have temporary quarters until the Tenth arrives. It may be some time. Pontius Pilate is also delayed." He summoned an aide. "Show Cornelius to his quarters, then take him to the dining hall."

After a meal, a bath, and a night's sleep, I decided to begin my study of the Aramaic language while waiting for Pilate to arrive. I donned my red tunic and returned to the centurion's office.

"I hope you dined well and slept well," he said. "What can I do for you?"

"As the legion is not to arrive for some time, I would like to reside in the community to learn the language, reporting to the fortress as often as you wish. Would you prepare a document which will allow me to enter and leave the fortress in local dress? Also, I wish to draw two months' pay."

"I am pleased to arrange both. You may leave your military items here. Report once a week. If you need longer intervals, that can be arranged. Tomorrow I will have your pay and the pass."

I returned to my quarters, separated my personal items from the military ones, and donned the Jewish tunic. It was discolored with road dust but would serve better than a clean one.

At the fortress gate, I said to the legionnaire on duty, "My name is Cornelius, centurion, Tenth Fretensis. I wish to leave the fortress in local dress. If I have not returned before the guard changes, tell your replacement I have gone into town. I do not wish to disturb the centurion on my return."

"Yes, sir, I will tell my replacement, if you have not returned."

Walking north, I met a man in a formal tunic and mantle complete with tassels. I raised my hand and said in my best Greek, "I am a stranger in Caesarea. Would you direct me to the nearest synagogue?"

"Peace be to you, my friend. Welcome to our community. There is one on the street to your right, a short distance."

The synagogue was beautiful, well constructed and well cared for.

I passed through the courtyard and in the space behind the building saw an old man dressed as the man in the street. "I am new to Caesarea and would like to talk with a priest or a teacher."

"Welcome to our city and to this humble synagogue," he said. "Perhaps I can be of assistance."

"My name is Cornelius. I am to join the Tenth Legion when it arrives. A Jewish friend suggested I learn Aramaic. I am seeking a teacher."

"Cornelius, it is my pleasure to meet you," he said in perfect Greek. "Perhaps your god, may his name be praised, arranged this meeting."

"Can you assist me?"

"Teaching is the purpose of our synagogue. This is, however, the first request from a soldier, and one who is a Gentile. There are procedural matters, but we can overcome those. We have instructors both young and old."

"I prefer an older one. Would you consider teaching me?"

"The honor is mine. I will make the arrangements. Return tomorrow at this time, and we will discuss the matter further."

"I will be here. Thank you for your kind reception. Peace be with you."

"Peace be with you."

At the fortress, the new guard stopped me but allowed me to pass when I identified myself. As I rested on my pallet, I wondered about the woman from the caravan and her children, then fell asleep.

The next morning, I walked to the centurion's office. He smiled at my appearance. "You look the part of a local. Did you find a place in the community?"

"I believe so."

"I commend you on learning the language," he said. "You carry a reputation. Someday I would like to hear your experience with the Fifth Alaudae."

"I would like to tell you about it," I said. "Each Monday morning,

I will report here. If anything changes, I will let you know. Thank you for the pass and the money."

From the fortress, I walked toward the man-made harbor. It was an impressive sight, complete with a breakwater and signal towers, and more merchant ships than navy. I had imagined Caesarea to be a military port, but it was as much a commercial city. A row of shops provided goods to satisfy any desire, and two aqueducts brought water into the city. Caesarea was a small Tarsus.

I made my way to the synagogue at the agreed time to meet my teacher.

"Peace be unto you and your house. My name is Enoch. I am a rabbi, a teacher of the Talmud. Welcome to our synagogue. Please follow me."

We entered a small room built into the wall surrounding the synagogue, furnished with a table, two chairs, and a pallet. Scrolls of varying sizes stored in a series of shelves reached to the low ceiling. On the table, a small lamp provided little light.

"I have been granted permission to teach you Aramaic. I had difficulty convincing the young teachers the merit of the undertaking. They never leave the synagogue and do not remember Rabbi Hillel. You must observe certain conditions: enter by the garden, wear Jewish dress, and speak to no one. You may not attend on the Sabbath. Are you agreeable?"

"Yes, but caution me if I fail to observe these or any other restrictions."

"I look forward to our venture. The synagogue scrolls are in Hebrew and are used to teach our own people. Most of my scrolls are in Aramaic," he said. "You must know the development of the language before you can read and speak it, and you must learn to think in Aramaic."

For the rest of the afternoon, Enoch explained the source of the Aramaic alphabet and the language itself, as well as the differences in the Aramaic and the Greek languages.

With his help, I arranged living space near the synagogue. I spent mornings with him, and during afternoons, I studied in my room or in the courtyard. I spent the Sabbath in the fortress.

A few months later, I had occasion to use my Aramaic while passing through an older section of Caesarea. Several young boys began taunting me. I ignored them, but soon they began to throw small stones, meant more to insult than to injure. I dropped to my knees, placed my mantle over my head, and trembled. The leader approached, making remarks about old people. I withdrew my knife. When he was near enough, I grabbed his arm, pulled him down and held him firmly by the back of his neck. I placed the blade against his throat, careful not to injure him. He struggled to free himself until he felt the blade. His friends hurried away.

In my best Aramaic, I whispered in his ear, "Do not insult old people. Some may not be as kind as I. You should be in school or helping your father. If you promise to help you father, I will let you go. Otherwise, I am going to make a eunuch of you. Do you understand?"

The heel of my left hand felt the pounding of his blood. His eyes were wide with fright.

"Do you promise to help your father?"

"I do."

"Good. If I see you again on the street, I will make you a eunuch. Do not forget an old Gentile spared your life one day when you insulted him." I released him and watched as he disappeared down a side street.

After several more weeks, I could read and speak the language adequately. Enoch suggested I visit friends of his in Jerusalem who were continuing the academy established by the Jewish Rabbi Hillel. It favored a moderate approach to the study of the Talmud. He said learning from their viewpoint would be of great value. I arranged a leave and traveled to Jerusalem.

✝

In Jerusalem, the House of Hillel welcomed me and assured me my presence as a Gentile was not an issue. The teachers were interested in my reason for being there and were eager to help me learn.

After several days of instruction, I became aware of great differences between Aramaic and Greek. I had difficulty translating certain words and concepts from one language into the other. The Greek world *soul* was difficult to express in Aramaic.

"Do you believe in an afterlife?" I asked one of the teachers.

"We believe in the resurrection of the dead. Is that the same as an afterlife?"

"Does *resurrection of the dead* mean we each have a soul which survives the death of the body?"

"Our word for the Greek *soul* is *the breath of life.*"

"Let us return to Aramaic words such as *fish*, *tunic*, and *sandals*," I said. "Using those words, I can think in Aramaic."

Some weeks after my return to Caesarea, I learned the Tenth Legion was on its way from Damascus, and Pontius Pilate was to arrive in a matter of days. I concluded my lessons with Enoch. Our last discussions were in Aramaic, and he corrected me only a few times.

When we parted, Enoch said, "In one of our discussions, you indicated an interest in the manuscript called *Job*. I have several. One is very old, written in Aramaic during the time we were captives in Babylon, and the script is difficult to read. I also have one in Greek and one in Aramaic, transcribed a few years ago. For you, I suggest the copy in Greek, for the words are forceful yet subtle in meaning. Perhaps it will help you with our language. Consider it my gift for mastering the language and a personal gift as a friend. This experience has been my pleasure."

"I am reluctant to take one of your manuscripts as you consider each an old friend."

Enoch removed a scroll from the shelves. "Please accept this with my blessing. You are perceptive and care for such matters. I am an old man and do not know what will happen to my manuscripts. It will be safe in your care."

"Thank you, my friend. I will care for it and master the subtleties. I am deeply in your debt. Peace be with you."

"Peace be with you," Enoch said.

A few days later, I asked a Jewish scribe to remove the pages from the scroll and fold them back and forth into a codex. During the next several months, I read it several times and came to believe it might have exceeded the Greek dramas in intensity.

✝

Pontius Pilate and his family arrived at Caesarea Maritima. Avitus had remained in Rome to study law. The garrison provided a proper reception, escorting Pilate to Herod's palace. I was part of the reception group.

A few days later, I visited Pilate's office. "Cornelius, it is good to see you. The Tenth Fretensis will be here in a few days. Let us adjourn to the palace. We can talk there."

We walked the short distance to Herod's palace, and I followed him into a spacious room. We sat on a carpet facing one other, each leaning on large cushions.

"The centurion said you have been here some time and have been living in the community."

"Yes, it has been a pleasant time. I have learned Aramaic and have been to Jerusalem," I said. "It is good to see you again. I hope the trip from Rome was uneventful."

"It is good finally to be here," said Pilate. "Sejanus is concerned there will be disturbances unless Rome establishes its authority over Palestine. He made very clear I am to use the three legions stationed here to bring order. He has promised greater responsibilities if I do well. Quirinius approved my request to move the Tenth Legion to Judea. I plan to locate seven cohorts in Jerusalem to be responsible for all Judea, and three cohorts here to look after the coast. We may need to send a detachment to Galilee, as most of the unrest is there. The Tenth has no mercenaries. There should be no problem in enforcing order."

"I have been studying the language, not the politics," I said, "but your plan seems reasonable. Why is Sejanus concerned?"

"He said the greatest threat to the empire is failure of the Jewish nation to accept defeat. With Quirinius's approval, the Sanhedrin governs Palestine through the sons of Herod the Great. I am to make the Jews understand they are a conquered people and owe allegiance to their conquerors."

"The temple in Jerusalem is the center of their religion and their government. Both are administered by the same officials," I said. "Most of my time was spent with religious groups, not those involved in administering the government. I am not aware of any unrest or rebellion."

"I am told the uprisings were suppressed with small detachments of soldiers. Dispersing the Tenth will increase the Roman presence. I would like to send you to Jerusalem as centurion of one of the cohorts. I will remain in Caesarea until I become more familiar with Palestine and Judea."

Pilate stood, and we walked to the palace entrance. As I was leaving, someone called my name. I turned to see Portia.

"Do you have time to talk?"

"Yes, I have no assignment."

"Let us go to the porch," she said.

I followed, noticing how gracefully she walked, head erect and shoulders back, black hair cascading from under her scarf. At the far parapet, she turned to me. "Father said you are to go to Jerusalem with the Tenth. I was afraid you might leave before we had a chance to talk. It seems much longer since we last spoke. I thought about you many times."

"We never finished our conversation that last night in Rome. I wanted to know how you learned Greek."

"When we were in Rome," she said, "you were leaving for Caesarea. Now that I am in Caesarea, you are leaving for Jerusalem."

We seated ourselves on a beach. "When I arrived in Antioch, I dressed as a Palestinian laborer and joined a merchant caravan," I said.

"That was clever."

"Since arriving, I have learned Aramaic."

"Did Father mention Sejanus?"

"Yes, he did. He spoke of his feelings about the Jews and the unrest in the province. Your father is to suppress it and bring order to Palestine. It seems a reasonable request."

"Father holds no ill will, but Sejanus is ordering him to punish the Jews. Father does not see that. He sees only an opportunity. I am fearful he will fall out of favor with Tiberius. I regret burdening you with this. Mother and I talk about it but never to anyone else." Portia took a deep breath. "My apology. Let us talk about more cordial matters."

"Do not worry about your father. I have not forgotten the warning you gave me in Rome, and I am aware of your concern," I said. "During that last evening in Rome, you were talking about your Greek teacher. Did he ever discuss whether our lives are planned from the beginning, that we are not free to make our decisions?"

Portia smiled. "You remembered. I feared you thought I was foolish. He taught Mother and me to read and write both Greek and Latin. We write the letters which Father wishes to be private. In Rome, the scribes and attorneys traffic on information gained from the letters they write. Even Sejanus inquired about my father's plans for Germanicus. It is a good arrangement for Father. It could never have been so well planned, so it must have been destined."

"You and Claudia wrote the letters to Germanicus! That is why no one knew of your Father's assignment to the Fifth Alaudae until he arrived."

"Yes. Father suspected the defeat of the three legions in the Teutoburg Forest was because Arminius had spies in Rome and in Varus's camp. Arminius knew more about Varus's legions than Varus himself."

"Portia, you may be better in Latin and Greek than I. I must be careful how I speak in the presence of you and your Mother."

"When the family left home for Rome, I brought many of the best manuscripts with me. To Father's dismay, I brought them to Caesarea.

I read one or two on the way from Rome. I am out of practice with the old Greek."

"I would like to see them and compare them with the manuscripts I read at the university."

"I wish we could look at them now, but it can wait," she said. "I will bring the best ones to Jerusalem. I look forward to discussing them, but I must read them again."

"Caesarea is a fine Roman town, with shops selling merchandise from all over the world," I said. "The water here is sweeter to the taste than the water in Rome, and the air is always fresh and clean. Jerusalem is not far away."

"I look forward to the day Father moves to Jerusalem. I have heard about it from the time we moved to Rome."

"It is good to see you again," I said. "I have enjoyed this meeting."

"I will study the manuscripts," she said. "Except for our Greek teacher, I have never discussed the subject matter. I am eager to hear your interpretation."

"It may be some time before I go," I said. "We can study the manuscripts during our next meeting."

"I look forward to it."

I found my time with Portia strange and exciting. She might well be a better student of Greek matters. I needed a Simmias.

✝

I looked forward to Jerusalem. It was the center of Palestine in many ways, set upon the high ridge running north and south through the province. The temple with its gold dome and marble columns was more impressive than any in Rome.

One day, an aide summoned me to Pilate's office. Pilate pointed to a document lying on his desk. "The Tenth Legion left Damascus a week ago. It is now in Galilee and will be here in three days. I plan to meet their vanguard and make the entry into Caesarea with them. Would you like to join me?"

"It would be my honor to accompany you. However, I am fearful my joining you in the van of the Tenth would cloud my authority when I am assigned one of the cohorts by giving the impression I was granted command rather than earning it."

Pilate bowed his head. "Well said. I understand your concern. It is especially important in the infantry that everyone have the ability to support his authority. As soon as I have learned the organization of the Tenth, we will talk again. Until then, I believe the expression in the infantry is 'For the Senate and the people of Rome.'" He saluted.

I stood and returned his salute. "For the Senate and the people of Rome."

At Pilate's direction, the leadership of the fortress in Caesarea had prepared the old campsite north of the city to receive the Tenth Legion. The legion was to arrive in early afternoon. Pilate, resplendent in his armor, rode out to meet it.

The garrison force in military array, in light armor and shield, marched out to the campsite. The commander of the fortress invited me to join him and his staff making up the van of the garrison. It was good to be part of the special glory.

Caesarea Maritima and the neighboring villages turned out for the occasion. By way of the Maris Road, the Tenth Legion, six thousand strong, with a unit of trumpeters and drummers and escorted by a small troop of cavalry, entered the campsite. With the legion's battle standard to his left, Pilate led the vanguard.

I remember to this day the moment I first saw the legion's standard. Under the polished bronze eagle, its wings outspread, was the crest of Tiberius and under it a tablet with the numeral X. On the crossbar below appeared the image of a Roman galley, Neptune with trident, and a wild boar. That battle standard was the history and the spirit of the Tenth Legion.

The Tenth settled into the old campsite, and Pilate immediately set his plan in motion. He relocated the three weakest cohorts to the fortress at Caesarea and ordered seven cohorts to Jerusalem. As the centurion of the Fifth Cohort was nearing the end of his service, he was assigned to the fortress at Caesarea. At the campsite, with some ceremony, I joined the Tenth Legion Fretensis as centurion of the Fifth Cohort.

Jerusalem was three marching days' distance and required the construction of two camps on existing sites. I ordered the Fifth Cohort to form for inspection, full military equipment, including baggage carts. After the inspection, I secured a cart from livery and drove to the fortress.

Pilate was in his office. I presented my request for replacement equipment. With a smile, he stamped it. The supply centurion was pleased to expedite the filling of the request, including its loading. I returned to the campsite, pleased with the efficiency with which it had been filled.

The next morning, with the Fifth Cohort in formation, accompanied by the centurion of each century, I introduced myself to each legionnaire. All were Roman citizens. Mercenaries were good legionnaires, but when grouped with Roman citizens, especially from Italy, they restricted the camaraderie and cohesion of a unit.

I had hoped to see Portia that evening, but preparing for the move to Jerusalem required my attention. The following day, seven cohorts began the march to Jerusalem. I was anxious whether I could maintain the pace and was pleased to arrive at the first site. The next day, I was stiff and sore but by noon had recovered. The third day, we arrived at the permanent camp outside Jerusalem.

After we had prepared for the night, the commander of the Antonia Fortress met with the centurions. "Welcome to Jerusalem. This is the principal city of the province and the center of the Jewish religion. Their religion prohibits any image entering the city, even that of Tiberius on your standards. To observe that tradition, you will cover your standards and enter the city tonight after the second watch."

We had no choice but to do as commanded. I ordered each of my centurions to cover the standard for his century. After setting the sentries, we slept until the end of the second watch. About midnight, each cohort formed an array and marched into the city and into the fortress with its standard covered. There were no disturbances, although it was a sullen procession.

Settling into a routine required several days. The fortress was a massive walled structure built by Herod the Great, adjacent to the temple with one tower overlooking the temple court.

Some weeks later, a messenger from Caesarea Maritima delivered troubling news. Several thousand Jews from Jerusalem had surrounded Pilate's office, protesting the presence of the legion's standards within the city. For several days, Pilate attempted to negotiate, but the leaders remained adamant that the standards be removed. He then ordered Syrian mercenaries in Jewish clothing to mingle with the protesters and kill them. When the soldiers drew their swords, the Jews fell to the ground and exposed their necks, shouting they would rather die than have the Holy City desecrated.

Pilate withdrew the mercenaries and sent an order to the fortress commander to move the legion's battle standards to the campsite outside the city. I was surprised by Pilate's capitulation and feared his reputation with Sejanus would suffer. Sejanus could not anticipate the response of the Jewish nation to a merciless slaughter. The protesters had been incited by religious leaders in Jerusalem, not one of whom was present in Caesarea.

✝

I began a training program to improve the stamina and discipline of the Fifth Cohort. Unless there was rain or snow, I led the cohort weekly on a ten- to fifteen-mile march into the areas around Jerusalem, followed by an afternoon of weapons training. With regular patrols in the areas around the city and assignments to street intersections, life at Fortress Antonia settled into a routine.

Men from the numerous farms of southern Italy made the best legionnaires. They were conditioned to long hours of hard labor and meager fare, and possessed the ability to gain the maximum use from inadequate equipment. Soon our discipline exceeded that of the other cohorts.

When a disturbance occurred, the fortress commander dispatched a force more than adequate to quell it. The appearance of a Roman unit was usually sufficient to disperse the crowd. The incident of the standards, however, had been different.

I requested and was granted a meeting with the fortress commander. "Cornelius, I am pleased to meet you. Pilate tells me you were with him and Germanicus at the Weser River. That was a great day for Rome. The Teutoburg Forest was a lesson the legions should never forget. Pilate did not receive the recognition he should have. We are fortunate to have him here."

"He believes in the legion," I said, "and is a good commander. He was prefect of the Fifth Alaudae when we met. The battle at the Weser River was my first battle as centurion. It is the high point of my life."

"What can I do for you?"

"Because of the incident of the standards, I feel I must learn more about the politics and religion of the Jews. I have Jewish garments and speak Aramaic. I request permission to leave the fortress dressed as a Jew to visit friends. Will you provide me with a pass to allow me through the gate?"

"Certainly. Your plan is commendable but dangerous. There are assassins in the city."

"I must know the issue from a Jewish point of view. I am willing to take the risk. Is there an obscure entrance I might use?"

"There are several such entrances, but there is no guard, as the doors are locked. I will show them to you."

All were in remote areas except one near a passageway. The door there had a barred window. In the fortress livery, I removed a bell from an abandoned camel harness, then obtained sandal laces from supply. With one of the laces, I secured the bell to a bar above the door. I tied another lace to the bell, then attached it to a bar in the window. Now I could ring the bell to gain entrance. I opened the bolt locking the door, cleared out an accumulation of sand and leaves, then moved into a recess with steps leading up to a deserted street lined with old buildings.

The following day, I met again with the commander and assured him I could use the remote door. He prepared a document allowing me to leave and to enter the fortress in Jewish dress. I returned to the guard room and showed the centurion my pass. I advised him I would be changing to Jewish clothing, leaving by a particular door, and that a guard would have to bolt the door behind me.

"There are assassins in the city," he said. "It is especially dangerous at night. Being inside the fortress in Jewish garments can itself be dangerous."

"I have Jewish friends in the city, and I speak Aramaic. If I am careful, there is little danger. I expect to return before darkness. I will enter by the door and report here on my return," I said. "For the Senate and the people of Rome." He did not know the significance of that benediction.

In my quarters, I rolled up the Jewish garments, including a small turban. They were showing wear and in need of laundering. I would purchase some fiber sandals, for the legionnaire sandals disclosed my identity. I reported to the centurion of the guard, who ordered another guard to accompany me. In the passageway, I donned the garments and left by the door with the bell.

I went directly to the Hillel School. The teachers were aware of the incident of the standards and were supportive of the protesters. I explained I was interested in a religion that could foster in its people such dedication. "Would you explain your system to me?"

The eldest, an old rabbi who managed the school, said, "You must understand our society. We believe we are God's chosen people, that he governs our nation and has given us laws we must obey. We have been conquered many times, but we never abandoned our belief. Three hundred years ago, Alexander brought Greek culture, so we speak Greek. Then the Romans came. They allow us to govern ourselves, but we yet hold to the religion of our forefathers and keep its laws. Our allegiance is to our God, but in political matters, we owe allegiance to Rome."

He paused. "In our society, the landowners are the wealthiest among us and are the religious and political leaders. Most are Sadducees. The high priest is the most powerful office in Jerusalem, appointed by Rome to lead the Sanhedrin, the governing body. Most members of the Sanhedrin are Sadducees who cooperate with Rome to protect their wealth, compromising their allegiance to God."

A young teacher interrupted. "The Hillel School is dedicated to teaching Jewish law to anyone who will study. We try to remain above the politics of allegiance."

"The next groups are the Scribes and the Pharisees," said the old rabbi. "The Scribes interpret law and try to keep our religion pure. The Pharisees try to maintain religious correctness. Both object to cooperating with Rome, as it compromises our allegiance, and both oppose the Sadducees because of the difference in allegiance."

Again, the younger man interrupted. "Our school tries to be at peace with all people, especially the Scribes, Pharisees, and the Sadducees," he said. "We believe the Jewish religion is broad enough to include all Jews."

The rabbi raised his hand to silence the teacher. "Within the Pharisees is a minor group, the Zealots, who believe the Jewish people should end Roman occupation. Within the Zealots are the Sicarii, the assassins, who are even more adamant in trying to end Roman rule. They kill Jewish collaborators," he said. "Of the people, one of a hundred is wealthy. The other ninety-nine barely exist. Most cannot read or write and must rely on the Scribes and Pharisees for guidance."

A large rat ran along the wall and disappeared into an opening, but no one moved to kill it. One of the older teachers smiled. "We do not bother the rats. Our friend will provide a meal for one of the ninety-nine."

"The Sanhedrin was apprehensive when it learned a large group was protesting in Caesarea," said the rabbi. "The Scribes and Pharisees said bringing the standards into our city violated religious laws. There was, however, neither a Scribe nor a Pharisee among the protesters. I am surprised Pilate did not kill them all. The Sanhedrin cooperates with him, but religious leaders would like to see him and the Romans gone."

"You believe the unrest will continue?" I asked. "There are three Roman legions, one here and two in Damascus. That should allow Pilate to control the situation."

"To establish the old Jewish kingdom," he said, "messiahs lead their followers in revolt against Rome. The incidents are growing in frequency. Today, somewhere in the province, one is promising the people he is chosen by God to remove the Roman yoke. One day a group may become strong enough to do that."

"Where do these leaders come from?"

"Most come from the desert to the east or from Galilee to the north," he said. "Galilee seems to have the most unrest. It is in the hill country. The people there do not respond well to any authority, be it religious or Roman, but as long as the Sanhedrin is in control, Pilate should have no problem.

"What I have told you is true, but our society is more complicated than I have presented it," said the rabbi. "Within our society, there are other groups which do not agree. The Hillel School and the Shammai School agree on some things, but on most we do not. The Shammai is popular with the Zealots, as it opposes Roman rule. The School of Hillel favors a conciliatory approach to Roman rule and is out of favor with the religious leaders. It will be interesting to see which school time will favor." He stood. "That is enough for one day. I trust this has been of help."

"It has been a great help," I said. "I look forward to our next meeting. May your god bless your school and you. Peace be with you."

"Peace be with you also."

It was late afternoon when I walked toward the fortress, burdened with what I had learned. Jewish society was unstable in its very structure. Pilate's only option was to disperse the legion over the province, moving one of the legions from Damascus if the Tenth could not assure order.

At the obscure entrance, I had to ring the bell several times before a legionnaire opened the door.

✝

A rumor Pilate was coming to the fortress was confirmed when he and his family arrived with little ceremony. The following day, I visited the section of the fortress reserved for the prefect. I identified myself to the guard, who directed me to Pilate's office.

"How good to see you, Cornelius. Thank you for coming. How is Jerusalem?"

"It is different from the Fifth and Germany. I appreciate the people and look forward to serving here," I said. "I would like to hear your interpretation of the standards incident."

"I have considered whether I did the right thing," Pilate said. "Would you join me and my family for the evening meal tomorrow? You and I can discuss matters then without interruption."

The evening of the next day, I donned my red tunic and walked to Pilate's quarters. Herod the Great had built the huge fortress and immense living quarters. Pilate and I sat opposite each other at a massive table.

"Allow me to welcome you to my quarters. Being prefect of Judea has some advantages. I am pleased with the furnishings," he said. "I do not understand the reaction of the Jews to the standards. We covered Tiberius's image and entered the fortress during the night. There should have been no problem. The image inside the city, covered or not, was the issue. Sejanus would have killed all the protesters. I could not give the order. Tiberius is tolerant of the Jews, although they fail to give him allegiance."

"The people are divided," I said. "After the incident, I visited Jewish friends. They owe allegiance only to their god. Some leaders govern in accordance with Roman law in spite of their religious obligations, but others oppose Rome. I see why there is unrest."

"Sejanus insists I break their spirit. I believe my best option is to disperse the legion throughout the province."

"Their religion is more oppressive than Roman law," I said. "If the protests were religious in nature, it is a local issue, as their allegiance is to their god rather than to Tiberius. However, it may be difficult to determine whether a protest is political or religious."

"Your Jewish friends may sense problems before I do," he said. "Let us join Claudia and Portia. They will be happy to see you."

Claudia apologized for the meager selection. "There is not a great variety of foods here, but the cooks are skilled in preparing any dish many ways."

Portia and her mother took great pleasure recounting hardships endured during the journey to Jerusalem, especially nights spent in a legion camp.

A guard came to the door and spoke with Pilate. "There is a problem I must attend to," he said. "Please excuse me."

After her husband left, Claudia said, "Rumors continue to circulate Sejanus is planning to overthrow Tiberius. He already governs, as Tiberius spends his time in Capri, but Tiberius is sure to discover the conspiracy, if there is one. We are fearful Father may be caught in the net. The standards incident will not set well with Sejanus. What do you think, Cornelius?"

"Pilate is well in command. He is here, and Sejanus is in Rome. I have a pass which allows me to leave and enter the fortress dressed as a Jew, and I have Jewish friends in the city."

"Dress as a Jew and mingle with the people!" Claudia said. "They are strange, and the Greek is different. Portia and I met the wives of some of the Roman officials. They are excited about a religious man from the desert attracting large crowds at the Jordan River."

"What did you learn about him?" I said.

"He is a wild man dressed in animal skins, living in the desert. He predicts the end of the world. For those who believe him, he immerses them in the Jordan. The people call him the Baptizer. I would like to hear him, but the Jordan is far away, and I would not understand him."

We talked for some time about the man from the desert and shared other gossip. I then said to Portia, "You brought manuscripts from Rome to Caesarea. Did you bring them to Jerusalem?"

"Yes, I brought the ones I like best. I am getting better at reading old text."

"I have not read an old manuscript in many years," I said. "I will try at our next meeting."

The hour was late, and Pilate had not returned. We said our benedictions, and I returned to the barracks, thinking about the man at the Jordan River.

Early the next morning, after advising the guard, I left by the obscure door, rented a mule and a cart, and followed a crowd to the Jordan River. It was as Claudia said. The man was dressed in animal skins, his hair and beard were long, and he spoke a different Greek from that of Jerusalem. He spoke well, with conviction and excitement. His images of the end times made the hair on the back of my neck rise. I understood why people who listened to him wanted to be baptized.

More than once, he shouted, pointing accusingly to all listeners, from the religious leaders in their magnificent raiment to the gaunt day laborers in their shabby dress. "Bear fruit worthy of repentance or be ready to flee the wrath to come. For the tree that does not bear good fruit, the ax is already at the root. That tree will be cut down and cast into unquenchable fire."

By the middle of the afternoon, the crowd began to diminish. Later, after letting my mule drink from the Jordon above where people were being baptized, I pulled away from the crowd and prepared for the night.

I climbed into the bed of the cart, wrapped myself in my mantle, and marveled at the brightness of the stars. I was shaken by the Baptizer's message. Must I, too, bring forth fruit worthy of repentance? I had heard few who spoke with such authority. There was nothing political about his message. It threatened religious leaders.

The next day, as I listened to his vivid imagery and dire predictions,

a young man approached the speaker. He was about my age, power-
fully built, with an air of command. He was gentle in demeanor yet
with a bearing of utmost confidence. Had it not been for his shabby
dress, I would have taken him for a king or ruler. The two men spoke
for a few minutes, then the speaker led him into the water and baptized him.

When the young man came up from the water, his countenance
emanated a radiance like diffused sunlight, his bearing now more impressive. He walked from the Jordan and disappeared into the crowd.

✝

My return to Jerusalem was uneventful, and I was thankful to
have a mule and cart, for the road to the crest was steep. As I ascended
the high ridge, I recalled the incident at the Weser River when the
leader of Arminius's force led the charge against my unit. His radiant countenance had been like that of the young laborer's after his
baptism. It was dark when I reached the city, returned the cart, and
entered the fortress.

A few days later, I reported to Pilate on my visit to the Jordan. I
assured him the gatherings were religious in nature, as the speaker's
message was one of proper conduct, not resistance to Roman authority.

✝

Time at the fortress consisted of guard duty at significant street
intersections and patrols through the communities around the city.
Pilate met regularly with leaders of the Sanhedrin. Preparing for
Passover each year, he would move the cohorts from Caesarea to
Jerusalem. The weeklong religious event attracted Jews from all the
world. Every inn, roadside park, and courtyard was filled. The people
of Jerusalem opened their hearts as they did their homes.

During the festival, usually near the temple, there were assassinations. The acts were committed so discreetly they were attributed

to the Sicarii. Pilate was never able to identify their leaders or the assassins.

During evening meals with Pilate and his family, Claudia and Portia continued their interest in the man baptizing in the Jordan, excited by experiences of wives of local officials and my journey to hear him. Half in jest, I suggested that the three of us go to the Jordan. They readily agreed.

To discourage them, I reminded them of the distance, that it would be an overnight stay, and that they would have to dress as Jewish women. I assured them, however, if Pilate approved of such a venture, I would arrange the trip.

A few days later, at the evening meal, Pilate approved the journey, provided I accompany them. We spent the remaining time discussing the trip. I agreed to purchase their raiment. Because Claudia and Portia would have to be fully covered, I purchased two dark-colored, well-worn, full-length, full-sleeved women's tunics and head coverings with veils.

On my way to the fortress, I visited several liveries to find a good mule and cart. I returned to the livery with the best cart, although it was old and worn, and a mule in the same state. As a condition to my hiring them for two days, I requested the proprietor clean both. After some haggling as to the price, we agreed I would pick up the cart the next morning.

At the palace that evening, we prepared for the trip. Donning the clothing embarrassed Claudia and Portia, as it suggested a sinister purpose. When I left Pilate's quarters, I carried with me two bedrolls and the Jewish attire. The next morning at the end of the fourth night watch, we were to meet at the door with the bell.

I reported to the centurion of the guard that the three of us in Jewish dress were going to spend two days away from the fortress. I explained we were going to the Jordan to hear the man from the desert.

Early the next morning, the guard and I arrived at the fortress door to find Claudia and Portia already there, each carrying a small bundle.

As the hour was early, no one was in the passageway. Withdrawing into the small alcove, Claudia and Portia donned their garments. We left by way of the heavy door and entered the deserted street. I reminded them to walk behind me and to let me do any talking.

At the livery, the cart was ready. After placing the bedrolls, my pouch, and their small bundles in the bed of the cart, I assisted each to a seat. Our raiment, that of impoverished travelers, matched the state of our mule and cart. I climbed to the seat next to Portia, and we joined travelers on the road to Jericho.

As we crossed the crest of the ridge, I said, "If you look back, you will see the temple and Jerusalem in the morning sun."

We immediately began the steep descent into the valley. I adjusted the crude brake to prevent the cart from overtaking the mule and had difficulty slowing the pace of the cart to that of the travelers.

Off to my right, I could see the Jordan River and its tributaries below, green ribbons in sharp contrast to the barren expanse of Perea to the east and the steep rock formations of the high ridge to the west.

Claudia and Portia placed their feet on the front baffle to steady their positions on the bench seat. "Cornelius, I have difficulty believing Pontius allowed us to pass the night at the Jordan," said Claudia. "Our Roman friends call the wild man John the Baptizer. They say his Greek is easy to understand."

She was quiet for a moment. "Our Greek teacher said everyone is here for a purpose. I believed him but never committed myself to find my purpose. There is a difference between believing and doing what you believe. I have missed something very important in my life without knowing what it is."

"I know how you feel," Portia said. "Our teacher had a sense of urgency that I never felt. When I see what others have accomplished, I feel I have wasted my life."

We completed the descent and turned east to cross by shallow fords a tributary to the Jordan. Most travelers continued to the King's Highway, but we turned south along the west bank of the Jordan to an open area where a large crowd had gathered. John the Baptizer was encircled by spectators, including officials and leaders from the temple, their opulence in sharp contrast to the others.

I drove the mule into vegetation suitable for foraging, a place close to the crowd, and assisted Portia and Claudia from the cart. We walked to the back where I lifted them to its bed.

In a clear, strong voice, John addressed the officials. "You snakes! Do you believe you can flee the wrath to come? You must change your ways. You must show repentance. If you have ears, hear what I say. You have laden the people with burdens grievous to bear, yet you yourselves live lives of ease. You carefully tithe the smallest herb yet ignore the weightier matters of the law. You clean the outside of the cup, but it is filled with wickedness. You are like the tree that bears no fruit and is cut down."

From time to time, the crowd voiced its approval, while the officials, by demeanor and gesture, expressed contempt for both the man and his message. Claudia was transfixed, her eyes on John.

"Whoever has two cloaks, give one to the man who has none. If you have food, share it with the man who is hungry. Slaves, obey your masters and do good work for them. Laborers, do good work and do not complain about your wages. Wives, serve your husbands; husbands, provide for your wives. Soldiers, be content with your service. All these things you should do cheerfully with no complaint. Repent and make it so."

Late in the afternoon, the crowd began to depart. John waded into the shallow water, urging those who would repent to be baptized. Many were going to the river. Claudia began to sob softly. "I feel I must go. My heart is touched. I will do better."

"If you feel you must be baptized, do you want me to go with you?"

She looked at me, tears streaming down her cheeks. "I do not need baptism. My heart is changed. I am already different. Oh, Portia, do you understand?"

"Yes." She wiped tears from her eyes and embraced her mother. "I, too, am changed."

I found a secluded place not far from the river and prepared for the night. We sat under the back of the cart, eating in silence as twilight filled the valley.

"This day has been all I hoped it would be," Claudia said.

We rose with the sun. I rolled our bedding, packed the cart, and drove to the site where people were already gathering. It was a repeat of the previous day, except there was a new element in John's preaching.

"There is one coming who is greater than I am. I am not worthy to loosen his sandals. I baptize with water; he will baptize with spirit and with fire. He will separate the wheat from the chaff, gather the wheat into its bin, and burn the chaff with unquenchable fire. He is the expected one, make straight his way."

In early afternoon, we departed for Jerusalem. Claudia and Portia were in a pensive mood. More than once it appeared either the cart or the mule might not complete the journey. Darkness was beginning to fill the streets when we reached the fortress. I stopped at the door, allowed them to remove the Jewish garments, and rang the bell to gain entrance.

Claudia touched my arm. "Thank you again for arranging this trip."

A few days later, at the evening meal, Pilate and I discussed new rumors involving Sejanus and Tiberius. "That is enough for one evening," he said. "Cornelius, your presence is a joy. Thank you for taking Claudia and Portia to hear John. They seem much happier. Unlike Rome or even Caesarea, Jerusalem does not offer much for women. I commend you for making the trip."

Claudia and Portia talked excitedly of being dressed as Jewish women, of the poor condition of the cart and the mule, of how John criticized the temple leaders, and of the enthusiasm of the crowd. Neither mentioned her own response to John's message.

Jerusalem's water supply was from cisterns and pools fed by a few small springs and runoff from winter rain. Pilate considered this inadequate. As prefect, it was his duty to provide good water. The temple treasury contained much of the wealth of Judea. He reasoned as the city would be the beneficiary of fresh water, the temple should pay for the construction of an aqueduct.

Pilate demanded the Sanhedrin provide the money. Temple leaders objected to sacred money being wasted on a civil project. Amid this controversy, Pilate ordered construction to begin.

†

One day thousands of Jews incited by the Pharisees besieged Fortress Antonia. After several days of disorder, Pilate ordered mercenaries to dress as Jews, arm themselves with clubs, mingle with the protesters, and assault them. In the chaos, many Jews were trampled. Others were beaten to death.

Pilate ordered the bodies removed and the streets cleaned. He increased patrols in the city and the number of legionnaires assigned to each. In the Sanhedrin, Sadducees justified Pilate's action, but the Pharisees protested. In his report to Tiberius, prepared by Claudia and Portia, Pilate attributed all the deaths to being trampled by others.

Pilate continued to control unrest at its source. He and I discussed how to assure stability, especially around Galilee and Perea. This area, under the administration of Herod Antipas, was sparsely settled except for the cities along the great inland trade route from Africa, and from Damascus to Antioch. We considered a station there, if Antipas would allow Roman soldiers to keep order.

At one of the evening meals, Pilate outlined his plan. "There is a toll station in Capernaum. We should establish a unit there," he said. "I am making your cohort First Cohort, Tenth Legion Fretensis. You are now first centurion of the First Cohort, second in command. You have earned the rank, and I am pleased to bestow it. Your cohort is the most disciplined unit I have, the one most qualified for this assignment."

"Thank you, sir."

"Galilee is two days' distance by horseback. I can rotate you to Caesarea or Jerusalem when your cohort must act as a unit," Pilate said. "One of our officials has been recalled to Rome. He owns a villa at Caesarea Philippi, north of Galilee. I have been a guest there many times. You may want to consider acquiring it, but visit there before you make your decision."

When my cohort next formed its array, I announced with great pride it was now the First Cohort of the Tenth Legion. I thanked them for their dedication and spirit, their work and discipline, all which allowed me to become first centurion. That night before falling asleep, I silently thanked others who brought me to this moment: Simmias, who encouraged me to make the commitment; Gaius, who gave me the glove; Remus, who helped me become a centurion of infantry; and Titus, who gave me the benefit of his years in the legion and saved my life. To repay this great debt, I resolved to assist any whose way I might make easier.

Days later, I arranged a trip to Galilee, planning to be away a week. I reviewed with the centurion of the First Century the duties he was to assume and then selected a good horse to cover the distance in two days. In Jewish raiment, I set out for Galilee.

I followed the inland trade route, the King's Highway, north along the east bank of the Jordan. On each side of the river, the land was heavily cultivated. The road was in fair condition but quite inferior to Roman roads. I passed caravans, some northbound, others coming south, all with groups traveling with them. I spent the night with one.

Late the second day, I crossed west over the Jordan, then traveled north along the west side of the Sea of Galilee. There were fishing sites and drying racks all along the coast. By nightfall, I entered Capernaum and stopped at the first hostel.

The proprietor recognized me as a legionnaire. He welcomed me, showing enough hostility to assure me of his lack of respect for Rome but not enough to lose a paying traveler. When I addressed him in Aramaic, however, he dropped an old harness he was repairing. "Your Aramaic surprised me. Welcome to Capernaum. Thank you for gracing our establishment. Please inspect the accommodations." He led me to a small room with a pallet on the floor. I wrapped myself in my mantle and passed the night.

In the morning, I left the horse with the proprietor, as a Jew in shabby raiment riding a fine mount would attract attention, and ventured into the city. Along the shore and in the marketplaces, all Capernaum was at work, loading and unloading goods. Caravans were encamped near the city, preparing for the next portion of their journey. It was a good place to quarter the unit.

On my way back to the hostel, I spoke in Aramaic to a merchant. "Peace be with you. How do I find Caesarea Philippi?"

"Peace be unto you. Caesarea Philippi is north of Capernaum, then east. Follow the river north a day's journey to the foot of Mount Hermon, then looking to the east you will see a Roman temple, to the disgrace of our ancestors. That is Caesarea Philippi."

"You answered well. Peace be unto you."

I returned to the hostel and found the proprietor at work. "I wish to visit Caesarea Philippi tomorrow. May I rest here again tonight?"

Laying aside his tools, he said, "Please be my guest. You again grace my establishment. I will care for your horse. I have no food, but there is a market down the way. Last evening, I told my family about the Roman guest who spoke Aramaic."

The market was noisy and provided a fine meal. Afterward, I returned to the hostel, pleased my presence at the market had attracted no attention.

The next morning, the proprietor greeted me. "Your horse is ready. I fed and watered him a short time ago. Last evening, my son curried him. He is a fine animal."

"I plan to travel to Caesarea Philippi today and return tomorrow night. Allow me to settle my account should I change my plans, but hold the accommodations until it is apparent I will not return."

The proprietor bowed slightly. "Allow me to charge two denarii for your lodging and for the care of the horse. I trust you find it reasonable."

I gave him three denarii, for he wore no sandals and the hem of his tunic was worn away. "Thank you for your attention to my horse and for your hospitality. Peace be unto your house."

I took the road north and by late afternoon reached the foot of Mount Hermon, and then turned east from the river. I rode into a broad vale watered by numerous springs, some of substantial size. Some distance to my left, I could see the alabaster temple. Far right of the temple, near a series of springs, stood the villa.

The courtyard gate was open. I dismounted and tied my horse. A man, the hem of his tunic tied to his waist, approached me from the garden. I greeted him in Aramaic with the customary salutation and asked, "Is this the villa owned by the Roman official Publius?"

"It is. I am chief steward. May I be of assistance?"

"I understand your master is returning to Rome and wishes to dispose of this property. Is that true?"

"That is true. I am here only to look after it and care for the animals. Do you know Publius?"

"I do not know him, but we have a mutual friend who told me of the villa. Would you allow me to view it?"

"It is my pleasure. Please follow me."

The steward showed me the rooms, then the animals, and we walked the boundaries. It was an impressive site. Some distance down the valley, I could see the temple to Jupiter set in a magnificent green vale.

"My master wishes to sell the property as it is. He has removed those items he did not wish to sell. You should discuss the price with him."

We returned to the entrance. "I will do so. The day is spent. May I pass the night in the courtyard? I can pay for grain for the horse and something for myself."

The steward bowed his head. "Please be my master's guest. I will care for your horse, and you are welcome to spend the night. The fare is simple, but it would please me to provide you an evening meal and breakfast."

I entered a large room furnished with a number of tables and chairs and laid my pouch on the nearest table. The steward returned. He had been cautious in his conversation but showed great hospitality.

"Your horse is a fine animal. It is a pleasure to care for such a creature." He pointed to some melons on a workbench against the wall. "These are from the garden," he said. "There are vegetables, but I have none prepared. I can make some wheat porridge. There is yet good wheat my master brought from Jerusalem."

"A melon will do well. It will wash down the dust. For breakfast, I would like some good porridge. You are very kind."

The steward sliced a ripe melon, removed the seeds, and set both halves before me, along with a small knife. Its sweet savor filled the room. I cut a small portion, speared it with the knife, and placed it in my mouth. The cool, sweet taste exceeded my expectations. It did indeed wash down the dust.

"Will you join me?"

"I would be pleased to do so, but there are tasks I must complete before nightfall," he said. "I shall return by the time you finish the melon."

When the steward returned, I said, "You must have a very fine garden."

"My master took great pride in it."

"May I retire for the night? I would like to leave early for Capernaum."

He removed a lamp from the shelf over the bench, careful not to spill the oil. He lit it and led me to a room with a number of bunks, all with thick pallets. He placed the lamp on a table, and I stretched out on the bunk next to it and fell asleep.

When I awoke, it was not yet light, and the lamp was still burning. I donned and laced my sandals, straightened my tunic, and tightened my belt. Picking up the lamp, I went to the kitchen and found the steward preparing breakfast. "Good morning. I've never slept on a pallet so comfortable."

"My master ordered them especially made from Antioch, or

perhaps Damascus. He is very proud of the villa," he said. "Are you ready to eat?" He set before me a bowl of steaming porridge made from good wheat, not the thin grains from which the legion's was made.

"The porridge is good. You have done well."

"I save the good wheat for special occasions. Allow me to prepare the horse for the journey."

I was finishing my porridge when he returned. "Your horse is fed and watered. He is at the door."

I retrieved my pouch from my room, removed three denarii from my belt, and placed them on the kitchen table. "You have been a good host. Allow me to pay for the care of my mount and for my meals. Is this sufficient?"

"You owe nothing. You are a guest. I hope you have had a pleasant stay."

"Please do not take offense. I did not want to take advantage of your generosity. You master is fortunate to have a loyal steward."

In the courtyard, he helped secure my pouch behind the saddle, bowed, and cupped his hands to assist me in mounting. "This is a fine villa, and you are a good steward," I said. "Perhaps we shall meet again."

I walked the horse to the gate and then gently kicked his flanks to increase his pace, for it was already light enough to see the road. It was late afternoon when I reached Capernaum, where I dined well on wine and fresh fish, and then returned to the hostel.

"I trust your visit to Caesarea Philippi was successful," said the proprietor. "Thank you for again gracing our establishment. With your consent, I will provide for your horse."

He assisted me in removing my pouch, took my horse to an enclosure, and led me to the same room. I passed the night, more comfortable in those austere surroundings than in the elegance of the villa.

Early the next morning, the proprietor was already at work. "Your horse is ready. I fed and watered him."

I settled with him and set out for Jerusalem. During the journey, I considered the assignment to Galilee. I regretted splitting the cohort now that it was the First Cohort, but a major engagement was unlikely. Pilate had assessed the situation correctly. It was best to spread the legion throughout Palestine, making it difficult for any unrest to grow undetected. One century in Galilee should be sufficient to keep order. If I could acquire the villa, I would accept the assignment.

Late in the afternoon of the second day, I began the steep ascent to Jerusalem. As I passed the crest, I caught sight of the city. The late last light illuminated the gold temple dome, towers of Antonia Fortress, and alabaster buildings.

Early the next day, I met with Pilate. "I understand you have been to Galilee," he said. "I hope you bring good news."

"I have been to Galilee. Capernaum is suitable for a post. I also visited the villa. I would welcome the assignment, if I can acquire it."

"I am pleased and will talk with Publius. The relocation process will take more time than acquiring the villa," he said. "Join us this evening. It is little notice, but you are like family."

"As always, I am pleased."

That evening, I enjoyed the conversation and meal more than usual. Portia walked with me to the entrance. "Once again, you are to leave us. It seems always you are leaving just as we arrive. I will miss you at the meals."

"I will be of greater assistance to your father in Galilee than here. Perhaps you can visit. It is a pleasant place, with open spaces and fresh air."

She placed her hand on my arm. "It is a pleasure to be with you. Thank you for arranging our trip to the Jordan. Mother and I have talked about it many times. Please know that you are welcome here any time. If I ever can be of assistance, please let me know. I feel very much in your debt."

Her touch was so light I was tempted to place my hand over hers. "Portia, once again we have not studied the manuscripts. I will try to visit again before I leave. Return to the palace. The night air, especially in Jerusalem, is filled with vapors that are not good for anyone. Until our next meeting, goodnight." I stepped into the passageway to the fortress, still aware of the warmth of her touch.

✝

As first centurion of the First Cohort of a Roman legion, my responsibilities were as great as those of the commanding officer. Since my appointment, I had established a training routine to improve the legion's performance.

Galilee and Perea were centers of unrest. I was the one best qualified to command the post in Galilee. I resolved to negotiate carefully for the villa and devote my best effort to the success of my assignment.

Pilate arranged a meeting with Publius. He had done well as an administrator for the former prefect and had been helpful to Pilate. He was fortunate to have a prospective buyer. The villa was far from Jerusalem and remote, being distant from the towns around the sea.

Publius's office was in a large building not far from the fortress. A laborer would be overwhelmed by its size. In the giant hallway, I stopped an official and inquired as to the location of Publius's office.

Publius was a large man of middle age, with accumulated girth from idle days and fine food and a sallow complexion from time in the city. His tunic displayed the stripe of his order, and he wore a magnificent toga.

"My name is Cornelius, centurion with the Tenth Fretensis. I am to be posted to Galilee. I have visited your villa at Caesarea Phillip. It is far from my post, but the house is much to my liking. Have you arrived at a price?"

"I am pleased to see you. Pilate speaks highly of you and said you were to be posted to Galilee. He said you were with him at the Weser River. That was a great day for Rome."

"It was a significant victory," I said.

"I am to return to Rome as soon as I dispose of the property. It is well built and overlooks the springs at Caesarea Philippi. I would go there in the summer when the heat made Jerusalem unlivable. I am asking 15,000 denarii, though it is worth far more."

"There are other properties, but none as fine as yours. But the most I could arrange is 10,000 denarii. Thank you for your time." I turned toward the door.

"If you can get 10,000 denarii, the villa is yours."

"It may take a few days," I said. "It has been a pleasure to talk with you."

"Thank you. I will see you soon," Publius said, smiling, for he had disposed of the last hindrance to leaving Jerusalem, Judea, and the discomforts of the province.

At the office of the paymaster, I requested backpay in the amount of 10,000 denarii. I had several times that amount in my account, for Pilate paid me well, and I was careful not to squander a denarius. "I am being transferred to Galilee where I purchased a villa," I said. "Can you have the money ready day after tomorrow?"

"My compliments on your appointment as first centurion. Good fortune in your new assignment," said the paymaster. "Your money will be ready by late tomorrow."

"Thank you. It has been a pleasure to serve at the fortress."

On the morning of the third day, I picked up the leather pouch, heavy with gold. In Publius's office, I exchanged my payment for a document in Aramaic transferring his property to me. I now owned land in Galilee, a lovely villa, large and well built in the Roman style, set among the many springs at the foot of Mount Hermon and the headwaters of the Jordan River, the most beautiful site in all Palestine.

In less than a week, the First Century of the First Cohort was on its way to Galilee. I regretted not making an occasion to visit the castle and Portia, but the relocation required all my attention.

†

On arriving in Capernaum, I settled my century in an old warehouse and commenced its repair. Laborers assisted in the heavy work, and I spoke to them in Aramaic, as they pretended not to understand Greek. There had never been a problem when I was in Jewish raiment. Their resentment was against Roman armor.

I visited the toll stations, inquiring about their operations. The tax collectors were cooperative but responded better when the discussions were in Aramaic. We agreed the soldiers were there to maintain order, not to interfere with the collection of tolls.

A century of eighty men kept order. I assigned half to live in the towns from Sabbath to Sabbath, the other half to remain in Capernaum. We changed guards each Sabbath. The centurion of the century acted as my assistant. I brought with us two horses, two mules, and a baggage cart and placed them with the local livery. I visited the toll stations each day for the first week, then only occasionally.

When I decided to visit my villa, the centurion assumed my duties. Dressed in my Jewish tunic and mantle, I saddled a horse and was on my way by first light. I stopped only to rest and water the horse, arriving at the villa late that afternoon. I rode into the courtyard and found the steward attending the garden.

"Peace be with you. Can we adjourn to a suitable place to talk?"

He led me into a large room, and we sat at a table. I removed my turban, revealing the legionnaire haircut, and laid before him the parchment recording the sale of the property. "My name is Cornelius, centurion, Tenth Fretensis. I have acquired the villa."

"I learned of it some time ago," he said. "Allow me to welcome you to your new home. I know also that you have established a Roman outpost in Capernaum. I welcome your soldiers to Galilee."

"How long were you Publius's steward?"

"For many years. He was a difficult man to serve. He was not comfortable with local people, just his fellow Romans. I have maintained the villa during his absences. Since the sale, I have continued to do so. I am pleased to do whatever you wish."

"Would you continue as my steward?" I asked. "I believe you will find me comfortable with local people, even my fellow Romans."

"Thank you for your confidence. My name is Joshua. I will do my best to please you, but if you become dissatisfied, I will leave."

"Good. I plan to spend two days here. We will inspect the property and list the things you need. If you need laborers, you are authorized to hire them," I said. "Do you have food in the house? I have not eaten since breakfast."

Joshua set out a platter of fresh sliced vegetables, a portion of cheese and some bread, and a container of wine.

"Will you join me?" I said.

"You are very gracious."

As we ate, I inquired about the condition of the house and livestock. Joshua described the repairs and their urgency. The hour grew late.

"On hearing you had purchased the villa, I prepared the bedroom." He led me to a room with two large bunks, one with an elaborate cover. "I hope you rest well," he said, placing a lamp on a small table between the bunks.

In the soft light, I sat on the edge of the smaller bunk. As I extinguished the lamp and lay down, I planned to think about the next day but was immediately asleep.

When I awoke, it was already dawn. I straightened my tunic and hurried to the kitchen.

"I trust you slept well," said Joshua. "We yet have fine wheat your friend Publius brought from Jerusalem. I ground enough for a good serving of porridge."

"I look forward to it. Please join me."

After breakfast, Joshua conducted me about the house. It was in good repair. We next visited the animal pens and the barn, where he gave a brief history of each animal and pointed out low feed stocks. Then we walked among the farm equipment. Publius had purchased fine implements.

"I am well pleased. That is more to your credit than to Publius."

We returned to the kitchen, and Joshua prepared our noon meal. "It is meager fare."

We ate amid cordial conversation. I asked him at length about his background. His family lived near Bethsaida, his father a day laborer working in town. His brothers and sisters had married and lived in the towns around the sea. He had first worked for Publius as a day laborer. As he tolerated his attitude, Publius gave him more authority, employing him to care for the villa while he was away. When he visited, Joshua would hire workers, depending on the needs at the time.

I described to him my duties as a centurion. He inquired about the Jewish garments. I explained I had learned Aramaic and wore them to visit Jewish friends and that it was easier to travel in them.

"When you visited the first time, I suspected you were a Roman soldier. You cannot hide the erect bearing and measured walk. But your deception was good, speaking Aramaic and dressed in well-worn raiment. What confused me most was the respect you showed."

"Your reception was cordial. I merely responded as you did," I said. "Tomorrow we will take a cart and a mule and purchase supplies and feed for the animals. Can we make the trip in a single day?"

"Yes, but it will be a long day. I would like for you to meet the merchants and approve my purchases."

We were both up at first light. During breakfast, I asked Joshua if the attire I wore was suitable.

He laughed. "If you appear dressed as a Jew, it will start many tongues going. Everyone knows a centurion purchased the villa. There are tales of what to expect."

After breakfast, Joshua hitched the best mule to the cart, and we were on our way to Bethsaida. With his encouragement, I took the lead in dealing with the merchants but relied on his judgment as to the quality and the final price. I told him to buy food of his choice for the house.

It was my first experience haggling prices in Aramaic. The

negotiations were cordial, and by the time we completed the list, I felt I had friends among them.

On our way back, Joshua said, "Your demeanor in dealing with the merchants will be the subject of many conversations in the marketplace. You did well."

We arrived at the villa by late afternoon.

The next morning, I reviewed my expectations with him, gave him money to repair the house, and granted him authority to spend it as he thought best. I then returned to Capernaum.

When I entered the city, a large caravan with many travelers was passing through. I was negotiating my horse through the crowd when someone shouted my name. An older man in shabby raiment worked his way toward me.

"Cornelius!" He removed his ragged turban.

"Moshe! What a surprise. What are you doing here? Why are you dressed this way?"

"Cornelius, what a pleasure. What are you doing here?"

I hailed a legionnaire at the edge of the crowd, handed him the reins, and told him to take the horse to the livery and place my pouch in my room. Then I turned and embraced Moshe.

"Let us get away from the crowd," I said. "You must tell me why you are here, dressed as you are."

"I live a few houses away. Follow me."

He wore a tattered tunic and cloak. His fiber sandals were beyond repair. I wondered if he had fallen into misfortune.

Moshe stooped to enter a small structure, a single room built into a corner between two buildings. I followed. A small opening in the roof provided the only light. The air was foul and smelled of stale wood smoke. We sat on a small carpet spread near the fire pit.

"So much has happened," he said. "Long after you left, a fever swept through Tarsus. Many became ill, my wife among them. She died within a week."

I remembered her always in peasant dress attending to duties about the house. "I am saddened to hear of her death. She was always cordial to me. I am sure you miss her."

"Adjusting was difficult. Cyrus and your mother helped. The business prospered, but after she died, I lost interest. Cyrus and I decided to sell and found a group of buyers from Antioch," he said. "From the money, I provided a dowry for my daughter and arranged a marriage in which she was more pleased than I was. I gave a sum to all the stewards and laborers and was able to prevail on Cyrus and Myrrine to take a sum. They moved to the farm, content to live out their years there. They both remain in good health. I kept a small amount for myself, arranged passage to Caesarea Maritima, and joined a caravan to Jerusalem and then to Capernaum. An old friend allows me to use this place. It is exactly what I wanted."

"I am saddened to see you in this state. Why did you not buy a villa?"

"I was tired of problems. I changed. Do you remember Crassus the Elder and his default on the note?"

"Yes," I replied. "It was one of Father's favorite stories."

"I have become Crassus the Elder. This is my home. These garments are all I have. I meet caravans and assist those who appear destitute. Usually I assist someone who pays me, and the amount is sufficient for my needs. Cornelius, my dear friend, I have never been happier. I think about it in the evenings in the lamplight, or in the darkness if I feel the lamp is not necessary."

"Nevertheless, it saddens me to see you in this state."

"Please, I would not exchange places with anyone. I do have one regret, however. I am sorry there is no food in the house."

"I will return to the barracks. I have been away several days and must determine whether there is any matter which needs my attention. I will return as soon as I can."

"As you wish. I will be here."

When I returned, Moshe and I walked to a small market. He ordered only a small quantity of fish and sour wine. Despite the meager fare, it was a fine meal.

I told him all that had happened, that I was now first centurion of the Tenth Legion and assigned to Capernaum. We talked into the night until the proprietor, by his constant attention, indicated it was time for us to leave.

I visited Moshe regularly and found him always in good spirits. I offered many times to assist him, but he would not permit it. I have known old cynics who, like him, found happiness by not being burdened with things. One day, I asked through the door, "May I come in?"

"Please do. I was thinking about something I heard today."

I entered and sat on the carpet opposite him.

"There is a young Pharisee from Nazareth," he said, "attracting large crowds with his teaching. I have heard him several times. He is like Simmias, but his style is different. I find I agree with him. In Nazareth, the council attempted to kill him because of his teaching and expelled his family. His family and some followers are here in Capernaum. It is late in the year, and winter rains will soon be here. They are stonemasons and have nothing. I am concerned about their welfare."

In the dim light from the opening in the roof, I could see Moshe's features. "Have you eaten today?"

"I will eat later. I am concerned about the young teacher."

"Let us go to the market. I have not eaten."

As I stepped out of the room into the sunshine, I took several breaths of fresh air. My eyes required a moment to adjust. At a small market, I purchased some cheese and bread, and we walked to the shore where small groups had gathered. We joined one.

A man said, "Jesus and his friends are staying at Peter's house, sleeping in the courtyard. People are beginning to gather there, and the city council is displeased."

"He was at the sea today," said another. "He withdrew to Peter's house a short time ago."

"He has been coming to the sea for the past few days," said a third. "I am sure he will be here tomorrow. I heard him speak today. He is different from the rabbis."

Withdrawing from the small circle, we went to a secluded place on the shore, sat down, and ate. We dined quite well. I handed Moshe what remained, and he placed it in his pouch.

"Let us return tomorrow," Moshe said. "Jesus has been attracting crowds since spring. You speak Aramaic and can reconcile his teachings in Aramaic with those of Simmias in Greek. I speak Greek, but many of Simmias's words I did not understand. Wear your Jewish raiment."

"I will be here," I said. "Are you ready to return?"

"I will stay awhile. It is pleasant here."

I left him sitting by the sea.

The next morning, when I arrived at Moshe's house, he was sitting on a large stone, basking in the early sunlight. We walked to the shore and joined those congregating there. Soon, excited voices announced the teacher's arrival. It was the young man I saw baptized that day at the Jordan.

On reaching the water's edge, he stepped into a small boat and sat in the stern, facing the people. His voice was clear and firm, loud enough for all to hear. When he began to speak, the crowd fell silent.

His Aramaic was simple, with vivid images and a clear message. The words were everyday words used in simple stories. I was reminded of Simmias. Learn from nature, be at peace with the world, provide for those in need, be good, always tell the truth. I heard nothing in his message that should anger anyone. He had captured the crowd.

It was midday when he stood and stepped from the boat. Moshe and I sat for a while. I had not heard teaching like this since the university.

"Winter will be here soon," Moshe said. "There are about fifteen in his group, too many to stay with Peter. Do you know of a place they might stay?"

"It will be difficult to find a place in Capernaum. My villa can accommodate them, but it is in Caesarea Philippi. The rooms are open and face the courtyard, but there is plenty of space. I can meet with their leader to determine whether the arrangement is acceptable."

"With the hostility in Nazareth and no place to stay in Capernaum, your villa may be the best arrangement. I will see whether there is any interest," Moshe said.

Several days later, I found Moshe seated outside his house. "I thought we might go to the market this afternoon."

"I am agreeable." He stood, and as we walked, he said, "I am pleased to see you. I inquired about the living arrangements of the young teacher and his friends. They have no place to go. I talked with one of their leaders. He is interested in your arrangement and wants to meet with you. The others call him Judas the Sicarii. Do you know of the Sicarii?"

"Yes, they are Zealots who wish to be free of Rome. I have never met one."

"I am fearful if he is Sicarii he may recognize you as a Roman. Will you meet with him?"

"If he is comfortable with me, I am comfortable with him."

"I will arrange a meeting in the courtyard of this market. Wear your Jewish tunic and cloak."

As we entered the marketplace, Moshe said, "Judas is from Judea, north of Jerusalem. He is the only Judean among the group. There is a story that years ago in Jerusalem he killed a collaborator. It may be only gossip, but I thought you should know."

"I will consider it gossip."

On entering the market, the proprietor motioned us toward the small courtyard. I requested a traditional meal, and we dined well. Moshe talked little during the meal. After eating, we walked back to his house. He was right about winter coming. The night breeze had a chill.

Several days later when I returned from changing the men at the various posts, the guard on watch told me an old Jew had requested I meet him at the market before the first night watch. I donned my Jewish clothing and went to meet Moshe. With him was a man taller than I and heavily built, his hair short in the style of the Palestinian laborer and his beard close-cropped. He wore a laborer's woven straw sandals. His eyes were bright and deep set, his face burned dark from days in the sun. Although his raiment was worn, it was clean and added to his striking appearance.

"Cornelius, this is Judas. He would like to know more about the house in Caesarea Philippi."

"Peace be unto you," I said in my best Aramaic. "I am pleased you are here."

"Peace be unto you, also," Judas said. "I know who you are. The people are impressed with the discipline of your soldiers. They also know that you are a friend to Moshe and dress as one of us. You speak Aramaic well. Welcome to Capernaum."

"Capernaum is a good place," I said. "I have found the people friendly and cooperative."

"Moshe says you have a house in Caesarea Philippi that might afford us a place for the winter."

Judas was confident and spoke well. He wore a cloak, so I could not determine whether he carried a sica, but there was no hostility about him. I described the villa.

"We would like to use it through the winter," he said. "I will purchase fabric to cover the openings and provide our own food. What will you require to allow us to stay there?"

"Please, be my guests. You may stay there as long as you wish. I will send word to Joshua, my steward. He is a good man and will help you prepare for the winter. He has a cart should you have baggage."

Judas stood. "You are very kind. If anything displeases you, let me know. We are deeply in your debt. Until we meet again, peace be with you."

"Let me know if either Joshua or I can be of assistance. Peace be unto you."

After Judas departed, Moshe said, "You both were commendable. I was fearful there might be differences."

"Moshe, I would be pleased to have an old friend abide with me. Would you like to spend the winter at Caesarea Philippi?"

"Yes," he said. "I can now look forward to winter."

✝

The number of caravans passing through Capernaum was declining. It was time to plan for winter. I reviewed with my centurion matters to be addressed during my absence, and on the next clear day journeyed to Jerusalem. At the fortress, the food, bath, and sleeping arrangements seemed strange after the summer in Galilee.

The following morning, I waited for Pilate at his office. He was thinner and had aged.

"Cornelius, welcome back. Antipas has not complained. You must be doing well."

"We keep order in the towns," I said, "and the people tolerate us. What are your plans for the winter?"

"When the number of caravans falls to one or two per week, return to Jerusalem. Passover will be our next problem. Did you learn of any Sicarii or Zealots in Galilee?"

"Sicarii and Zealots are in Galilee," I said, "but there have been no incidents involving either group. The only excitement is a young Pharisee with a following."

"Unrest here is between the people and the chief priest and his temple guard. On the tower, we station archers during the religious festivals. Regardless of our security, the Sicarii assassinate one or two collaborators, but it is done discreetly so no one is aware. When we investigate, the one who laments the loudest is probably the assassin."

"What do you hear from Rome?"

"Sejanus insists the Jews pay allegiance to Tiberius," Pilate said. "Tiberius's heirs died mysteriously, and Sejanus is suspected. I am glad to be far from Rome. Please join Claudia, Portia, and me this evening. They will be pleased to see you."

I returned to the barracks, enjoyed time at the bath, and donned my best red tunic. The meal was a simple, delightful affair made more so by pleasant conversation.

"Have you heard any more of John the Baptizer?"

Everyone fell silent. "He is in prison at Machaerus for criticizing

Antipas's marriage," Claudia said. "We do not expect him to be released. I regret I did not hear him again."

Pilate said, "The wives of the officials take great delight in eastern religions. Claudia and Portia enjoy talking with them."

"You never heard him," Claudia said to her husband. "He was a far better teacher than the ones in the academy. Unlike them, he believed what he said."

"I believe you would enter the temple, if the guards would allow you."

Portia turned to me. "Cornelius, what are your plans?"

"For a day or two, I plan to visit friends here at the fortress and in the city, then go to Caesarea to visit friends there. I will return in about a week," I said. "I am saddened to learn of John's imprisonment. He made the hair on the back of my neck bristle with his descriptions of what is in store if we do not do better."

After a few exchanges about John the Baptizer and the circumstances of his arrest, I stood. "It has been a pleasant evening. Thank you for allowing me to join you."

Portia escorted me to the door. "Sejanus had Tiberius's heirs killed. He is in line now to be emperor. I am fearful for Father."

"Your father heard those rumors. He is beginning to doubt Sejanus. If he can maintain order, the issue with Sejanus may resolve itself."

"Cornelius, I have read the manuscripts. Do you know Sophocles's *Antigone*? I have read it so many times I am Antigone. Father is convinced he is right in administering the law, but I see in him the traits which brought low Creon, the king," she said. "I can now read the old manuscripts as well as I could when our Greek teacher was with us."

"I have not forgotten my promise to read the manuscripts. I should have made time for that. I will do better."

Portia laughed softly. "I am not complaining. I enjoy the manuscripts. It passes the time, and each time I read a portion, I see another way to interpret the passage. *Antigone*, though, is different. The words speak to me as though I am saying them. I see Father and myself as the characters. That may be why I am compelled to read it again and again."

"At the university," I said, "I read it many times and also attended presentations. I still caution myself not to be proud or overconfident lest I suffer the same fate as Creon. I would do well to read it again."

"Take my copy. You can keep it as long as you wish."

"I will take it to Galilee."

"Mother and I associate with the wives and consorts of officials, but they are not in touch with the people. It is as though we are on an island in the middle of Jerusalem. In Rome, we knew more about the happenings in Palestine than we do here."

"I plan to visit Jewish friends here and in Caesarea. We will talk when I return."

"I look forward to that."

The following day, I visited the Hillel School. After an exchange of pleasantries, I asked, "Who are the Sicarii and how influential are they?"

The old rabbi said, "They are a group within the Zealots, but they are different. They take action against Jews, especially those who co-operate with Rome. On holy days, when the temple courts are filled, a collaborator mingling with the crowd is in danger. The Sicarii carry a small dagger, the sica. One can kill with it so quickly and quietly no one is aware until the assassin is well away."

"Do you know any Sicarii?" I said.

"We know a number of Zealots. Any one of them may be Sicarii."

Another teacher said, "We spend our lives studying the Talmud. We are not politicians or priests. We associate with everyone, including Zealots and Sicarii. They are people, and people are our friends."

I thanked them for their hospitality and returned to the fortress.

Two days later, after an uneventful trip, I arrived in Caesarea Maritima. Although I was in Jewish dress, the guard at the fortress recognized me and allowed me to pass. I reported to the centurion of the guard, requesting permission to remain at the fortress a few days.

"You are welcome any time. I will prepare the document. It is always good to have you here. Congratulations on becoming first centurion of the First Cohort."

"Thank you. I will pass your congratulations to my men. They are the ones who earned the distinction."

I visited my friend and teacher Enoch the next day in the garden behind the synagogue. "Peace be to your house," I said. "It is good to see you again. I now speak Aramaic more than Greek. Are you still teaching?"

"My Gentile friend, welcome to my house. I have no students at present. The young ones think my teaching is no longer relevant, but I am not offended. There is no place I would rather be."

"You are more in touch with the people," I said, "than the teachers at the Hillel School. Can you tell me what the people think of Pilate and his administration?"

Enoch seated himself on a nearby bench. "Pilate lost his first encounter with the religious Jews when he was ordered to remove the standards from Antonia Fortress. He made friends when he constructed the aqueduct. It was appropriate for the temple to pay for it, to spend some of its wealth to help the people. My young teacher friends, however, believe otherwise." After a moment, he continued. "Herod built Caesarea's aqueducts with the help of Roman engineers. Caesarea and Jerusalem would be much less without them. My young friends still complain about Herod's use of Jewish labor to build them. They do not remember how it was before."

"Can you tell me how Pilate is doing? I have been in Galilee for almost a year. For the people there, Rome is just another burden. They are too poor to support an insurrection. There are Zealots and Sicarii in Galilee, but I do not sense a problem. Am I correct?"

"In Galilee," he said, "the people, especially the religious, live free compared to the people in Jerusalem. Yet when a leader promises to defeat the Romans, the people in Galilee respond more intently, especially if he promises freedom from both Rome and the temple. Galileans resent authority. Most want to live their lives as best they can. As long as the legionnaires do not extort money and no young savior incites them, they will tolerate Pilate. If any trouble starts, though, it will start in Galilee."

"What do you know about the Zealots and the Sicarii?"

"I know they are a party of the people. I never hear of them in Caesarea. I do hear of them in Jerusalem. If Pilate continues his control, the Zealots and the Sicarii will be no problem."

"You have answered my questions," I said. "This has been an enjoyable afternoon. Thank you for your hospitality. May your god bless you as you study the scrolls."

I renewed friendships that evening at the barracks and departed for Jerusalem the next morning. What I had learned of the Zealots and Sicarii and of Pilate and his administration would be good news. At the fortress, my bringing good news added to the enjoyment of time in the bath and the prepared meals.

Late the next morning, I visited Pilate's office.

"Welcome back. I trust your trip went well."

"It was good to visit old friends. The people I talked with believe by continuing your present policies you will prevent any incidents. In Jerusalem, the Zealots and the Sicarii should be no problem. Most of the Jewish working class here are more resentful of the temple than the Roman presence. Those issues are Jewish problems."

"That is reassuring," Pilate said. "This winter, I plan to relocate all cohorts except the First to Caesarea. The next major holy day is Passover in April. We can relocate them here at that time. I need to keep the First here should I need to show my authority." He added, "Please join us for the evening. I am sure you need to return to Galilee."

That evening, after the meal, we discussed news from Rome, then Pilate and Claudia excused themselves. Portia said, "I asked Mother to arrange for us to be together. I knew you would leave for Galilee tomorrow. Father allows me to read the reports from Rome, and Mother and I still write his letters and reports. I also read the manuscripts each day. That is the best part of the day."

"As a Gentile woman, there is not much you can do. It is as though you are a prisoner."

"I am reconciled to that. I picture myself as Antigone, waiting to be sealed in my tomb," she said. "What did you learn about Father?"

"Your father is doing well. The incidents of the standards and the aqueduct are in the past. There are no serious problems ahead."

"I am concerned about Sejanus. Father tries to follow his polices, although he does not agree with them. His friends among the Sanhedrin believe the relationship between Rome and Jerusalem would improve if Tiberius would take a stronger position against Sejanus. I still fear he may become emperor."

"Commander of the guard is an important position, but winter is coming, and even Rome slows during the cold weather. Nothing should happen until next summer."

"Thank you for assurance. I welcome your return for the winter. Mother and I still talk of the trip to the Jordan. You are the only good thing that has happened since coming here. I will accompany you to the entrance. My copy of *Antigone* is there," she said. "It is the story of my life."

"I will read it again, but with greater interest than before."

✝

I arrived in Galilee two days later. My unit had performed well during my absence. I announced when the number of caravans declined we were to return to Jerusalem and for them to prepare to close the operation.

I visited Moshe's house a few days later and found it empty.

After several days of routine inspections, I arranged a trip to the villa. I departed early and arrived in Caesarea Philippi late in the day. As I approached the villa, the slanting rays bathed the landscape in golden light. I stopped the horse. The Temple to Augustus, off to the left, set in a vast expanse of grasses, gleamed in the late last light, and trees showed their color.

At the villa, I found Joshua, Moshe, and others building a wall to close off one of the rooms. Judas, the lower portion of his tunic tied around his waist, said, "We are preparing the room for winter. Jesus has gone to Tyre with most of the disciples. We stayed to enclose the room. Joshua thought you would approve."

"Certainly, I approve. You do fine work."

"By trade, I am a stonemason. We will finish tomorrow."

Joshua, Moshe, and I entered the room. In the center sat a long table with benches. I touched the smooth surface, feeling the adze marks.

"How did you manage this?"

"When Judas said the disciples needed a table, Joshua brought out heavy timbers from the shed. Jesus marked them to make benches and a table long enough to seat eight on a side," said Moshe. "It took some practice to keep the surface level and smooth."

After feeding and watering my horse, I found Joshua in the kitchen preparing two platters of food. Judas invited him, Moshe, and me to join the disciples at the table. They were laborers, hard and lean, with hair close cropped and beards closely trimmed. All wore traditional Jewish tunics. Joshua set the food before us and filled our cups before finding a place at the table. We enjoyed a congenial meal.

When the laughter and conversation quieted, I stood and said in my best Aramaic, "My name is Cornelius, centurion, First Cohort, Tenth Fretensis. My unit is assigned to Galilee. Of all Palestine, Caesarea Philippi is the most beautiful. I am pleased you are here. To know you better, tell me your name and your skill."

"I am Judas from Judea, the hill country north of Jerusalem. My family are stonemasons. We have done well. Our father insisted the sons attend the synagogue each morning, then do a day's work. I joined this group because Jesus is a leader."

"My name is Simon. I worked on a farm. Now I do what Judas tells me. They call me Simon the Zealot."

"I am James. My family are laborers and help build in the towns. Judas works us hard, but we eat regularly. I am called James the Less, because I am small when compared to James, the son of Zebedee."

"My name is Bartholomew. My family helped build houses.

Working for Judas is hard, but I enjoy it. This group can accomplish anything. That is why I am here."

"I, Jude, grew up on the streets of Capernaum and have no family. When I could not find work, I gave up and was waiting to die. Then I heard Jesus. He took me in, and I became one of this group. It has changed me."

"My name is Thomas, and like everyone else except Judas, I am from Galilee. All my family are day laborers. We helped build some of the finest houses in Tiberius. I would follow Jesus anywhere."

Judas stood. "Let us end the day. We will finish the wall tomorrow. Until first light."

Each picked up a thin pallet and unrolled it on the floor. The room was warm, with a single lamp providing sufficient light. Moshe, Joshua, and I retired to the main part of the house.

The next morning, it was yet dark when I awoke. Joshua and Judas were preparing breakfast. I asked if I could assist in completing the wall.

"No," Judas said. "The laborers have worked with me and know what I need."

I joined Moshe and the others seated around the long table. Joshua and Judas carried in platters of food. Again, the meal was noisy and congenial. When all had finished and left the room, Moshe and I sat across from each other.

"Tell me about these men," I said.

"I've known them for almost a year. Jesus is their leader and knows what he wants to accomplish. Judas sees to its completion. He can with little effort have on his hip any man here and throw him to the ground."

"I determined that the first time I saw him. They call him Judas Iscariot—the sica. Does he know he is so called?"

"Yes, but do not be concerned," Moshe said.

"Do they have political aims?"

"In Galilee, people are too poor to be concerned with religious and political parties. Jesus is a Pharisee and takes his religion very seriously. I suspect many of the disciples are Zealots."

"Is Jesus a Zealot?"

"I believe him to be a Zealot in belief but not as committed as Judas. Jesus says he is building a spiritual kingdom."

"Then he is not a revolutionary," I said.

"No, he states very clearly his is a spiritual kingdom. However, Pilate might not understand."

"Man is part of the spiritual order and at the same time owes allegiance to a social system. I do not see a conflict."

"Yes, but you are Greek, and Pilate is Roman," Moshe said. "I am a Jew. If we understood each other, we might agree."

We sat in silence. "Let us talk about work that needs to be done," I said.

"There are freshwater springs above the villa. Judas suggested an aqueduct to bring water into the courtyard to make Joshua's work easier."

We joined Joshua in the main room, and I inquired of him regarding the money available.

"I have used very little," he said, "though Moshe and I do not require much."

"Judas suggested an aqueduct to bring water into the courtyard. If you think the springs provide enough water to justify the effort, purchase the tiles for Judas, but only if he is enthusiastic about the venture. There may be other work which is more important," I said. "Let us join the others."

I spent the day helping clear the area of rejected stones and other clutter. Late in the afternoon, Jesus and the rest of his disciples returned. Like the others, they were clothed in Jewish tunics and neatly groomed. Any one of them might have me on his hip should there be a personal encounter.

Again, Judas invited Moshe, Joshua, and me to join the group for the evening meal. Amidst laughter and talking, all dined well. Judas spoke loudly to gain attention. "This is Cornelius. He is our host and provides us this fine place."

"Welcome to my house. You have made it a fine place. Last evening, those present introduced themselves. Let us do the same tonight."

Jesus stood. "My name is Jesus. My family are stonemasons from Nazareth. When I spoke in the synagogue there, I angered the council, and we are no longer welcome. Thank you for providing us this place to abide the winter."

A giant of a man with a rough demeanor said, "My name is Simon. I have acquired the name 'Peter' since joining this group. My brother Andrew and I are fishermen. The Sea of Galilee has served our family well. We believe Jesus will accomplish great things."

"I am Peter's brother, Andrew. We are from Bethsaida, by the sea. Thank you, Cornelius, for the use of this place. We were becoming a problem for Peter's mother-in-law."

"My name is James, brother to John. Our family is from Bethsaida, and we are fishermen. We have been with Jesus from the beginning."

"I am John, brother to James. Working with this group has given my life meaning, something I never felt as a fisherman."

"My name is Philip," said the next. "I am also a fisherman from Bethsaida. I was a follower of John the Baptizer until he encouraged me to follow Jesus."

The last one stood. "My name is Matthew. I am a collector of tolls in Capernaum. Cornelius, you were the first soldier to use Aramaic to settle an argument. I commend you. It is my pleasure to meet you again." He paused. "I am pleased to be with this group. I am despised by most."

"Thank you for your kind remarks, Matthew," I said. "I remember the incident. You helped settle the issue with the caravan leader. Where did you learn Greek?"

"My father is a Pharisee. He made us attend the synagogue and learn to read the scrolls. Our rabbi had attended a university in Athens, so my father arranged for him to teach all of us Greek. Reading and writing Greek has been a great help."

"Jesus, I am impressed with the men you have selected," I said. "Any one of them would make a good legionnaire."

"They are all good men. I chose them carefully." Jesus smiled. "May I prevail upon your good nature, Cornelius? Mary, my mother, and my sisters are still at Simon's house in Capernaum. Their presence is difficult for everyone. May we convert a room for their use?"

"I would be pleased if you would allow me to do so. We can enclose the last room on this wing. That will allow them more privacy."

"You are generous. Thank you on behalf of my family. I look forward to your friendship. Would you consider joining twelve other good men in an effort to change the world?"

The next morning, Moshe and I joined Judas and the group building the wall to provide the room for Jesus's mother and sisters. The other disciples unpacked their cart, removing a large quantity of badly soiled clothing along with carpenter's tools and equipment.

During the next two days, Judas and his laborers completed the wall enclosing the second open space while the others salvaged and laundered the clothing.

After the evening meal on the second day, Jesus and Judas discussed plans for the winter and agreed it was time to begin preparing houses. In the morning, Judas assigned tasks for the day, then took the cart to Bethsaida and Capernaum to replenish the supplies of food and to acquire building materials.

After breakfast, Moshe and I lingered at the long table with Jesus. "I happened to be at the Jordan the day John the Baptizer baptized you," I said. "As you came out of the water, your countenance glowed as if there was an inner fire. I once witnessed a similar occurrence."

"I would like to hear of it."

"Once when I commanded a unit in the Roman army, it was in battle formation ready to receive an enemy assault. Their leader, a young man, was directly in front of me. About his face was a radiance like pale sunlight. I was distracted and delayed raising my shield to deflect his sword. The legionnaire to my left caught on his own shield the young man's blade and thrust him in the side. Had that thrust not been successful, the young man's sword would have split my crest. I shall never forget the young man's countenance or that day. I never again witnessed a similar radiance until I saw you come up from the water."

"I well remember," Jesus said. "I had dedicated myself to the people of Palestine. When John baptized me, I heard a voice affirming that promise. The young man in your story considered his life a small price to pay for his commitment. For such a person, his life becomes a weapon."

He paused. "After my baptism, I spent forty days in the desert to determine what I must do. The tempter appeared to me in a vision so intense he seemed to be real. He offered me three ways to fulfill my commitment. His first offer was to turn stones into bread. People who are always hungry have lost the desire for bread. This could not satisfy my commitment. The second temptation he offered was spectacular events, such as leaping from the high wall of the temple. But this, too, dulls the senses. This, too, could not satisfy my commitment."

Jesus looked me full in the face. "Then the tempter carried me to a high mountain from which I could see the power and glory of the legions of Rome, the splendor of Athens and the cities of the world, and the hanging gardens of Babylon with their fountains and cool water. With that power, had I twelve committed men, there was nothing I could not do.

"Any one of the ways required I abandon my commitment. The cost would be my soul, a seller in the marketplace haggling for wealth and power, my soul in the cup of the scales. How much would the wrongs of the world weigh in comparison to the weight of my soul?

"I wrestled with this as surely as Jacob wrestled with the angel. And as surely as Jacob prevailed, I renewed my vow to give my life for my people."

We sat in silence. I recalled the warfare raging in my own soul when I pledged myself, without equivocation, to my destiny. No one, not even Simmias, knew my struggle.

"Commitment creates the radiance," Jesus said. "Such commitment is more intense than the desert sun at noonday and death lighter than a wisp of morning fog. For those so committed, there is a radiance."

✝

To this day, I recall the image of weighing one's soul in a balance scale, the soul in one cup and the wrongs of the world in the other. How simple an image—a man attempting to weigh his own soul compared to the weight of wrongs.

Would that I could weigh my own soul. With a set of balance scales in my hand, my soul in one cup and in the other the sum of my life, would the arm of the scale tip in favor of the sum? Would that indicate a profit from the exchange? In the marketplace in Capernaum, in Jerusalem, or in Rome, how much would my soul purchase? If I gain the whole world yet lose my own soul, what is the profit?

✝

The next morning, I gave Joshua money to cover repairs at the villa and set out for Capernaum. There everything was in readiness for the return to Jerusalem.

The march from Capernaum to Jerusalem required two days. After the long ascent from the Jordan River, it was good to see the city and finally to enter the cleanliness of Fortress Antonia.

Pilate and I agreed the First Cohort and two others would spend the winter at Antonia. All others would be relocated to Caesarea. He also discontinued postings in the city and patrols throughout the province. I requested for each legionnaire two extra tunics and a heavy cloak.

"Would Damascus approve instruction in the Greek language for my men? The better they understand each other, the better they perform. In any engagement, the cohort must be of one mind."

Pilate smiled as he rejected my request, but I was pleased to assume the cost and arranged for teachers from the Hillel School to instruct them. Pilate did agree, however, to furnish each legionnaire a tablet and stylus.

When the weather was acceptable, I scheduled long marches, and with the extra clothing, the men handled the colder days. Morale was high. The men were always ready. We were like members of a family. With standards held high, we marched in perfect order through Jerusalem under the sullen gazes of onlookers. We were Rome at its best.

✝

Winter passed without incident. Staying warm and providing food was more important to the Palestinians than contesting the presence of Rome. Each week, I spent pleasant evenings with Pilate and his family.

"Jesus and his group are spending the winter at my villa," I said. "The council in Nazareth, his hometown, expelled him and his family. They had no place to go."

Pilate said nothing.

"I can see why the Sanhedrin is concerned about him. The temple makes religion a burden. Jesus believes both should consider the welfare of the people."

"I am pleased John the Baptizer is in prison," Pilate said. "He enraged the Sanhedrin when he said God could raise up from stones children to Abraham. One can understand their anger." He paused. "Jesus is in Antipas's province. The Sanhedrin believes his popularity will become more than Antipas can handle."

"John and Jesus are religious leaders and offer no political threat. Palestine and the world would be better off if they heeded their message," I said. "Jewish people distrust their leaders because they are more interested in keeping themselves in power than in the welfare of the people."

Claudia and Portia were quiet during our conversation. Some days later, a guard from Pilate's quarters requested I join the two women for the evening meal.

"It is kind of you to come," said Claudia. "My husband is in Caesarea. Portia and I wanted to talk with you."

"It is always a pleasure to be here."

"New gossip suggests Sejanus will become emperor, allowing Tiberius to retire to Capri. Should that happen, Portia and I are fearful Sejanus will force Father to take stronger action against the Jews, especially the Sanhedrin. We wanted you to be aware."

"I've heard the same rumor," I said. "It has long been circulating."

"Father relies more and more on the Sanhedrin," Claudia said. "It sees Jesus and John as revolutionaries. Antipas has John in prison, and his palace guard keeps order in Galilee. The high priest and the Sanhedrin have their own guard in Jerusalem."

"Mother and I were surprised to learn you are allowing Jesus to use your villa," Portia said. "I am amazed Father did not take issue with you the other night."

"Pilate can handle the matter. Jesus is no threat, and John is in prison," I said.

Claudia and Portia talked of the trip to the Jordan, of their own efforts to help those less fortunate, and affirmed their belief that John should not be in prison.

"I have here some money Portia and I have saved. Please give it to Jesus. It would do John no good."

I accepted the money.

Portia said, "Have you had the opportunity to read *Antigone*?"

"I have great difficulty since it has been a long time since I studied old Greek."

Portia laughed lightly. "Do not apologize. I, too, had trouble reading it."

At the barracks, my thoughts returned to Jesus and the disciples. He could, like John the Baptizer, add a political dimension to his message. As a revolutionary, he could build a following with little effort. But I believed the agitators were the Sanhedrin and the Sadducees.

✝

Weekly marches, weapons training, and language classes became routine. The weather turned clear and cold, and I arranged a trip to Galilee. Joshua and Moshe greeted me and shared news about my guests.

"Jesus and the disciples come and go depending on the weather. I often see Mary and her daughters," Joshua said. "You must see the aqueduct. I no longer carry water from the spring."

I turned to Moshe. "Antipas imprisoned John the Baptizer. Do you believe Jesus's message is political?"

"No, he spends his time helping others. Is he in danger of arrest?"

"I am trying to determine that," I said. "Joshua, are Jesus and the disciples here?"

"Yes."

"They will be pleased to see you," Moshe said. "They inquire about you."

Jesus and his disciples were still at the long table. Three lamps provided sufficient light, and a fire warmed the room. We exchanged greetings. Judas left, followed by the other men, except for Jesus.

"They have work to do. Judas must replenish the cart," he said. "Thank you for making the room available for my mother and sisters and the others. I am in your debt."

"I am the beneficiary."

"What brings you so far from Jerusalem with bad weather always threatening?"

"I am a friend to Pilate. While he has been prefect, there has been little unrest, even in Galilee," I said. "Pilate relies on the Sanhedrin, but orders from Rome require Jews recognize Tiberius as god. Trying to please both Rome and the Sanhedrin is a problem."

Jesus said, "I understand."

"Pilate is concerned groups like yours and John the Baptizer's cause unrest, that you object to the Roman presence and also challenge religious leaders."

"Your concerns are ill-founded," Jesus said. "I have no quarrel with the Sanhedrin. But religious leaders in Jerusalem should be concerned whether their people have enough to eat. In Galilee, the Roman presence is not oppressive. There have been no incidents of your men abusing the people. My purpose is to live at peace with all men and to assist those who cannot provide for themselves."

"That is what I have reported to Pilate. But some of your men appear to be Zealots and some Sicarii. How do they fit into your effort to live at peace with everyone?"

"A man should be free to choose his belief," Jesus said. "All of the disciples understand my teaching, and our actions are peaceful. Judas and others carry the sica as a warning to those who prey on the defenseless."

"I attended Jewish schools to learn Aramaic but need further instruction," I said. "Would you help me?"

"I would welcome such a session. Let us meet tonight after the evening meal."

That night, a fire burned brightly, and lamps sat at each end of the table. The room smelled of burning olive oil and wood smoke. Moshe and I seated ourselves with the disciples.

"Matthew is best in Greek and Aramaic. Judas is also knowledgeable in both."

I addressed Jesus in Aramaic. "One day as you returned to Capernaum, a paralytic and his friends pleaded for a cure. You said his sins were forgiven. The Scribes accused you of blasphemy. Then you told the paralyzed man to walk and that you, indeed, had the power to grant him forgiveness. Who gives you this authority?"

"Cornelius, I have seen you give the order to form an array, and immediately from the crowd appear a number of legionnaires, some in Jewish raiment, who do as you command. How did you know the legionnaires would form an array?"

"By my authority," I said. "But yours comes from a higher source."

"Authority is authority."

"Most Pharisees believe in the resurrection. Does that mean there is a part of me which will survive my death and exist in another world?"

"We do not believe we will exist in another world. We will be new," Matthew said.

"Your memories, the things you have learned, all the things you hoped for, you will remember none of these?"

"We believe the breath of life returns to God who gave it," he said. "It will not remember our life here. We will be new, whatever form it may take."

"The Greek word *soul* describes that which identifies us and makes us different from all others. It is our spiritual identity and transcends our death. Does the Aramaic *breath of life* mean the same?"

"It is very close," Matthew said, "but I do not believe my *breath of life* will recall my experiences here."

"Moshe," I asked, "what is the difference between those words?"

"I assumed they had the same meaning."

"I have used the Greek word *soul* to express *breath of life*," said Judas. "I know now that it means something different to you."

We exchanged good wishes for the evening. Moshe added wood to the fire, then went to his room. On the table, a single lamp burned. In the soft light, I longed for someone to talk with. I missed being with Portia and wished I had remembered to bring her copy of *Antigone* to Caesarea Philippi.

The next morning, after Joshua cleared the table, I said to Moshe, "Last evening, I learned more about Jewish religion than when I studied Aramaic. It is unfortunate our discussions are not written so we can study them."

"You could record the comments in Greek, and I could record them in Aramaic," he said.

"Yes, let us begin a chronicle. I will bring materials on my next trip."

The two of us spent the day assisting Joshua. When we finished, I stood in the courtyard, looking to the south. The white marble of the temple contrasted sharply with the dull gray of the countryside. Sunlight reflected from the surface of a spring. I longed for the rich smell of deep woods.

After the evening meal, I said to Jesus, "I heard you caused a blind man to see by making a poultice and telling him to wash his eyes at a spring. If you could restore his vision, why did he need a poultice?"

"There were a number of issues at hand that day," Jesus said. "The Scribes alleged the man had been blind from birth as a result of the sins of his parents. Another issue was the faith of the blind man, whether he believed I could cure him. When I asked if he truly wished to be cured, he assured me he did. I mixed spittle and clay as he believed the mixture would cure him. His belief, his faith, assisted the cure as much as my authority."

Jesus invited another question. I chose Aramaic words to convey the Greek intent I sought. "Are we free to live our lives, or are we, like the blind man, governed by an outside force?"

"God knows what is to happen to us, but we are free to make the decisions and live our lives as best we can," said Matthew.

"I believe just as you do," I said. "But when something which happened today was the result of a decision I made years ago, was I really free years ago when I made the decision?"

"Freedom is a state of mind," he said. "Liberty allows us to say and to do what we wish. If you are free to make decisions, then you are free. If you are prevented from carrying out decisions, your liberty is restricted."

"Natural law gives order to the world. If freedom is the ability to make decisions in keeping with natural law, then we are free," I said. "Judas, what do you think?"

"How to keep the cart filled is easier to ponder than whether I am free or not free to fill it. One day I may fill the cart to my disadvantage. I can then speculate whether I was free to do so."

"Moshe, what do you think?" I asked.

"I agree with everything that has been said. I can see no contradictions, yet there must be contradictions."

The following morning, I returned to Jerusalem and assured Pilate that Jesus was no threat to his administration.

Winter settled in. I joined my cohort in marches and weapons drills. Their Greek lessons progressed well. I set aside time each morning to study *Antigone*. The meals with Pilate's family were the brightest events in my routine.

On a trip into the city, I purchased writing materials, and on my next trip to Caesarea Philippi, Moshe and I each began a chronicle of Jesus's teachings, recording them in Aramaic and Greek.

The days grew longer, and the land showed traces of green. I had mastered old Greek sufficiently to read *Antigone* and follow the dialogue. Pilate moved the cohorts to Antonia Fortress, and Jerusalem began to fill with pilgrims. To assure order during Passover, Pilate posted two legionnaires on each street crossing.

Assassination of collaborators continued. Pilate regretted the loss of his informers but made no investigation. He seemed to be accepting Sejanus's policies and was weary of the contempt for Rome shown by the stiff-necked religious leaders who would not accept defeat. At times, I shared his weariness.

The number of caravans passing through Galilee increased, and Jesus was attracting large crowds. Pilate again assigned a century of my cohort to Antipas's Galilee. We prepared our base and posted guards there. I assigned four legionnaires armed with shortened hastae to stand at the crowd's edge.

Each day I studied the manuscript of *Antigone*. Creon the king was brought low when he obeyed the laws of the state rather than doing what was right. I understood why the drama enthralled Portia.

When Jesus was preaching in Capernaum or a nearby city, Moshe attended and chronicled his experiences in Aramaic. I translated them into Greek. Late in the summer, Herod Antipas beheaded John the Baptist at the request of his wife's young daughter. I wondered if Antipas's palace guard was a threat to Jesus. The guard was no match for my legionnaires, but Antipas had been clever enough not to engage even the smallest element of my century.

Late one afternoon, Moshe and I sat by the sea. The sun bathed the opposite shore and upland in a soft rose. "Why is Antipas such a poor governor?" I asked.

"His father, Herod the Great, did more than anyone to reestablish the kingdom of David," Moshe said. "As a young man, in spite of his own bad decisions, with Rome's help, he became the most powerful man in Palestine. In Jerusalem, he restored the temple Pompey destroyed when he captured the city. He built the Fortress Antonia and the castle. In Caesarea Maritima, he constructed the harbor, the fortress, and a castle. He also assisted with the two aqueducts bringing water into the city. He built the castle at Machaerus and the fortress at Masada. For the people of Palestine, it was not the best of times, but it was better than today. In his old age, he became a sick man and a tyrant. All the good he did was lost when his sons inherited his tyrannical ways."

He paused. "Antipas lives under Rome's wing, as did his father, and believes he is due the power granted by Rome. He has no concern for people. They are *am ha-aretz*, filth of the earth, and are to serve him. Polite people do not use the Aramaic word *am ha-aretz*, but use the Greek *hoi polloi*," Moshe said. "Herod the Great killed anyone who threatened his rule, even family members. Antipas is the same. He fears for his life, and that makes him a prisoner in his own palace."

"He is Jewish, yet fearful of his own people?"

"If the people are incited to rise up against him, they possess unlimited power. That is why he killed John."

"I heard John was beheaded to satisfy the whim of his wife."

"That is gossip among old men in the marketplace. The poorest laborer in Galilee or Perea may have no food for tomorrow, may only possess one tunic, yet he is more content than Antipas. Only those who are free from fear can be happy."

As summer passed, Jesus continued to attract large crowds and anger religious leaders. In Jerusalem, the Scribes and the Pharisees joined in their effort to trap him. In Galilee, they confronted Jesus only to have their challenge turned against them. Moshe said the Sadducees were sending delegations to the city.

Late that summer, I had accompanied a unit of legionnaires to the north of Capernaum, visiting the toll booths along the way, and received a report of an incident involving a delegation from Jerusalem. I returned to find Judas in the guard room, bound. His tunic was badly torn and streaked with blood. He had cuts and bruises on his head and arms. I ordered the guard to free him.

"What happened?"

"It had been a good day with everyone in good spirits until a group of Scribes from Jerusalem challenged Jesus, trying to provoke a fight."

"You have been one who stepped in to prevent such encounters."

"Today was different. The Scribes surrounded Jesus, separating him from the rest of us, and challenged him on what he had said."

"What did he say that angered them?"

"He said all Jews were Abraham's children and his teaching would make them free."

"That seems a small issue to provoke a confrontation."

"When Jesus tried to reconcile differences, they grew angrier. I stepped inside the circle and stood at Jesus's back. One of the Scribes then shouted, 'We are born of Abraham; we are Abraham's seed. We were not born of fornication.' I considered using my sica but felt pity for these men. But when they began casting stones at us, I observed the law of the Scribes, 'a bruise for a bruise.' A centurion arrested me."

I looked at the centurion in charge. "Is it true what this man says?"

"Yes. If I had not intervened, this man might have killed one or more."

"You were fortunate not to be injured, Judas. Had you killed one of them, I would have had to detain you and report the matter."

"They were as little children playing a man's game. They did not have the ability to stone a man," he said. "One or two protected by the centurion may brag about the lesson they taught some rowdy Galileans."

"Was Jesus injured?"

"No, we deflected most of stones. He may have some bruises. I regret he heard the accusation. I know it is whispered about."

"There is water and wine in the back if you would like to cleanse the bruises."

"It is strange, but I now regret I dealt so harshly with them," Judas said. "They spend their lives in the darkness of the temple, studying old scrolls by lamplight, discussing whether a mark is a jot or a tittle and speculating as to the intent of the Scribe who made it. For them, the world is a strange place filled with crude people. They seldom see it in sunlight and reject those of us who work for our bread. They should remain in the dark sanctuary and not venture into the bright, wonderful, and raucous world which you and I love so much."

"Judas, we will soon eat our evening meal. It is sparse, but you are welcome. Will you remain here tonight?"

"No. I must return, as the others will be concerned. Thank you for the manner in which you resolved the issue."

I loaned him a Jewish tunic and a pair of sandals, for he was barefooted. As we walked through the guard room to the outside door, he said, "I am anxious to hear what Jesus will say. The Scribes intended to kill him. Until we meet again, may peace be on your house."

Judas then left for the sea.

With the onset of cooler weather, fewer attended the occasional gatherings to hear Jesus. Galilee gradually settled in for the winter, and Pilate recalled the century to Jerusalem. Another year had passed without major incident.

My cohort was again selected to spend the winter at the Antonia Fortress, the others returning to Caesarea Maritima. I resumed the training and employed a teacher to conduct classes in Aramaic. My men began referring to me as "Mother Cornelius."

I reported to Pilate. "It is good to have you back. I was apprehensive about Galilee with Jesus attracting such large crowds and Antipas executing John the Baptizer. Claudia and Portia were greatly saddened. If Jesus continues to attract such crowds, I am fearful of what may happen. The Sanhedrin and the high priest are also concerned," he said. "But to more pleasant matters. Please join us tomorrow evening. There is news from Rome."

When I arrived, Pilate, Claudia, and Portia were in the large reception room reclining on cushions, facing each other. "Tiberius discovered the plot by Sejanus to become emperor," he said. "He believed Sejanus was the chief conspirator and ordered he be executed and his body thrown to a mob. His wife and their two children were also killed. Other conspirators were executed without a trial. Tiberius affirmed his policy to treat people of the provinces as Roman citizens. I regret the loss of Sejanus as an advocate but welcome the affirmation of Tiberius's policy."

Pilate looked at me. "My work here will now be easier. I can allow the Sanhedrin and the chief priest to assist in administering Judea. Galilee is in Antipas's tetrarch, and he is as anxious as anyone to keep peace with Rome."

"Cornelius, you knew Antipas executed John the Baptizer?" said Claudia.

"Yes. John had a large following along the Jordan to the south of Galilee, but Antipas must have known there was little danger."

"The loss of John is felt by people I know in Jerusalem," she said. "The wives talk of another teacher in Galilee. He attracts more people than John and heals those who are sick. Portia and I would like to hear him, but Galilee is as far as Rome."

"What do you know about him?" Portia said.

"He is like John. He and his disciples spend their time helping people who cannot help themselves. Some women here in Jerusalem send him money."

"The religious leaders see him as a threat, although he is a good Pharisee and a good Jew," I said. "If all the people were like him and his disciples, Judea and Galilee would be better places."

I glanced at Pilate. He knew Jesus was using my villa. I would have to convince him it was prudent for me to have him there if he posed a threat to Rome.

Portia accompanied me to the door. "I see in Father the traits in Creon. He was greatly distressed to hear about the execution of Sejanus without a trial and the murder of his wife and children. I am not sure Father will be able to choose what is right over following the law."

I bade her good evening and walked slowly to the barracks. Should I travel to Galilee to warn Jesus? And how could I continue to be friends to both Pilate and Jesus without betraying one of them?

I decided to visit the Hillel School. "Do you expect any problem in Galilee next spring with Jesus and his followers?"

"He is a Pharisee and keeps the law as he sees it. We find no fault in his message," said one of the older teachers. "But the Shammai believe the chief priest should arrest him."

"Are the differences between Jesus and those who oppose him religious only?"

"We see it as a religious issue. As long as he remains in Galilee, there will be no problem. If he and his disciples come to Jerusalem for Passover next spring and he teaches or heals in the city, there will be trouble. Pilate's soldiers will take charge."

"Is there a political element in Jesus's teachings?" I asked.

"Certainly, everything he says can be political, but the people in Galilee are too poor to support a political movement."

"Thank you for your comments," I said, "and for teaching at the fortress. My men learning Aramaic might lessen the chance a small disturbance grows out of control."

I decided to delay traveling to Caesarea Philippi until the weather improved.

✝

In the winter, it was always a joy to pass by the Sea of Galilee and journey up the river. There was a stillness about the land that reminded me of the deep woods at the farm. In the courtyard of my villa, I turned my horse into an empty stall and fed him. I joined Joshua and Moshe in the main house, warming myself by the fire while Joshua prepared our meal.

"It is good to see both of you again. Are things going well?" I asked.

They both assured me all was well.

"Are the disciples here now?"

"Yes," said Joshua. "They have been here more this winter than last and spent many long hours around the table."

"In Jerusalem, we are preparing for Passover and summer. Pilate is relying on the Sanhedrin for information about Jesus. The religious groups may be more hostile toward him."

"Jesus is determined to continue his teaching," Moshe said. "I see in him the leader promised to Israel. We will soon know whether he is the promised one, the Messiah."

"If the Scribes, the Pharisees, or the Sanhedrin start a disturbance, Jesus will have both the temple guard and Pilate's legionnaires upon him," I said as I withdrew to my room.

In the morning, I spoke with Jesus and his disciples. "Pilate believes there will be trouble if you enter Jerusalem during Passover. You say your kingdom is a spiritual one, but the religious leaders accuse you of inciting the people. What are your plans?"

"My kingdom is spiritual, but we will lighten the burden laid upon the people. There is no affront to Pilate. He should listen to the people," said Jesus. "As for my plan, I am not absolutely certain of it."

"Are you and the disciples going to enter Jerusalem this Passover?"

"It is what we must do."

"The Sanhedrin, the chief priest, and others will try to provoke you to make a statement against Rome. To keep order, Pilate plans to increase his presence. If you will assist us, Pilate and I can help you."

"I see you are committed to what you are called to do," Jesus said.

At our next meeting, I said to Pilate, "Jesus and his disciples plan to enter the city during Passover. They are committed and disciplined. It will be the Sanhedrin or the religious leaders who provoke a confrontation. Keep me aware of reports from them so that I may verify my own information. Can the Tenth Legion control Jerusalem?"

"If we disperse wisely," Pilate said, "we can control the city. The Sanhedrin promises the temple guard will assist. Relocating the two legions is not necessary."

"It is early to plan for the summer," I said, "but I assume you will assign me to Galilee. With two centuries, I can maintain order there. I need thirty sets of Jewish garments, including turbans. I also need fifty shortened hastae."

He did not respond. I said, "At the toll stations, I will keep the same number as before. Legionnaires in Jewish dress will be in the streets and in Jesus's crowds. They speak Aramaic and can handle any problem."

"According to the Sanhedrin," Pilate said, "Jesus already is a problem. What you report is quite different. If you are agreeable to going again to Galilee, I will arrange it. I can give you as many men as you need. I will place an order for the Jewish clothing and the fifty shortened hastae. I rely on your report."

My chest tightened at Pilate's statement. After the meeting, I visited the teacher of Aramaic, attending the remainder of the session. When it was over, we discussed the group's progress. I requested he continue his teaching until Passover and then provide me with a list of the fifty best students.

I returned to the barracks. Lying on my bunk, I reviewed all that had happened and concluded the plan was sound. I was ready for Passover.

✝

Winter passed, and the land was green. I made a trip to Caesarea Philippi. I met with Jesus and his disciples and inquired about their plans for Passover. They were to spend Passover with friends in Bethany and had decided not to make a formal entry into the city. I requested when they entered as a group to let me know. I was fearful the temple guard might attempt to arrest them.

Pilate moved the cohorts to Jerusalem. Everything was ready for Passover. Jerusalem filled with pilgrims. Jesus and his disciples entered Jerusalem on several occasions, but as we knew the time and the route they were to take, we posted additional legionnaires. Passover week was without serious incident.

On Wednesday, however, for me there was an incident. Hoping to reduce the number of assassinations, Pilate ordered the centurion of the guard to go into the lower city and bring in for questioning any suspected Sicarii. By early afternoon, the unit returned with a number of suspects, Judas among them.

The centurion questioned each suspect and released some. When questioned, Judas asked to speak with me. The centurion sent an aide requesting that I report to the guard room. When I arrived, he explained that his unit had brought in a number of Sicarii and then added, "When I questioned this one, he requested your presence."

"Thank you for summoning me, Centurion. I know this man. He is a friend. Allow me to talk with him."

"Certainly, but I will dismiss him. He is my responsibility."

"I will do so. May I use the adjoining room?"

The centurion nodded assent.

I motioned Judas into the room and followed. After closing the door, I pointed to a bench and moved a chair to its front. He was dressed in his worn tunic and fabric sandals. He had no cloak, so his sica was visible. I was surprised he was detained, for his appearance was inconsistent with that of the Sicarii.

"What were you doing in the lower city?" I asked.

"I have friends there, some are Sicarii. The legionnaires picked up a number of us. They were speaking Greek, and I was fearful of execution."

"Pilate is attempting to reduce the number of assassinations. I can attest that you are from Galilee and here for Passover. There is no danger of execution."

"I was fearful the centurion would associate me with the assassination of a mercenary. Gratus was prefect of Judea, so it was before Pilate. At the time, I worked in Jerusalem as a stonemason and had joined a group of young Sicarii. One night, four of us were out most of the night and had too much wine. On our way home, we encountered an acquaintance who had been with the legion in Damascus. My friends considered him more Roman than Jewish and provoked a fight. Each of us drew our sica only to find he had a knife. As he engaged my friends, I was able to get behind him and bring him to the ground. I held him while my friends cut his throat. Two of my friends, however, were cut seriously enough they died there in the street. My other friend was cut but was able to escape. I was not injured."

I was surprised but said nothing.

Judas bowed his head. "I had never seen a man die from a knife wound. He died in my arms as I held him to the ground. He showed no fear and fought as desperately as we did. If I had not put him on the ground, he would have killed us all."

Judas continued, "Gratus, the prefect, concluded the mercenary had killed the two Sicarii who had killed him. I sought out the mercenary's wife. He was the father of three young children, two sons and a daughter. I explained to the wife what had happened, although I did not tell her my part. With her approval, I requested a prominent Pharisee for whom I had worked to recover his body. I paid for his burial."

Judas glanced at me, only to lower his eyes again. "For a number of years, I worked very hard to be assured work and to have money to give to her. The boys are now with the legion in Damascus, and the daughter is married. The wife lives with her daughter and takes care of the grandchildren. I visit her when I am in Jerusalem."

Judas stood. "I wanted you to know of the incident before you talked with the centurion. He may inquire about it. I am willing to do what must be done. The punishment may be crucifixion."

I stood. "Pilate is attempting to reduce the number of assassinations. There is no record of the killing of the mercenary. I will assume responsibility for you."

Judas again bowed his head, his countenance falling. "You are the only one who knows of this. A day seldom passes that I do not recall the incident. We knew the man. He was not an adversary." Judas raised his head and said, "Later, in Jerusalem, I met Jesus. I felt he could help me lay the regret aside. It has helped, but I still regret the incident."

I knew Pilate was to bring in some Sicarii, and I also knew there was no record of assassinations.

As we walked toward the door, I said, "Allow me to speak for you. The centurion will question you in Greek."

As Judas and I approached, I said, "Centurion, I know this man well. He is from Galilee and was visiting friends in the lower city. He will return to Galilee after Passover. He is a Sicarii but from Galilee. He is not an assassin. With your permission, I will assume responsibility for his conduct while he is in Jerusalem."

He said, "I release the suspect into your hands. He is free to go. We are looking for assassins."

I walked with Judas to the entrance. As we parted, I said, "Judas, you did well to call me. If you had admitted killing the mercenary, however, things might have ended differently. Enjoy the trip to Bethany."

Judas replied as he turned toward the street, "I was fearful of what was in store for me. It is with great joy I journey to Bethany. Peace be upon your house."

I watched Judas disappear into the crowded street.

✝

Pilate relocated three cohorts to Caesarea Maritima and left seven in Jerusalem, including the First Cohort, which he assigned to Herod's Palace, with two centuries scheduled for Galilee.

I asked each of the best students of Aramaic whether he was agreeable to assignment to Galilee. Each was planning to volunteer. I selected the First Century and the fifty on the teacher's list, unless they happened to be in the First Century. I asked the centurions of the other centuries to select five good men to complete the unit. They were as fine a group as I ever led.

In Galilee, we established the post. I divided the unit into two sections, one to provide security for the toll stations and the other in Jewish dress to mingle with the crowds.

Jesus attracted large crowds, and the town councils had difficulty keeping order. He cooperated by teaching from a boat just off the shore and with frequent withdrawals to the countryside. The crowds grew larger, and the issues more severe.

Delegations from Jerusalem were attending the sessions, their sleek appearance in sharp contrast to the hoi polloi. When a delegation created a disturbance, a legionnaire with the shortened hasta would confront the leader, requesting he soften his speech. On those few occasions when the leader was hesitant, the legionnaire placed the point of the hasta against some part of the leader's body.

Groups normally hostile to each other were cooperating in their effort to trap Jesus into a confrontation with Pilate. I could handle the confrontations in Galilee if Pilate could handle the issues in Jerusalem.

As long as Jesus was in Antipas's tetrarch, I remained in Capernaum. There were occasional disputes, but my legionnaires were becoming better at settling them. When Jesus journeyed to other areas, I visited the villa.

I made occasional trips to Jerusalem to review the situation in Galilee as reported by the Sanhedrin and others. Pilate was apprehensive. The Sanhedrin and the chief priest accused Jesus of sedition. I assured Pilate there was no sedition in Galilee, but I was never able to convince him Jesus was not a revolutionary.

The summer passed without incident, and the number of caravans declined. My unit returned to Jerusalem. Pilate continued to rely on the reports form the Sanhedrin, although they were false or at least overstated. After my report, Pilate invited me for the evening meal.

Being with his family was a pleasure, for the welcome and cordiality reminded me of home. Pilate was showing the strain of his office. Claudia was gracious as the wife of the prefect, and Portia, dressed in a plain stola, was as attractive as ever. After the meal, we talked of Jesus.

"During all the time I have served here," Pilate began, "Jesus is the first revolutionary to remain free after he came to my attention. I hoped the temple guard or the Sanhedrin by now would have arrested him. It is dangerous to let him continue."

"All summer," I said, "the Sanhedrin and the chief priest and others challenged Jesus. He states his kingdom is a spiritual kingdom. The Sanhedrin reads sedition into that. On my next trip to Galilee, I will make sure I have not misinterpreted Jesus's teaching."

Pilate said, "We have all winter to resolve the matter. But whether or not you are correct, the Sanhedrin considers him guilty. There will be serious problems ahead if the Sanhedrin insists on his guilt."

The conversation then turned to news from Rome.

It was late when Pilate stood, with Claudia and Portia also standing, each expressing a benediction. Portia accompanied me to the entrance. I felt the warmth of her hand on my arm. She said, "Be careful. Father relies on the Sanhedrin and collaborators. They have convinced him Jesus incites the people to revolt against Rome."

I hesitated to reply, and Portia continued, "Father is hopeful Tiberius will recall him to Rome and award him a position in the government. An incident would jeopardize that. You see the issue as it is in Galilee. Although it may be the truth, sometimes it does not prevail."

"It is important that I know what is happening. We discussed how your father might react. After studying *Antigone*, I see myself facing similar issues."

"With the death of Sejanus," Portia said, "Father is more at ease. At least the issues are local and do not involve conflicting policies set in Rome. I would like to hear your interpretation of the drama, however. It was very real for me."

"With so many groups intent on killing Jesus," I said, "I feel Jesus and I are actors in a Greek drama pursued by the Furies. I am moving toward a disaster I cannot avoid."

Her hand rested on my arm, and I grasped it in my right hand and held it, then said, "Peace be unto your house." I released her hand and turned toward the barracks.

†

The cohort settled into winter quarters as Pilate's personal guard. The Aramaic lessons continued on a voluntary basis. After the winter routine had established itself, I arranged a trip to Galilee.

When I left Jerusalem, it was a clear day, but by the time I reached the villa, a cold, light rain was falling. Joshua took the horse to the stall to wipe him dry. I joined Moshe by the fire in the main room. Joshua joined us and prepared a meal for me.

Moshe said, "Jesus and his disciples returned a few days ago. They had been to Jerusalem, spending time in Perea on the return trip. They are more serious now. All believe Jesus is the Messiah, yet he refers to his kingdom as a spiritual one."

"Let me end my day," I said. "We will talk with him tomorrow. Joshua, thank you for caring for the horse. You are indeed a good steward."

The next morning when I arose, it was much colder, and a light rain was yet falling. After breakfast, Moshe and I went to the disciples' room.

After jovial exchanges in rough Galilean style, I sat across from Jesus. Moshe sat next to me. I said, "I never thanked you for your assistance during the last Passover. With it, Pilate was able to keep your entries peaceful. It was a joyous occasion."

Jesus replied, "We were very much aware that Pilate was in control. It was also a good summer."

"You and your disciples did enjoy a good summer. I have difficulty believing so many people can congregate in one place and there not be disputes. You handled the delegations well."

Jesus nodded but did not speak.

"As you know, I report to Pilate," I said. "The reports of the Sanhedrin, the religious groups, and his collaborators accuse you of inciting the people to revolt against Roman authority. Although I assure him otherwise, Pilate is beginning to accept the reports. I am here to verify my report. Is there a political aspect to your kingdom?"

"Our prophets of old," Jesus said, "promised someday there would be a leader who would establish the kingdom of David. I believe I may be the one, although I still have difficulty with the concept of Messiah." Jesus paused and then said, "There is a political aspect to my kingdom. Our complaint is against the religious leaders. The temple is a burden to the people. That is the political aspect of my kingdom. I have no complaint against Rome. Both the Sanhedrin and the chief priest fear a confrontation. By going to the temple in Jerusalem for the last two Passovers, I hoped to assure myself of my mission, but I yet have doubts."

I understood Jesus's dilemma. "Last year, you spent most of Passover week in Bethany. What will you do this year?"

"We discuss that daily. I will be arrested if I enter Jerusalem. The leaders of all the groups conspire to kill me. It will be dangerous for us to go, but we are committed to doing so. We plan to make a public entry into Jerusalem in keeping with the prophesies of old, entering by the Golden Gate. For me, this has become part of the commitment I made with the baptism at the Jordan."

"Your comments are well received. The purpose for my being here has been accomplished. I understand your dilemma. By the end of our days, each of us will know whether he has been faithful. Until then, we do what we can." I stood and addressed the group. "I will tell no one of your plans. I do assure you, however, Pilate will keep order when you enter the city."

Jesus stood. "Thank you, Cornelius." He then motioned for me to come nearer. As I leaned toward him, in a whisper he said, "Tonight after the session, may I join you in your house? My heart is indeed heavy."

I replied in like manner. "Certainly, I will be pleased to see you." I then said to the entire group, "Until we meet again, may peace be upon your house."

I stepped into the darkness followed by Moshe. It was raining and much colder. We entered our room to find Joshua dozing.

I said to him as he stood, "Place more wood on the fire. Jesus is to visit us. Leave the lamps on the table."

Joshua placed several pieces of wood on the fire, and he and Moshe excused themselves. I sat close to the brazier and pulled my cloak tightly around me. Just beyond the glow of the fire and the lamps, darkness and cold hung like a pall.

When Jesus entered, I stood and pointed to a stool close to the brazier.

After Jesus had seated himself, he said, "Thank you for allowing me to visit. I know you will soon depart for Jerusalem, and I might not see you for some time."

"I am pleased you are here. I plan to leave in the morning, but only if the rain has ceased."

Tightening his robe, he said, "I have difficulty believing that I, a good Pharisee, am sitting in the house of a Gentile, not only a Gentile but a Roman soldier, speaking Aramaic, as friend to friend."

"You are very gracious. I am much richer from the presence of you and your group."

"During the past summer," Jesus said, "the hostility of the delegations grew. I am amazed you prevented an incident. There were orders for my arrest and the arrest of my disciples, but your presence prevented any attempt. Each time we visited Jerusalem, it was more dangerous. The confrontations during the coming Passover and in Galilee will increase."

I nodded in agreement but did not speak.

"I must talk with someone who understands my circumstances," Jesus said. "I am committed to my mission. Occasionally, however, I sense great fear—fear of arrest and execution and fear of failure. Of the friends I have, you are the only one who might understand."

I was not surprised by Jesus's comments, although I was surprised at his voicing them so openly. I said, "My good friend, I, myself, have sensed those same fears. I have also sensed failure in my mission. If it will assist, I am pleased to talk about those things."

"I often wondered whether you ever felt fear or sensed failure. Your demeanor never revealed such feelings."

"When last I discussed such matters," I said, "it was with a teacher at the university. I had known him for many years and found his teachings to be true."

"I never had such a teacher," Jesus said. "The rabbi in Nazareth did the best he could, but he was not experienced at facing controversy. A room in his house with an old cabinet holding the Torah was the synagogue. Many times, there were fewer than ten men present to conduct the service. The city council also met there. He was among those who expelled me and my family from Nazareth."

"From my teacher," I said, "I learned that everyone coming into this world has a purpose. To help us succeed in that purpose, we are born with a desire to be a member of a family, to be part of a community, and to use our skills to make it a better place. We are born to believe there is order and purpose in the world and to enjoy its beauty. Occasionally, I have doubts, but something always happens to assure me the teaching is true."

"I believe what you say," Jesus said, "but never heard it so well stated."

"When we discover our purpose, there are signs we have found it. There is genuine contentment in committing ourselves to the task. Someone helps us along the way or says something that reassures us we are moving in the right direction."

Jesus nodded. "I have found that to be so."

"Your life is proof. Your mother told me about your birth and the flight into Egypt when Herod killed the young boys of Bethlehem. Many people at great risk assisted her and Joseph and you. That assistance was not by chance. It was part of the plan. You have mentioned your baptism and sensing its approval. That also affirmed the plan. What you have accomplished and all you do to help the people of Palestine show you are doing what you were destined to do."

I glanced at him. Jesus was staring into the fire. I continued. "Some acts were significant to each of us. The one I remember most, however, was my good friend who gave his life to save mine when I failed to perform my duty. Because of these acts, I am compelled to pursue my plan, for the assistance was provided at so great a price."

Jesus still gazed into the fire. I said, "Occurrences in your life which I know about tell me that you were born to be who you are and to do what you are doing. As strong as the signs are in my own life, they are much stronger in yours."

Jesus looked at me. "I understand what you are saying, and it reassures me of the plan for my life. But what of the fear of death and the fear of failure? Those fears weigh heavily upon me."

"Such fears are common when waiting for an encounter," I said. "I can assure you, when it occurs, you will be so engrossed in performing your task you will not think of the outcome. I am sure in past encounters you did not think of fear and failure. And you will not think of them when you face the encounters for which you were destined."

Jesus again turned his attention to the fire, which was now burning low. Neither of us spoke.

After some time, I said, "After the encounter, there follows an elation like no other. It far outweighs the anxieties and the fears and adds to the contentment of knowing you succeeded."

Jesus looked at me again. "This has been time well spent. I am overly concerned about pain and failure. If we plan carefully, the coming Passover and summer in Galilee will be as the others. Hostility will increase, but with people supporting me and with you keeping Pilate informed, we shall have another year of work. My disciples and I will continue as we always have."

Jesus stood and added, "My good friend, I am confident of our plan. It was the purpose of my visit. I now look forward to the journey to Jerusalem. Until we meet again, may peace be upon your house."

I also stood. "Until we meet again, may peace and good fortune be upon your house."

We walked to the door, and then Jesus vanished into the darkness. I placed more wood on the fire and returned to my seat. One of the lamps had died, but the fire was again burning brightly. I sat until it again burned low, marveling at the significant gift of this life and feeling again the contentment that flowed from having lived according to a plan.

I stared into the embers recalling events that had given meaning to my life. I noticed a small flame rekindled itself again and again, although it became weaker and lasted a shorter time.

I pulled my cloak tightly around me, for the pall had drawn closer. The more I thought about Jesus, the more I was convinced there would be a confrontation. I longed for someone to talk with. For a moment, I regretted not encouraging Jesus to abide longer.

Staring into the brazier, I became aware that the solitary flame had failed to rekindle itself. The flame of the second lamp had died from lack of oil. It was very late. I picked up the third lamp and went to my room.

As soon as I lay down, it seemed I was awakened by talking from the kitchen. Still wrapped in my cloak, I walked to the kitchen and joined Joshua and Moshe for breakfast.

After breakfast, as the rain continued, Moshe and I decided to work on our chronicles. I transcribed into my chronicle in Greek his notes in Aramaic.

As I recorded, Moshe observed, "There are differences in the nature of the languages which make it almost impossible to translate some words. In Aramaic, an object is defined by how it is used." He reached for a flat stone at the edge of the brazier. "If I write on this," he said, as he formed an Aramaic letter, "it is a tablet." He then set a lamp on the stone. "Now it is a lamp stand." Then he laid the stone on sheets of vellum. "It is now a weight. Since Aristotle, in the Greek language, everything is classified by what it is. A stone is described as a stone whether it is used as a tablet, a lamp stand, or a weight. I am never sure the Aramaic words Jesus used create in my mind the same image he had in his. If I did have the same image, did I select from all the possible Greek words the correct word to convey it? I am anxious how accurate the images we create are when the Greek is read by another."

I nodded assent. "You have well explained the problem, but it does not make the translation easier."

Moshe had recorded a saying in Aramaic that was causing me difficulty translating it into Greek, one about rendering to Caesar things that were Caesar's and to God things that were God's. When I read it, I felt I could translate it with little difficulty, the words being everyday words in both languages, but I hesitated at the word *render*. I believed Jesus was encouraging the people to give to Caesar that which was Caesar's, but Moshe was quick to enlighten me that this was an expression favored by the Zealots, to justify that nothing belonged to Rome, but everything to God, as Tiberius had no authority except that granted by God.

The following day, the rain ceased, and the weather was much improved. During my return trip to Jerusalem, I envisioned what would happen at the next Passover when Jesus entered the city. The hoi polloi could neither read a scroll nor sign their names. They relied on others to tell them what was required of them. The presence of a Pharisee frightened them, but a forceful leader could incite them to action. During Passover, there might be as many as a million pilgrims in Jerusalem and the neighboring villages.

The morning after my return, while waiting for Pilate, I reviewed the points I wished to cover, for I was anxious how he would respond to my report and to Jesus's plans.

Pilate entered his office and said, "Already back from Galilee. You traveled in some bad weather."

"The weather could have been much worse. My horse endured more than I did. I met with Jesus and his disciples. He is a more forceful leader. Last summer, the leaders of the religious groups attempted to entrap him. He is a clever adversary and turned the questions to entrap him into a trap for them."

Pilate nodded agreement but said nothing.

I continued. "Jesus is more confident in his teaching. Those sending the delegations want him arrested, for he is winning the loyalty of the people. I can control Galilee next summer with the additional legionnaires. Keeping Jerusalem calm during the next Passover may be the biggest problem. Jesus plans to enter Jerusalem with a large group."

Pilate said, "You see the issue as one between Jesus and the leaders, and the leaders see it as one between Jesus and Rome. I must determine whether it makes a difference. This recalls a discussion we had in Germany. We never agreed on Roman justice. You asserted justice was a religious concept based on natural law, but it does not explain the world you and I see from day to day. Roman law is based on eight hundred years of experience gained from building the greatest nation the world has known. I will apply Roman law and justice to the situation in Jerusalem. Perhaps the result will be justice by your definition."

I left his office greatly concerned.

I visited the Hillel School, and the teachers did assure me the religious groups were cooperating to bring a charge of sedition against Jesus.

I walked to the entrance to the fortress. Jerusalem seemed as orderly as ever. Perhaps we could keep it that way.

Two weeks before Passover, Pilate moved the Tenth Legion to Jerusalem. At the same time, he transferred enough legionnaires from Damascus to bring the legion to its full strength.

During that time, I was in the guard room at the entrance to the fortress when a disturbance occurred in the street just outside. A crowd was attempting to stone a man, and the centurion of the guard sent a group of legionnaires to rescue him.

The crowd's anger was so great it was yet attempting to kill him after he was in the hands of the guard. It was the Egyptian who had planned an insurrection some years ago. I instructed the centurion to take him into a room for questioning. The man addressed the centurion in perfect Greek. I recognized the voice. To my great surprise, it was Moshe's son, Saul, my good friend from Tarsus.

I stepped in front of him, and he recognized me, yet he was reserved. We barely exchanged greetings. I pointed to a bench nearby.

"I thought you were the Egyptian revolutionary. I was going to have you arrested. The crowd was angry enough to kill you."

Straightening his raiment, Saul said, "I took a follower of Jesus into the temple, a Greek under arrest. The crowd objected to a Gentile entering even though he was under arrest. Fortunately, it happened near the fortress." Saul then said, "Cornelius, it is good to see you. I see you have your red tunic. I knew you would. Are you stationed here in Jerusalem?"

"Yes, I am here with the legion for Passover. Why were you bringing the Greek into the temple when it is not allowed?"

"I assist Caiaphas, the high priest, by arresting those who mislead the people. Jesus in Galilee is giving us concern."

"You were coming to Jerusalem to study under Gamaliel. How did you join with Caiaphas?"

"I attended the Hillel School until I discovered it was not in strict obedience to the law. Then I attended the Shammai School and, after completing my studies, joined the temple. We keep the law and see that others do the same. The Hillel School is corrupting the people and needs to be disbanded."

"Your father thought you would build on your Greek background."

Saul glanced away. "That was long ago. The world has changed, and I have changed. The Torah is the law."

"Have you heard Jesus?"

"No, but I know of him, and he is offensive to me. He associates with the filth of the earth. He is not fit to be a Pharisee. The temple guards will arrest him when he comes to Jerusalem."

"Saul, I have heard his teaching. The temple and the priests make religion a burden heavier than the Roman one."

"You do not know the Torah. Moses gave to us the law as God gave it to him. To know God, you must obey God's law. You are Greek; I am Jew. We are different. There is no reconciliation."

Attempting to reduce the hostility, I asked, "Did you know Moshe is in Galilee, in Capernaum?"

"Yes, when he came to Jerusalem, he inquired about me and

found me in the temple. He is more Greek than Jew. We could not understand each other. He is in Capernaum, and I am in Jerusalem. It is better that way."

"That is unfortunate."

"I am pleased you have done well," Saul said. "I am distressed to see you with the Roman legion here in Jerusalem. The Shammai have no use for Romans, but I appreciate the rescue. For that I owe you a debt. If I am free to go, I must return to the temple."

"You are free to go, and you owe me no debt."

As Saul left the guard room, I noticed he yet favored his right leg. He might be in greater danger than Jesus, being so tightly bound to the temple.

I returned to my duties. Passover was at hand. I made my last trip to Caesarea Philippi to verify Jesus's plans, especially after hearing Saul's comments. The morning after my arrival, Moshe and I joined Jesus and the disciples. He was leaner in appearance but with the same commitment and discipline.

The disciples were in high spirits. I stood at the table across from Jesus and said, "Pilate is strengthening Jerusalem. The full Tenth Legion is to be dispersed, six thousand men. He is a friend to the Jews but will tolerate no disturbance. Are you planning to make a formal entrance into the city?"

"Yes," Jesus said, "we are committed. If there is to be a confrontation, we feel it is better to die in it than to live regretting the lost opportunity."

Jesus stood, extended his hand, and grasped mine tightly in his. "My dear friend, you and I understand each other. I am not certain going to Jerusalem is the purpose I came into this world, but I must go. I am fearful of what may happen, but it will happen. Pilate and all his legions cannot stop me."

"I will assist you," I said, "to the extent I am able."

"Well spoken, my friend," Jesus said, releasing my hand.

"Tell me where you will stay during Passover, should I need to find you."

Jesus answered without hesitation. "We will stay in Bethany at the home of my good friend Lazarus. We have yet to make plans for the Passover meal."

My anxiety in confronting Jesus had been for nothing. We sat at the long table and talked of things past and of things to come.

In the flickering firelight and light from the lamps, I recalled the assault on my cohort. That young man led a formidable group. Jesus's commitment to enter Jerusalem might become a similar confrontation. I was committed not to let it happen. I felt a sense of pride in being associated with such men. I wished them well.

The next morning, Moshe reminded me Jesus would enter Jerusalem by the Eastern or Golden Gate, fulfilling an old prophecy that the Messiah would by that gate enter Jerusalem. He speculated his entry was his announcement to all the world he was the Messiah.

At my request, Moshe agreed to accompany me to Jerusalem. The following morning, we began our long ride.

I arranged lodging for Moshe in a sparse hostel on a back street not far from the fortress. He was to keep in touch with Jesus and the disciples.

On returning to the fortress, I reported to Pilate that Jesus and his followers were coming to Jerusalem and would enter by the Eastern or Golden Gate. The chief priest would have the temple guard just inside the gate. Jesus's disciples would be armed.

Pilate was at his best. Each day, as we gained new information, we reviewed the possible confrontations and how best to suppress them. Jerusalem was ready.

At one of the evening meals with Pilate and his family, Claudia and Portia asked if they might attend one of Jesus's sessions. I suggested that Moshe arrange for them to attend. Pilate was concerned as to their safety. We agreed Moshe should accompany them.

Several days before Passover, I rode down to Jericho, then north along the Jordan. Jesus and his disciples were traveling with a large group from Galilee. Jesus was talking with a small group. I dismounted and, leading my horse, joined Judas walking by their baggage cart.

After an exchange of greetings, I asked, "Has anything changed since our last meeting?"

"Nothing has changed. On Sunday, we will enter Jerusalem by the Golden Gate and go to the temple. You see the crowd following us, and we have Zealot friends in the city. Jesus is the Messiah. He is to establish his kingdom. You are forewarned."

"Pilate is prepared. Any attempt to seize the temple will fail. It will be a bloody, efficient, killing match. Calculate the cost." I then mounted and moved slowly through the crowd.

Saturday Pilate's scouts—spies—dressed in Jewish clothing, reported Jesus and his disciples, along with a large crowd, were collecting in the Kedron Valley and planned to enter the city on Sunday.

Sunday morning, Pilate dispersed a reserve cohort, almost six hundred men, along the way from the gate to the temple, with strict orders to protect the pilgrims.

Jesus's entry was suitable for a king. The crowd accompanying him was in a joyous mood, singing and shouting, proceeding slowly to the temple, many entering it, then later slowly, joyously returning to the gate and down into the valley.

During the time Jesus was in the city, the First Cohort had duties inside Antonia Fortress. I was on the roof of the tower overlooking the temple court, standing by a parapet. I saw his group enter the Court of the Gentiles, Jesus in the lead. He walked to the columns, turned, and addressed the crowd as they formed a semicircle about him. I could not hear what he said, but a short time later, he walked to the cages containing the doves and opened the doors and then to the pens, releasing the lambs. The archers strung their bows, nocked their arrows, preparing to shoot, but I ordered them to hold their arrows until I gave the order to release them. I was anxious whether the temple guard would arrest Jesus. He moved to the tables of the money changers and overturned them. He then walked out of the court, the crowd making a way for him.

Had the temple guard attempted to arrest Jesus, there would have been a contest. With archers on the roof and legionnaires at the temple entrance, any disturbance would have been suppressed quickly, possibly inside the court itself. The chief priest that day in his rage ripped his tunic to his waist.

On Monday, Jesus came and went as he pleased. When I visited Moshe that afternoon, he suggested that he escort Claudia and Portia to the temple Tuesday morning. I promised to have them at the hostel early the next morning.

I visited Herod's palace and told Claudia and Portia they were to visit the temple and to be at the fortress entrance early the next morning carrying their Jewish clothing.

The next morning, we donned our Jewish garments and journeyed to Moshe's hostel. I returned to the fortress.

Tuesday passed without incident. That evening when I visited Moshe, I inquired about the visit to the temple. Moshe said, "Much of Jesus's teaching was in Greek, as there were many pilgrims present. The three of us mingled with the pilgrims and were able to stand close to where Jesus spoke. Claudia and Portia were good pilgrims."

It was yet three days before Passover. I visited with Moshe each day. We walked the main streets of the city.

On Wednesday, Jesus entered the city, and Pilate again posted legionnaires along his route. He continued to attract large crowds that became part of the joyous chaos.

Wednesday passed without incident.

Thursday morning, Moshe and I were on our way to Bethany. In the Kedron Valley, we met two of Jesus's disciples, the ones called Peter and John, the brother of James, in a cart going to Jerusalem. We inquired as to their plans to eat the Passover meal.

Peter said, "We are on our way to Jerusalem to the place we are to have a meal this evening, but it is not the Passover meal. We have not dined as a group since we left Galilee. We go now to make sure everything is ready. Please join us."

He handed the reins to John, dismounted, and joined Moshe and me as we turned back toward Jerusalem. With the great mass of pilgrims, we began the ascent to the city, everyone in a joyous and festive mood. After entering, we followed the cart into the lower city.

As we neared a house, two men approached us, one carrying a water pitcher.

"This is the place," Peter said.

The man with the pitcher said, "May we assist you?"

Peter said, "The master said where is the guest chamber? We are to arrange for the meeting."

The man said, "Welcome to our house. Please enter and take the steps to the upper room. If you require anything, we are to assist you."

We entered the courtyard and climbed the steps, followed by the two men. Inside the room was a long table fully set for a number of guests. After inspecting the arrangement, both Peter and John indicated their approval and thanked the men.

As we turned to leave, Moshe said to Peter, "Tomorrow night will you celebrate Passover in this room?"

"Tomorrow morning," Peter said, "we will plan for the Passover meal. The meal tonight is to celebrate our good fortune in being together."

"I am alone in the city," Moshe said. "For the Passover meal, will your door be open and will you have a vacant chair? May I be your Elijah?"

"Moshe, you are as one of us," Peter said. "Join us tonight, and we will make sure you will be our Elijah tomorrow night. You can be our Elijah tonight as well."

"You are very gracious," Moshe said. "I am pleased to attend. I wish for you a successful sojourn in Jerusalem and a safe return to Galilee. May Elijah make it so."

Peter then looked at me and said, "Cornelius, you also are welcome. With you and Moshe present, it will be like the pleasant times in Galilee."

I delayed a moment, caught off guard by the cordial invitation, and then said, "Indeed, you are very gracious. It would be my pleasure to attend, but I am compelled to be at the fortress. May your meal be a joyous time."

The disciples left the room and began the return journey to Bethany. Moshe and I returned to his hostel.

Neither of us spoke on the way, but on arriving, I voiced my concern. "I am fearful the temple guard will arrest Jesus when he returns to the city."

"Do not be fearful," Moshe said. "The man with the water pitcher and all that about the master's need was to identify Peter and John as Jesus's disciples. Judas arranged the meal with a family friendly to Jesus. Except for us, no one knows where Jesus and the disciples will be tonight."

I marveled at the audacity of Jesus and his disciples. I said to Moshe, "I am concerned. If you become aware of an attempt to arrest anyone, go to the entrance to the fortress and tell the guard to summon me."

"I will do as you have instructed," replied Moshe as we parted.

As I returned to the fortress, I wondered about the cart. Today it was well covered, and no one removed anything from it. Both it and the mule remained inside the courtyard.

Early in the second night watch, the centurion of the guard sent an aide advising me an old Jew was at the entrance. I hurried there to find Moshe in the shadows.

"Jesus and his disciples have gone to Gethsemane," Moshe said. "The cart is filled with weapons, and they took it with them. The Zealots are to help them occupy the temple. To lure the temple guard away, Jesus sent Judas to tell the chief priest where he can be found. Some of the Zealots are to ambush the guard outside the gate, and the rest are to enter and occupy the temple. Galileans will join them."

I went to the centurion of the guard and said, "There may be trouble tonight. Wake Pilate. Tell him to send two centuries to the Eastern Gate to keep any trouble there outside the walls and send one to the entrance to the temple to keep it secure. I am going to the Garden of Gethsemane."

It was a short distance to the Eastern Gate. Moshe and I passed through taking the road east to the garden. The valley was filled with pilgrims lining both sides of the road, some sitting around small fires. The entrance to the garden was also filled with pilgrims. At the far end of the garden, among the olive trees, I saw the cart. I walked slowly, for I was not sure who was there. As I approached, Phillip, one of Jesus's disciples, stepped in front of us but let us pass when he recognized me.

"Where is Jesus?" I asked.

"There," he said, pointing to a group by the cart.

As I approached, Jesus welcomed me. The disciples were arming themselves. Jesus started to explain what was to happen when Judas joined us.

He said to Jesus, "I told the chief priest you were here. He dispatched the temple guard, then handed me the money. I met with the Zealots. They say our effort will fail. Pilate controls the city. The guard is almost here! The twelve of us cannot overcome them. Call angels to assist us. Only with their help can we occupy the temple."

Jesus bowed his head. I could barely discern his features, but I saw his shoulders droop. After a moment, he said, "Judas, Judas, my dear Judas. You! You have become the tempter. He has entered you and has again offered me the kingdoms of this world." Jesus hesitated and then said, "I know now who I am and what I must do. Let the guard arrest me. I take the cup without hesitation."

Jesus placed his hand on Judas's shoulder and said, "My friend, I came to change the world. For that, one life is a small price to pay. The temple guard is here. I will meet them."

Judas walked to the cart and picked up one of the heavy, curved Greek swords used like a battle-ax. He withdrew the sword, casting the scabbard aside. Peter then drew his sword, and both stepped toward the path the guard would use.

Judas turned and shouted, "Form an array. Engage the guard. This is the moment!"

He then stepped alongside Peter, and with both hands on the hilt of his sword, he raised it above his head to engage the first soldier.

The temple guard approached along the narrow path, their torches showing their number and their weapons. Again, with a shout of defiance, Judas stepped in front of the first soldier, bringing the heavy blade of his sword down toward the soldier's head. A soldier to the right of the first soldier deflected it with his stave, and another with his stave landed a heavy blow to Judas's head. Judas fell to the ground.

Peter landed a severe blow to the head of one of the guards but was easily disarmed by blows from several guards.

The captain of the guard shouted, "Which one is Jesus?"

Jesus stepped into the torchlight and said, "I am he."

The calm reply caught everyone by surprise, and the shouting ceased. In the sudden stillness, Jesus stood in the flickering light and raised his hands to halt the advance of the guard. He moved toward the injured guard, now on his knees holding the left side of his head. Peter's blow had opened a long, slicing wound, severing his ear. The guard was holding his ear in place, blood cascading over his hand and down his face. Jesus placed his hand on the guard's head. He leaned over and whispered into the guard's right ear. The guard removed his hand. The wound was healed!

Meanwhile, the remaining disciples with swords drawn had formed a double line between Jesus and the temple guard.

In the circle of torchlight, Jesus again raised his hands, calling to the disciples, "Put away the swords. This is my hour. My kingdom is not of this world. I submit to arrest."

The disciples returned their swords to the cart and one by one withdrew behind Jesus. At a signal from the captain of the guard, two men stepped forward. One bound Jesus's hands behind his back, the other passed a cord twice around his chest and arms and bound him tightly. The captain ordered the guard to turn, then withdrew toward the road with Jesus secure in their midst.

The garden was silent. The pilgrims along the roadside and in the garden entrance were not aware anything had happened. In the semi-darkness, I saw Moshe and John standing to the side. John replaced his sword into its scabbard and laid it in the cart.

I was fearful the blow had killed Judas. I motioned to Moshe and John, and we pulled Judas under the tree, propping him in a sitting position against a large stone. The other disciples had slipped away.

In the brook flowing through the valley, Moshe wet the corner of his cloak, returned, and wiped much of the blood from Judas's head and face. Judas pushed his hand away.

When Judas had recovered sufficiently, Moshe, John, and I lifted him to his feet and assisted him into the cart. Moshe and John retrieved the swords of Judas and Peter and placed them in the cart alongside Judas. Moshe mounted the cart, and I sent John ahead to warn Lazarus we were coming. I walked beside the cart as we started the journey to Bethany and Lazarus's house.

The journey required some time as Moshe drove slowly to make the ride for Judas as gentle as possible. As we entered the courtyard, Lazarus, Martha, Mary, and John were waiting at the entrance. It required all of us to get Judas into the house and onto a pallet.

In the pale light of a single lamp, Martha cleansed Judas's wound, applying ointment but leaving the wound exposed. "It is a grievous wound," she said. "The ointment will stop the flow of blood. I am fearful he will fall to the fever, but the wound is well cleansed. There is little more I can do. I pray his strength will carry him through."

I knew Judas would fall to the fever. Had we cauterized the wound, he would not be in danger, but it was not accepted here. Martha looked at me and motioned for me to come closer. I leaned in her direction to hear what she might say.

She handed me a pouch of coins and said, "This was in Judas's tunic and fell out when I loosened his belt. I cleaned the blood away. It is safer in your care than with any of us."

Lazarus said, "Judas should be safe here. No one saw you enter the courtyard. John told us Jesus was arrested. I am fearful it will not go well for him." He thought a moment, then said, "Martha stopped the bleeding. The danger will be the fever. She used all the ointment. I will go to Jerusalem tomorrow. Although it is Passover and I owe him money, the apothecary is faithful to his calling."

I handed Lazarus several denarii from my pouch, enough to pay for the ointment. It would be costly, for I could smell the savor of the myrrh as Martha had applied it.

John, Moshe, and I set out for Jerusalem. For John and Moshe, it was the Day of Preparation. For me, it was Friday, with a hint in the east of the new day.

✝

It was dawn when I entered the fortress. Pilate was at the entrance to the guard room. As I approached, he said, "You handled the event well. The threat is over. There will be no incident. Jesus is in the hands of the temple guard. I have recalled the centuries from the Eastern Gate and the entrance to the temple. Much has happened since Jesus's arrest. He has been tried by the high priest and by the Sanhedrin and found guilty of sedition. The Sanhedrin is meeting now to confirm its findings. It had to wait until dawn to make its proceedings legal. I expect them shortly. They accuse Jesus of perverting the people with his teaching, which is not my problem. They accuse him also of saying he is king of the Jews, which is my problem."

He pointed to the entrance to the fortress and said, "The porch will be my praetorium. We will receive the Sanhedrin there."

A number of us accompanied him to the open porch. We could hear the shouts of the crowd approaching the fortress. The Sanhedrin and temple priests led the crowd with Jesus at their front, still tightly bound. Everyone stopped at the edge of the porch. Pilate walked to where Jesus was standing and asked the charge against him.

"He claims to be king of the Jews," the leader said. "We have no king but Caesar."

Pilate turned to Jesus and asked, "You have heard the charge against you. Are you king of the Jews?"

"Do you believe I am king of the Jews or did someone tell you this?"

"Am I a Jew?" Pilate replied. "How am I to know whether you are king of the Jews? What crime have you committed that the Sanhedrin has delivered you to me for judgment?"

"I have committed no crime. My kingdom is not of this world, but from the beginning was I born to bear witness of this truth. Those who hear me know the truth."

"What is truth?" Pilate said. "Would that I knew."

Receiving no answer, Pilate addressed the priest holding Jesus. "I find no fault in this man. By his dialect, he is Galilean. Galilee is not in my jurisdiction. Let Herod Antipas decide his case."

Pilate remained on the praetorium as the leaders of the Sanhedrin and the priests argued among themselves.

Again, Pilate said, "I find no fault in this man. He is not guilty of any crime." He then turned toward the fortress, leaving the mob at the edge of the porch. After a few moments, the leaders, with Jesus still bound, left the fortress with the mob following.

As Pilate entered the doorway to the fortress, an aide handed him a small document. After reading it, he rolled it tightly and placed inside his tunic. Later, Claudia told me she had written the note to warn him she had had terrible dreams about Jesus. The dreams convinced her Jesus was innocent, and she was compelled to warn him he should have nothing to do with his punishment.

Sometime later, one of the guards entered the guard room stating that the leaders of the Sanhedrin and the chief priest had returned with Jesus still a prisoner.

Pilate again walked onto the porch to the edge where the leaders stood. "Why are you here a second time?"

The chief priest replied, "Herod Antipas found no fault in him. He sent us back to you. Jesus claims to be king of the Jews, but we have no king but Tiberius."

The acknowledgment of allegiance to Tiberius surprised me. Even the crowd fell silent. It was false witness. He had perjured himself, and in the presence of the Sanhedrin and the crowd. I held my breath, waiting for Pilate's response.

On hearing the statement, Pilate bowed his head. After a few moments, he shouted to the crowd, "It is my custom at Passover to release to you a prisoner of your choice. I hold Barabbas prisoner. Would you rather I release to you Jesus of Nazareth or Barabbas?"

The priest's supporters shouted loudly, "Barabbas. Release unto us Barabbas."

Pilate then said to an aide, "Bring Jesus to me." The aide summoned Jesus to stand before Pilate. Pilate again asked Jesus, "What crime have you committed?"

"I have committed no crime," Jesus said.

"Are you king of the Jews?" he asked.

"You have said it. My kingdom is not of this world."

Pilate did not respond but again attempted to return Jesus to the leader of the Sanhedrin, saying, "You take him. I find no fault in him."

The chief priest stepped to the edge of the porch and said, "By claiming to be king of the Jews, this man speaks against Tiberius. If you release him, you are no friend of Tiberius. He will hear of this."

At best, Pilate was unsure of Tiberius's support. "What would you have me do with him?"

"Crucify him! Crucify him!" they shouted in unison.

Pilate summoned an aide and, to my dismay, ordered Jesus taken to the prison to be scourged. He then announced to the crowd, "Jesus is to be scourged. Return to your homes. It is Passover."

Pilate turned and entered the fortress. The crowd remained, its hostility growing, encouraged by the leaders.

Later, Pilate, accompanied by Jesus, returned to the porch. As Jesus stood before the crowd, the shouts were replaced with murmuring, for his tunic was wet with blood, a small pool collecting at his feet. He stood erect, facing the crowd. Pilate pointed to Jesus and shouted to the crowd, "Behold, the man!"

Pilate again said to the chief priest, "I find no fault in this man."

The chief priest was furious, ripping the front of his tunic, shouting louder than ever, "Crucify him! Crucify him!"

The shouting grew louder and was drawing more people. Pilate summoned an aide and instructed him to bring a basin with water. When he returned, Pilate faced the aide, washed his hands in the basin for all to see, and said, loud enough for them to hear, "I find no guilt in this man. I am innocent of his blood. See you to it."

With great pomposity, the chief priest shouted, "He claims to be king of the Jews. Let his blood be on our hands and the hands of our children."

The crowd fell silent, and even those on the praetorium were astonished.

Pilate stood with his head bowed. After several moments, he summoned a guard and pointed to Jesus. "Take him to the prison. Crucify him with the other two."

I marveled at Jesus's demeanor. Should I come to a similar end, my hope was that I could endure with as much grace. Ecce homo.

THE CRUCIFIXION

After the priest accepted responsibility for the death sentence and Jesus was taken away, the crowd diminished. I returned to the barracks and sat on my bunk. Would that the issue could be resolved by Pilate washing his hands and the priest assuming the guilt.

Crucifixion was a bloody, brutal ordeal designed to inflict the utmost pain on the condemned. The worst assignment a legionnaire could have was to carry out a crucifixion. It was so demoralizing Pilate assigned the task to a small group of fortress mercenaries. By now they were scourging Jesus with special whips with metal studs. His ordeal was just beginning.

Jesus needed a friend. Then like a lightning flash, I decided I should be the centurion in command of the crucifixion. I could not alter the course of events, but I could see that things were handled properly and provide what support I might. I donned my armor and walked to Pilate's office. He was seated at his desk, staring at the opposite wall.

He motioned me in, saying, "I do not wish to discuss the matter at this time."

"I wish to command the party assigned to crucify Jesus," I said.

"As your friend, Cornelius, I cannot permit it."

"I have considered the matter. Jesus is my friend. I am compelled to be with him."

After some moments, Pilate said, "He will certainly need a friend. You have my permission to command the party."

He then reached for a tablet on his desk. "Here is the inscription to place at the top of the cross. The chief priest objected to the wording, but I was not inclined to appease him further."

"I will see to it," I said, picking up the tablet. Then saluting smartly, I turned and left the office.

On the way to the prison area, I looked at the inscription. It read "Jesus of Nazareth, the King of the Jews" written in Greek, Latin, and Aramaic. Pilate had the last barb.

As I walked the long corridor leading to the holding area, I became apprehensive. I had never been present at a crucifixion, nor had I ever been in command of a crucifixion party. I had seen prisoners on crosses but never so close as to talk to one.

Jesus was my friend. If it was his hour, it was also my hour. If from the beginning, he was destined to be here, it was possible that I, also, from the beginning was destined to be here. As I approached the area where prisoners were held, my confidence returned, and I was prepared to do what I was destined to do.

The crucifixion site was northwest of the city, visible from a number of roads. For a joyous and festive season, this was a stark reminder of the power of Rome. The first day watch was half complete, and Passover started at sundown. Two other prisoners were to be crucified, their groups already having left the prison.

I had obtained a shortened hasta at the guard station. In full centurion armor and my cloak, I entered the area where prisoners were held. The mercenaries, who appeared to be Syrian, were carrying out the lashing with Jesus strapped to a table designed for that purpose.

I was taken aback by the indifference with which they acted. Jesus's back to his waist was bleeding badly, with a part of a rib exposed. A mercenary unbuckled the straps and assisted him to his feet. Jesus placed one hand on the table to steady himself and stood erectly as another helped him don his tunic.

Four mercenaries collected their equipment, and two others brought out the crossbeam that bore evidence of many crucifixions and was dark in color, as though wet from winter rain. I tasted the sour wine to make sure enough myrrh was present to dull any pain.

When it was time to begin the journey, I removed my helmet, for Jesus had never seen me in my armor, stepped close to him, and called his name.

He raised his eyes to mine, and I held out my hand, as much to steady him as to assure him. He gripped my hand firmly.

He said, "I knew you would be here."

"I am grieved to see you so. There is little I can do to alter the process. I will assist when I can."

Jesus nodded. "I understand."

One of the mercenaries handed him his robe, and Jesus released my hand. Two of the mercenaries lifted the crossbeam to rest on his shoulders, then picked up their equipment and formed a square with Jesus in the center. I stepped to the front, walking ahead into the street, motioning to the pilgrims to clear the way.

We had traveled a very short distance when I heard a murmur from the crowd. I turned. Jesus had fallen. His tunic was soaked with blood. I lifted the beam to free him.

In the crowd, I saw a giant of a man, a Cyrenean by his dress and complexion. He stood alongside our formation watching Jesus. In Greek, I ordered him to take up the beam. He stepped forward and lifted the beam to his shoulder. I assisted Jesus to his feet, then, to steady him, I placed his right hand on the left shoulder of the Cyrenean. The procession continued its journey, the crowd lining each side of the way.

Arriving at the site, I marveled Jesus had completed the journey. He was bleeding badly, leaving a trail of blood. The two prisoners were on their crosses, positioned a short distance apart, each facing the place where Jesus's cross would stand.

The vertical beam lay on the stony ground between the crosses, near the hole to receive Jesus's cross. The Cyrenean placed the cross-beam by it. I thanked him, and he gave a casual salute in return, withdrawing to the crowd, watching.

In Aramaic, I ordered the mercenaries to begin. With military precision, they fitted the crossbeam to the top of the vertical beam.

Jesus stood alone. Our eyes met, and in his face was a trace of the radiance I had seen at his baptism. I hoped the elation of fulfilling his mission might in some way lessen the pain.

Overwhelmed by what was happening, I removed my helmet and placed it near the pail of wine and myrrh. It was not appropriate for me to be here with my head covered.

After removing Jesus's robe, one of the mercenaries motioned to him to take off his tunic. Jesus's effort failed, as it adhered to his back. The mercenary removed the tunic, revealing the lacerated and bleeding back, tossed the bloody garment on top of the cloak, then motioned for Jesus to take off his loin garment.

As Jesus started to remove it, I placed my hand on the mercenary's shoulder. "No, leave the garment."

He hesitated a moment, then motioned for Jesus to position himself on the cross.

Jesus straddled the vertical beam, sat, then reclined and spread his arms on the crossbeam. One mercenary held his arm in place, another positioned a spike over his wrist, and the third drove it through with a single hammer blow. Jesus grimaced but uttered no sound. The process was repeated with the other hand.

A mercenary then positioned Jesus's feet on the small pedestals low on each side of the vertical beam. Again, with a single hammer blow, the mercenary drove a spike through the soft area behind each ankle into the vertical beam.

As the mercenary with the hammer stood, I handed him the tablet with the inscription, which he nailed above Jesus's head.

Then as one mercenary guided the foot of the cross toward the hole, the other three lifted it to a vertical position, allowing it to slip into the hole, and braced it with wedges.

Once the crosses were in place, each prisoner faced the other two. The crosses were heavily made, each holding the crucified a few inches above the ground. I could easily touch the tablet above Jesus's head while standing in front of his cross. Prisoners were usually crucified facing a road. I had never witnessed prisoners crucified facing each other, so close as to carry on a conversation.

When the final wedge braced the cross, Mary, mother of Jesus, softly sobbing, came forward and kneeled but looked only at the ground at its base. A number of the women who had assisted Jesus in Galilee accompanied her. John the disciple was there, but only John.

The chief priest and a number of the priests from the temple began to shout insults and railed against Jesus, taunting him. "If you are king of the Jews, come down from the cross."

With my hasta, I was able to keep them some distance away.

The mercenaries cast lots to determine who should have the garments, and the winner placed them with his equipment.

As I stood near Jesus's cross, I heard him say, "Father, forgive them, for they know not what they do."

At the time, I thought the prayer was for the mercenaries or the religious leaders, but they knew well what they were doing. Perhaps the prayer was for those in the crowd and in Jerusalem who should have known better but did not attempt to know, avoiding responsibility for this event. The prayer was for those of us who find security in not knowing.

The crucifixion complete, I ordered the mercenaries to return to the fortress. I moved the container of sour wine and my helmet to a safer place within the area of the crosses, for the religious leaders were inciting the crowd.

After the mercenaries left, I stood alone between the crosses and the crowd. The leaders continued to incite the crowd. As the hostility increased, I removed the glove from my belt and slipped it onto my right hand.

The crowd moved closer to the crosses. My back was to the two crosses facing Jesus. I transferred the hasta to my left hand and drew my sword. If the religious leaders wanted a confrontation, I would provide it. As I gripped tightly the hilt of my sword, I felt strength flow through my body like a flood.

One of the leaders made a rapid, hostile move toward me. I neatly nicked his forearm with my sword, knowing the wound would bleed profusely and hopefully deter any further movement. A murmur went up from the crowd as the leader looked down in disbelief. He withdrew, and others took up the hostility. I took my defensive stance.

The Cyrenean stepped to my left side and faced the crowd. I handed him my hasta. As he and I stood side by side, another man, this one a common laborer, stepped forward and stood by my right side. Then another joined and another. Soon there was a line between the crosses and the crowd. The shouting gradually decreased, and the crowd began to thin as many started toward the road below.

One of the first crucified prisoners began to taunt Jesus, saying, "If you are the Christ, save yourself and us also."

The second prisoner admonished him. "Do you not fear God? We are here because of our wrongdoing, and justly so, but this man has done nothing wrong." He looked at Jesus. "Remember me when you come into your kingdom."

Jesus said, "Today you will be with me in paradise."

All my hopes were confirmed. The afterlife was real, a new beginning to which all may aspire. In how many manuscripts, in how many languages had I questioned whether there was a paradise?

Jesus struggled to lift himself, his breathing becoming difficult.

Mary and the other women and John were by the cross. The women were kneeling, weeping, never looking up. I moved closer to the cross, hoping I might comfort Mary.

I had reached her side when I saw Jesus again attempt to lift himself. After the effort, Jesus opened his eyes, saw us at his feet, then looked from Mary to John and said, "Mary, behold your son."

At the sound of her name, Mary glanced up but quickly looked down.

Jesus then looked to John and said, "John, behold your mother."

John stepped closer to Mary, placed his hand on her shoulder, both to comfort her and to let Jesus know he understood, but did not speak.

Mary looked up at me through her tears and said, "That day at the temple in Jerusalem, when Joseph and I dedicated Jesus, an old man there said a sword would pierce my very soul. So long ago, Cornelius, how did he know?"

Standing by Mary and John, it occurred to me that Jesus and the other prisoners had nothing to drink since the previous day. I removed the sponge from the container, stepped in front of Jesus, and placed the dripping sponge against his lips. I held it in place, but he did not respond.

I felt compassion for the two prisoners, for no one was present to mourn their suffering. I again dipped the sponge into the container, walked to their crosses and lifted the sponge to each. The myrrh would soften but not end their pain.

The crowd was no longer hostile, and many were making their way to the road. I returned to the line formed to protect Jesus and thanked them in Aramaic and in Greek, for many were pilgrims.

A short distance away, the tragedy of the crucifixion was offset by the joyous spirit of the high holy day. Most knew nothing of what had happened during the previous night.

Many years ago in Egypt, in each household an innocent lamb had been slain, its blood spread on the door posts to protect the first-born from the Angel of Death. Here today, the holiest day of the year, an innocent man had been sacrificed, his sacred blood now spreading over the stony ground.

Jesus struggled for breath, then said, "My God, my God, why have you forsaken me?"

It was a plaintive cry. I dropped to my knees, my head bowed. I had never been forsaken, not by family, not by friends, certainly not by God. I recalled the plight of Job, forsaken by his family, his friends, and his God. How must it feel to lose hope, to be destroyed among adversaries.

To provide some comfort, Mary, his mother, was here, John, always the faithful disciple, was here, and I was here. We would all be here until the end.

Jesus had been on the cross for about five hours. There were hours remaining. For the first time in my life, I felt helpless. For a moment, I regretted requesting the assignment but instantly dismissed it.

I heard Jesus say, barely above a whisper, "I thirst."

I rushed to the container, removed the sponge, and lifted it to his lips. He was able to drink! It would wet his lips, mouth, and throat. I held the sponge for some time, then returned it to the container and took my station.

A little later, exerting great effort, Jesus raised his head and took a breath. The wine had wetted his mouth and throat, allowing him to shout, "It is finished."

In it I heard his elation in achieving the purpose for which he had been born. He knew who he was beyond any doubt and what he had accomplished.

A moment later, barely audible, I heard, "Father, into your hands I commit my spirit."

I had difficulty believing Jesus was dead. He had been on the cross six hours. Two mercenaries approached. One carried the special hammer used to break thigh bones to speed death. One explained, "The chief priest wanted all three dead by sundown. He said he did not want anyone alive on a cross for Passover."

With military precision, the one with the hammer broke the bones of the two prisoners, each prisoner emitting a painful cry as the hammer struck. On arriving at Jesus's side, the mercenary said, "This one is already dead."

Most men live at least a day, some much longer. With great reluctance, but to verify the observation of the mercenary, I thrust the point of my hasta into Jesus's side. There was no response. Jesus was dead. His journey was complete. His suffering was over. Jesus was already in paradise, with the prisoner soon to follow.

For some time, there had been a spring storm gathering, with the wind increasing and dark clouds rolling in. The storm broke over us suddenly with heavy rain. The small crowd remaining hurried to find shelter. At the foot of the cross, John draped his cloak over Mary and the other women who reluctantly allowed him to lead them away. Soon I was alone.

The storm grew in intensity. I considered donning my cloak but decided not to do so, as it might lessen the significance of my being there. It was the end of the third watch, the middle of the afternoon, yet it was growing dark. Flashes of lightning lit the crosses in stark detail. A great earthquake shook the ground. The earth was devouring itself, slipping into eternal darkness. I feared I might be the last man alive. I steadied myself, placing my left hand on the upright beam of Jesus's cross and holding the hasta in my right hand.

The storm continued to rage. The lightning flashes became like giant fiery bolts launched from a massive crossbow, splitting the darkness and striking the earth. After the flashes, darkness crashed around me with claps of thunder.

When I looked up during the flashes, the brightness seared into my memory the image of the two prisoners. When I looked down, I saw on the stony ground my centurion's helmet, the red plume erect against the storm, like the last standard facing final defeat. Then the darkness like a giant pall fell again. The earth continued to tremble, and in the darkness, I grasped tightly the upright beam of the cross beside me.

For the first time in my life, I felt stark, numbing, paralyzing fear. I had sensed it before, but that was momentary. Now it gripped my very being like a giant, cold hand crushing my chest or a terrible winding sheet immobilizing me. The fear grew, and my left hand gripped tightly the upright beam of the cross. In my right hand, I continued to grip the hasta with all my strength, for I felt I was slipping into a vast, eternal, and unknown abyss.

At last the lightning flashes became less frequent, and the rain abated. The earth ceased its trembling. I released my grip on the beam of Jesus's cross and placed my hasta on the stony ground like a shepherd's staff. My legs were weak and unsteady.

I had witnessed on this hill a contest to the death between Rome and Jesus. Jesus won the encounter. He remained faithful to his commitment. He had overcome the world. I took a deep breath and shouted into the abating storm for the entire world to hear, "Truly, this was the Son of God."

A few moments later, the skies began to lighten. Then suddenly the western clouds broke, and the full sun appeared just above the horizon. The entire world filled with glorious light. Jerusalem was bathed in it, and the gold of the temple dome gleamed like a precious stone. The remaining dark clouds took on a red glow, and all the land appeared fresh and clean.

✝

In the twilight, I considered whether I should abandon Jesus and the crosses when two shadows approached. The hair on the back of my neck rose, and I tightened my grip on the hasta. One of the forms, to my great relief, announced in Aramaic, "I am Joseph of Arimathea, a member of the Sanhedrin and a follower of Jesus. The prefect Pilate granted us permission to remove Jesus from the cross."

Pointing to the other figure and then to the nearby garden, Joseph said, "This is Nicodemus. He is to help me carry the body to a tomb there."

As the men approached, I could see by their raiment and demeanor they were men of distinction. Joseph said, "We are friends of Jesus and believe him to be a man sent from God. We were fearful no one would attend his body. We are here to do what we can. Will you allow us to remove him from the cross?"

"Of a truth, you may," I replied. "Allow me to assist you."

Joseph and Nicodemus approached the crosses, and Nicodemus placed the burden he carried on the ground nearby.

Both men stood by the cross, their heads bowed. After a few moments, Joseph said, "Jesus was my friend. I am saddened to see him come to this end. He was among the best of men." He paused.

"Without a landmark, how will we find our way? As the God of our fathers will receive us, may his Father receive his own Son, his journey complete."

Joseph raised his head and said, "Let us look forward to the day when all of us shall be together as at a celebration. Let us now to the task."

"Today in Israel, a prince has fallen, and all of us are poorer for it," Nicodemus said. "May the God of our fathers forgive us our failure to keep holy this holy day, and may the righteousness of our endeavor outweigh the unrighteousness we do."

Nicodemus then opened the burden, revealing an array of carpenter's tools, and removed a large hammer. He said, "I'll first loosen the spikes through his feet. You should be able to withdraw the spikes with this bar."

He set about loosening the first spike, and then Joseph, with some difficulty, engaged the head of the spike and slowly withdrew it. By then, Joseph had loosened the spike through Jesus's other foot, and Nicodemus slowly withdrew it, freeing both feet. I then stepped to the front and embraced Jesus's body as they removed the spikes through the wrists. With increased confidence, Nicodemus loosened the spike in the left, then the right wrist, with Joseph removing them. With the removal of the last spike and with the tenderness afforded a newborn child, Nicodemus and Joseph lowered Jesus until his body draped across my shoulder.

We placed Jesus on the cloak Joseph had spread and wrapped it around him. Joseph and I then carried him to the tomb nearby, and Nicodemus followed with the tools, my hasta and helmet, and our cloaks. In the darkness, we stumbled more than once.

We stooped as we entered the tomb. It was newly carved with a large, table-like stone in the center on which to place the body for preparation. Joseph had left a lighted lamp there. We laid Jesus on the smooth surface and removed the cloak. The rain had washed away portions of the blood, but crusts remained.

Joseph arranged the body of Jesus, laying him full length on his back, and folded his hands over his chest. With his hands resting on the folded hands of Jesus, he bowed his head, closed his eyes, and in the soft light of the lamp, tears streamed down his cheeks onto the table. I looked at Nicodemus. The lamplight reflected his tears.

I stood in silence.

Jesus appeared smaller in stature as he lay on the table. Joseph stepped to the corner of the tomb where materials were stored, removed a linen shroud, unfolded it, held it to the ceiling of the tomb, and then draped it over the body and the table.

After aligning the shroud, Joseph said, "I sent word to his mother we would lay him here. She and others will prepare him for burial. I regret we have no water with which to cleanse his body. It will pain her to see the effects of the scourging, but such is the lot of mothers."

Standing at the table close to both Joseph and Nicodemus, I noticed neither wore symbols indicating they were Pharisees. Most Pharisees wore distinctive garments displaying their religious order and rank, with devices on their head, chest, and arms. The plainness of their raiment, along with their demeanor, told of their religious nature.

Their task complete, Joseph and Nicodemus donned their cloaks, walked to the entrance, and sat on the step, facing the body of Jesus. I followed and sat cross-legged on my cloak on the floor in front of them. It was good to sit down, for I had been standing all day. In the quietness of the tomb, I heard Joseph and Nicodemus breathing.

After a few moments, Joseph said, "Nicodemus, my good friend, the task is finished. For your assistance, I owe a debt. From the cross, I removed the tablet identifying Jesus. Please take it for risking everything to assist me."

Nicodemus shook his head. "No, Joseph, you keep it. You saw the need, did the planning, and took the risks. The recollection is sufficient reward."

After a moment, Joseph replied, "Thank you, my friend. It will be the most precious possession I pass to my children. Better yet, I will place it in the recess for Jesus. It will remind all who enter that he is buried here. Later when we place his remains in his container, I will place it with them."

"Yes, that is a better disposition," Nicodemus said. "The recollection is sufficient."

"I was anxious I might find no one to assist," Joseph said. "I then remembered your intercession for Jesus before the Sanhedrin the day they clamored for his arrest and execution. You stood and spoke in his defense. I marveled at your courage, for I was fearful the Sanhedrin might accuse you. I learned that day a good man with courage can accomplish much."

Nicodemus replied, "We are friends of Jesus. I happened to be present in the Court of the Gentiles the day he opened the cages and overturned the tables. Others of the Sanhedrin were present, some so enraged they ripped their tunics, but no one lifted a hand to challenge him. To be so affrighted must be a terrible burden. Joseph, do not be overawed by my defense of Jesus. I knew well my adversaries. I was surprised at your request for assistance. I marveled at the audacity of requesting of Pilate Jesus's body, to risk everything on a favorable response."

"I owed Jesus the effort," Joseph said. "He was my friend."

"Of a truth, I am a better man for my knowing him, but requesting the body put you in great danger. Why did you undertake such a venture?"

"When Pilate granted us permission, he seemed grateful. It was the only time I ever saw him without armor and robe. I do not recall ever hearing anything good about him. His speech was cordial and put me at ease, for his demeanor was pleasant."

"In his office, I was fearful of arrest. Your confidence was my assurance," Joseph said. "Centurion, thank you for your assistance. It made our task much easier. When you raised your spear, I expected you to drive us away. That is why I spoke so quickly but in Aramaic. You understand Aramaic."

"My name is Cornelius," I said, "centurion with the Tenth Legion. When I came to Palestine, I studied Aramaic at one of your synagogues. That effort has served me well, for I came to know Jesus and his disciples. In my own way, I am a follower. I am pleased you removed his body, as I did not know what to do. I have followed your conversation with great interest. How did you as members of the Sanhedrin and Pharisees become followers of Jesus? Most of the Sanhedrin are Sadducees."

Joseph replied, "Most are indeed Sadducees but never knew him. They live anxious lives and avoid any conduct which might offend Pilate or any Roman. Their wealth and position are inherited or gained as favors. Nicodemus and I earned our wealth and would risk it all to assist a friend. Although Pharisees, we enjoyed the presence of Jesus and his disciples."

Nicodemus added, "Joseph and I felt a kinship to him and his disciples. We knew his visit to Jerusalem might end this way. He was, indeed, faithful to the end. I greatly admire him for that. The Sanhedrin erred in condemning him. I am fearful there will be a price to pay, but today the Sanhedrin is pleased with his death."

Nicodemus stood. "Let us return to Jerusalem. The hour is late, and we do violate this holy day in many ways. Joseph, may you be long remembered for your deeds. I am sure the God of our fathers will forgive us both for our misdeeds this day, for he looks on the heart."

Joseph and I stepped into the darkness. Nicodemus extinguished the lamp and followed.

Outside the tomb, our eyes became accustomed to the darkness, and there was enough light for us to see the path to the road below.

During the journey to the city, Joseph and Nicodemus discussed whether Jesus would have removed the two prisoners from their crosses. Nicodemus said to Joseph, "Jesus would have removed them. Would you consider doing so, it being Passover?"

"I have thought of nothing else," he said. "If we meet at the crosses early, we could complete the task by sunup. Jesus would welcome them to his tomb. He was content to share the lot of the abandoned. Only the two of us would know. It would be our memorial. I will meet you at the Fish Gate before sunrise. I will bring spices if you will bring two robes. Let us see to it."

Nicodemus said, "I will bring the robes."

"Allow me to join you," I said. "I will speak for Pilate should there be any question and report the event to him at the proper time."

"Cornelius, we welcome your assistance," Joseph said. "We are agreed then, to meet here before sunrise this day."

Nicodemus and I both agreed. We then parted, each going his own way.

Entering the fortress, I reported to the guard, requesting that I be awakened when the fourth night watch was half completed. As soon as I lay down, it seemed I was awakened. In the dim light of the barracks lamp, I donned my Jewish dress. I reported my departure, stating that I expected to return by midmorning.

As I approached the gate, I saw Joseph standing under the arch.

"I would never have recognized you in Jewish apparel," he said. "I commend you. Someone comes."

Nicodemus approached and inquired, "Joseph?"

"Yes," Joseph said. "Cornelius is here. We must hurry."

We passed through the gate, Joseph leading the way, Nicodemus following, with me last. To the east was the first hint of dawn. The road rose gently toward the hill where the crosses stood, and Joseph turned into the well-worn path leading there.

Joseph said, "Nicodemus, spread the robes on the ground and hand me the hammer. Cornelius, give him the bar and be ready to receive the body, just as we did for Jesus."

As Nicodemus removed the last spike, I lowered the prisoner onto the cloak and wrapped the body. By the time I walked to the second cross, they had already loosened the spikes. I carried the prisoner to the other cloak and wrapped him. The eastern sky was beginning to brighten.

Joseph and I carried the bodies into the tomb while Nicodemus carried the spices and tools.

Aware of their reluctance to touch the bodies, I said, "I am pleased to apply the spices, if you will direct me."

With both Joseph and Nicodemus giving instruction, I applied the spices and the oils to the body of the first prisoner, and then all of us wrapped the robe tightly around the body and lifted it into the recess to the right of where Jesus would lie.

Joseph opened the robe to expose the body of the second prisoner and I applied the spices and oils, the sweet savor filling the tomb. Together we wrapped the body. Nicodemus and I lifted it onto the shelf to the left of where Jesus would lie.

Joseph said, "The task is done. I sent word to Mary there was no water here. She and her friends will be here at dawn tomorrow to complete the preparation. Let us return to the city."

"We have done well," Nicodemus said. "I believe Jesus would commend us. My contentment from helping far outweighs my discomfort from violating this holy day. What we have done here was the right thing to do. We all know what happened here. That is sufficient."

We stepped out of the tomb into the cool morning air. There was yet no activity on the road below. From a bush nearby, a sparrow made its excited call, and in the early sunlight a group of swallows overhead circled and darted.

"We will leave the entrance open to allow the women to enter," said Joseph as we started toward the road.

On the way to the city, there was little discourse. I did feel, however, I now had two friends among the Sanhedrin. We passed through the gate, and I was pleased to be on my way to the fortress.

I marveled at the audacity of two men who risked so much for their friend. Would I be so fortunate as to have two friends provide me an honorable burial when I completed my journey?

†

Pilate had survived another Passover, but I feared he had cast aside faithful service to a fine legal system to satisfy the wishes of a few religious men.

"Has there been any disturbance?" I asked the centurion of the guard.

"Not since yesterday morning."

"Is the legion deployed?"

"It is."

"Have you seen Pilate?"

"No, sir, not since yesterday morning. But his orders are to deploy the Tenth throughout the city and the outlying areas."

I thought of the dilemma Pilate faced. All the work of a lifetime lost in a single morning. I feared he had lost the vision of a Rome that would last a thousand years.

✝

I changed to my Jewish dress, advised the guard I would be away for most of the day, and set out for Bethany. Lazarus and his sisters, Mary and Martha, were at risk for sheltering Judas. I found them and Moshe sitting on a bench under an olive tree.

"The blow would have killed an ordinary man. Martha cleansed the grievous wound and stopped the bleeding," Moshe said.

Inside a dimly lit room, Judas lay on a pallet, his eyes swollen shut. The wound was open and the ointment glistened, giving forth a pleasing savor. Lazarus's goats were in a pen in the corner.

I knelt beside Judas. "It is Cornelius. How do you feel?"

"My head hurts, and I can barely see, but Lazarus and the women provide good care," Judas said. "I do not know what happened. I remember the temple guard approaching and us drawing our swords. I did not see the man who struck me." His voice dropped to a whisper. "You heard Jesus call me the tempter. The Zealots were to seize the temple while the guard went to Gethsemane, but soldiers were everywhere. Had we attempted, they would have killed us all. After all the planning, I did not want to fail. He was not angry when he called me that."

"Since we brought you here, much has happened," I said.

"I will go to the villa in Galilee. We can start again. The work will hold us together. Would that I could have talked with Jesus."

I stepped outside and breathed the sweet air, for the savor of Lazarus's goats had filled the room. "Continue to assist Martha," I said to Moshe, handing him coins from my pouch.

My journey to the fortress was long. Part of my world had ended. The temple priests and the Sanhedrin had killed Jesus. The disciples and Lazarus and his sisters were in danger of arrest.

The day was far spent when I arrived at the fortress. I did not sleep well, for my mind kept returning to the sight of Jesus on the cross.

The next morning, I was called to Pilate's residence. He was alone, his countenance haggard, his eyes swollen.

"Thank you for coming so promptly. I regret being terse with you when you visited my office. Please do not take offense. This Passover has been a bad two days. I sent an innocent man to his death."

"It was a hard choice," I said. "To release Jesus or not to release him, each carried an injustice. As it was, Jesus gave his life for the people. He himself believed he was destined to do so."

"I can neither justify nor condemn my act. You once said justice was a moral concept and required a higher law by which to judge an act."

"At first, I thought you had erred. But events during the past two days were part of a far greater plan. Jesus believed that from the beginning of the world he was to give his life for the people. His death allowed him to accomplish that. We will never know for a truth, but I believe it to be so."

"Claudia and Peoria are deeply distraught," Pilate said. "They believe I should have released Jesus."

"I will encourage them why you could not release him," I said. "You were trapped like the principal in a Greek drama who seeks to learn the truth, but it eludes him. In seeking the truth, he makes decisions which bring about the tragic end the audience expected. It does not address the issue, but find comfort in the chief priest taking onto himself the responsibility for Jesus's death. He spoke in a rage, but had I been a member of the Sanhedrin or a priest or even a Jew, I would have trembled at the confession. You washed your hands, saying you found no fault in him."

"I do find a little comfort in that," Pilate said. "As prefect, however, I am responsible for administering Roman law. I do not believe I am so easily relieved. I am thankful the festival is over and the threat has passed. I will recall the legion and prepare for its return to Caesarea Maritima. With your approval, I will keep the First Cohort here as palace guard. I will see you tonight at the regular time."

I returned to the barracks and joined other legionnaires in a steam room at the bathhouse. I closed my eyes and let the heat remove the cold and ache from my world. My thoughts turned to Pilate. By condemning Jesus, he had suffered a defeat as devastating as one on the battlefield. The Roman constitution and law were unwritten, but for Pilate both existed as a body of legal principles to be mastered by those who loved the law and sought to administer justice.

Among surgeons, lawyers, statesmen, teachers, and soldiers, there exists a body of knowledge unique to each profession, which is to be mastered during a lifetime devoted to its study and application. Pilate refused to acknowledge the gradual replacement of those unwritten principles with rules and regulations guiding politicians and lawyers in its administration without requiring of them any understanding of the law or of the body of knowledge. Among the young, there were no longer professionals who mastered their field and took pride in its practice.

When it was time to prepare for the evening, I donned my red tunic, made sure my sandals were free from dust, and walked to the palace, anxious whether Pilate would be in a pleasant state. He, Claudia, and Portia greeted me more formally than usual. "It seems a long time since I last was here," I said. "I hope you are doing well."

"Portia and I are not doing well," said Claudia. "We believe Jesus was innocent and should have been released."

Her remarks caught me off guard. "There was more than the decision whether to release Jesus," I said. "The religious leaders and the Sanhedrin were anxious a disturbance would cause Pilate to order the legion to suppress it. If Pilate had released Jesus, there would have been a riot, and many would have been killed, regardless of the number of legionnaires in place. Also, people were planning to seize the temple. Pilate did the correct thing. It was a hard decision, but it was the correct one."

"I understand what you are saying, but it does not seem right to crucify an innocent man," said Claudia. "Portia and I heard Jesus speak when your friend took us into the temple court. He was a more forceful speaker than John the Baptizer. I did not see anything wrong in what he said."

"His disciples will continue to spread his teachings."

"I hope things will be quiet for a while," she said. "The past two days have been difficult for all of us. Pilate has not slept well."

"Cornelius believes I did the right thing. He is in a better position to know. I have put the matter aside," Pilate said. "Tomorrow I will re-call the legion. The next day, they will depart for Caesarea Maritima. Now that winter and the festival have passed, all Judea will settle into its old routine. I will welcome springtime."

The meal was more enjoyable than usual. Claudia resumed her pleasant demeanor, and there was no further discussion of the crucifixion.

As I departed, Portia accompanied me. "I do not understand everything that has happened, but Father was in good spirits this evening for the first time in a long time," she said. "He seems to have accepted what happened. When there is time, Mother and I would like for you to tell us more about Jesus. His words were forceful, but I am not sure what they mean."

"When the turmoil has ceased, we will do so. Do not concern yourself about your father. In *Antigone*, Creon the king is brought low when he does not do right. Your father was brought low when he faced a decision where Roman law was silent. Whether or not to release Jesus was not a matter of law; it was a decision based on what was right. Your father made the right one."

Portia looked down. "How well you have said it. Father was different this evening. He was more sympathetic. He did not have the arrogance he always had."

In her pensive state, Portia was especially attractive. All I could say was, "The night air yet has a chill. You should return to the living area. I hope to return soon." In the soft lamplight, I marveled at her beauty as she turned and entered the palace.

I rested well that night. The next morning, I journeyed to Bethany, concerned for Judas and the others. The high priest did not consider the matter closed. After a pleasant journey on a fine spring day, I found Lazarus, Martha, and Mary sitting in the courtyard. "Peace be unto you and unto your house," I said.

"Peace be unto you, also," Lazarus said.

"How is Judas?"

"We are pleased," Lazarus said. "He has no fever. The wound is healing, although it is unsightly. His eyes are yet swollen shut."

Moshe appeared at the doorway and motioned me into the room. In the dim light, Judas looked like a dead man. I knelt beside him. "How do you feel?"

"Cornelius. Thank you for coming. I am greatly improved. If I do not move, there is no pain." He lowered his voice. "You heard Jesus call me the tempter. Occupying the temple was the easiest way to establish a spiritual kingdom."

"Do you remember Jesus discussing his temptations while in the desert?" I asked.

"Yes."

"Occupying the temple would establish a political kingdom. You were the tempter. You lured the temple guard to the garden and asked Jesus to call angels to assist. When the plan failed, the temptation failed, and Jesus committed himself to a spiritual kingdom."

Judas lay quiet for a time, then asked, "Have you seen any of the disciples?"

"No, except for you and John. They expect to be arrested. Tomorrow, Moshe will go to the lower city to the house with the upper room, for we believe they are there."

Outside I said to Moshe, "Judas's belt and sica are missing. Did you remove them?"

"Martha removed his tunic," he replied, "and got him into a clean one. She gave me his belt and sica to clean. I have concealed them."

"Good. Keep them concealed until we know how he responds."

I exchanged a parting benediction and set out for the city. Judas would recover, but the scar would mark him. If the disciples were hunted men, they would have difficulty hiding him.

✝

Passover had come and gone, and it was now time for the Tenth Legion to relocate to Caesarea Maritima. With limited space in the Fortress Antonia, most of the legion was camped just outside the western gate. The plan was to start those cohorts on their way, joined by the cohorts quartered at the fortress.

Everyone had been alerted. The next morning, Pilate, with characteristic ceremony, amid trumpets and drums, formally ordered the Tenth Legion to Caesarea Maritima, leaving the First Cohort behind as palace guard. It would be the last formation and, as a formality, would leave the fortress and march through the city to Herod's palace.

At the campsite outside the fortress, with order and precision, the standard bearers received their standards and took their stations. It was a memorable sight, the cohort of six hundred men in perfect array, aligned on their standards, ready to respond to Pilate's command.

When the Tenth Legion formed for any occasion, Pilate in his armor, holding in both hands his special pilum, stood on the platform overlooking the parade ground and slowly raised his pilum. Each legionnaire struck his sword against his shield in unison. When Pilate lowered his pilum, the noise ceased abruptly and was replaced by a raucous battle shout. Then, as a farewell gesture, Pilate the Pilum saluted the centurions who returned the salute.

On his command, relayed like a religious litany by the officers and centurions, augmented by the trumpets and drums, the unit moved down the road to the sea. By noon, all cohorts were away, and a stillness settled over the campsite.

That afternoon, when Pilate entered the parade ground of Antonia Fortress, a command went up for a cohort to form an array. He mounted the stage at the edge of the parade ground, his bearing as straight as his pilum. His features, barely visible under the helmet, were stern and demanding as prefect of Judea and commander of the Tenth Legion. Again, with a cohort forming itself out of the chaos, Pilate raised and lowered his pilum with the cohort responding accordingly.

Finally, it was time for the First Cohort to form. On my command, we formed in marching array, facing Pilate. He raised the pilum, and I heard behind me the sound of swords striking shields in unison. Then as he lowered the pilum, the sound ceased, replaced by the raucous shout echoing off the towers and filling the fortress compound.

My heart surged with pride as I repeated, like a call to battle, Pilate's command to march. We were the last to leave Fortress Antonia, and the trumpeters and drummers accompanied us as we marched into the city. We represented Rome at its best, marching through a thousand years of history. Six hundred legionnaires in perfect order, moving as a single man. Sunlight flashed from burnished helmets, the plumes a rippling sea of red filling the fortress square. Would we had our battle standards for the entire world to see and remember forever this cohort, my cohort, the Italian Cohort. Would we could march through the temple gate and through the holy court, that the conquered might know the name of their conqueror and pay homage to the victor.

This was the glory of infantry, and it filled the skies. Infantry without equal, daughter of Mars, god of war, and queen of battle. Where were adversaries worthy of defeat by such men? For a moment, I regretted my enlistment was almost over and longed to lead the First Cohort, Tenth Fretensis, until my dying breath.

✝

The following day, I began preparing for the summer in Galilee. Pilate, the centurions, and I reviewed the plans. My centurions and I inspected the equipment, including animals and carts, then inspected each century to be sure the armor and clothing were acceptable. By the end of the day, all was in readiness.

It had been three days since I had seen Judas. The next morning, I attended to detail, completing everything by noon. I checked out with the guard and traveled to Bethany. When I arrived, Moshe and Martha were sitting under the large olive tree.

When Moshe saw me, he shouted, "Jesus is alive! I went to the upper room. All the disciples were there. Sunday morning, Mary and some friends saw Jesus alive at the tomb, but no one believed her. He then appeared to them in the room and talked with them. They all believe Jesus is alive. But without Jesus or Judas to lead them, they are not sure what to do. They are fearful of arrest."

"Are the disciples sure Jesus is alive?" I asked.

"Yes. They are to return to Galilee where Jesus will meet them. They believe Judas betrayed them and they will be arrested. I did not tell them Judas is here," Moshe said. "He has no fever and can sit up and eat."

I sat on a smooth stone near Moshe. Jesus was alive, as he promised. It was not that I doubted his ability, for I had seen him heal the temple guard. For me, at that moment, the news that the disciples believed Judas had betrayed Jesus overshadowed the word that he was alive. "Judas will be more concerned than ever with the accusations of betrayal," I said.

I entered the room where Judas was lying on the pallet. His face was swollen, but his eyes were open. I knelt beside him. "It is Cornelius. How are you?"

"I am doing well," he replied in a low voice. "I overheard part of your conversation with Moshe. Did he say the disciples saw Jesus? Did he escape the guard?"

"Judas, much has happened. Jesus did not escape the guard, but it is more than that."

"Did Moshe say the disciples believe I betrayed Jesus? Only you and I heard him call me the tempter."

"You must prepare to go to Galilee," I said.

"Did the others escape?"

"Judas, get better. You must get to Galilee. Jesus is to meet you there. I must go, but I will return tomorrow." I placed my hand on his. "Moshe will tell you everything that happened. At the fortress, we are planning for the summer. I will again be in Galilee. You must be there."

When I left, Judas was staring at the ceiling.

The road crossed the crest of the Mount of Olives, and I saw the temple in the distance. I followed the road down into the Kedron Valley and entered the Garden of Gethsemane. There had been few travelers on the road, and no one was at the entrance to the garden. I walked the narrow, stony path past a grove of ancient trees and an old olive press to several giant trees at the far end where Jesus had been arrested.

Under one of the trees, I found two scabbards and placed them on the lowest branch. I would return them to the cart on my next passing. I turned toward Jerusalem. Through the leaves, old and new, I saw the high eastern wall. The fragrance of the small white blossoms, half-hidden among the leaves, filled the spring air.

I sat down on a large stone. How quiet it was. The twisted, gnarled trunks, gray and massive, had served as sentinels for hundreds of years, providing seclusion from the garish world. The clusters of leaves softened the noise of the city, but I could hear the murmur of the stream, full from winter rains, as it flowed toward the Salt Sea.

The shadow from the city wall had deepened when I returned to the road, crossed the Brook Kedron, and began the ascent to the Eastern Gate. I passed tombs of prominent people long forgotten, the dust of strangers now resting there. I entered the gate the expected Messiah was to enter and, perhaps, through which he had already passed. The massive stone wall, the gate, and the giant pillars just inside amazed me. How quiet it was now compared to the welcoming shouts two weeks ago when Jesus entered, and a week later during the confusion on the night of his arrest.

In the road, palm fronds and abandoned cloaks were reminders of the crowds once present. As I walked toward the fortress along the massive eastern wall of the temple, I beheld a piteous sight, like a battlefield strewn with the dead and dying. Old men, worse than helpless, many blind, some missing limbs, all with gaunt faces and bony arms, were propped against the temple wall. Their tunics were tattered and soiled, their bodies needed cleansing, and their stench spoiled the air. Small children held up their tiny, dirty hands to the passing stranger.

The sight struck me harder than usual. This was the outward wall of the temple itself. On the other side was the heart of the Jewish religion, with opulent furnishings, handsome priests, and a treasury large enough to provide for all the needs of Judea. Would there were priests attentive to these people. Would there was incense to sweeten the air and obscure the sight. Would there were oblations holy enough to cleanse and make whole their existence, especially the little ones with their wide and pleading eyes.

I removed several denarii from my pouch and placed one in each of the upraised hands. The children shouted, handing the coin to an elder. An old one rose like a specter and threw his coin into the street with an expression of contempt for one of Gentile birth. I wondered why a man, his body whole, would seek an existence depending on a child and then throw away a day's wage because its source was not acceptable.

Several children fought for that coin. One finally grasped it firmly and held it high over his head like a victory prize, his dirty face radiant as he handed it to his elder. I felt sorrow for the other children, for I had added to the despair of those who had so little.

The austerity and cleanliness of the fortress was a welcome sight.

The next afternoon, I again journeyed to Bethany, stopping at the garden to retrieve the scabbards. On entering the courtyard to Lazarus's house, I returned the scabbards to the cart. Moshe was still assisting in the care for Judas. Martha alone could not manage the great size of him. Lazarus and his sister Mary had gone to Jerusalem.

Moshe motioned me to follow him into the house. In the darkened room, Judas was sitting at the edge of the pallet eating with Martha assisting him. As we entered, she smiled and bowed slightly.

"Thank you for the money for the ointment," she said. "The wound is healing well, and the risk of fever has passed. Without the ointment, he would have died. We are in your debt."

"You appear much improved," I said to Judas.

"I am."

"Did Moshe tell you what happened after the guard struck you?"

Judas lowered his head. "He told me about the arrest and crucifixion." He covered his face with his hands. "I am aware of my failure. Crucifixion is a terrible way to die. I wish the blow from the guard had killed me. I yet do not understand why Jesus did not escape with the others." He looked at me. "Moshe also told me Mary, his mother, and the disciples have seen and talked with Jesus since the crucifixion. I have difficulty believing he is alive. I cannot face him."

"You remember Jesus saying, more than once, the third temptation was the most difficult. It kept recurring," I said. "That night in the garden, after the guard struck you, as they were binding him, Jesus told us by yielding to the arrest, he had conquered the third temptation."

Judas's hands still covered his face.

"Many times Jesus said he was born to give his life to establish his kingdom. Judas, his death accomplished that. It was the purpose for which he was born. That is why he did not escape with the others. He believed his death was necessary."

After a few moments, Judas dropped his hands. "The others think I betrayed him by going to the high priest. My betrayal was calling for angels to assist him in establishing his kingdom. That was the betrayal. It was my betrayal." He looked down and whispered, "I must decide what I must do."

"Judas, you understand better than the rest of us that Jesus succeeded after all. He has established his kingdom."

I myself understood. Jesus's return from the dead validated all I had said without understanding. He was the Messiah, as he said. From the foundation of the world, he was to establish a new kingdom. I now understood why from the cross Jesus shouted the defiant victory cry, "It is finished." He knew then, without a doubt, who he was and that he had accomplished his purpose. More than ever before, I was convinced Jesus was the Son of God. I was engulfed in elation.

His head yet bowed, Judas said, "Now I have a new concern. I was the betrayer and will face judgment. I must calculate the gain in recovering." He lifted his head. "You are the only Gentile friend I ever had. Those were good days in Galilee. I learned about myself. I am fearful now I will not join you in the resurrection. Cornelius, my prayer is for peace to be upon you and upon your house forever."

I felt compassion for Judas, for in his countenance I saw his great despair. "Judas, my good friend, Jesus is alive. He is to meet all of you in Galilee. We must get you there."

With some effort, I controlled my elation. Moshe, Martha, and I helped Judas lie down. He placed his hands over his ears, keeping the weight of his head from causing even greater pain. Moshe and I held his shoulders and lowered him while Martha lifted his feet onto the pallet. For Judas, it was a painful event, but he made not a sound. He closed his eyes.

Moshe, Martha, and I filed from the room and sat on the bench under the tree. Martha looked at me. "Cornelius, your countenance changed as you talked to Judas. Did something happen?"

I was taken aback by Martha's observation. I looked at her in the bright sunlight, so gaunt and frail, so small in stature, yet in good spirits, as always. How could that be, with unending toil her lot, with never enough food to get through the day, with Lazarus providing better fare for his goats than for her?

I loved her very much. She assisted the rest of us through the day, wore shabby garments that we might wear better, and provided us food at her expense. Each day she was first to rise and last to re-tire, never complaining but seeing such dedication as her reasonable service.

I was helpless in her presence. I could not compensate her for her goodness. I understood what Jesus meant when he said, "Those who lose their lives for my sake will find it." Martha had, indeed, found her life in losing it for others and in so doing had found a contentment that others would have purchased for a great price.

I was not prepared to answer her question or to discuss with anyone my epiphany until I myself had considered what it meant. "Martha, I cannot repay the debt I owe you for all you have done." I would have embraced her, but it was not permitted. "Would you allow me to give you money enough to pay in full the apothecary for all he has provided for Lazarus?"

She smiled. "The money you gave Lazarus was sufficient for Judas's care. Without your help, Judas would have died, if not that night in the garden, then here at our house," she said. "Lazarus would be of-fended at my accepting money from a Gentile, and a Roman at that, to pay a personal debt. Your gesture warms my heart. I am indebted to you for your concern."

I turned to Moshe. "I must go. I am again to command the de-tachment in Galilee. I must prepare for the trip but will return before I go. We must get Judas to Galilee."

†

During the next few days at the fortress, I devoted my attention to the move to Galilee. Early one morning, a guard said a Jew at the entrance wanted to see me. I walked to the entrance thinking it must be Moshe, but there stood Judas wearing a fresh tunic and fiber san-dals. He broke into a broad smile when he saw me.

"Cornelius, Jesus *is* alive. Yesterday as I slept, someone touched me. When I opened my eyes, he was bending over me. I moved my head, and the pain was gone. I touched my forehead, and it was healed.

It's as smooth as before. See?" He held his head toward the sun. "I am yet his disciple and in his kingdom. The spreading of his kingdom is the purpose of it all. I am on my way to Caesarea Maritima to board a ship to any place wanting to hear the good news. Before I left, I wanted you to know what happened."

"Judas, let me purchase for you a new tunic and better sandals."

"Oh, no, I have all I need. My Gentile friend, I regret this may be our last meeting in this world. The hard going, the long days, the discussions we and the others had, all that is a part of me forever. Thank you for that. I know now why I was born into this world. Jesus did what he had to do. I go now to complete that which I must do."

"How good to see you healed," I said, grasping his strong, calloused hand. "I feared for your life when I saw the soldier strike you. I am so pleased, Judas, my dear, dear friend. I wish you well. We shall meet again."

I handed him his pouch, which Martha had given me. "On the night we brought you to Bethany, Martha gave me this for safekeeping. You will need it."

"I wondered what happened to it. That is the money the high priest gave me when I told him where he could find Jesus. It is not my money. Give it to Lazarus. He will know what to do with it."

"Judas, let me give you some money."

"No, Cornelius, I have everything I need. You have been my true friend. Indeed, we shall meet again. I look forward to the day."

He turned and walked into the street leading out of the city. In his demeanor, I saw myself advancing to the battle line. I noticed his sica on his belt. He still showed all the traits of the old Judas Iscariot, Judas the Sica.

With Jesus and now Judas gone, Galilee would not be the same.

✝

There was never word from Judas. Stories are told that he founded a church in Africa and wrote his own chronicle. The world may never know the man. Unlike the world, however, I believe his redemption is assured. I look forward to seeing him again.

I often recall that last meeting. Judas seemed intoxicated at the time with his beaming countenance, his great happiness, his love for his fellow man and for the world. I have not witnessed a similar incident since. Is it possible that one could become intoxicated on his love for Jesus and the good news of his kingdom? It is possible. In fact, I can attest to it.

✝

The day after Judas left, I journeyed to Bethany. When I entered the courtyard, Lazarus and Mary were seated under the tree. I was pleased to see in the corner of the courtyard a pen for the goats with Martha tending them.

"Peace be upon your house," Lazarus said. "We are pleased to see you. Have you seen Judas? He went to Jerusalem yesterday to find you."

"Peace be upon your house. Yes, he told me Jesus healed him. He was on his way to Caesarea Maritima," I said.

"I was sitting here when Jesus and Judas came out of the house. I was so surprised I could not speak," Lazarus said. "Jesus spoke to me only to say he was on his way to Galilee. I have difficulty believing what happened."

"Judas is pleased to be one of the disciples. I also have difficulty believing, except he is healed." I seated myself on a stone opposite Lazarus and Mary. Martha, in a worn garment and head scarf, joined us and sat near me. I said to her, "You gave me Judas's pouch. When I offered it to him, he said it was the money from the high priest and I should give it to Lazarus."

"I cannot take it," said Lazarus. "It is blood money. You keep it."

"I cannot accept it. Find a good purpose for it."

"Cornelius," Martha said, "count the money. Let us see how much is there, and we can decide then what to do with it."

I opened the pouch and poured the money on to the hem of my robe. "Thirty silver coins."

"That is more than a year's wages," Lazarus said.

Martha looked at the ground. "During Passover, a stranger died at our neighbor's house. We could not find anyone who knew him. We finally agreed he was a Gentile mingling with the pilgrims. None of the men would assist us. We wrapped him in his worn cloak, sewed it around him, and placed him on a cart taking refuse to the Valley of Gehenna. We were saddened to so dispose of one who had breathed the breath of life only the day before. I am sure someone longs for his return. Could we use the money to bury such ones?"

"The law forbids men to touch a corpse," Lazarus said. "It was Passover. I was saddened to see the corpse disposed of in such a manner, but he was a Gentile."

Martha, still looking down, said, "At the far end of the valley is a parcel of rocky land with ravines and caves. Only small bushes and brambles grow there. It would provide a far better place to bury such ones than to dispose of them with the refuse of the city. In Gehenna, they are food for worms and vultures. It is not a fit burial site."

"Martha, you and the other women spend your time on such tasks rather than looking after your own household," said Lazarus. "The death of the man was the only such incident ever in this neighborhood. It may never happen again."

I was embarrassed for her. It was in keeping with her demeanor to assist the other women. I spoke cordially to Lazarus, not wanting to offend him. "Let us consider what Martha has said. Allow me to give you the money. Inquire about the parcel. If it can be acquired with these thirty pieces of silver, that would be good use of the money. If more is required, I will provide it. As Martha said, all of us are endowed with God's breath of life."

With a trace of petulance, Lazarus took the pouch. "On behalf of Judas, I will acquire the parcel. It would be a fitting memorial to him for all he has done for us."

We engaged in conversation for some time before I bade them all goodbye and returned to the fortress.

†

The summer in Galilee passed without incident, and Moshe and I completed our chronicles. Each one consisted of about thirty pages, written on both sides, laced at the left edge. Preparing them had been an enlightening process.

When my unit returned to Galilee, Matthew had resumed his duties as tax collector. Through him I learned the disciples were spreading the good news, as they called it, in the synagogues in Galilee, through Perea, and south into Judea. No one attempted to rebuild the group led by Jesus. Religious leaders in Jerusalem were displeased by the new teaching, saying it corrupted the purity and discipline of the law. However, some were pleased for it was a return to religion by the hoi polloi. A tree bearing poor fruit was preferred to a tree bearing no fruit.

There were no further incidents worth of description as Pilate continued his strict administration. He relocated the prefect's office to Herod's palace in Caesarea Maritima, as the city afforded better accommodations, both for his administration and for the legion.

As Herod Antipas was content to let Pilate include Galilee and Perea in his jurisdiction, I continued to be in command of the post in Galilee during the summers.

In Samaria, there appeared a leader who was attracting large crowds and claiming to know where Moses had buried the sacred vessels from the tabernacle. His followers were in camp at the base of Mount Gerizim. That was in Pilate's area of responsibility, a two-day march northeast from Caesarea Maritima. The group continued to grow and was arming itself, preparing to climb the mountain to recover the lost vessels.

The rapid growth and arming of the group caused Pilate to

dispatch a messenger to Capernaum requesting that I visit the group and prepare a report sufficient to plan a response. I discussed the characteristics of Samaritan laborers with Moshe. With Joshua's help, from old clothing left by the disciples, I selected a laborer's tunic, a cloak, and sandals woven from the leaves of the rush plant. He provided me with a short-handled pruning hook.

Dressed as an impoverished Samaritan farm laborer, I was prepared to go. Joshua and I rode well into the night until we saw the fires of the Samaritan camp. I dismounted, gave the reins to Joshua, removed my legionnaire sandals, put on the rush sandals, and bid goodbye to him.

I walked into the camp, found a group similarly dressed, and sat just inside the circle of firelight. Most were already asleep. I spoke with the few by the fire, wrapped my cloak around me, and was instantly asleep.

I awoke at first light, moved closer to the fire, and opened my pouch. To my surprise, there was a quantity of bread and several cuts of cheese. I marveled that Joshua knew what to pack. Food was more valuable here than silver coins. I removed a piece of cheese and some bread, sliced them, and offered them to those around the fire.

I engaged them in casual conversation, speaking Aramaic with a rural Galilean accent. "I am from the hill country near Nain. I learned of the new Moses from a traveler and thought it worth my time to see for myself. What do you know of him?"

An older man said, "Thank you for the food. We have had little to eat. Something must happen soon or we will return to the farm. The leader is the new Moses who will take us to where Moses, on entering the Promised Land, buried the tabernacle vessels. If the leader knew where the vessels were buried, he could have recovered them first and then led us to victory over the Romans. Wait until you hear him. You may become a believer. Thank you again for the food. You are very generous. May the Lord make his face to shine upon you."

"May peace be with you. I will go now to find the new Moses." I stood and picked up my pruning hook.

I walked through the camp, if it could be described as a camp. There were as many as two thousand scattered about in small groups, mostly young men, armed with long- or short-handled pruning hooks or with long-handled five-pronged sifters. The long-handled pruning hooks and sifters would be deadly weapons in the hands of trained fighters, but these young men had no conception of their use as weapons. I counted only two hundred heavy Greek swords. There were more, I was sure, but probably not more than four hundred. These swords were slashing weapons no longer used by the military. I could see no organization to provide food, water, or shelter to these men.

It was close to noon when activity indicated the leader was arriving. He reminded me of John the Baptizer, except this man was older with streaks of gray in his beard and hair. His stride was firm and his bearing one of command. He was dressed in a simple laborer's tunic and traditional cloak but carried a long shepherd's hook. He walked to a small rocky mound and spread his arms, calling for attention. Many moved toward him and sat in a large circle around him.

In a commanding voice, he said, "Children of Israel, descendants of Ephraim and Manasseh, followers of the true religion, the time has come to possess the Promised Land and restore the vessels of the tabernacle. Jehovah will again lead us with a pillar of cloud by day and a pillar of fire by night. We will soon be strong enough to take the land. Be patient. Trust in the Lord. The day of deliverance is at hand."

Not since John the Baptizer had I heard anyone who could so enthrall a crowd. I looked at the young men around me. They were all gazing at him, entranced by his words. I listened with great fascination as he continued to speak with zeal and encouragement.

Later, when the speaker paused, I rose and slipped away. I had collected sufficient information for my report. It was early afternoon. If I maintained a steady pace, I would reach Caesarea Maritima by midnight.

By nightfall, I had reached the smoother coastal road, but the rocky road leading there had demolished my sandals. I removed my cloak, cut two wide strips from its border, and wrapped a strip around each sandal. My new sandals were not as comfortable as the old ones, but I soon adjusted to their feel.

It was midnight when I approached the fortress. I shouted a greeting, for I was apprehensive a sentinel might mistake me for an adversary as I yet carried the pruning hook. I stood by a lamp near the entrance. He recognized me and welcomed me to the fortress. In my room, I fell into my bunk and was instantly asleep.

The next morning, by the first day watch, I woke, donned my light armor, and reported to Pilate's office. His aide welcomed me and sent another aide to fetch him. Before the aide completed his summary of happenings at the fortress, Pilate arrived.

"Cornelius, it is good to see you," he said, returning my salute. "What did you find?"

"The group is gathering on the south side of Mount Gerizim," I said, as Pilate unrolled a large map on the table before us. "Here." I pointed to a symbol on the map. "The leader is another messiah from the desert. This one believes he is Moses reborn and plans to lead the Samaritans to the top of Mount Gerizim to recover sacred vessels buried there. The vessels will give him authority to lead the people."

"What do you know about the sacred vessels?" Pilate asked.

"The leader assured everyone the vessels are there. Samaritans believe their own messiah will someday lead them to a promised land. This one is a new Moses who will lead them from bondage, as did the first Moses. According to tradition, no one was present at Moses's death. He disappeared into a cloud, the legend says, atop Mount Gerizim. It is reasonable he would carry vessels with him, as his people were desert tribesmen searching for a promised land. It is a myth. All of us search for a promised land."

"I never heard any of those stories," said Pilate.

"The leader is a revolutionary. He is planning to lead his followers against our forces in Judea. If they find the vessels, they will believe him, and when they start toward Jerusalem, he will gain more. He must be stopped before he leads them up the mountain."

Pilate studied the map before him, tracing with his finger the distance from Caesarea to Mount Gerizim. "What size force should we send?"

"They number about two thousand," I said. "A single cohort with support units would be sufficient if we intercept him before he ascends the mountain. His followers are young men, laborers and farmers, armed with pruning hooks and wheat sifters. The sifters are similar to the tridents favored by some gladiators. They also have some heavy Greek swords, but none of them are trained in its use. On my way here, I developed a plan."

"Tell me your plan."

"The young men are not soldiers. They should be home threshing wheat or working for the Romans. I doubt any have seen someone die from an arrow or from an acorn from a slinger. If we array a cohort to block access to the mountaintop, we will be on higher ground with the Samaritans coming up the mountain. Our archers and slingers will have the advantage. With the first volley of arrows and acorns, as the first casualties occur, it will be such a shock to the others they will lose interest. If the advance is not halted, legionnaires carrying two pila each will discourage them. I do not believe the Samaritans have the spirit for an engagement. By the second volley, they will turn back. The pila will be used if necessary."

I paused to allow Pilate time to follow my plan. "Their weapons will present no problem. If they were well trained in the use of the long pruning hook and sifter as weapons and the two were paired against a single legionnaire, he might be in danger. It is a waste of good laborers to send these men against our troops. I am in favor of keeping their losses low but capturing their leaders."

"I understand your plan," Pilate said. "How will we implement it?"

"I walked the distance, about forty miles, in less than ten hours. A cohort leaving by noon today could be on the mountain by midnight. The problem is the baggage. The cohort needs to be in light armor carrying only a short sword. We can put weapons and personal baggage in the carts. Should we also load the shields? How can we get the baggage train to the mountain by the time we need the weapons?"

Pilate thought a moment. "We can delay the engagement from tomorrow morning until the following morning. If we load and start the carts by noon today, the train should arrive at the mountain the day after tomorrow in the afternoon. If the cohort leaves early tomorrow morning, it would arrive at the mountain about the same time. Do we need a special unit of archers and slingers?"

"The First Cohort can do the march and provide both the archers and slingers. As it is a forty-mile march without interruption, the First Cohort is the most dependable. Two centuries are in Galilee, leaving four centuries here. Each man is trained as an archer and a slinger, but some are better than others. You will need a unit of cavalry to get behind the leaders should they try to flee."

"Are you sure four centuries is sufficient? You said there were two thousand of them."

"I wish the whole cohort were here, but there is not time. We have all the advantages. I am confident four centuries will be sufficient. I know my men."

"If you are confident, I am confident. Let us prepare the orders. We need to get the carts under way."

"Most of these Samaritans haven't eaten a meal in days. The engagement will be a disaster for them. If you are agreeable, may we add to the train two carts of rations? I will pay for one if Tiberius will pay for the other."

"We are planning a military campaign, not a relief expedition." Pilate placed his hand on the place on the map marking Mount Gerizim. "What audacity! It is a great idea. I will pay for the second cart. The Samaritans will remember the rations rather than their dead. Perhaps they might support us against the Jews."

He rolled up the map, cleared the table, and said, "We must not delay."

Pilate began drafting the order dispatching the four centuries of the First Cohort. He then signed it, affixed his seal, and added *SPQR* under his name and seal. He fanned the air with the document to dry the ink, then held it motionless for me to witness. I saw the signature with the initials and nodded my approval. All orders were so signed.

He then prepared the order for the weapons. "I'm ordering five hundred pila, forty bows with the standard lot of arrows, and forty slings. What acorns do you want?"

"The practice clay ones. Lead and stone would be too much. I'm planning to keep their casualties low. They are farmers. Too many casualties would complicate their return."

We worked steadily until all the orders were prepared, then handed them to the aides to be delivered. Pilate pushed his chair from the table, leaned back, folded his hands, and said, "Cornelius, what will I do when you are gone? I never worked with anyone who could anticipate my needs before I voiced them. You have served me well. May good fortune bring you back safely."

Embarrassed by his praise, I saluted. "Thank you, sir. For the Senate and the people of Rome."

"For the Senate and the people of Rome. Let us now to the work."

We walked together into the morning sunlight.

As usual with Pilate, everything proceeded according to plan. By noon, the baggage train departed. The men of the First Cohort spent the afternoon preparing for the engagement. Early the next morning, with some ceremony, the cohort was ready for departure.

I joined my standard bearer at the front of the detachment. He acknowledged my presence. I identified with our standard. It was my family crest. Everyone longs to be a member of a family. We are so born. The cohort fulfilled that longing. It was closer to me than my brothers and sisters. The standard at my side proclaimed to all the world who we were.

The greatest honor bestowed upon a legionnaire is to be named the unit's standard bearer. His life becomes a small price to pay to keep it always to the front. In temples in Rome, standards are displayed in places of honor. The standard of the Tenth Legion Equestris, Julius Caesar's own legion and personal guard, is so displayed. Captured standards of enemy units that fought with special valor are also displayed. Battle standards represent a nation's gallant defenders and deserve the highest honor and deepest respect. The glory of a battle standard should never fade.

We arrived at the assembly area during the first night watch. There was yet sufficient light to position the men. I had sent scouts ahead to mark the line along which we would deploy. The baggage train and the cavalry unit had already arrived.

To ease tensions, I spoke to the assembled group in a hushed voice. "Do not underestimate the enemy. They number about two thousand. They are farmers and laborers and should be back on their farms or at work. I am counting on the archers and slingers to discourage the advance. Be careful of the slingers. I once saw a young Palestinian bring down a falcon as it stooped on a swallow. They are your first target. Take your positions, enjoy your rations, but no fires, no noise, and sleep well. Tomorrow will be here soon. For the Senate and the people of Rome."

I divided the men into two ranks of two hundred, with the tenth man an archer and eleventh man a slinger. The centurions were to select the best archers and slingers. Everyone else carried two pila. After deployment, I walked along the line, making sure everyone was prepared. Each man took a ration from his pouch, sat down, and enjoyed his evening meal, resting from the hard march.

Well before sunrise, the centurions woke their men and formed the array. The sun appeared on the horizon as bright as noon, for there was no morning mist. The legionnaires stood shield to shield in two ranks, with an archer and a slinger placed uniformly along the front, arrows and acorns at their sides. The centurions with their standard bearers stood in front of their century, and I took my place in front of the array. The formation was, indeed, beautiful as the sun bathed the plumes and helmets in glorious light, reflecting off the armor and weapons. Even the shields were spectacular.

I turned to face the Samaritan camp about three hundred yards below us. I had feared we would face the rising sun, but it was far enough to our left it did not hinder the archers or slingers. I hoped the sight of the array might discourage the Samaritans. The activity in their camp, however, indicated they were preparing to advance. I wished they were a military unit worthy to engage us.

In a great mass, the Samaritans began to move up the mountain. By the time they were two hundred yards distant, they had dispersed and the more aggressive were moving rapidly toward us. I raised my sword to signal the archers and slingers to prepare the first volley. After allowing them time, I lowered my sword, and the first volley was away.

When the volley struck, the forward motion hesitated but then resumed. By the time the second volley was released, the nearest Samaritans were fifty yards distant. The second volley stopped their advance, and few were coming toward us. The archers and slingers selected specific targets. The main body turned and began moving down the mountainside in great disorder, followed by the wounded. I ordered the activity to cease. The cavalry had corralled a small group of leaders, the self-proclaimed messiah among them.

I ordered my men to the assembly area occupied by the baggage train. After all had arrived but were still in formation, I commended them, for it had been a typical Pilate victory. We had suppressed the Samaritans with minimum loss of life on their part and no injuries to the legionnaires.

"Enter the Samaritan camp and order them up the mountain to assist the wounded and to recover their dead," I said. "Tell them to return to their homes. Centurions, make sure the wounded are provided a way and the dead are returned to their families. After that, take the two carts of rations and distribute the food. If anyone attacks you, make him a prisoner. Assemble here by the end of the last day watch."

The legionnaires completed their tasks and returned to the campsite. We set about preparing for the night, making sure we were secure from attack by the Samaritans. The men then formed their cooking groups and prepared their evening meals. I visited their sites, complimenting them on the march and the engagement.

The drivers had erected a small tent for me, although I preferred to sleep in my cloak. I appreciated the gesture and did not wish to disappoint them. I entered the tent and sat on the pallet in a pensive mood. I thought I could hear the lamentation of the mothers of Samaria weeping for their lost and wounded children.

I sent a messenger to Pilate to report the victory, although I was reluctant to call it that. On the return trip, I broke the march into two days, allowing the cohort and baggage train to enter Caesarea Maritima in a victory parade. It was not the celebration when the Fifth Alaudae entered Rome, but for Palestine, it was a significant event.

✝

I related in detail the Mount Gerizim incident as rumors overstated the number of Samaritans killed, causing Tiberius to interpret the incident as a direct violation of his policy of leniency to the Jews. He should have known the Samaritans were not Jews. In fact, there was great animosity between them. I was surprised the incident was reported to Rome at all. To the delight of his adversaries, Tiberius ordered Pilate to Rome to account for his violation of the policy of leniency toward the Jews.

Pilate was apprehensive about the real purpose for his recall to Rome. After the execution of Sejanus, he had been anxious his name might be linked to that conspiracy.

✝

As winter was approaching and there was no evidence of any disorder in Palestine, Pilate arranged for the Tenth Legion to winter in Caesarea Maritima. To provide more room in the fortress there, he moved his office to Herod's palace, assigning my cohort to be Praetorian Guard there. At the next assembly of the cohort, I announced, "In keeping with your reputation as the Italian Cohort, I am pleased to report Pilate named you his Praetorian Guard again this winter. Unfortunately, you will reside in the palace rather than the fortress. Enjoy your hardship. You have earned the distinction."

I welcomed the news, as the fortress at Caesarea could quarter the legion more easily than Antonia Fortress in Jerusalem. The city of Caesarea was Roman, and we could conduct ourselves in keeping with Roman customs. There was a Jewish quarter in the city, but it conducted its own affairs, refusing to assimilate.

As the time for Pilate's departure neared, he invited me for an evening meal. As we sat in the large entertainment hall of the palace, he said, "I am anxious why Tiberius recalled me to Rome. My report on the Mount Gerizim incident clearly stated the Samaritans were planning a revolt against the Roman presence. I included collaborating statements with the report attesting to the actual number killed. I also explained that Samaritans are not Jews. It is for some other reason he is recalling me."

"Do you believe your life to be in danger?" I asked.

"Yes, I do. Why would Tiberius use such a minor incident to recall me? I may be linked with Sejanus. That conspiracy may still be under review."

"It would be unfortunate to be linked with Sejanus now. Are you considering not going to Rome?"

"Yes, I am. My family still has estates in southern Italy, but that is the first place Tiberius would search. Alexandria may be the safest place, but I have never been there."

"I regret you are in danger. We will get you to a safe place."

"The ship to Rome is to sail in about a week. Let me think about it."

After the meal, Portia suggested she and I walk to the porch overlooking the harbor. I was surprised, for the sun had set. As we walked to the far side of the porch, Portia said, "Father has been called to Rome to account for the incident in Samaria. He did not mention it during the meal, but he must have discussed it with you. Mother and I prepared the report, which clearly indicated the Samaritans were beginning a revolt. We are sure the recall means trouble for Father."

In the semidarkness, I could see her gazing out to sea. Finally, she said, "Many times I wished we could have shared our lives." Laying her hand on my arm, she whispered, "I have complained enough. Please forgive me."

I placed my hand on hers, felt its warmth, and said, "You do not know how many times I would have exchanged my life in the legion to spend my days with you. My time in the legion is almost completed. Let us resolve your father's problem, and then we can consider what we can do. The hour is late. Let us return to the room."

During the next day, I busied myself with minor chores about the castle while considering how we might arrange for Pilate to disappear. He invited me to join him that evening, and at the agreed time, I entered his quarters. He was sitting alone in a corner section of the palace hall.

He greeted me, then said, "I have decided it is too dangerous to return to Rome. Claudia and Portia agree. Tiberius is old and in poor health. Nothing good can come of my return." He paused. "Over the years, I looked forward to spending my last days there, but the world is different now, and Rome is not what it was. I would like to withdraw to an unknown place."

"It has been a long time since the days in Germany with the Fifth Alaudae," I said. "Indeed, the world has changed. The republic became the empire under Augustus, and now the empire is dying under Tiberius. We can get you, Claudia, and Portia away from here. I am saddened to see it come to this. All the world is in decline." I stood. "Alexandria would be the best place to begin again. It is much like Rome."

Our meal was as cordial as ever, but the conversation was subdued.

✝

Caesarea Maritima was the administrative capital of Judea, built by Herod the Great, named after Caesar Augustus. Herod's palace, built on a cliff extending into the sea, served as Pilate's headquarters.

The success of the city can be attributed to its large seaport, far larger and better than Tarsus, and to the two aqueducts bringing fresh water into the harbor. I would have no difficulty finding a vessel destined for an obscure place. Herod the Great had built a fine harbor, and the harbormaster was keeping it so. It was reassuring to see Roman excellence.

The day following my visit with Pilate, I checked with the harbormaster to confirm the departure of the ship for Rome. He said it was scheduled to leave in four to five days, depending on the arrival of officials from Jerusalem. I advised him Pilate was planning to board the ship the afternoon prior to sailing, and I would return in two or three days to verify the time.

I complimented him on the order in his harbor evidenced by the number of ships coming and going. I inquired about merchant ships leaving for Alexandria or North Africa. He said there were always such merchantmen putting in at Caesarea for water and supplies.

I walked to the breakwater to familiarize myself with the harbor, the ships present, and the activity on the piers. The harbormaster had been cooperative, and the noise and activity on the piers reminded me of working for Moshe. I returned to the mainland, sat on a secluded bench, and watched the sun sink toward the horizon. I thought of Pilate and our ventures, his family, and Portia. A part of my life was coming to an end. I felt also a sense of remorse as though I was committing a wrongful act, but I convinced myself I must plan their departure. It was the right thing to do. By sundown, I had a plan.

The next afternoon, I again visited Pilate. We sat amidst the cushions, and I explained my plan. "Late on the day prior to sailing, you board the ship for Rome, sign a passenger manifest, direct the storing of your baggage, and go to your assigned quarters. During the night, a boatman and I will come alongside your ship and take you aboard. In all the confusion of getting under way the next morning, no one will notice you are not on board. When you are discovered missing, everyone will assume you fell overboard, or someone killed you and dropped your body overboard. Your name on the manifest will be proof you were on board when the ship left Caesarea. We will hide you until we find a ship for Alexandria, or wherever you would like to go. When you pick a destination, you, Claudia, and Portia, dressed in Jewish garments, will board the ship and sign the manifest with assumed names. I will arrange passage, tell the officer you do not speak their particular Greek but understand some, and request he make sure you disembark at the port you wish."

I paused. "Think about the plan. I believe we can make it work."

"It seems simple enough. My personal affairs are in order. I will make the final plans for my office. You explain the plan to Portia. I'll tell her you are here."

I stood and waited for Portia to arrive. "It is good to see you again," I said to her and pointed to the open porch. We walked to the far parapet.

"Father said you had a plan."

"Yes, but I wanted you to assure us we can make it work."

"I will do what I can." She leaned on the smooth surface of the parapet, gazing at the beauty around us.

To the north, the setting sun gave the towers of the breakwater a rosy glow and reflected off the polished stones of the buildings in the city. The ships were afloat on a crimson sea.

I explained the plan to Portia. "Do you think it will work?"

"Yes, I do. Mother and I have worn Jewish garments enough to feel comfortable. You can secure garments for Father." She was quiet for a moment. "Once more, we must part. This time I do not know where I am going. Will I ever see you again?"

The sun was slipping below the horizon, and twilight was deepening. The lamps in the signal towers along the breakwater were being lit, one by one. The last rays of the sun bathed Portia in a soft glow. How perfect were her features: the dark eyes, the delicate high bridge of her nose, the smooth, thin lips. At that moment, I would have exchanged everything to escape with her to a secluded garden.

"Let me serve out my time with the legion," I said. "Then I will go to Tarsus and establish my life there. After that, I will find you.

We can live where you wish or we can return to my home in Cilicia. It is beautiful there. Together we can live out our days."

"Oh, what a pleasure that would be. I will look forward to the day," she said. "But I am fearful it will never happen. How will you find me?"

I took her in my arms and kissed her. Embarrassed by my boldness, I quickly released her.

"After waiting so long, it was my pleasure," she said softly.

I was filled with elation. "Portia, I will find you. I will not be content until you are at my side. Any place then will be paradise. Would that it happened today! Never be discouraged. I will find you."

It had grown dark, and stars were beginning to appear. The signal towers were lit. As we walked toward the palace, I placed my arm around her waist. At the entrance, I wished her goodnight, embraced her gently, marveled at her delicateness, and then walked toward the barracks.

The next day, I purchased a cloak, tunic, and turban for Pilate. At one time, they had been fine clothing but were now worn enough not to attract attention.

Pilate prepared for the trip to Rome. I would take charge of the palace guard, and Roman officials would administer his office. He withdrew a significant sum from his accumulated pay account and arranged to have his baggage delivered to the dock.

A few days previously, I had asked the harbormaster to notify me of ships destined for Alexandria or any North African port. A clerk from his office requested the guard call me to the palace entrance. He told me a Greek ship destined for Alexandria had arrived to replenish food and water and would put to sea in two or three days.

Early the next morning, I inquired of the harbormaster about the ship. "The *Lucretia* is an old ship and has been a regular visitor since the port opened," he said. "Her captain is an old seaman name Timaeus. He and his family are part owners. He is among the last of the old captains. To him and his kind, being a ship's officer is still the highest of callings. Of all the vessels in the harbor, I would say the *Lucretia* is safer than most, and her captain is the best of the lot."

He pointed to the far breakwater. "He is moored at the first small pier on the outward breakwater where he can better load the water casks and supplies. He tells me we have the best water among all the ports, and our supplies are available and reasonable. He is loading now and should finish tomorrow, then sail the next day. You can see the name *Lucretia* in gold letters on the ship's bow. The captain chose that name because as long as he owns part of her, he has wealth. You will find him a good man."

I thanked him for his assistance, complimented him on his harbor and its operation, and walked to where the *Lucretia* was loading. The crew and laborers on the pier stepped aside, and I walked up the gangplank to the captain. He had a pleasant demeanor, his face bearing evidence of many years at sea. I held out my hand. "Welcome to Caesarea Maritima. I hope your stay has been pleasant. Is there anything I can do for you on behalf of Pontius Pilate, Prefect?"

"Centurion, you honor our ship," he said, grasping my hand. "I do not recall ever a welcome from a centurion and certainly never one on behalf of a prefect. Thank you. Caesarea is a fine port, the finest on the Great Sea. There is nothing you can do to improve our stay. Please convey my compliments to Pontius Pilate. May I be of assistance to you?"

"Yes, I have a friend, his wife, and daughter who request passage to Alexandria. They are Jewish but not among the wealthy and have little baggage. Can you accommodate them?"

"I am pleased to do so," he replied. "They can occupy my quarters. Have them board two days from today. I would like to sail the third morning from today. Let me show you my quarters to see if they are acceptable. They are adequate for me but may be austere for another."

He took me to a small room at the stern of the ship. The decking was old and showed signs of wear, but the seams were tight. As the harbormaster had said, the *Lucretia* was old but in good condition. The captain opened the door to his quarters. As he said, everything was austere but clean. It was all Pilate and his family would need.

The next morning in the palace hall, Pilate, Claudia, and Portia donned their Jewish garments to become accustomed to them. Selecting what to take was difficult. Finally, they were reduced to items filling two large pouches. Portia was saddened to the point of a few tears to leave behind the manuscripts. I was so moved by her state that I promised to make sure they reached the farm.

The ship to Rome was to sail early the following day. In my Jewish dress, I arranged with a local boatman to be alongside Pilate's ship at the end of the second night watch. I had him repeat my instructions and then asked him to meet me at his pier at the end of the first night watch. I paid him and promised an equal amount if our venture succeeded.

Late that afternoon, Pilate and I walked to the ship destined for Rome. His baggage had been loaded and stored, and he carried only a small pouch. He boarded and signed the passenger manifest, and an officer conducted us to his room. Pilate thanked the officer, and we returned to stroll around the deck, paying particular attention to the location of a fixed ladder on the side of the ship. As darkness fell, I made a great display of leaving Pilate, wishing him well on his voyage.

That night, allowing plenty of time, I arrived at the dock and boarded the boat that would take me to Pilate's ship. Suspecting the nature of our venture, the boatman had wrapped woolen cloth around the oars and lined the oar locks with fabric. Without a sound, we proceeded to the ship and positioned the boat near the fixed ladder.

We were early. To avoid detection, the boatman kept our vessel close by until I saw a figure come over the rail and down the ladder. I assisted Pilate into the boat, and we slipped away. The boatman delivered us to a designated place, a deserted boathouse on the outward breakwater. I paid double the amount promised, placing my index finger over my lips. He smiled, placed his finger over his lips, and gave a slight wave of his hand to show me he understood.

I left Pilate in the boathouse where he would remain most of the next day. When I arrived at the palace, Claudia and Portia were asleep on cushions in the great hall. I went to my quarters.

The next afternoon, I donned Jewish dress and informed the

fortress guard I would be gone overnight. At the livery, I selected a legion baggage cart and horse and returned to the palace entrance. Claudia and Portia were waiting. I picked up the two pouches, and Claudia picked up a small bundle of clothing. I loaded the cart, assisted the two women to the seat, and started toward the harbor. It was yet an hour until darkness. This late in the day, there would be little activity at the harbor and none on the pier with the abandoned boathouse. I tied the horse to a post at the end of the breakwater, assisted Claudia and Portia from the cart, picked up the pouches, and the three of us walked along the breakwater onto the pier.

At the boathouse, Pilate, Claudia, and Portia changed into Jewish garments. I rolled the abandoned clothing into a small bundle and dropped it into the water. The three of them looked the part of a Jewish family. We walked along the breakwater to the pier where the *Lucretia* was still loading. I boarded and talked to the captain, allowing him time to recognize me. It took him several moments, then he broke into a hearty laugh and welcomed me with great cordiality.

"The passengers are friends of mine," I said. "They speak a special dialect, but the gentleman does understand Greek. Be sure they disembark at Alexandria. They will be good passengers. I wish I could accompany them. I am pleased they are in your care." I paid him the quoted fare plus a gratuity.

"Thank you for the gratuity. You are very generous. I will provide for them. It will be my pleasure to be of service. We will sail at first light. You may stay as long as you wish." He led us to his quarters, removed some personal items, and left us.

They were aboard a ship for Alexandria! This departure had surely been destined, for the timing had been a miracle. A wave of sadness engulfed me, for this might be the last time I would see Portia, or any of them.

What would Judea be without Pilate? I thought. He had been a landmark. Without him, I was lost, without direction, without a vision of what should be. I felt all Judea would be adrift, without anyone to guide us.

I wondered how he must feel, having given a lifetime of service to Rome and now leaving, disguised as an impoverished Jew. The thought passed in a moment.

Portia and Claudia sat on the edge of the bunk, Pilate in the available chair, and I sat on a storage locker, each facing the others.

"I have difficulty realizing I am not bound for Rome. Tiberius abandoned his office for pleasures at Capri. There was no reason to call me to Rome. I am convinced I was to be arrested on my arrival. I wish I knew the reason," Pilate said. "I have never been to Alexandria. I am sure opportunities are there, but I can think about that later."

He turned to me. "Your time in the legion is almost up. What will you do when it ends?"

"Less than a year remains. I look forward to being with my family and working the farm," I said. "I would like to join you and Claudia and Portia wherever you settle and, with your permission, marry Portia and do whatever Portia wishes to do." I was embarrassed to request permission to marry Portia in such a manner.

"Nothing would please me more, if my daughter is agreeable."

"Father, nothing would please me more than to marry Cornelius and go with him wherever he wishes. I should regret leaving you and Mother, but I would go with him today if it were possible."

"I am well pleased," said Pilate. "Would that we were already settled and could arrange the wedding."

"Cornelius, you do not know how many times Portia and I speculated whether you would ever ask," Claudia said. "This is now a happy occasion."

The parting developed into a pleasant evening, although the sadness of parting was only a thought away. We continued talking until the hour was late. I got up and looked outside. No one was on deck. It must have been well past midnight.

I extended my hand to Pilate. "Thank you for all you have done for me. With your assistance, I became the best I could be. I shall never forget."

Pilate grasped my hand. "Cornelius, without your help, I could not have administered my office with the success I achieved. You will be pleased to know I have come to believe law may well be based on a higher order. I shall miss our discussions. I look forward to seeing you again."

I moved toward Claudia and embraced her as she wiped away her tears.

"Cornelius," she said, "I look forward to the day when we shall meet again."

Portia was smiling through her tears. I embraced and kissed her on the lips. "Portia, I will count the days. Do not lament the loss of your manuscripts. At the farm, they will join a roomful of others. Together, we will read them all. Never be discouraged. I will find you."

I saluted Pilate and, despite my Jewish dress, said, "For the Senate and the people of Rome."

I turned and walked out of the room and along the gangplank, bidding goodnight to the sentinel. The walk to the cart and the ride to the fortress was a long journey I recalled many times.

That night as I lay on my pallet, my sadness was dispelled as the darkness was dispelled at sundown on the day of the crucifixion. I recalled Pilate and me standing shoulder to shoulder, studying a map and planning the placement of the legion. Like an experienced judge, time will deliberate his case, tally the facts, then hand down his decision.

The loss of Portia was different.

†

Sometime later, we heard Pilate and others had been lost in a storm at sea. There were also rumors the Sicarii had killed him and tossed his body overboard. I prepared Portia's manuscripts for shipping. I packed them all in a single pouch, including my copy of *Job*. It remained in my quarters until I boarded ship.

†

We received word of Pilate's replacement, and on the day of Marcellus's arrival, I formed the Tenth Legion in battle dress with unit standards to welcome him to Judea with full military honors. To my dismay, however, he and his vanguard passed in front of the legion without looking our way, not so much as a salute from any in his group. To assuage my disappointment and anger, I conducted the reception formalities as though he were present.

I expected a summons from him to review his expectations of the legion. Learning he had assumed his duties as prefect, in my light armor I went to his office, expecting to spend time with him. I introduced myself to his aide who, much to my surprise, was dressed as a Roman citizen. I requested permission to see Marcellus. The aide excused himself, left the office, then returned and suggested that I be seated. I waited some time, my anger rising, before the aide motioned me into Marcellus's office. To my surprise, he wore a Roman toga and tunic with the stripe of his equestrian order.

I stood before his desk, saluted, then said, "My name is Cornelius, first centurion, First Cohort, Tenth Legion Fretensis. On behalf of the legion, welcome to Caesarea Maritima and to Judea. I am here to receive orders for the Tenth Legion."

Marcellus did not return my salute but replaced a stylus to its holder. In a pleasant voice, he replied, "Thank you, Centurion, for the welcome. I noticed the legion was in formation on my arrival. I do not rely on such formalities. Is there anything I can do for you?"

"For Pontius Pilate, I was liaison with the Sanhedrin and the temple leaders in Jerusalem. I speak Aramaic. I will be pleased to be of service."

"Thank you for your offer, but I am confident the officials here and in Jerusalem can perform those duties."

I turned without saluting and left his office. I resolved to limit my duties to keeping the legion in readiness, including those duties performed by Pilate to make sure it received its supplies on time and the quality was the best we could obtain. I scheduled a training program. It was not rigorous, but it was sufficient to keep the men in good condition.

Marcellus proved a pleasant person and easy to work with. He conducted his office from Herod's palace in Caesarea Maritima, seldom if ever going to Jerusalem. Pilate's discipline made Marcellus's assumption of the prefect's duties easy. But he was different. His arms and shoulders were like those of the wife of a Roman official. He had never worked at common labor, and his features did not have the firmness that comes from a rigorous lifestyle. I suspected he was a stranger to the short sword and the pilum. I was apprehensive how he would handle a prefect's office in this harsh and demanding land.

Marcellus abandoned the post in Galilee as it was under the jurisdiction of Herod Antipas. He also withdrew all the Tenth from Jerusalem to Caesarea Maritima.

In Jerusalem, there were already subtle changes that he did not perceive. The Sanhedrin exceeded its authority in several incidents, each more serious than the one preceding. The Roman officials in Jerusalem voiced their concern. Because I spoke Aramaic, I became the liaison between Marcellus and the Sanhedrin.

The religious leaders assumed more control over the administration of the city. Soon they were comfortable making arrests of those who perverted the law. The Sanhedrin and the chief priest were anxious about the growth of the followers of Jesus, who called themselves Followers of the Way.

During my visits to Jerusalem as liaison, I met with the Sanhedrin at designated sites, for many were Pharisees and careful not to defile themselves. As a condition to the meeting, I had to attend without weapons or armor.

At one of the meetings held adjacent to the temple court, four temple guards led me into a room, instructed me to remove my Roman military garments and gave me a Jewish tunic, then led me to a small waiting room. After some time, I was escorted into large room with long tables and chairs alongside. After sitting there some time, my anger rising as the time lagged, the Sanhedrin entered, pompous in their demeanor and opulent in their appearance. I looked carefully at each as he entered. Not one had the lean, hard features of a leader but appeared soft and indolent, indicative of a lifestyle in keeping with their elegant raiment. Most wore their hair long, and all had luxurious, well-groomed beards. By legionnaire standards, there was not a man among them.

After seating themselves by some official sequence, one of the younger members stood and inquired, "It is our understanding you desire a meeting with this group. You may now state your purpose."

I replied in my best Aramaic, "It has come to Marcellus's attention that you arrested a Follower of the Way named Stephen, tried him, found him guilty of blasphemy, and sentenced him to death. No one can be put to death without Marcellus's approval."

"The Sanhedrin," he replied, "found him guilty of the sin of blasphemy, an act punishable by death under our law. Marcellus administers Roman law and is in Caesarea Maritima. The blasphemy occurred in Jerusalem. Stephen was tried here and is to be stoned here."

"It is Roman policy that you cannot execute anyone without the prefect's approval."

"You are a message carrier. You have no authority here. The execution will take place as scheduled. Take that message to your prefect."

The Sanhedrin was bluffing. However, I had no legionnaires to enforce Roman policy. The few legionnaires in the fortress were there to monitor activity in the temple court.

"I will bring the matter to Marcellus's attention."

"Please do." After conferring with two of the older members, the spokesman turned to me and said, "We see no need to continue the meeting."

Again, in keeping with their ranking, the Sanhedrin filed from the room. As the last member left, the four guards entered and motioned for me to follow them. They led me to the room where my raiment lay on the floor and motioned for me to dress. After I had donned my red tunic, the guard led me with great ceremony to the entrance to the temple.

On my release, I strode briskly toward the fortress. My body fairly shook with rage. The special nails in my sandals struck sharply the paving stones, a warning to anyone in my way to stand aside. In my anger, I pictured the hardened nails striking fire.

Suddenly, two old men carrying a lame man between them on a frame stepped into my path. I did not break my stride, knocking down the first of the two men and causing the lame man to fall to the street. The two men abandoned their passenger. The lame man cowered as he knelt, his hands clasped as in prayer, his head bowed to receive the expected blow. Immediately my anger softened. I knelt beside the man and assisted him onto his frame. I called to the two old men to pick it up. They stared at me. To allay their fear, I said, "I am a Follower of the Way. Please forgive me. I regret I have caused this incident."

Both men came to assist the lame man. I removed several denarii from my pouch, giving two to each man. As the men left, one gave the traditional parting, "Peace be unto your house."

I resumed my journey but at a normal pace. I recalled an admonition by Simmias. "Anger and reason are like two spirited horses pulling in opposite directions. Anger jeopardizes any task. Reason reduces the likelihood of error."

No longer angry, my thoughts returned to my report to Marcellus. I resolved that I would urge him to correct the usurpation of Roman authority by the Sanhedrin. That was the best I could do. I could not correct the situation. By the time I reached the fortress, I had recovered myself and entered the eating hall. Although it was late when I finished my meal, I visited the bath. The legionnaires present were assigned permanently to the fortress, but I knew them well.

One of them said, "We heard you provided a great reception for Marcellus. To your credit, you handled that situation much better than I would have. I am pleased to be here at the fortress. I am fearful the Tenth will soon be assigned to the desert to chase scorpions."

I replied, "Do not be too harsh with Marcellus. He was not as fortunate as we. He was never a mule. Can you imagine growing up with nothing to do but eat and sleep? It is no wonder he is the way he is."

I had difficulty sleeping that night, for I kept recalling the effrontery of the young Sadducee. He was convinced he was right, but he carried the false message. Any messenger absolutely convinced his message is absolutely right is dangerous not only to himself but to the entire world. I feared for Jerusalem.

While yet in Jerusalem, after the meeting with the Sanhedrin, I visited my friends at the Hillel School. We exchanged greetings, then I asked, "What do you hear now of issues existing between the religious leaders and Rome?"

The eldest teacher said, "We do not take sides in such issues. We are concerned; however, the Sanhedrin and the chief priest will continue to usurp Roman authority until one day there will be a confrontation. The longer the delay, the greater the confrontation and the greater the force Rome will apply. Rome will be successful. We are fearful Jerusalem will be destroyed."

Another teacher said, "We cannot understand why the Sanhedrin cannot see how it must end. It would be better for us not to be here when it does. I have heard how Rome handles insurrections."

"All the old ones who remember a siege are dead," another added. "Their children who heard of the destruction are dead. Jerusalem encounters the same disaster over and over, sooner or later. I am fearful it will happen to my children, certainly to my grandchildren."

"I agree," I said. "Marcellus is allowing it to happen. He sees Judea as in a dream."

After more exchanges among us, I thanked them for their honesty and bade them goodbye, for my report to Marcellus had been verified.

While in Jerusalem, I visited Galilee. In Capernaum, I found no one present when I visited Moshe's house. I then visited Matthew, for I was anxious what had transpired since the crucifixion.

I was not sure how Matthew was disposed toward me. He knew by now of the stoning of Stephen and of other arrests of Followers of the Way. Even in Galilee, Matthew was yet subject to arrest.

Matthew stood when he saw me and said, "Cornelius, my dear friend, may peace be unto your house. It is good to see you again. I am pleased to join you, as there is at present no caravan to tally. There is a small courtyard behind the building. It will be cooler there and quieter."

Matthew led the way, and we seated ourselves on a bench under a large tree. He said, "The last time I saw you was the night of Jesus's arrest. That seems long ago. You had just joined us when the temple guard arrived. I had drawn my sword and joined the others to defend Jesus when he stepped to our front and ordered us to put our swords away."

Matthew looked downward, then added, "I saw a soldier strike Judas a killing blow and other soldiers easily disarm Peter. The guard attempted to arrest us, but in the darkness and confusion, we were able to slip away. We were fearful of arrest and returned to the room where we had observed the evening meal. We expected the temple guard to break in at any moment and arrest us."

Matthew looked at me and said, "You have heard by now that Jesus appeared to us, although we had secured the doors. In spite of all the doubts, he convinced us he was alive. I yet have difficulty, fearing somehow it never happened."

Then, looking away, he said, "He was again our leader and instructed us to meet him in Galilee by the Sea. We left Jerusalem one by one. I made my way here and on the appointed day went to the meeting place. Jesus and some of the disciples were already there. He had prepared a breakfast of fresh fish as in the old days."

Again, he looked at me and said, "Jesus assured us we were to establish his kingdom, and he would always be with us. Never before had I felt such dedication. My heart ached to be on my way. Then he was gone, and we were all alone."

"What has happened since that morning by the sea?" I asked.

"I attend to the collection of tolls," he said, "but I also teach in Galilee and Perea and plan to give up my position here. No one attempted to reestablish our group, but each in his own way is spreading the good news."

We had been some time in the courtyard, and Matthew had acknowledged a summons from those in his booth more than once. I stood, as did Matthew, and we wished each other well.

I rode on to Caesarea Philippi, arriving at the villa late in the day.

Moshe and Joshua were working in the garden. To my great surprise, I saw John with them. Later, as all of us sat at the large table in the disciples' room, I asked for news.

Moshe said he was meeting caravans as they entered Capernaum but was spending more time at the villa, for John had joined them along with Mary, mother of Jesus, her daughters, and the other women. With John and the women present, Joshua said it was becoming more like home.

I looked at John. His beard and hair had grown, adding to his commanding demeanor. I said, "John, my friend, it seems a long time since that night in Gethsemane. Without your help, we could never have placed Judas in the cart. Your presence at the crucifixion was a bold gesture. It is good to see you here. Do you provide for Mary?"

"Yes," he said, "but there are other reasons. I mourn the loss of my friend. I hoped you might be here. Your presence at the crucifixion made a difference. I was fearful harm would come to the women. It also prevented my arrest."

"I was destined to be there." Encouraging him to continue, I said, "Why are you here?"

"Jesus's crucifixion and departure weigh heavily upon me. When he left us there by the sea, I did not know what to do. I had no place to go. Mary and the others were here, so I came here. Moshe showed me the chronicles. I am a fisherman and unclean. I never learned to read and to write, but now I am a disciple of Moshe. He is teaching me both Aramaic and Greek. Reading and writing are miracles."

John continued, "That night after we left Judas with Lazarus, I returned to Jerusalem and was there when Jesus presented himself. I was confused and deeply moved. I did not tell them about Judas. He was my friend, and I should have defended him. On my way to Galilee, I visited Lazarus. He said Jesus had healed Judas and had gone to Jerusalem to find you. I never told anyone about Judas. He was my friend, but I was not strong enough to defend him. Purchasing the land on his behalf was a fitting gesture."

When John paused, I said, "I saw Judas after he was healed. He

was like the Judas in Galilee. Jesus welcomed him into his kingdom and urged him to spread the good news. He was on his way to
Caesarea Maritima to find a ship."

"I was among the last to leave Jerusalem," John said, "and after
visiting Lazarus, I hurried to Galilee, for I feared Jesus might arrive
before I did. When I arrived, he was not yet there. Peter and Andrew
acquired a boat from their father, and we fished. We fished all night
and caught nothing. At dawn, we saw Jesus on the shore. He shouted
to us to cast our net on the other side of the boat, which we did, and
hauled in a net full of big fish. We pulled it to shore and joined Jesus.
He prepared breakfast for all of us. It was like the good days. I wish
you could have been present at a conversation between Jesus and Peter.
Jesus used Greek words in his Aramaic. It recalled discussions at
this very table, when we discussed the difficulty conveying a concept
from one language into another. I now find myself thinking about the
meaning of words and whether they convey the exact thought I have."

John paused. "I remember discussing the number of Greek words
for different types of love compared to so very few in Aramaic. At
this table, I learned the Greek word *agape* describes the highest form
of love, a sacrificial, completely unselfish love, as the love of a mother
for her child. One of the other words for *love* was the Greek *philia*,
which describes the love among close family members, or among
those exposed to great danger."

He looked at me. "In Galilee by the Sea, before Jesus arrived,
Peter was apprehensive concerning Jesus's arrival. From a conversation
later between Jesus and Peter, I learned that after the arrest of Jesus,
at great risk of arrest himself, he followed the crowd to the house of
Caiaphas, the high priest. He stood by a fire close to the porch where
Caiaphas was questioning Jesus. A serving woman recognized him
and identified him in the presence of the guard. When challenged
three times by an officer, Peter three times denied he knew Jesus. The
denial was loud enough for Jesus to hear, for Peter said Jesus looked
in his direction.

"That morning by the sea, after we finished breakfast, I was with

Peter when Jesus motioned for him to come nearer. I was by his side. His countenance had fallen, and his head was bowed. In a most tender voice and manner, placing his hand on Peter's shoulder, Jesus said, 'Peter, look at me. Do you love me?' using for *love* the Greek word *agape*. Peter delayed a response, raised his head, looked at Jesus, then bowed his head again and answered in a whisper, 'You know I love you,' using for *love* the Greek word *philia*.

"Jesus, his hand still on Peter's shoulder and with more compassion, said again, 'Peter, look at me. Do you love me?' Again, using for *love, agape*. Peter did not raise his head but said barely above a whisper, 'Yes, Lord, you know I love you,' using again the word *philia*.

"Jesus said, 'Peter, my dear friend, look at me. Do you love me?' This time, however, Jesus used for *love* the word *philia*. Peter then raised his head, tears streaming down his face, and answered, 'Lord, you know everything. You know I love you," using the same word for love Jesus had used, *philia*. He bowed his head and broke into great sobs. Jesus laid his hands on Peter's head, and he stood, yet weeping, and embraced Jesus. He knew Jesus had forgiven him.

"Jesus used Greek words to welcome Peter into the fold, although for Jesus he never was outside. Had we not discussed the meanings of words like *love*, I would not have understood why Peter was so heartbroken when Jesus ceased using the word *agape* and used instead the word *philia*.

"Later, when Peter had recovered his demeanor, the three of us were standing together. He asked of Jesus, 'What about John?'"

John delayed for a moment and then said, "Jesus looked at me, then at Peter, and said, 'Peter, you have a difficult way to go. You will be tested more severely than you can imagine. John, too, has a difficult way, but if I desired him to tarry until I return, that is between John and me.'"

John looked at me. "What did Jesus intend? Am I to tarry until he returns?"

I glanced at Moshe and Joshua. Both were transfixed by what John had related.

"John," I said, "you knew Jesus better than any of us. The incident you related merits remembering. Prepare your own chronicle of what you have seen and heard. Otherwise, no one will know."

John bowed his head but did not reply. I said, "I am pleased you are here and pleased to see the women here. My time in the legion is almost complete. Since that spring day twenty years ago, the world has changed. Of the world I loved so much, you here alone are all that remain."

I turned to the purpose of my visit. "I regret to do so, but I must dispose of the villa. Moshe, I will transfer it to you with the understanding that everyone can remain."

No one responded. We sat a long time in the lamplight in silence.

The next day, with a sense of sadness, I departed for Jerusalem. I kept the horse at a steady trot until I passed Capernaum. Then I let it walk at its own pace.

My world was coming undone. Pilate was gone. I did not know where Portia was. I would soon leave Moshe, Joshua, and the villa, and I would no longer be first centurion of the First Cohort.

†

After a night in Jerusalem, I selected my favorite mount and began the journey to Caesarea Maritima. I entered the costal road by early afternoon. Over the years, I had noticed the grain fields of a particular farmer were consistently better than those of his neighbors. The wheat was as good as that grown in Cilicia. I turned into the way to the farm, and when I reached the gate to the courtyard, I shouted a greeting.

An older man approached, his face like weathered leather. "Peace be unto your house," I said. "I have passed your farm many times, and your wheat always is good, the stalks tall and the heads full."

"Welcome, my friend. May peace abide with you. Sit here in the shade. By your sandals and horse, you are a legionnaire. The Jewish raiment is inconsistent."

"Yes, I am Cornelius, centurion, the Italian Cohort, Tenth Legion, returning to the fortress. I travel in Jewish raiment."

The farmer nodded. "My name is Jacob. You grace my humble dwelling."

"I am a farmer from Cilicia," I said. "We grow fine wheat there, but your wheat is as good. How do you accomplish this?"

He smiled and said, "May I offer sour wine or, if you prefer, good wine?"

"I am pleased to take sour wine."

He shouted to someone in the house to fetch sour wine and then said, "You noticed the difference between my fields and the others? Most people see only a field, not the quality. My Gentile friend, it is indeed a pleasure to talk with a Roman who can speak Aramaic and who notices the difference in wheat. You are indeed welcome."

An elderly woman in peasant dress placed a cup of wine before each of us and returned to the house.

He continued. "No one ever asked me to account for the difference. Before the winter rains, I make a trip to the Salt Sea with two pack mules and fill four containers with salt cakes. I spread the salt from three containers over the fields where I will next plant the wheat. The fourth container, during the winter and spring, I mix with manure for my garden. Among us, there is a saying: 'Cast your good salt upon the soil and upon the manure pile, but throw away your bad salt to be trod under foot.'"

He stood, looked over his fields, and said, "Allow me to show you my farm."

We walked the outside of the courtyard, the farmer pointing out the crops, animal pens, olive trees, and vineyard. He was especially proud of a cistern built into the ground, looking much like a well with a counterbalanced beam to lift the water.

I felt a bond with him based on our love of the land.

We returned to the table. Still standing, I finished my wine and thanked him for his hospitality. He accompanied me to my horse.

"May our Lord bless you now and forever," he said, bowing slightly.

"Peace be with you and your house," I replied as I mounted and turned toward the coastal road.

On reaching the road, I dismounted where one of his fields of wheat joined it and walked along its edge. The grain was waist high. I extended my right palm over the heads of wheat, feeling them brush against my open palm. I could smell the grain ripening in the sun. I recalled the wheat fields at home.

The shrill cry from a desert eagle overhead woke me from my reverie. I collected two full heads of wheat, as I had done so many times on the farm, rolled them between my palms, and blew the chaff from the cup of my hands. I tossed the grain into my mouth and savored the taste. Once again, I longed to return to my home.

I placed my arms over the saddle, resting my forehead against it, savoring the taste of the wheat, thinking what a paradise this earth affords. She brings forth her goodness, which sustains us and gives us the taste of ripened wheat. In my reverie, I walked again with my father and the others the long path from the lower fields toward our home where Mother would have ready the evening meal.

My horse stamped his left foot, interrupting my dream. I stepped to his shoulder and stroked his mane, talking softly. Beyond us was the coast and the sea, with the fields in the foreground, the sea blending into the horizon. I recalled standing on the step in front of the kitchen door, looking at the snowcapped mountains with their dark ridges and gray outcroppings, awed by the beauty. I longed to feel in summer the cool breeze from the Taurus Mountains and on a frosty winter morning to smell the faint smell of wood smoke, more pleasing than fine incense. This earth, like a mother, provides for us not only our needs but a quality that makes our existence a paradise.

Jesus's words, "Today you will be with me in paradise," flashed through my mind. How can that paradise exceed the one here and now?

As I gazed into the distance, my horse placed his head gently on my right shoulder, as he had done so many times. I stroked his head from forehead to muzzle. My Jewish friends believed God breathed into the nostrils of animals the breath of life, just as he had breathed it into mankind. This remains one of the most pleasing of all my memories of Palestine.

I roused myself from my reverie, mounted, and continued my journey. A short time later, I entered the fortress at Caesarea Maritima.

✝

The next morning, I visited Marcellus's office and left a message I was ready to report. Later, his aide visited the guard room to tell me Marcellus was ready to see me.

I had removed the Jewish garments, bathed, eaten, and then dressed in my red tunic and light armor. I reported to Marcellus, saluted, and waited for his acknowledgment. He returned my salute in a casual manner and asked for my report.

"I visited my friends in Jerusalem. They are teachers of Jewish law and are aware of political happenings. They are concerned the Sanhedrin and the religious leaders are assuming authority in political matters."

Marcellus interrupted. "Jewish teachers may be experts in Jewish religion, but what do they know of Roman law?"

I was taken aback by his dismissal but continued. "While in Jerusalem, the chief priest arrested a member of a new sect, tried him, found him guilty of blasphemy, and sentenced him to death by stoning. I advised the Sanhedrin it did not have the authority to condemn anyone to death without Roman approval. They replied the issue was a religious matter and within their authority—not yours to make."

"Blasphemy is a religious, not a political, offense," Marcellus said. "Local officials have authority to handle such matters. I do not see a challenge to Roman authority in the stoning of a blaspheming Jew."

"My Jewish friends and I believe the Sanhedrin will continue to usurp Roman authority. I recommend a cohort of the Tenth be assigned to Jerusalem and you establish your office there until the situation returns to normal."

"The Sanhedrin is the local government," Marcellus said, "and Roman policy is to allow local government to govern until such time as there is a clear indication it cannot do so. The death of a local Jew does not seem to be a challenge to Roman authority. Thank you for your report. I will keep it in mind."

He picked up his stylus to let me know the meeting was over. I saluted. He did not return it. I turned and left his office.

It was one of my worst days in the legion. I sat on my bunk, my head in my hands, thinking about what had transpired. I did not sleep well that night, but by the next morning, I was reconciled to attending my duties as first centurion and no longer concerned myself with the affairs of the prefect's office.

†

Some weeks later, I was attracted to activity at the entrance to the fortress. When I arrived, a detachment was escorting a prisoner into the courtyard. I recognized the prisoner. It was Saul, Moshe's son.

With proper ceremony, the centurion of the detachment released Saul to our authority. I walked to the guard room, hoping to learn the circumstances of Saul's imprisonment. He was delivering some documents to our centurion of the guard. I could not recall his name.

I waited until he had completed the delivery and then said, "I am Cornelius, first centurion, Tenth. Welcome to our post. May I get you anything, some wine or water?"

The centurion recognized me, stepped forward, and extended his hand. "Cornelius, it is good to see you. No, I will join my unit in the dining hall after I finish here. Thank you for your welcome. How are you bearing the rigors of serving Rome here in Caesarea Maritima?"

"I bear the burden without complaint like any good legionnaire. Regarding the prisoner you brought in, he and I grew up together. Do you know the charge against him?"

"All I know is that he is a Roman citizen charged with a civil offense. He needs a surgeon. I was anxious he would not complete the
journey. He said it was an old injury. He is a tough Jew."

"Yes, I remember when he was injured. It gave him trouble."

"I am happy to be rid of him," said the centurion as he walked
toward the door. "From the time we received him, he never ceased
talking—too many lotus blooms. He was friendly and never complained about the pace or the chains, although the leg injury must
have pained him greatly."

"Thank you. I will be aware."

In the doorway, he turned and said, "If I were in authority, I
would turn him loose in the desert to talk with the locusts and the
scorpions. He's harmless." He then added, "Endure the burden of
serving here."

"Thank you for the prisoner. Give the men in Jerusalem my best
wishes."

"For the Senate and people of Rome," he said as he left the office.

Visiting Saul was no small task. I could not imagine what crime he
had committed to be in chains on the way to Rome. I feared what lay
ahead for him. To access the prisoner in some prisons, the visitor was
lowered by a rope into the prisoner's cell. I was anxious about being
lowered into a cell in the darkness and the filth, but I owed Saul the
visit, regardless of the circumstances.

The next day, I entered the prison area and inquired of the guard
the location of Saul's cell. He led me to the area and, at my request,
opened the door. I was encouraged, for here the cells were on a sub-
terranean level with bars overhead allowing some light to enter. The
air was stale and damp but far better than in the cells at Antonia
Fortress in Jerusalem.

As I entered, Saul was standing at the extremity of his chain and
fairly shouted, "Cornelius, you are here! Once again, I am in trouble,
but this is of my own doing."

He was in good spirits, not dismayed by the chain or the conditions. I was reluctant to start the conversation, as we had not parted

as friends. He returned to the bed of straw and sat down, motioning for me to sit on a small box nearby.

"Much has happened since our last meeting," Saul said. "At that time, I was an officer carrying out arrest orders and bringing in violators of religious laws. One day I was on my way to Damascus with arrest orders for some Followers of the Way, as they call themselves. About noon, a flash of light, brighter than the sun, knocked me to the ground. I heard a voice say, 'Saul, Saul, why do you persecute me?' I shouted, 'Who is it?' The reply came, 'I am Jesus, whom you are persecuting.' I saw Jesus just as surely as Stephen did as he was being stoned."

I had difficulty believing what he said. "How is that related to your being here in chains?"

"Most of the Followers of the Way are Pharisees and good Jews. They now include Greeks who wish to become Jewish converts. I was bringing Greek converts to the temple to take Jewish vows when the temple guard attempted to arrest me. The fortress guard again rescued me, took me into the fortress, and was preparing to scourge me for creating a disturbance. I declared I was a Roman citizen and was not subject to such punishment without a trial. In the process of the civil trials, I appealed my case to be heard in Rome. I have been granted that request."

"You are a prisoner," I said, "and will be so treated. Because you are a Roman citizen and charged with a civil crime, you have been given the best of the cells. At least it receives some light. The chain is longer than those in other cells. You must clean your own cell. Prisoners are fed well enough but only once a day. If your trial is to be in Rome, you may be here for months. Imprisonment will be worse than any punishment."

"I know all that," Saul replied. "The cell in Antonia Fortress was not as nice as this. I am reconciled to my lot. I am more than reconciled. I am a true believer born to this end. There is no doubt in my mind that Jesus is risen. Simmias said the pattern of our lives was laid from the beginning of the world. I believe that to be true. No prison cell can deter me from what I am appointed to do."

"I am greatly distressed you are here," I said. "I will do what I can."

"Cornelius, I am a believer, a Follower of the Way. I am no longer Saul. My new name is Paul. What happens is meant to happen. I will endure any hardship, scourging, death itself. Jesus is my witness. He will vindicate me when I stand at the judgment bar, for I am his faithful servant."

I was awed by his conviction. "Should I call you Paul?" I said.

"Yes, my new name is Paul. I have answered to none other since the day I saw Jesus."

"Paul," I replied, "the name does not come easily. The centurion of your escort said you should see a surgeon."

He laughed and said, "Oh, that. You remember I injured my leg working in the warehouse. It yet gives me trouble. From time to time, a splinter rises to the surface, and I must remove it. It happened on our way from Jerusalem. It is no problem."

"The centurion was concerned you might not complete the journey. It must have presented a problem for him."

"On that first day," Paul said, "I felt the splinter deep under the skin. By evening, it was so painful I could barely walk. I borrowed his knife, opened the skin over the splinter, and removed it. I have performed the task many times. It is painful, and the bleeding is difficult to stop, but once it is done, the pain from the splinter is gone."

"Why was the centurion so concerned?"

"When I removed the splinter, it bled badly, but I placed shredded bark from a willow tree over the cut and wrapped it in a bandage cut from my cloak. The centurion was fearful I would bleed to death and walked beside me the next day. We became good friends. He is from Thessalonica. His family owns a small farm there. He hopes one day to return. I was surprised to find he was Greek."

"Some freedom is allowed prisoners," I said, "who can afford it. I can arrange for someone to clean your cell, replace the straw, and remove the waste. I can bring you food, good water, some wine, and a fresh bandage. Your father will want to be with you. I will go to Capernaum and be away almost a week. My heart is broken to see you in these circumstances."

"I have never been happier," he said. "I am doing that which I was born to do. I am a runner trained to run the race. May God send me adversaries worthy of my effort. No Roman prison can deter me from my appointed journey. I can change the world."

Although encouraged by his spirit, I doubted his ability to survive. I said, "I will leave you now. Cooperate with your guards. They can make your time here some better or unbelievably worse. They are not necessarily your adversaries."

I motioned to the guard to open the cell door.

†

I prepared for the journey to Galilee. I withdrew a sum from my accumulated pay and arranged for one of the freed men who frequented the area to clean Paul's cell. The centurion of the First Cohort assumed my duties, and I arranged with the guard to leave the fortress.

How would Moshe respond on learning Saul's name was no longer a Jewish name, beautiful in its sound, but Paul, a Roman name that fell harshly on the ears like a dog barking? How would he react to his being a Follower of the Way and a prisoner in chains?

Early the next morning, I selected a good horse, secured my cloak and a waterskin behind the saddle, and set out for Galilee by way of Cana and Nazareth, it being about a day's journey northeast from the fortress. I concealed my short sword in the folds of my cloak. The road was not well traveled, nor did it qualify as a road by Roman standards.

As I climbed the mountain ridge running north to south, the terrain consisted primarily of stone outcroppings with dried vegetation in the thin soil. On reaching the crest, I could see Mount Hermon to the northeast, still snowcapped this late in the year. I dismounted, retrieved the waterskin, and let water cascade into my mouth. I poured some into a leather cup and allowed the horse to drink.

This was the first time I traveled this road. To the northwest, the Jezreel Valley stretched as far as I could see, the site of battles between armies from Egypt and Syria. From vantage points high on the southern ridge, the commander of an army could watch the battle develop.

I imagined myself commander of six or eight Roman legions against any foe in the world. The level land by the stream was ideal for my chariots and cavalry, and the rolling land to the north ideal to maneuver light infantry. I could watch the tide of battle change from errors in judgment. Seeing a mistake as it developed, I could respond before it became critical. Someday perhaps.

The road descended into the upper valley, winding south of Cana, a small town with a single well. It was a far different country than the coastal plain but beautiful in its own way. I could see Capernaum in the distance.

Arriving in Capernaum, I passed by Moshe's house and went on to Caesarea Philippi, arriving well after dark. Announcing my arrival as I entered the courtyard, I dismounted and walked toward the main room. Moshe and Joshua had opened the door by the time I reached it. Joshua took the horse, and I entered to a reception by Moshe. Until Joshua returned, I engaged in light conversation, for Paul's plight would affect both of them.

When Joshua returned, I said, "Moshe, Saul is a prisoner in the fortress at Caesarea Maritima on his way to Rome. The charge is not serious under Roman law, and if he had not appealed to Rome, he would have been freed by the governor. Regardless, he is in prison, and you both know what that means. He now goes by the name of Paul. He did not tell me why he changed his name, but I believe he wanted a Roman name to allow him to associate with Romans and Greeks. What is of greater importance is that Paul claims to have seen Jesus, talked with him, and he is now a follower of his. I could not believe in what high spirits he is, knowing what lies ahead, but he says that he has never been happier. Paul is like the old Saul in Tarsus. He needs your help while in prison."

"My greatest wish," Moshe said, "is to be reconciled with him. Our last parting broke my heart, not so much from his activity, but he rejected me as less than a good Jew. If he is reconciled to you, a Greek

Gentile, surely he will accept me, a less than faithful Jew. I will assist him as I am permitted. The good news of Saul's change outweighs the bad news of imprisonment."

I said to Joshua, "My dear steward, my dear friend, again the villa is in your hands. While Paul is in prison, Moshe can help him better than anyone else."

Handing him a pouch, I said, "Here is money for the villa, enough to last a year. In addition, there is two year's wages, for indeed you have been the faithful steward. My enlistment ends in less than a year. As I said before, this may be the last time I will see you. I shall never forget you, my dear friend."

Joshua accepted the pouch. "Once again I am saddened by your departure. Being your steward has been my great pleasure. As you have said many times, we shall meet again. May peace be upon your house forever."

That night, Moshe, Joshua, and I talked of many things long into the night. I announced my plan to transfer the villa to Moshe and to offer my chronicle of Jesus's sayings to Matthew.

The next morning, Joshua prepared the best mount for Moshe. After breakfast together, the three of us walked to the entrance to the courtyard, each embraced the other, and then Moshe and I mounted and turned toward Capernaum, waving to Joshua from down the road. I well remember that last view of him in the early sunlight. He was one of the kindest men I ever knew. It was the last time I saw him.

In Capernaum, Moshe and I visited a scribe and transferred the villa to Moshe. We then rode to Matthew's toll station and found him at his post.

"Matthew, my dear friend," I said, "my duty in Palestine is nearing its end. Some time ago, Moshe and I completed chronicles of the teachings of Jesus. Moshe's chronicle is in Aramaic, and mine is in Greek. I would like for you to have my chronicle."

Matthew welcomed us and motioned for us to follow him to the small courtyard. He took the chronicle, sat on a bench, and opened it. He examined the page and studied the reverse side. He turned through several pages, reading a line or two on each.

He turned to me and said, "It is fine work, well written. I am deeply in your debt." Closing the chronicle, he said, "I am saddened your time here is ending. From you I learned people are the same and struggle to survive their own problems. May the God of us all favor your ventures forever."

I replied, "And may God favor your effort to spread the good news. Perhaps we shall meet again."

"Perhaps we shall. I look forward to the day."

Moshe and I mounted and wound our way out of Capernaum, up the road to the mountain crest, me for the last time. We rode steadily, resting our horses occasionally, and arrived at the livery in Caesarea Maritima late during the first night watch. The guard allowed us to spend the rest of the night in the hay loft.

The next morning, Moshe and I agreed I would return to the fortress, resume my duties, and obtain the necessary documents for him to visit Paul. He was to come to the fortress entrance at noon.

I was ready when an aide announced I had a visitor. I followed him to the entrance and welcomed Moshe to the fortress. I gave him the pass, and both of us entered the guard room. I explained to the centurion I was a friend of Paul, introduced Moshe as his father, and indicated he would be attending to his needs.

We walked the passageway around the courtyard square and into the long corridor leading to the prison cells. When Moshe showed the guard the pass, he motioned for us to follow him.

Paul's cell had been cleaned. The straw was new, there was a pot for waste, and he was wearing a clean tunic. On the box serving as a table was a small container with fruit and cheese. The caretaker had exceeded my expectation.

Paul was standing at the extremity of his chain, his face beaming. Moshe walked quickly to him and embraced him. The guard and I stepped outside, the guard locking the cell door.

I thanked the guard for allowing the caretaker to clean Paul's cell and take care of him. I then returned to the main fortress area. I entered the open square, imagining Moshe and Paul rebuilding the relationship they had in Tarsus.

I realized Moshe would need money to pay for his own living arrangement and for meeting Paul's needs. I visited the office of the paymaster and made another withdrawal. To pass the time, I joined my cohort in their training routine. After the evening meal, I returned to the prison. Paul and Moshe were sitting on the edge of the bed of straw. Both stood as I entered.

Paul spoke first. "My father and I are together. It is as it was in Tarsus. I regret my conduct when we met in Jerusalem. That is now a lifetime ago, in a different world. I am interested in hearing about you being with Jesus in Galilee. My father told me of his chronicle of Jesus's sayings." Paul delayed, then added, "I owe you a debt I can never repay. My father and I are together again, and you see how orderly my cell is, including the pitcher of water and the fruit."

"Paul, I owe a debt to your father and to you for the goodness you showed while I was at the university. That was a turning point in my life. Without your help, I would never have joined the legion and never known another world."

Looking toward Moshe, I said, "You can provide Paul some benefit while he is here. Today we will find you a place to stay."

Looking at Paul, I said, "Is there anything you need? We can bring it to you in the morning. Your father and I must go."

"There is nothing I need. I look forward to seeing you in the morning."

I motioned to the guard to open the cell door. I again thanked him for his tolerance, and Moshe and I walked down the long corridor. We entered the guard room, and I arranged to leave the fortress in my Jewish raiment. I asked Moshe to wait at the entrance until I changed.

Moshe and I went to the house where I stayed while studying Aramaic and arranged for Moshe to stay an extended period. The owner conducted us to the room Moshe was to occupy. The room was as austere as my room at the barracks, but it was sufficient. I thanked the owner, then Moshe sat in the only chair, and I sat on the pallet.

"Paul has a hard journey ahead of him," I said. "You see how to enter the fortress with the pass. The guard at the entrance will provide you an escort to Paul's cell. Always ask permission to bring anything into the cell. As Paul is not a criminal awaiting execution, the guards can make concessions. Have you eaten today?"

"No, I never thought of eating."

"Let us find a place."

I returned to one of the eating establishments I frequented when I lived in the section. I ordered a traditional meal, and Moshe and I talked.

"I will be leaving in a few weeks," I said. "By that time, you will be comfortable taking care of Paul. Here is money to last until I go. If you should need anything or have trouble, give a message to one of the aides at the fortress entrance, and he will find me.

"Paul is in good spirits. That will help him more than anything else. He is convinced he is one of Jesus's disciples and was meant to be where he is and doing what he is doing." After a moment, I added, "You can find your way to the house. You are free to visit Paul anytime. You and Paul work out a schedule. May peace be with you and Paul."

Moshe replied, "You have been to me as a son. May peace be with you also."

We walked out of the establishment, Moshe turning toward his house and I returning to the fortress.

To pass time until my enlistment was up, I gave my full attention to the Tenth, but the cohort remained my greatest joy.

✝

The world and the legion had changed since that spring day so long ago. The legion continued to present an image of Rome at its best, but its loyalty was now to its commander. Talk among travelers arriving in Palestine indicated Rome no longer presented the image it once did, or perhaps never did. Palestine was also different. The Italian Cohort was my only interest.

I continued to visit Paul and Moshe and was amazed that Paul continued to be in high spirits. Moshe had replaced the straw with a thin pallet, and there were some scrolls, although the light was poor for reading. Most encouraging of all, the guard arranged for a lighter and longer chain to be substituted for the original. A comradeship between the guards and Paul had grown almost to cordiality. All that was encouraging, for soon it was my last visit.

On the evening prior to my last day in the legion, I arranged a celebration with the cohort, with permission to use the parade ground. The fortress cooks were to prepare legion fare but of the highest quality. To commemorate the dead and our time together, I had arranged the construction of a funeral pyre to the side of the platform. As it burned, it would shed light over all the gathering. This was to be my recognition of the First Cohort, the Italian Cohort, of the Tenth Fretensis, as the best of all the good that Rome had given the world, and to thank the men for allowing me to be their first centurion.

On the morning of my last day, I carried a small crate of assorted fruits and cheeses to Paul's cell. Moshe and I sat on the edge of his pallet, and he sat on a small box. "This is my last visit," I said. "Today is my last day as a member of the legion. This evening, there is a celebration with my cohort. Tomorrow I will board a ship for Tarsus. I would like for this to be a happy occasion. When I recall the good times we had together, the things you both taught me, and the opportunities which followed, life has been for me a great adventure."

"Well said, Cornelius," Paul said. "There are things Simmias taught which explain what I believe better than any words I could use. I do not see any conflict between Moshe's belief as a Pharisee and the teachings of Jesus. Once a person becomes a true believer, all the differences disappear, and he is truly free, directed by his love of his fellow man."

"I agree," Moshe said. "Knowing Simmias and Jesus helped me understand the Torah. Indeed, it is a landmark guiding me in the direction I should go. I am free to live my life guiding on my own landmark."

I stood. "I must leave you now. From my deepest being, I wish both of you the strength and wisdom to live as we have discussed. Knowing each of you has been a high mark. I look forward to knowing you again, unless by some chance we meet in this world."

I embraced each in turn and then motioned to the guard to open the cell door. I walked the long corridor, then stepped into the glare of the open courtyard.

✝

It was late afternoon when I emerged and time to go to the parade ground. On arrival there, I was pleased with what I saw. The tables were prepared, each cook standing by his table. The pyre had been constructed. I stepped up on the small platform and ordered the trumpeter to call for an array. Everyone, including myself, was dressed in light armor. Once the array was formed, I instructed the standard bearer of each century to place his standard at the designated table, then shouted, "Welcome to the best fare in Palestine! Break your array!"

I visited each table to be sure the meal was to my expectation.

After everyone had finished, I sent an aide to light the pyre. Each centurion, beginning with Century Six, was to lead his unit across the platform so that I could bid farewell to each legionnaire. When the Sixth Century reached the platform, it halted, and the centurion of the First Century stepped forward and raised his hands for silence.

"On behalf of the First Cohort of the Tenth Fretensis," he said, "I present this medal to you, Cornelius, First Centurion, in recognition of your leadership making this the First Cohort of the Tenth Legion."

Holding the medal aloft for all to see, the centurion continued. "This medal was cast in Damascus of the finest silver mixed with elements to make it durable as the finest steel. It will last a thousand years. The front is a replica of the standard of the Tenth Fretensis, under which appears the phrase 'For the Senate and the people of Rome.' On the reverse is the inscription, in Latin, in Greek, and in Aramaic, 'Mother Cornelius, First Centurion, Tenth Fretensis, in appreciation.'"

The centurion stepped forward, placed the leather thong over my head, and then stepped back. At his signal, the legionnaires began to clap hands in unison, imitating the sound of a sword striking a shield, then, again on his signal, all gave a raucous, victorious battle shout.

A silence then fell over the group. During the past few days, I had been thinking of some parting remarks I might make. I stepped to the front of the platform and in my command voice said, "Legionnaires of the First Cohort, the Italian Cohort, the Tenth Fretensis, may that name last a thousand years. Thank you for the medal. It will be my honor to wear it always in remembrance of this cohort.

"Someday someone will recover it from my ashes and will, even then, appreciate its significance. During these years, I have watched with great pride your performance. You are an example to the world of what it is to be a legionnaire. You are the best Rome has to offer. We have shared the danger, the hard going, and the great reward of being comrades. I commend you for your courage, wisdom, tolerance, but most of all, your honor. These are the virtues of the legionnaire, and you have them in abundance."

After hesitating a moment, I added, "I must leave you now." I then shouted, "May the standard of the Italian Cohort never know defeat!"

With my heart filled with pride, I saluted the men of the cohort, holding the salute for some time. When I dropped my arm, the cohort responded again, as one man, with the raucous shout.

When the roar died away, I called out, "For the Senate and the people of Rome!"

By that time, the first legionnaire had stepped in front of me. In the light cast by the pyre, I shook the hand of each, calling him by name, and wished him well, for I had recruited him especially for the cohort.

The last legionnaire was the centurion, First Century. I grasped his hand firmly, for he had acted in my stead for many years. As he stepped aside, he gave a command, and the cohort formed a column of two ranks, each facing the other, the arm of each raised, creating a corridor. The centurion pointed to it and entered.

I shouted again for all to hear, "For the Senate and the people of Rome!" and joined him.

It had been a night to remember. Before I fall asleep and when I first wake in the morning, I recall that event.

As I lay on my pallet, I felt a deep contentment. My life had been a great adventure. I marveled at the gift of life. To be born of Cyrus and Myrrine and to grow in that family was a gift. To serve as a Marius mule and to see the Fifth Alaudae deployed for battle was a gift. My time with Pilate and with Jesus had been a gift.

There must be a plan for my life. I wondered whether it might be complete. Then I fell asleep.

†

On the day of my departure, more to my pleasure than displeasure, there was no ceremony. The centurion of the First Century accompanied me to the ship. Earlier he had placed my baggage on board.

On reaching the gangplank, I turned, faced him, grasped his hand, and said, "My good friend, our comradeship has come to an end. You have indeed served me well. Assume my role as first centurion until someone challenges you. May all the gods of Rome give you good counsel."

I then saluted him smartly and said, "For the Senate and the people of Rome."

He returned the salute and said, "On behalf of the Italian Cohort, I wish you well. For the Senate and people of Rome."

CONCLUSION

I turned and walked up the gangplank. By the time I stowed my baggage, the ship was under way. I stood at the rail and watched Caesarea Maritima slip into the distance. Finally, I could no longer see the buildings, only the deep rose outline of the hills beyond, and then they were gone. The shadow of the ship glided effortlessly over the waves.

Some distance away, a trireme was moving toward Caesarea Maritima. It was beautiful, the square sail bright in the late-morning sun against the blue of the sky and the sea, sunlight reflecting from the oars. From its great size and majesty, it should travel for days without sight of land, but with as many as three hundred rowers and crew on board, it put ashore almost daily. The merchantman on which I stood was less impressive but could remain at sea for days.

Marcellus was like the trireme, Paul and Moshe like the merchantman. Marcellus required the support of others. He needed rowers to arrive at his destination. The sail was not sufficient. Paul and Moshe were different. They were capable of longer and more difficult passages. They were engaged in an effort that would succeed, eventually to arrive at a destination. Their belief was like the wind that drove the merchantman, keeping them moving in the right direction.

I thought about the farm and the life I left. I longed to live that life again, to return each evening to the same house, to a home. What good was a home without Portia? I knew what I must do. I resolved as soon as I established myself at the farm, I would begin my search for her. I needed her at my side to make the farm my home. With that gift, my life would be complete.

Some days later, without incident, the ship arrived in Tarsus Bay. To my surprise, merchantmen could no longer dock at the piers in the center of the city. The harbor had filled with silt, allowing only shallow-drafted boats to enter.

I transferred my baggage to such a boat and said to the boatman, "Do you know of a large warehouse located near the pier in the center of the city? It has been a long time since I was here."

"Yes, sir," replied the boatman, "I know it. Years ago, it was owned by an old Jew. He sold to some men from Antioch and returned to the Promised Land. It is used now to store merchandise. Today there is little activity on the pier. I can take you there. It will be my pleasure."

"How long since ships could not enter the center of the city?"

"I've been a boatman here for a number of years. When I started, it was dangerous for a merchantman to come to the pier, as the bay was already filling with silt. The Cydmus is muddy now and filled with silt. In another ten years, you will be able to walk to where your ship anchored. Whenever we have a heavy rain upriver, or when the snow melts, you can see the silt rolling in. I hope I can continue my work here, but I do not count on it. It is getting more difficult to load and unload ships."

"Is the shipyard still building ships?"

"No, sir," he replied. "When I first came to Tarsus, the shipyard was building shallow-drafted boats. I worked there for a while, but building even smaller boats became difficult. It was hard to get good lumber, and the best workmen could find better jobs. I could see what was going to happen, so I managed to acquire this boat."

"Is the university in operation? It was one of the best in the world when I left."

"I believe it is, although I have never been there. Occasionally I have a passenger from the university to take out to a ship, or pick one up to bring into the city. They do not have much to say, and they regret parting with the fare. I can recognize a university person a distance away, and I avoid them if there is a chance for a better fare. They act as though my boat is dirty or I am their hired man."

He hesitated, his voice becoming anxious. "Are you from the university?"

I laughed and replied, "No, my friend. I am not, but more than twenty years ago, I was. You will not find me regretting to part with the fare."

"No offense, sir. I feared for a moment I had offended a university person and my fare would suffer."

I recognized the pier. The boatman tied to the dock nearest the warehouse and assisted me unloading my baggage. I paid him his fare plus a generous gratuity, for his tunic was badly worn, and he had no sandals. He smiled broadly when he saw the silver coin, gave me a casual salute, and returned to his boat.

On the pier, I arranged my baggage in an orderly way and then walked to the warehouse. It had not changed but needed repairs. I entered the office and walked to a table where an older man was sorting papers.

"I just arrived by ship," I said. "I am returning home and do not know what circumstance I will find. I need to store my baggage for several days. May I entrust it to your care?"

"Welcome home. You have the manner of a legionnaire. Are you with the legion?"

I was not aware my manner gave me away. "Yes, I am a centurion with the Tenth Fretensis, Palestine. You are very observant."

"One of my sons is in the legion. After many years, he is now a centurion. He is with the Fourteenth Gemini now in Germany. His mother worries about him being so far from home. We miss him, but I am very proud of him. My respects to you, sir," he said as he stood. "I trust you had a pleasant trip. This is a good time of the year to travel. You may store your baggage here in the office. Do you need assistance?"

"I am pleased to know of your son. You should be very proud. May good fortune follow him until he returns. I will retrieve my baggage. Thank you for your offer."

I made two trips carrying the baggage, for two of the bags were heavy. I placed them neatly in the area he designated and then returned to the table where he sat.

"I have an additional request. The day is almost gone, and I do not know Tarsus. May I sleep in the warehouse tonight?"

"You may. Find you a place among the merchandise. I will tell the guard you are here for the night. I am pleased to be of service."

"Thank you for your kind reception. It is good to be home again. Please give my best greeting to your son and your wife. Again, you have been very kind," I said as I turned to leave the office.

In the warehouse, I found some bales of fabric of similar size and had no difficulty finding two on which to lie. I spread my cloak, sat on it, and removed some food from my pouch. It was good to be on land, and it was good to be in Tarsus with a comfortable place to sleep. I should be home in two days. I wrapped myself in my cloak, rested my head on my pouch, and dreamed of home.

The next morning when I awoke, it was yet dark, but there was sufficient light for me to find my way to the office. I thanked the guard for the night's lodging and walked toward the Jewish section of Tarsus.

The streets were empty. I found the eating place Paul and I had frequented. I entered it to find it as noisy and as hospitable as I remembered.

I sought the proprietor and then asked in my best Aramaic, "I am returned to Tarsus after many years. Is the original owner present?"

The proprietor was surprised by the question in Aramaic posed by a Roman. He said, "I am the present owner, but my father is in the back. Allow me to fetch him."

A few moments later, I saw an older gentleman in traditional Jewish dress walking toward me. "I am the former owner. May I be of assistance?"

"Yes, you may," I said. "Many years ago, Saul, the son of Moshe the Merchant, and I often visited this place. I remember you, but I do not expect you to remember me. I am Cornelius, Saul's friend."

The old man broke into a broad smile. He stared at me for a moment and then said, "Cornelius, you have become quite the handsome man. I well remember you and Saul. You were good customers. Please join me at the table." He pointed to a large table at the far side of the courtyard. "Saul went to Jerusalem to study and never returned. Later, Moshe's wife died, and then his daughter married. He sold everything and returned to his home in Galilee. I have heard nothing from either. Cornelius, Cornelius! How very good to see you. Your Aramaic is perfect. I am proud you mastered the language. As I remember, you joined the legion. You look the part. Welcome home."

I followed him to the far side of the courtyard where a number of older men, Jewish by their dress, were eating and talking. He motioned for me to sit at one of the open places across from him.

He announced, "This is Cornelius, my old friend from many years ago. Make him welcome. He speaks Aramaic better than most of us."

I sat in the designated place and joined in the meal. I told of my years in Palestine, of meeting Moshe and Saul, and answered their questions.

I then asked of the former proprietor, "How are you doing? You look well. The market seems to be doing well."

His countenance fell. "Tarsus is not like it was when you and Saul were here. Businesses are having a difficult time. There is less and less work. People cannot find work, and they beg or steal. My son does very well, but most of our friends do not. We keep hoping things will improve. Our life here, however, is better than the life we had in Palestine. Tarsus is home to us, although sometimes I long for Palestine."

I said, "I am sorry to learn Tarsus is not the city it once was. I remember there was always more work than there were laborers. It is good to know your family still owns the market. I know at least one good eating place in Tarsus. The sun is well up. I must begin my trip. I shall visit each time I am in Tarsus. It is good to see all of you again."

On my way to the street, I offered the son payment for my meal.

"Not this time. It has been our pleasure," he said.

The center of Tarsus had not changed but was in a state of disrepair. There was little activity, although the morning was far spent. To my great surprise, there were beggars in the streets. As I followed the road north, I was amazed at how far the city had grown. It was almost noon before I was in the country.

In my Roman tunic and my light sandals, I set for myself a good pace. As I had started late, it was almost dark when I reached the spring with the grassy area.

The area around the spring and the spring itself had changed. The spring coming from under a large rock outcropping was much smaller and flowed into a marsh nearby. I drank from it. The water was as good as ever. I cleared a space next to a small outcropping, enjoyed some cheese, then wrapped myself in my cloak and fell asleep.

The next morning, by good light, I was on the road, eating as I walked. By noon, I could see the pale outline of the Taurus Mountains and sensed the air was already sweeter and a bit cooler. By late afternoon, I could see the outlines of the ridges marking the boundaries to the farm. I breathed deeply and could smell the sweet, musky smell of the forests. A short time later, I entered the courtyard of the house I remembered so well. How great it would be to have Mother and Father greet me. I shouted to announce my arrival.

A young man appeared in the doorway followed by a young woman and three children. I recognized him but could not recall his name. I announced, "I am Cornelius, home from the legion."

"Uncle Cornelius!" the young man shouted. "We thought you were dead. We heard nothing since you visited on your way to Palestine. Welcome home. It is good to see you. Please come in. We are ready to eat. Please join us. My name is Animus. This is my wife, Juliana, my oldest son, Gaius, my daughter, Lavina, and my youngest son, Cornelius." He added, "When you visited us, your appearance and confidence impressed me. I wanted to join the legion, but I never brought myself to do it. The next best thing was to name one of my sons Cornelius. I hope you do not object."

I laughed and replied, "I am pleased. It is a good name."

Animus motioned his family into the house and me to follow. Through the open door, the late sunshine illumined the room. It had changed little since the day I left. There were more shelves and more devices hanging from pegs in the wall. In the pleasant smell of the freshly cooked meal was the fragrance of the spices and herbs I remembered from Mother's cooking. I took a deep breath, adding to my contentment at being home.

Animus, his two sons, and I sat at the table while his wife and daughter set food before us. The sons were asking questions faster than I could answer. It was good to be home, to be accepted, and to feel the contentment in this family and in this home.

Juliana set a fine meal before us, a welcome change from the fare at sea and the sparse legion food. I answered questions, especially from the boys. Rising from the table, Animus said, "We have had a good day. There are several fields to plant. The help will be here early. Let us get to bed."

The boys excused themselves and left the room. The daughter began clearing the table, and Juliana motioned for me to follow her, removing a lamp from the table.

"Cornelius," she said, "we are pleased you are here. Myrrine's room is as she left it. I must clear some things from the bed. I will prepare the room tomorrow. I hope you will be comfortable."

She placed the lamp on a table near the bed, removed some items from the bed, and withdrew. I looked about the room. Mother's mark was everywhere. I breathed deeply. The air was heavy with the fragrance of old manuscripts and scrolls.

Sitting on the edge of the bed, I enjoyed the sights and smells. How different from a room in the fortress. I wrapped my cloak around me and extinguished the flame. It was good to be home.

I was awakened by activity in the kitchen. I straightened my tunic and joined Juliana and her daughter, who were placing platters on the table in the dining area.

"I thought you might sleep late, but old traits never die," Juliana said. "I hope you slept well. Animus and the boys are in the courtyard. Select your food. Once the laborers are here, it will disappear rapidly."

I selected a bowl, filled it with steaming wheat porridge, adding honey and milk, and picked up a horn spoon. "Thank you. I did sleep well. How very good it is to be home. Thank you for the welcome."

Animus, the boys, and the laborers entered. Animus introduced me, inviting me to stand with them. They welcomed me, many reminding me they had met me in the past. It was a pleasant, cordial affair. After eating, as if on a signal, they all filed out, thanking Juliana and Lavina for the meal.

In a few minutes, Animus returned and said, "Cornelius, it is good to have you here. I hope you are pleased with our performance. We can move to another house, but we want to be part of the family. Cyrus and Myrrine missed you. When Myrrine saw a traveler on the road, she would watch until he passed the cutoff to the farm. Juliana will tell what has happened. I must go."

I placed my empty bowl on the table. Juliana stood beyond, facing me, and I thanked her for a fine breakfast.

She pointed to a stool beside me, indicating for me to move it closer to the table. Juliana then sat opposite me. Her simple beauty struck me. Her eyes were bright and her face aglow from the effort at breakfast. During the meal, she was a leader in a desperate struggle, moving from one crisis to another, never in doubt what to do.

She folded her hands, placed them on the table, and said, "Cornelius, I am so pleased you are here. After Cyrus died, Myrrine managed the farm. Animus and I moved in when she could no longer do the hard work. She gradually turned everything over to me. I tally how much we have. Most years, we sell more than we buy. We have accumulated enough to build a house, if we need to do so. There is also money from Animus, the Elder, and a good amount from Cyrus."

Lavina finished clearing the table, then excused herself.

"All the time I was away, I missed very much being a member of a family like yours," I said. "Let me tell you my plan. Tomorrow I will go to Tarsus to pick up my baggage and get anything you might need."

Juliana nodded. "I always need some things for the kitchen."

"I would like to be married. The woman I wish to marry left Palestine with her father to avoid his imprisonment or execution. They sailed for Alexandria. I must find her."

"I understand," she said. "Among the old ones here, loneliness is the greatest burden. She will make a difference."

"I would like to store my baggage here until I return. We can then decide what to do. I have money to do all I need to do. We may prefer to build a smaller house, but do not plan anything until I return. I have dreamed of that day."

"Certainly, you may store your things here."

"It has been more than ten years since I walked the farm and climbed the back ridges. I would like to do that today. As soon as I can, I will leave for Alexandria."

Rising from the table, Juliana said, "I will prepare something to eat. You look over the farm and then join us for the evening meal."

I retrieved my pouch from my room, and when I returned, Juliana handed me a slice of cheese and a portion of bread, still warm to the touch. I placed them in my pouch and said, "Juliana, again thank you for the welcome. Animus is indeed fortunate to have someone like you to be with him."

I stepped into the courtyard. The sun was well up, and the world a fresh new green. Among the grape leaves I saw small clusters of grapes, and the olive blooms added to the sweet air. It was springtime in Cilicia.

I walked toward the river, entered the road to Tarsus for a short distance, and then turned toward the ridge in back of the farm. I waved to laborers as I passed. When I reached the ridge line, I walked to the cove beyond and sat by the cascade. I was breathing heavily.

After a few minutes, I drank from the stream. The trees filtered the sunlight, and the air was heavy with the musk of decaying leaves.

I took several deep breaths. I cut a portion of the cheese and the bread and savored the good taste. The world could never be better than this.

Then I began to climb, working my way to the crest of the ridge to make climbing easier. The first outcropping towered above me, and I rested more than once before reaching the top. On reaching it, I walked to the edge and studied the mosaic below. Stepping away from the edge, I could see the higher outcroppings, bright gray in the sun.

I returned to the ridge to climb to the next outcropping. The cool air seared my throat. I was pleased to walk onto the top. I rested on a convenient stone, my legs weak from the effort. Above me loomed the highest outcropping. That view would have to wait for another day. I regretted I could not reach the spring at its base, for it was the one place in all the world I hoped would never change.

I walked to the edge of the outcropping and for some time studied the view. Looking to the south, I could see the great plain as it disappeared into the horizon. Looking then to the north, I could see the Taurus Mountains, snowcapped above the evergreen forests. How could paradise be so fair as this?

I worked my way toward the ridge and started down. The descent proved to be more tiring than the ascent. About halfway down the ridge, I worked my way to the stream and followed it to an eddy. At an opening among the trees where full sunlight came though, I sat on a smooth stone enjoying the warmth.

I listened to the cascade. After resting a few minutes, I drank from the stream and savored the last of the food. How good it was to be alive.

The sun was almost to the top of the far ridge. With some difficulty, I arose and made my way down the mountain, arriving at the house as Animus and the boys were putting away the tools.

I approached Animus and asked, "May I prepare the horse and cart for the trip to Tarsus?"

"It is ready," he said. "Both boys wanted to go with you, but I could not spare Gaius. Young Cornelius remained here after the noon meal to prepare it. I hope you do not object to him going."

"I am pleased to have him along," I said. "I will need help."

We entered the house and sat down to the evening meal. I had not planned on eating much, but I was hungrier than I realized, and Juliana was a good cook.

After Juliana and Lavina had cleared the table, but before we started the questions, I said, "I have a request."

"Anything you wish," Animus said, "we will try to do."

"One of my fondest memories is Mother reading from the *Iliad* the description of Achilles putting on his armor as he prepares for battle. I can recite the passage. Before I left for Rome, Mother removed that page from its binder, and Father made a hard-leather case to protect it. We planned to replace it when I returned. In the room, the binder is yet open where Mother removed the page. I would like to replace it."

Animus, Juliana, and the children listened.

"You are my closest family," I said. "Allow me to bring the binder here and insert the page while you watch. I am saddened Mother is not here, although from the battlements of paradise, I believe both are watching. May I fetch the binder?"

Animus agreed. "Certainly. It is a gentle gesture. Sure, bring the binder."

Juliana said, "How like Myrrine to make such a token. It is a fine thing. It will add to our memories of her."

I stood and said, "Cornelius, bring one of the lamps."

With Cornelius standing in the doorway to the room, I picked up the leather case containing the page and walked to the shelf with the open binder. I laid the case on the open page, then closed the binder. Cornelius and I returned to the kitchen. I placed the binder on the kitchen table and opened it. I then removed the page from its case and unrolled it, as I had so many times in so many places. I placed it in the binder, aligning the holes for lacing, and then closed the binder. The page had been returned to its original place as Mother and I had planned. Placing my hand on the cover, I said, "In remembrance of Mother and all those who have gone before, until we meet again."

Then I said, "Thank you for allowing me to complete the obligation.
Now, does anyone have a question?"

Again we talked into the night until Animus stood, indicating it
was time to retire. I picked up the unlaced binder and a lamp and went
to my room. I placed the binder and the lamp on the table. I would
lace it tomorrow. I removed my sandals and wrapped myself in my
cloak. I thought, *Mother, the journey is complete and the page returned.*

The next morning after breakfast, Juliana placed food in my pouch
and filled a waterskin from the aqueduct, and I placed them on the
cart. Cornelius mounted on the driver side, and I on the passenger
side. He turned the horse toward the gate, and we waved goodbye.

Cornelius entered the road to Tarsus and kept the horse at a steady
trot. He inquired about the legion and my experiences. About noon,
as we approached the spring, I said, "This is a good place to rest and
water the horse. I'll see what Juliana has prepared."

Cornelius turned off the road, guided the horse to an eddy, and
tied the reins at the edge of the cart. I withdrew the food Juliana
had prepared and cut a portion for Cornelius and for myself. After
finishing the meal, I decided not to linger at the spring and requested
Cornelius continue our journey.

Late in the afternoon, we came upon an open area with grass for
the horse, and I indicated to Cornelius to drive into it. He unhitched
the horse, then fed and hobbled it. We sat by the cart and enjoyed the
evening meal. Then each of us wrapped in his cloak and passed the
night in the bed of the cart.

We arose early, donned our cloaks, for the sun was not yet up,
and I mounted to the driver's seat. We arrived in Tarsus and enjoyed
a good breakfast at the eating place I had visited a few days previously.
I then drove to the warehouse and loaded my baggage, thanking the
man in the office for his hospitality.

In the city, I purchased two pairs of sandals of good quality and
a plain tunic. At a market, Cornelius purchased salt and spices for
Juliana, and I purchased food for the return journey. I then drove to
the legion post north of the city, introduced myself to the centurion

there, presented my pay record, and requested a withdrawal to be picked up in two or three days. After examining my record, the centurion introduced us to the group, reciting my service. I did not know any of them, but we enjoyed a cordial visit.

I slapped the horse with the reins, and we resumed our journey. We rode in silence until we turned off at the spring. The next morning, by sunup, we were on the road again and entered the courtyard by late afternoon. Cornelius helped carry the baggage into my room. There were three pouches containing my clothing and equipment and one containing Portia's manuscripts.

After the evening meal, I asked if Cornelius could remain behind the next day to help unpack my baggage so I could show him how to care for my equipment. I also announced I would leave in a few days to begin my search for Portia.

"Cornelius, you do not mind caring for my equipment?" I asked.

"I will be pleased to do so," he said.

Juliana asked, "How do you know where to look?"

"She sailed for Alexandria with her mother and father about a year ago. He was prefect of Judea, but changes in Rome caused him to fear for his life. He is the kind that cannot hide easily. He will make a name for himself. By finding him, I will find her. One day, a year or so from now, you will see Portia and me, and perhaps Portia's mother and father, arriving in a fine cart. We may build a house above this one, where the ridge runs into the farmland. Regardless, I look forward to living out my days here, as did Mother and Father."

I was enjoying questions when Animus stood and announced it was time to end the day and that Cornelius would remain at the house the next day.

The next morning after breakfast, Cornelius and I unpacked the pouches, except the manuscripts, and I showed him how to clean and care for everything. By the end of the day, all was in order.

On unpacking my glove, I regretted not giving it to the centurion of the First Century to express my appreciation for his service to me and to the cohort. I would take it with me. I might need it or find someone who might use it. I also laid the medal the cohort had given me on top of the other items I was to take.

I had grouped Mother's manuscripts into one section of shelves and then opened the pouch containing Portia's. With Cornelius's help, we soon had hers in the shelves.

"Would you take me to Tarsus tomorrow?" I said. "You know the way there and through the town."

"Nothing would please me more. I can manage the trip."

We walked to the kitchen and joined the family. After the meal, we sat at the table. I was home with my family.

At the proper time, Animus announced the day had ended.

I stood and said, "My return has been everything I hoped it would be. I thank all of you for your welcome." I then said to Animus, "Tomorrow, please allow Cornelius to accompany me to Tarsus. He is a fine young man, and he and I have become friends. He has agreed to go, subject to your approval."

"I hoped you would stay longer," Animus said. "Yes, if Cornelius wants to go, he has my permission. Everyone to bed, so we can get an early start."

I returned to my room and set the lamp on the table by the bed. In the corner, my helmet with its red plume rested on my armor, both reflecting the soft light. It was an appropriate setting—old manuscripts filling the shelf space and my helmet and armor in the corner. I was content. I took a deep breath and savored the smell of burning olive oil, the musky smell of old manuscripts, and the sweet, pungent smell of the oil treating the leather. It was indeed home. It was a good end to the journey. Tomorrow would begin a new venture. I extinguished the lamp.

When I awoke, I heard talking in the kitchen. They were already at breakfast! I quickly donned my sandals and entered the kitchen. Everyone was present and waiting. Juliana had prepared a special breakfast. It was a great time. We talked and laughed about many things, but the time arrived.

I picked up a lamp and returned to my room. I packed the items laid out and passed over my head the medal from the cohort. I looked one last time around the room and returned to the kitchen.

Juliana motioned for my pouch and slipped into it a parcel of food wrapped in a piece of worn fabric. I passed the strap over my head and secured the pouch at my side.

I was saddened to be leaving the house that had always been my home. I said, "Portia and I will return. May good fortune smile upon each of you and upon this house and upon this family."

All of us walked into the courtyard, where the horse and cart waited. Cornelius mounted to the driver's side and I to the passenger side. We turned and waved as we cleared the courtyard gate. The rays of the morning sun were touching the crest of the ridge across the river.

The horse settled to a steady trot, and we shed our cloaks. "Cornelius," I said, "each summer your grandfather invited a teacher from the university to spend time with us. My favorite teacher was an old sophist named Simmias. Your father will want you to attend the university. When you do, find a teacher who teaches for the love of it."

I paused to look at Cornelius. He was attentive to his driving but immediately glanced at me.

"He can show you a new world," I said. "In it, each of us has a purpose. Find it. Happiness is making the journey."

"I believe Father wished he had joined the legion," Cornelius said. "He is happy farming, but sometimes he says something, or the way he says it, that makes me think he wished he had joined."

"You may be correct. He named you Cornelius. In Palestine, there was another teacher. He believed he was here to show people a better way to live. His teaching was no different from Simmias's. Knowing him convinced me all I had learned was true."

I glanced again at Cornelius to see whether he was listening. "What I have said sounds strange, but there is a fine, new world if you look for it. Remember you are here for a purpose. Life has meaning. If we never meet again, Cornelius, I lived the life I was born to live. Remember that."

"I think I understand," he replied. "Father says some little thing that lets us know. It is not that he is sad, but it seems to be, somehow, a regret. I love farming, but I see you, and I think I would like to be a centurion, to be like you."

About noontime, we again stopped at the spring. After the meal, I mounted to the driver's side, pulled into the road, and slapped the horse with the reins to increase his pace. Cornelius and I talked of many things. He was a fine young man. He would honor the name.

The sun had set by the time we entered the city. I stopped at the first livery. We unhitched the horse and turned it over to the livery, then prepared pallets in the cart for the night. Cornelius and I then sat under the edge of the cart and enjoyed the meal. After some light conversation, we crawled under the canvas, wrapped in our cloaks, and passed the night.

By good light, the horse and cart were ready. I drove into the Jewish section to the eating place. After an exchange of pleasantries in Aramaic, I ordered breakfast. The peasant woman set the platter on the table, and we enjoyed the meal.

I next drove to the legion camp. All except the centurion were retired from the legion, proud of their service, and welcomed a chance to talk about it. Cornelius listened intently and more than once asked a question for more information or to clarify a point. He may have enjoyed the exchanges more than I.

I excused myself from the group, motioned to the centurion, and we walked to his office. He handed me a small bag containing the money. I thanked him for his service, and he and I joined the others. After a cordial exchange of parting wishes, including the benediction, "For the Senate and the people of Rome," Cornelius and I returned to the cart.

As I drove to the office of the harbormaster, Cornelius was in a pensive mood. On arriving, we dismounted and walked to the back of the cart. I unpacked my pouch, lifted the false bottom, and filled the space with coins. With it full, I replaced the items except the remaining food. I gave the food to Cornelius, still wrapped in the cloth, and handed him the bag with the remainder of the coins.

"Put this with the other money," I said. "It is yours. It should last until I return. We will then talk again. Take care of the family. It will mean more to you than you realize. Be careful on the way home."

"Goodbye. I will take good care of everything. I look forward to your return with Portia."

We walked to the driver's side of the cart, and he mounted to the seat. I reached for the reins, slapped the horse, and stepped back. Cornelius took up the slack, looked back, waved, and was on his way.

I watched as the cart disappeared into a curve some distance away. I continued to look down the road for some time. I felt a sense of loneliness, but I now had my new home, and a family was waiting for my return.

I took a deep breath, squared my shoulders, walked into the harbormaster's office, and said, "My name is Cornelius. I wish to book passage as a member of the crew on a merchantman destined for Alexandria."

The harbormaster turned from his study of the harbor and said, "Cornelius, welcome to Tarsus. We can always use a strong hand. There are several ships to sail for Alexandria. Let me point them out."

I thought, *Portia, the long wait is almost over.*

✝

EPILOGUE

In the depth of winter, Portia and I find joy in the harbingers of spring. In the late sunshine and winter's cold of our lives, in conversations with family and friends, and in the recollection of things past, we see harbingers of the beyond. We are content in afternoons to sit for hours, enjoying the pleasure of each other, reading our manuscripts, and recalling events from days gone by.

I was never able to return to the spring at the top of the highest outcropping, but I hear it has not changed.